Such Outlaws

ISBN: 978-0692192054

Cover art by Jack Nevins @jacksketches

The quote on page 246 is from *A Feast of Lanterns* by L. Cranmer-Bying, 1916

The quote on page 378 is from *A Song of Harvest* by John Greenleaf Whittier, 1858

Contact me at Merv.Hamstead@gmail.com

This book is available for purchase on Amazon.com

for Amy

Such Outlaws

A novel by Adam Rann

Prologue: The Tender Tempest

A tired, weathered man rested his head on a lumpy bag for what felt like the millionth time. Maybe the last time. The park bench he had chosen that night was a familiar one. He'd slept there dozens of times, typically in the summers and milder autumn nights. On occasion, as tonight, he returned in winter for some faint sentimental comfort. His bony spine fit between two of the center boards like the final piece of a puzzle. As he puffed on his last cigarette, he realized he'd forgotten what a bed even felt like.

The park around him was a shell of its former beauty. Where flower patches and well-kept paths used to crisscross, now resided only overgrown weeds over bumpy trails. As a child his grandmother had taken him here, to the heart of the Inner District, a couple of blocks from the only house he had ever called home, to chase butterflies and play in the snow. He could remember when the May Day festivals were held here, on the other side of the lake. The fireworks had lit up the sky and, mirrored magnificently below, the water.

Warmer nights were cloud-covered, but tonight, buzzed off of an old friend's homebrew, he gazed into an open sky of stars. This week, or this month, marked his 9th cumulative year of homelessness. A year here, two years there. What was the difference? Unlike most homeless, he didn't bug people for money; he didn't nag people for a bite to eat. He typically kept to himself. He didn't care much anymore for the pursuit of people's sympathy or charity. Every few days he could find a good meal and something warm to drink at the local house of worship. Their kitchen wasn't spectacular, and he may not have been religious, but they did special things there.

Believe it or not this man had gone to college. How had such an educated man found himself homeless for such a span of time? Well that was simple: addiction. Name it, he'd tried it. Uppers, downers, hallucinogens, speed, tranqs, pills, powders, liquids and plants. Snort, smoke, inject or ingest, organic and inorganic. A life subjected to abuse and hatred from one's father and uncle could make any mind crack, fixated on forgetting both the past and future, begging to become consumed in the euphoric now. This was a man who had made and loved paintings, mostly those reflecting the evil he'd experienced. But those had all been sold to support his cowardly habits.

The unseasonable winter weather had turned his clothes ragged. Although the daytime temperatures were climbing, the nights still proved bitter cold when the wind was active. Tonight was such a night. He had tried his best to cover himself in a few pages of yesterday's newspaper. A feeble attempt, he knew, but it was better than nothing. He shifted slightly, exposing the headline of the *Fort Dearborn Ledger's* front page. In bold, it read 'TERRORISTS LINKED TO GOLDEN PARACHUTE INCIDENT.'

Since the day his grandmother died, he had never felt loved. Having her as a consistent part of life was a fleeting memory of his, a momentary glimpse into his fading dreams. What was life without love? Maybe one night he'd fall asleep and never wake up. As the years passed by, he felt more and more like the stars, less and less of him visible to the city, drowned out by the ever brighter lights until one day he would disappear entirely. Forgotten.

He closed his eyes for the last time that night. Slowly, he drifted.

In the distance, the sound of sirens approached. They drew nearer and nearer, practically deafening as they passed, yet the weathered homeless man remained still on his bench. He didn't bother to peek at the scene, no, he'd heard the sirens countless times and didn't much care to inquire after them this night.

The sound of leaves rustling in the wind continued for several moments after the screaming chase passed. The sound was foreign, though. It took him a second to realize that strangeness in what he heard. Was his mind tricking him again? Eyes closed, he squinted. There hadn't been leaves on the trees in months. . . Just as he came to this conclusion, the man felt a feather-like object land softly on his face. As he gradually opened his eyes and adjusted to the light of the lamps that lined the nearby street, he reached out to grab whatever had landed on him. He held a crisp hundred-dollar bill in his hand. Confused, he sat upright and became aware of the scene in front of him.

The illuminated street was caught amidst a shower of money.

Then, with the sirens some distance beyond, he heard a thundering crash.

PART 1: TO WHOM IT MAY CONCERN

"I rebel; therefore I exist." - Albert Camus

Chapter 1: Temporary Resident

The creaking floorboards in the entryway to Rob's cabin wished him a warm welcome home from his early morning adventure, as if he'd lived there his entire life instead of only two short months. Inside the mudroom, he took a seat on an oak bench to the left and slid his hiking boots off one by one. They dropped beside his hunting bow with a thud, and he leaned over to stack them neatly beside a variety of footwear lining the opposite wall. His wool socks were next off his feet, followed by a long flex of the toes and a rub of the heels, a meager attempt at undoing the ache brought on by hours spent in the woods. Rob stuffed his socks in his boots, stood, and hung his light camouflage jacket, hat, and facemask on three respective hooks. He ran a hand through his hair and stepped into the living room.

He took the cabin's silence as a sign that his roommate, Julius, was still sleeping, and decided to maintain the calm as best he could. Julius had come down with a rather severe respiratory infection and quarantined himself to his room a few days ago. The two had been good friends and roommates for almost three years, since Rob's Junior year of college, and Julius was hardly known to embrace hypochondria. If he was acting it, he was truly sick.

Rob quietly made his way across the cozy living room to the kitchen and opened the refrigerator. He removed a small plate of cheeses and cured meats, along with a pitcher of water, and grabbed two rolls from a countertop bin, a little firmer than they had been yesterday morning. He pressed his thumbs into the crusty exterior and ripped each roll open to build two modest sandwiches. Six months ago such a small plate of food wouldn't have put a dent in his appetite, let alone constituted an entire meal, but he had adapted to the local lifestyle much quicker than anticipated; his diet had been no exception. He found it interesting that the greater the distance from home, the easier it was to alter one's habits. Not to mention, dinner at the hotel in town was only a few hours away, so he needn't fill up now. Rob scarfed the sandwiches, washed the dish quickly, swept the crumbs off the counter into the trashcan, and took his glass of water around the corner to his bedroom.

The cabin was quite small, but what it lacked in size it made up for in charm and warmth. Two small bedrooms, perhaps ninety square feet each, shared a wall and opened onto the living room and adjoining kitchen, separated only by a change from floor tile to wood planks. The off-white walls were made of plaster and the ceiling slats of stained pine, as were the kitchen cabinets, doors, and about every piece of trim or accent in the house. The entire footprint of the cabin could likely fit into the living room of Rob's home apartment, but through his travels he had quickly learned that larger living space was in no way directly related to happiness.

In his bedroom, Rob placed the glass of water on the pine nightstand and tumbled into bed, succumbing to fatigue. He had been up before dawn, at a heightened state of awareness until noon, and at long last had a chance to relax. Presently, it was 1:30 p.m. A deep breath and a sigh forced his heavy eyelids to close, and he began to recount the morning, slowly drifting away into peacefulness.

Rob was suddenly awoken by a striking sound oddly similar to that of a frog croaking. A roll of the head revealed his bedside clock to read 4:45 p.m. He cursed, having slept much later than planned, and quickly rose to try to shake the grogginess. In the kitchen he found Julius bracing himself on the edge of the sink while working to hack up whatever remnants of his debilitating infection were surely lodged in his lungs.

"Oh, baby's awake," Rob joked.

Julius shook his head. "Shut up. . . Ugh."

"You alright?" Rob asked, assuming a tone of concern.

"Yeah, I guess. Still fighting the good fight," Julius replied. His voice was nasally and clogged. He looked terrible.

"You want me to ask your Aunt and Uncle if they can take you to the doctor? You still don't look so hot."

"*Nah.* There's nothing a doctor can do," he groaned. "Just gotta let it pass. Plus," he waved, "come look at this."

Rob went over to Julius and traced his attention towards the sink.

"Check it out. Green."

A downward look showed a quagmire of mucus Rob would much rather have heard about euphemistically than seen firsthand. He snapped his head away, mildly disgusted by the sight.

"Aw, dude. C'mon."

"Green's good, man. Means I'm at the tail end of this thing."

"If that's *good,* I don't wanna know what's been coming up the past few days."

"I'm telling ya. I took a semester of Bio. I know things."

"Whatever you say, Dr. J," Rob said as he leaned against the countertop. "Are you gonna try to rally for dinner?"

"Yeah, I'm gonna–" Julius's sentence was cut short by a coughing fit.

Rob smiled at him. "Go on."

Julius shook his head, as if would rid him of his plague. "Gonna *try.* What time are you leaving?"

"Like 6:30ish. Dinner's at 7 so I'm gonna shower and do a quick load of laundry in the meantime."

"Alright. I'm gonna lay back down for a little. Let's hope I wake up a new man," Julius resolved, and traipsed off to his sickroom.

By 6:15, Rob was about ready to start his walk to town. Yet there was no sign of Julius. He had been purposefully noisy over the past half hour in hopes of stirring him from his slumber, but such measures had proven ineffective. As a last effort, he decided to peek into Julius's room for signs of life. The door cracked open with a squeak, shining a bar of hallway light onto a resting body. Julius was on his side with his mouth open, a tissue rammed up each nostril, and completely asleep. *So much for the rally,* Rob thought, and decided to leave a note, just in case he woke in an hour or so.

Before departing, he remembered to charge the bulky cellular phone his stepfather had entrusted to him for his time abroad. It had been dead for days before Rob, having scoured the cabin, eventually found his charger in the pocket of a raincoat he hadn't used in weeks. He waited a moment to see if he had any missed calls, but the phone needed some juice before the display would change from a blinking pixelated image of a hollow battery. *Fuck it*, he decided, and rested the phone on his bed. It would be waiting all the same after dinner and, since it was set on vibrate mode, he needn't worry about any calls or notifications waking Julius.

Outside, Rob took a moment before descending the staircase to breathe in the pure, late-summer German air. He was still in the honeymoon phase with this country, and in the back of his mind he knew it would soon come to an end. He cherished like it would be the last each moment he was able to file away a mental image, a sensation, or sound. Pictures are special in that they capture an image in time and evoke a range of feelings, and of his recent journey he'd taken plenty, but nothing speaks to the soul like a memory. So Rob made it a point to take special memories with him from each leg of this journey in life, from the simplest to the outlandish. A moment admiring and memorizing the rural German landscape was just as important as any other.

It was a cool sixty-five degrees that evening, so Rob made sure to grab a light flannel shirt to take with him in case the temperature dipped before his after-dinner walk home. He wore his hiking boots from the morning hunt, worn denim jeans, and a white waffle-knit thermal shirt. He descended the staircase swiftly and made his way to the gravel roadway that ran adjacent to his cabin, which sat in the northwest corner of a twenty-five-acre property owned by Julius's aunt and uncle, Ana and Wilhelm. Alongside the road was a broad, open meadow that extended some distance to a patch of forest. The field looked magnificent in the setting sunlight, full of greens and golds, like a pasture out of a magazine or some dramatic cinematography. Some nights, he would see a small herd of red deer grazing in the field or a brazen fox after an evening meal. It was so foreign in a way, he being from a bustling metropolis. Even though he learned to appreciate the outdoors back in the States, this locale held an undeniable majesty. It was simply extraordinary.

The gravel road crunched beneath his feet, the sound propelling him forward with its audible energy. This path would take him past Ana and Wilhelm's main house in under five minutes and into town in about thirty. His first solo attempt had led him down some wrong turns, and taken closer to an hour, but he now knew the journey with the familiarity of a local. Gently, a rumble spoke up from the depths of his stomach. The promise of beer and heavy, carbohydrate-rich food awaiting him put some extra pep in his step and a small smile to his lightly bearded face.

Rob had arrived in Germany two months earlier, in late June. The previous December, he had concluded the fall semester of his 5th year of college and still been ineligible to graduate. It was a moderately embarrassing situation for him, but he did his best to stay positive and true to himself. His studies had varied widely. Rob enjoyed classes like Calculus, Philosophy, Ancient European History, Astronomy & Classical Physics, and so on. But while his thirst for knowledge was insatiable, his desire to limit his learning to merely one subject or focus was non-existent. And unfortunately, such a searching interest in knowledge hindered rather than advanced his ability to progress through college. Based on University standards, and real-world standards for that matter, he hadn't accumulated enough credits to become a scholar or a professional in any one subject. He had accumulated more credits over four years than most of his peers, but without enough in any one major to satisfy the graduation requirements he found himself stuck.

Having fallen behind, to appease his mother he enrolled in his 5th year in hopes of graduating. After the fall semester, however, it was clear that he was spinning his wheels. He simply didn't fit the mold of a "good" student, he supposed. This was a frustrating and sometimes inadequate feeling, but he had always stubbornly followed his natural path of interest, and, in doing so, found contentment. So when his friend Julius, having been able to finish up his degree in that time, told Rob that he planned to take a celebratory trip to Europe shortly after his December graduation, it didn't take much convincing for Rob to agree to come along. A trip was exactly what he needed in lieu of another fruitless, directionless semester at college.

To his surprise, Rob's mother didn't put up much of an argument. His charm and credit total at college were bargaining chips despite his lack of closure, and if a trip was necessary for him to find his path, what were a few more months? To convince his stepfather, he took the financial route, explaining that a trip to Europe would be a fraction of the cost of another semester as a full-time student. While his mother was able to massage the friction out of the tense discussion between the two, as she always did, his stepfather made it clear this was a one-time forbearance on his responsibilities as a young adult, not carte blanche. Rob had given empty nods at the "rules" and counted the days until their adventure commenced.

Their stereotypical trip abroad began in a stereotypical location: Amsterdam. Hostels, women, and partying had been plentiful in the early days, and so too had been the damage to their bank accounts and livers. It was a binge of sorts, and after three weeks of excess, their revelry leveled out. Rob confronted himself. He had claimed, and honestly meant, that one of the main motivations for his trip was to find direction, yet their initial actions provided none of worth. Over the following months, they moderated the craziness and hopped around from city to city—Brussels, London, Paris, a quick stop in Luxembourg, then Prague, Copenhagen, before finally calling for respite in the tiny town of Schmallenburg, Germany, a short hour east of Dusseldorf. Originally, their final destination was to be Zurich and a multi-week tour of the Swiss Alps, but with Julius's encouragement the pair decided to visit his family briefly before that last leg of the journey.

They arrived in Germany on month four of their trip, and before long found themselves forgoing the idea of Zurich altogether, opting for an open-ended stay in the glorious Rhineland. The people, the sights, the environment, the food, beer, and the convenient housing circumstances all lent merit to the decision. One week turned into one month and one month turned into two, with Rob conjuring a number of excuses for the delay in returning home. His stepfather had insisted on a global cellular package to keep tabs on him, and every few weeks, Rob would chat briefly with his mother over the phone and try to give some timeline of his homecoming. They had most recently spoken a month prior, and though he hadn't set a rigid return date, he had promised to be home before autumn. The loose plan left him with a mere three or four weeks remaining on this beloved adventure of freedom and experience. *Perhaps tonight I'll book the flight home*, he thought as he approached Wilhelm and Ana's pretty homestead beside the road. After all, the trip wouldn't end itself.

Rob paused at the fence in front of the couple's home, an equally charming, if not larger, version of the cabin he and Julius occupied. Rob was to be joining them for dinner down at the hotel, and wondered if they had yet departed or if he could accompany them for the remainder of the walk. It took but a moment to notice the lights off in the kitchen, bedroom, and bathroom. He took that as an answer to his inquiry, as they often arrived early to have a drink at the bar.

Shortly beyond the property, a wooded section of the road began. It was a lovely piece to walk along, being flanked on both sides by nature's diverse thumbprint. Towering green oak and pine trees lined the road, creating a tunnel of branches overhead. Thick shrubs grew between most trees and the occasional gap offered a window into the deep forest. Moss-covered rocks and ferns blanketed the ground, over which squirrels bounced along like some fairytale cartoon. He had half expected a knight on a horse to trot by the first time he journeyed down the road alone.

After a couple twists, Rob was greeted by the pointed spire and clock of Schmallenburg's bell tower peeping its way above the treetops. "Use the bell tower as your compass," Wilhelm had taught him during his early days in town. Despite Rob's claim to a good sense of direction, he had managed to get lost daily for the first week, both in town and on the outer roads, and always looked to the clock tower to help him correct his errant path. Over time, it came to serve as a friendly welcome as he entered or a genuine goodbye as he left. Presently, he wagered he was ten minutes from the town center.

Schmallenburg was located in the heart of the Rhineland with a population of but a few thousand people, making it relatively unknown to most. It was rich in history, and its residents enjoyed a lifestyle they were most proud of, evidenced by the local sock factory that employed - what seemed like - half the town. Just a few years back the factory had celebrated its 100th year of operation. In fact, the very socks Rob wore had been made not two miles from where he stood! These were the qualities that Rob admired from the moment he arrived. Authenticity of the architecture, the people, and their mindset toward life as well as the genuine nature in which they lived were all intriguing facets of a people so familiar yet so removed from his life experiences. It seemed daily he'd add an interesting observation to his growing list.

As he reached the end of the gravel roadway, the bordering trees peeled away and revealed the first official street. It took but a half-dozen blocks from that point to reach the town center and the base of the 12th century church that stood as a symbol of Schmallenburg's proud local history. The church's ever-present clock tower served as a reminder to residents that time was always marching forward. Even though the church seemed to defy that fact, time the residents wasted not, for that was the German way.

Rob approached Hotel Strom as the 7 p.m. church bells rung. Built in the late 1700s, Hotel Strom was a classic German building in style and construction, a two-story affair with charcoal-colored roof shingles that cascaded onto the face of the second story and wrapped around the windows, making the upper half of the building look like it was covered in scales. The ground floor exterior had new cloth awnings and some hanging flower pots with pretty pink blossoms stretching for the last of the sun's light. The hotel was owned and operated by Abigail and Claus Weiss and had been in the Weiss family since its establishment some two-hundred years earlier.

The street-side front entrance was edged by outdoor seating and umbrellas where a few couples now awaited service. In lieu of more technologically advanced space heaters, which might diminish the character of the building, the guests were provided with blankets to ensure that if the weather were to turn brisk, they'd surely stay warm. Rob ascended the three front steps with ease and pushed open the ornate front door, a beautifully inlaid piece with a large stained glass rendition of the German flag. He stepped onward and inward to the hotel's main hallway, which led to the lobby some thirty feet ahead. The low chatter of dinner guests percolated its way out of the dining hall to Rob's left, just short of the lobby, and lured him in with amiable sounds to accompany the delicious smells of the kitchen.

The dining room had original wood floors with small area rugs placed strategically to absorb some foot traffic. The walls were wood-paneled halfway up from the floor, with plaster finishing the journey to the ceiling. The ceilings, plaster as well, were sectioned off into long rectangles with rough-cut, ancient lengths of wood. Rob had attended dinner at Hotel Strom perhaps ten times, but each visit he paused for just a moment to take in the ambiance.

His concentration was broken by a wave from Wilhelm, seated at the back table beside the fireplace. Nestled behind a protruding wall, the table offered Rob a view of only half of the dinner party. Upon reaching the table he was greeted by a variety of warm welcomes from all—'Hello,' 'Hallo,' and 'Guten Abend,' sung in unison for the final guest as he made for his open seat at the head of the table.

"Guten Abend," Rob greeted them comfortably as he sat.

The elongated wooden table seated ten other friends, all of whom Rob had gotten to know well. On the left were Wilhelm and Ana, who had a tall glass of Pilsner waiting for him. Moving clockwise were Paul and Mia, who owned a small farm outside of town and provided Hotel Strom with many vegetables. Paul and Mia's son Tim was beside them, and across from him was his wife, Leah. Tim was the assistant brewer and cellarman at the small brewery Wilhem and Ana owned on the edge of town, and Leah worked as waitress at the hotel. Gladly for all, tonight was Leah's night off. Next to Leah were Jonas and Marie, who were Paul and Mia's neighbors. Finally, there was Lara, Jonas and Marie's daughter, occupying the seat to Rob's immediate right.

Rob said a quieter, personal hello to Lara, who beamed back. She always seemed to be seated beside him, whether he was last to arrive or first, and Rob respectfully allowed what appeared to be a matchmaking push regardless of his lack of feeling toward her. She was a pretty, shy girl with flowing blond hair and a rather fun sense of humor. Had she been older, Rob would've made a move in a heartbeat. At the age of 17, though, he couldn't bring himself to walk down that road. Sometimes, timing is everything.

The group resumed their conversation and Rob turned to Wilhelm, raising his beer to toast. "Thank you, Wilhelm," he said. "I've been looking forward to this all day."

"Prost!" Wilhelm cried, and clanked glasses with Rob.

Noticing the motion, Tim called over in a thick accent, "Rob, this is the batch we made together your first week here."

"It was ready?" Rob asked, leaning forward in surprise.

"Yah. I kegged it this morning. Tell me what you think."

Rob cracked a devious smile. The weeks of anticipation leading up to this moment had been indescribable. When Julius and Rob arrived in Schmallenburg, they felt eager to repay the generosity bestowed upon them. To be quite honest, four months of backpacking through Europe had left the boys quite rough around the edges. Seeing them sleep deprived, scruffy, dirty, and on the verge of keeling over, Wilhelm and Ana cleaned them up, arranged their rooms in the cabin, and put them to work at the brewery (volunteer work to repay said generosity so they needn't worry about work visas and the like). They did simple manual labor, but as a welcoming treat they were permitted to shadow Wilhelm and Tim through the brewing process one day during their first week. They mashed in, grained out, casted, learned of gravity measurements and yeast pitching techniques. It had been a wealth of technical knowledge to take in all at once, but it was a cherished memory Rob would not soon forget. Conveniently, Wilhelm had secured an order from a group of restaurants in

Dusseldorf, providing plenty of work to keep the boys busy during their stay.

He inspected his glass more closely than any ordinary beer, for he had a part in this divine concoction. It was his. Holding it up to the light revealed a brite, straw-colored beverage with a fluffy white head and delicate carbonation. The aroma was a heady balance of sweetness and German hops. He took a healthy drink, swirling the nectar in his mouth briefly with a resulting smile of pure ecstasy.

"It's the greatest thing I've ever tasted in my life," Rob announced, only somewhat facetiously, with a foamy moustache. It truly was delicious.

All following Rob's elaborate production chuckled.

Tim replied, "A good batch, yes. You have a future in the industry!"

"Prost!" Rob raised his glass.

"Tomorrow we make more," Tim concluded, and turned towards his wife.

Abigail Weiss came by the table shortly thereafter, dropped off the first plates of Bratkartoffeln, and took another round of drink orders. While the lunch and breakfast menu at Hotel Strom may have made Rob miss home, most of the dinner dishes caused him to nearly forget it entirely. Bratkartoffeln was one of those dinner dishes. Everyone's had pan fried potatoes before so maybe it was just Abigail's secret recipe, but her version made him salivate every time.

"Rob, how was your day off?" Wilhelm asked in thickly accented English.

Even though Rob had assimilated and picked up quite a good amount of German, his present friends, Tim especially, were more eager to speak English with him than to allow him to practice his German. Rob gladly obliged and snuck in some practice of his own when able. At first, he spoke English a bit too quickly and utilized too many grammatical shortcuts, but in short time, he learned to annunciate, make eye contact, and help whomever he was conversing with through any difficulties that arose, even if it meant simplifying to achieve a desired conversational outcome.

"It was a good day," he replied steadily. "I went hunting this morning and rested in the afternoon."

"Any luck with deer?"

"Not today. I think I figured it out, though. I'll just buy some venison next week and pretend I got it myself!"

Wilhelm offered a laugh. “My lips are closed,” he replied, and took a drink.

Leah called over, “Rob. I thought you were from a city. Where did you learn to hunt?”

As Leah worked most nights, she was a little less familiar with Rob than the others. She was a truly lovely woman that always had a bright smile painted on her fair face and kindness to follow. The forthcoming explanation was one Rob had given several times over, but he didn’t mind repeating himself.

“You cannot hunt where I live, in the city, but my uncle used to live upstate,” he began. “Beginning when I was ten my mom let me visit him every summer and during some holidays until he passed away two years ago. Every time I visited we would go in the woods either hunting, fishing, camping, or hiking.”

Leah nodded in acknowledgement. “Good skills to learn,” she called.

“I agree,” Rob replied. “I always liked the countryside better than the city.”

“I am sorry to hear you lost your uncle,” Ana chimed in kindly.

Rob turned his attention to give her a grave smile. “Yes. It was a sad time. He was the only family member besides my mother that I had a relationship with. But he taught me many things,” he added in an upbeat tone, “and I appreciate the memories I had with him.”

“Your memories are good ones.”

Lara spoke up, then. She had been following the conversation timidly since Rob sat down. “What is ‘upstate’?”

Rob smiled to himself, having missed the potential slang in his explanation. “Upstate means that he lived north of the city. Similar to here where there is a small town and a lot of woods.”

Lara nodded. “That sounds nice.”

“It was. Much quieter than where I am from.”

Leah called again from down the table. “Is your city like San Francisco?”

Leah had studied for two semesters in America during her time at the University and had lost much of her accent while there. Yet without the means to travel much while in the States, her only frame of reference was the Bay Area.

“Not really, Leah. I’m from Fort Dearborn, which is a little bigger and has fewer hills than San Francisco. A shorter plane ride too,” he finished with a smile.

"Oh, yes," she blurted with a nod. "I remember, now. I always wanted to travel there. They have such a great Fashion District."

"You're welcome to come anytime you want. All of you. Just tell me or Julius when you want to come and we'll host you."

It was as genuine a sentiment Rob could offer. He was indebted to these people, whether they agreed or not. To be welcomed the way he was, by what were largely strangers, was an experience he feared he'd never find again. His other months of travel in Europe, while wild and eye-opening, hadn't left as deep of an impression on him as the overwhelming feeling of acceptance here. Here, he was treated like family.

"Will you be staying much longer, Rob?" Lara asked.

"Ah. The big question," Wilhelm added before a drink. If Rob was to guess, Wilhelm was on his tenth beer and counting. The man was a tank.

Rob paused as all laid their eyes upon him. It had been an ongoing internal debate the past few weeks. One day he would be resigned to return home and resume his paused life, and the next day, he'd squander those thoughts and listen to the voice of encouragement within. Hell, just an hour past he had thought of booking his flight home. But here at the table he bounced back. Why leave? What was stopping him from staying here and letting life take him where it would? Home will always be home, he supposed, but was there anything wrong with having two homes? In his heart the answer to that question was always no. Tomorrow he would sit down with Julius and discuss this crossroads they had met. Not all was lost in terms of time, and perhaps they could arrange something further. Rob's family back home would just have to deal with it.

"*Well*. . .I haven't decided yet. But if Wilhelm and Ana will have me, I am really thinking about staying. Julius and I already looked into getting our work visas. It might be difficult, but I think I have a good chance to meet all of the requirements."

The group smiled hopefully, leaving Rob with a warm feeling of contentment.

"You are welcome as long as you like, Rob," said Wilhelm.

Ana's voice drew Rob's attention. "Have you asked your mother about your plans?"

"We haven't spoken for a few weeks, but I plan on calling her tonight or tomorrow morning to talk it over."

"Yah. She might be able to give you some good advice."

"Definitely," Rob concurred.

Dinner arrived to quiet the conversation. For the third night in a row, Rob had the weinerschnitzle with spätzle. And for the third night in a row, his excitement was written on his face. My, could Abagail cook. Clanging silverware and small talk filled the air as the group enjoyed their meals, a testament to the hearty deliciousness on their plates and the casual atmosphere Rob loved so.

As the hours went, the beer flowed, the conversation rose and fell, and Rob filled his belly to its brim. Judging by the German being quickly passed between Jonas and Marie, he had a sneaking sense that they would be inviting him to their house to spend more time with Lara. Rob decided to excuse himself before having to decline their offer in a way that may have come off as rude, not to mention after seven beers he was feeling the aftershock of the morning's physical exertion and didn't want to give his body any more excuses to catch whatever affliction had stricken Julius. After formal goodbyes, he made his way out of Hotel Strom and began the pleasant stroll back to his cabin.

As Rob's feet rolled over cobblestones, passing the church and accompanying bell tower, his thoughts turned to his mother, Amelia. He wondered what she would say if he told her he wanted to stay in Germany indefinitely. For as long as he could remember she had worked tirelessly to keep him out of trouble and on the path to success. *Would this path make her proud?* He hadn't lied at dinner when he said his only close family members were his late uncle and his mother, immediate family included. Rob was an only child and had no firsthand memory of his father. The man had left before Rob was more than an infant, forcing him to grow up on the fringe of financial stability, living off his mother's salary as an outpatient nurse in the city's hospital. There were no family holidays, celebrations, or casual visits. It was a lonesome stretch of time for him and his mother. But struggle breeds strength, and their relationship was a testament to that fact. She was his everything. Curiously, Rob never found himself with a yearning to inquire about the man who had left their lives. He never felt emptiness, never felt anger, for his circumstances were all he knew. At the age of ten, though, and much to his initial dismay, it was clear that his mother felt quite differently than he.

Amelia met Rob's stepfather, Wilson, at a fundraising event at the city hospital, and from then on, their lives changed dramatically. Dates led to vacations, which led to engagement. It happened quickly, too quickly for Rob. Suddenly he saw new life in his mother, like she had hatched from a cocoon and could spread her wings and fly. Before long, the two were married and a new wave of changes rolled ashore. Formerly tenants of a 700-square-foot loft on the fourth story of a walkup with views of a neighboring brick wall, marriage to Wilson saw an upgrade to a 4,200-square-foot penthouse apartment with views of the harbor and towering Financial District. Splitting a box of pork lo mein was upgraded to four-course dinners on the weekends and professionally prepared meals on the weekdays, once Amelia gave in to Wilson's pressures.

The list went on, and over time, a strained familial dynamic arose. Rob's relationship with his mother hadn't suffered, however, around Wilson, Rob always felt detached. Like a stranger of sorts. He had assimilated into their new lifestyle moderately well. New school, new opportunities, and new material wealth all fell into place, and an adolescent Rob went with the flow. He didn't understand what his mother saw in Wilson outside of providing them with wealth they never imagined, but he also realized that it really was none of his business what kept them together. Wilson made his mother happy. The man wasn't obligated to make Rob happy too, so he left it at that.

But as his teenage years came and went, he grew uncomfortable with this lifestyle. Wilson wasn't a bad guy necessarily, he just had a tendency to come off as a prick, whether he meant it or not. The man was pure business all the time, as if a chat with his own family was another meeting in the day's schedule. Beyond that, he always seemed critical of Rob's outlook on life. The older Rob became, the more palpable the tension. Their twelve-year relationship had been like oil and water. The last straw seemed to be Rob's trip to Europe, and in the back of his mind he felt anxious about the inevitable conversation concerning his questionable return home. He wanted his own path, rid of the association with Wilson's social circle and business ties. He wanted freedom. He wanted out.

Along the wooded path, the church bells rung in 11 p.m., causing Rob to turn back toward town. Invisible though it was, he knew the exact direction in which the tower lay and remained still until it finished its goodnight song. Because of the incline of the walk home, the turn forward made him notice the brilliant, speckled sky. It was a new moon, the stars out in full like glittering chain mail on the chest of the night. The view reminded him of his old Astronomy Club back in Fort Dearborn and their monthly trips north of the city. Some nights here he longed for a telescope.

The nighttime view was more impressive than the best nights at his uncle's house and dwarfed that of any night back home in Fort Dearborn. Trudging along, he could see Sagittarius, the archer, dotted low on the horizon between a gap in the trees. Despite their common interest in archery, Rob hadn't seen much blessing from the constellation during his mornings in the forest. Suddenly, the face of a beautiful girl smiled in his mind's eye. *Rose was a Sagittarius*, he thought. The months since he'd seen that face and felt so gentle a touch seemed like years. He shook the thought away, knowing that following it would surely lead to a sad ending on such a wondrous day.

Sometimes, Rob would share his interest in the stars with friends, and while they would temporarily indulge him in his joy, the expression seemed to fall on deaf ears. Perhaps they simply couldn't relate, yet something told him that wasn't the case. More and more he wished he had someone with which to gaze upon the universe's beauty.

He laughed to himself as a thought came. In the yearbook of his mind he saw his twenty closest friends, lined up by picture. It was as if he could take his finger and rattle off their careers. *Finance, Law, Med, Corporate, Finance, Law, Med, Corporate, Finance, Law. . .* And suddenly it would come to him! *Finance, Law, Med. . .Dropout.* And cue the music. *Dun-Dun-Dun!*

Rob smirked. Were such friendships true or merely fabricated due to proximity and association? If such friendships falter when people separate for a time, is that an indication? Likely, he supposed. What, then, would he be going back to? His friends were distant and he had broken the heart of the only girl he loved. It seemed an honest path to follow that which pulls one's heartstrings, be it glorious or be it simple. Was there ever a 'right' move when there was no precedent for his life, no guide on which to base his decisions? Feeling was all one had to stave off logic's choking grip. And if life was just borrowed time, some blip in the grand fabric of the universe, one might as well take one's time when lucky enough to walk a smooth and sunlit path. It might get bumpier farther along.

"Ehh," he breathed, hoping to shake the drifting, deepening thoughts. "How the hell should I know?" he mumbled.

In short time, the woodland cabin welcomed him back. Rob shed his layers in the entryway. Silence met him yet again, and the note he left Julius appeared untouched. Rob felt a passing sympathy for his fallen mate and decided to pour himself a finger or two of whisky and read until fatigue overwhelmed him. A pull and a pop had the top of a ceramic jug of some local booze free. The label was in German and Rob hadn't bothered to decipher it. A splash or two had his glass to a proper level. After stowing the jug, he entered his dark bedroom, placing the whiskey beside his water glass from the afternoon.

Sitting on his bed landed him square on his cellular phone. He cursed, reached under himself and grabbed the bulky thing. He pressed the sleeping phone awake, illuminating its frontal display. It read: 27 Voicemails. *What the. . .?* Rob squinted and froze, it taking a moment register.

". . .That's bad," Rob decided aloud.

At that very instant, before he could formulate a remote action plan, a call came through. The phone buzzed in his hand, sending a tingling twinge of anxiety radiating up his spine. Caller ID: Mom. Rob blinked and answered with alarm.

"*Hey*, what's going on?" he blurted.

"Rob, my God. Finally." It was a man's voice.

"*Wilson*? Where's Mom?"

The voice exhaled sharply. "I've been trying to reach you for a damn week."

"I'm sorry. I couldn't find the charger for this thing. What's going on?" he asked quickly. "Where's Mom?"

"She's resting."

"Is everything okay? Why do I have so many voicemails?"

He heard an inhale before the words. "Rob, you're going to need to come home. Your mom hasn't been feeling well recently."

"What do you mean? What's wrong with her?"

"Her cancer came back."

Chapter 2: A Tragic Smile

Sleep eluded Rob along his foggy nine-hour flight. He even slugged a few drinks in an attempt to calm his jittery system. Endless ocean views provided no peace and the incessant, whirring engine had his mind on the brink of collapse. But he stuck through the limbo of travel as best he could, determined to report home for the sake of his beloved.

The lens through which he had seen the world over the past eleven hours had been a blurry one. Like a broken microscope, the more he fought to adjust the focus and find clarity the farther he was from it. Wilhelm had graciously agreed to drive him to Dusseldorf before daybreak to make the flight his stepfather had arranged. Before he left, Rob had grabbed a notepad and pen to write Julius a message, but after two failed attempts to express his thoughts and explain the situation, had given up. Julius would just have to understand. He'd call his friend from the States once things settled. Ticketing, security and boarding had been a haze. Did he get aggressive with the ticketing agent? Had he knocked into that man and spilled his coffee? Did he even pay for the quick meal he ate before boarding? To the end of his days he would never truly be able to remember the events with certainty.

The wet, turbulent landing and car service left his memory as quickly as they entered. Rob spent the forty-five-minute, traffic-laden drive home from Fort Dearborn International Airport as he had the morning ride to Dusseldorf, peering out the window wide-eyed and unfocused. Rain blanketed the car in battering waves like a morose symphony. His ordinarily inquisitive mind was unable to fight away the stress of such a forthcoming unknown. Cars, overpasses, and growing heights of buildings went unseen through the opaque backseat window while Rob's mind raced.

At one point along the highway, two miles or so from the edge of the skyscrapers that constituted Downtown Fort Dearborn, two towering, unfinished apartment buildings loomed overhead like brotherly monuments of a fallen District. Usually an object of consideration and a sign that he was soon approaching home, on this day he hadn't taken notice. Even though he learned of the Inner District's collapse in school, the unfamiliar development atop it, in which those towers now lay, was altogether an afterthought. Though his curiosity of that forgotten place oftentimes had him musing, his mind's present haze fogged all higher order thought. The towers scrolled out of view, ignored as they had been for the better part of three decades. The closer his car towed him towards Downtown, the harder the rain fell. The city looked like it was weeping.

The car dropped him off under an overhang and Rob wordlessly walked into the lobby of his apartment building a physical and mental wreck. He'd only slept three hours or so in the past thirty-six, yet upon entering the familiar place, recognition that he was finally home tapped his energy reserves and offered him some hustle towards the rear elevators. Up the elevator went, higher and higher, like a straight delivery of this young man to the heavens. The higher he went, the harder his heart pounded, and in what seemed like a moment's time, the elevator sounded its gentle ping upon reaching the penthouse, indicating he finally must face the music of an uncertain future.

The doors separated to reveal a lavish living room. Rob's eyes flashed about, taking in the home he hadn't seen in many months. Beyond the living room was an exposed kitchen brandished with modern amenities, marble countertops, and stainless steel appliances. A tiny network of hallways beyond and on opposing sides of the open kitchen led to bedrooms, bathrooms, an office, and a billiards room/study. A dining room was out of sight, and to Rob's immediate right was a side section that held a white grand piano, it's lid propped up to expose the strings and hammers in all their glory - Rob's favorite accent in the otherwise excessive home. Floor to ceiling windows lined the perimeter of the apartment, including each bedroom's outside wall. The views could be quite stunning, truth be told.

The centerpiece of the living room was an imported Japanese Cyprus tree stump sat upon an antique oriental rug. The stump covered a majority of the area's hardwood floors, serving not only as a discussion piece but functionally as a coffee table. Suede couches hugged the stump from three sides, opening onto an ostentatious fireplace flanked with paintings that made it look like a museum exhibit. Rob had always felt the gaudy aesthetic additions to their living space out of place.

On the middle couch sat Wilson with a snifter of brandy on the table and a copy of *The Financial Times* in his hand. A single small reading lamp was all that lit the entire grey living room, perhaps setting the ambiance for an inevitable conversation. Behind Rob the elevator doors rolled shut in a tender delivery.

"Hi Rob," Wilson greeted soberly as Rob stepped into the space. "Welcome back."

"Hey," he breathed. "Where is she?"

Wilson folded his newspaper, leaned forward and placed it beside his drink. "She's sleeping right now." He motioned to the couch beside him. "Can we talk?"

Rob hesitated, looking down the dark hallway beside the kitchen towards the master bedroom. If not for the pelting rain, silence would have held the apartment in stasis. There was a ghostly, empty feel about.

"Ok," said Rob as he set his bag on the floor beside the elevator and walked to the couch. He ran a hand through his hair and plopped into the cushion. "Tell me what's going on."

Wilson was a sharp, well-built man with an immaculate haircut and wardrobe. He had a gold watch on his right wrist that Rob had never seen before. He hadn't missed him.

"I'll start at the beginning."

"Please."

"As you know," Wilson began deliberately, "since your mother's battle with cancer 5 years ago, her doctors administer yearly screenings as a precaution. Six weeks ago she went in for her scan and they found a rather large tumor in her lower abdomen. The treatment schedule was immediate and very aggressive."

Rob squeezed his eyes shut and heaved a breath. "*Six weeks ago*? Why wasn't I told about this then?"

"Your mom was. . .optimistic. When the news came she didn't want you to have to cut your trip short. She kept insisting on how important it was for you. It was her wish for you to return home on your own terms, at which point we could discuss the situation. She knew you'd be back by the end of September so she - stubbornly - decided to wait to tell you. But I'm sorry, Rob. Her body didn't share her mind's optimism. After four weeks of aggressive treatment, her condition began to decline and last week her kidneys failed. With that news, I immediately took it upon myself to call you. I'm sorry, Rob. I've been trying for the past seven, maybe eight days. I booked every flight available in hopes you'd answer. *Finally*, and thankfully, you did."

For a moment, Rob's aggravation approached a peak. His thoughts felt like a washing machine on spin cycle. Why hadn't she told him? Why hadn't he had that fucking phone charged? Why hadn't he just. . .

"I want to see her," he exclaimed.

Wilson swallowed heavily. "Certainly. But I have to, um. . ."

Rob squinted in disbelief as Wilson hesitated. Wilson's eyes searched while his mouth moved. Was the man at a loss for words? Finally, he looked Rob dead in the eye with a newfound intensity.

"I have to warn you. Your mother's condition is. . .not easy to see. She is very frail. You do not have to go in the room if you don't want to."

Rob couldn't hold his look, staring then into the wooden table. "How bad is it?"

"She may not make it through the night," he heard Wilson say. "If you're going to go in, it should be to say goodbye."

Rob buried his head in his hands. His voice became muffled as he spoke. "Oh, I can't fucking believe this. I don't understand. I just don't understand all this." He lifted his head. "I spoke with her a *month* ago. How does this happen in that time?"

"When it takes hold, it takes everything."

"No one said *anything*. *Why*? Why the *fuck* didn't you call me?"

"She. . .just wanted you to have fun, Rob." Wilson sighed with a tone of disapproval. "I tried to convince her, but she wouldn't budge. And then it was too late." He shrugged. "No one planned for you to come home like this."

Before Rob could muster a sentence, soft footsteps patting the wood hallway to the right of the kitchen caused him to perk up like a deer at the sound of a snapping twig. His heart felt as though it had stopped. For an instant, for the slimmest margin of time, he thought it was his mom. It wasn't.

Instead, he found a middle-aged woman dressed in white standing in the hallway, illuminated only slightly by the reading lamp and half-open window drapes. The lighting made it appear like she was floating on the dark backdrop of the hallway, as if she was an angel. Rob's heartbeats returned with a thud, and with it, wonder of whom this woman was and why she was in his home.

"Who are you?" Rob asked coldly.

"Hello, Rob," the woman returned softly. "My name is Betty. I'm a Hospice nurse helping to take care of your mother. We're all very glad you're home." The tip of her tongue rolled over her lips. "Have you had enough time to speak with your stepfather?"

"Yes," Wilson announced in Rob's stead. He was staring at the fireplace.

Betty motioned, then, to the hallway. "Would you like to see her?"

Rob delayed, and then nodded.

"Come with me." Her voice was kind.

Rob stood, ignoring the ache in his bones, and met the elderly woman in the entrance to the hallway. He could feel his face flush as the nurse led him along, the corridor closing in around them. His legs moved without feeling, robotically, like he was on a conveyor belt passing memories on each side of him, jogging pictorial flashes and sensations unfelt for months and years: a wall-mounted needlework his mother had sewn; picture frames littered with images from years and decades gone; his bedroom on the right, the site of adolescent angst, motherly advice, and teenage mischief; the bathroom where his twelve-year-old self had cried from broken bones, sickness, or sadness; a second bedroom where he'd watched movies and played board games with her.

The conveyor belt dropped him off at the end of the hallway, before his mother's bedroom door. Until the pair halted, Rob hadn't realized the nurse was holding his arm. After a quick squeeze to boost his confidence, she opened the door and he walked into the dim, storm-lit room. The endless hardwood floors, hallways to the bathroom, walk in closet, and sauna, the enormous drapes that could keep the magnificent sunset at bay, and the bed where he had spent his sick days greeted him familiarly. It was almost exactly as he had remembered it.

Almost. The alien feeling in the room began as a smell, a twinge of something foreign. He remembered his mother vividly by her perfume, a smell that even in his imagination would trigger goosebumps of sentimental joy. This was a severe opposite. The smell in the room could simply be explained as the smell of the end; a deathly odor. It made him cringe.

Then he saw her. At least what was left of her. There was a sleeping body in her place on the left side of the bed. It wasn't *her.* It was less, somehow fabricated or illusory, like a declining rendition of the vibrant woman he so cherished. His position above her showed tight, pale skin against black hair, hollow cheeks, and a slim wrist with a tube taped over the hand.

Rob was stunned. He couldn't move, he couldn't speak, he could only observe. The tube led to an IV bag next to beeping electronic machines hanging beside the bed. It was a makeshift hospital room. Another woman, he noticed, also a nurse, sat beside the machines with crossed legs. She was watching him.

"Amelia," she said, and looked over to the bed. "Your son is here to see you." The tone of optimism felt out of place.

The body beside the nurse didn't acknowledge her words. It lay there only in form, frail, withered, and so delicate. The nurse stood, then, and walked towards Rob and Betty. Standing before him, she offered a tragic smile.

"You take as much time as you need, okay?" she said, and the pair of nurses exited the room.

The door closed behind Rob, sealing him into the expiring situation. His legs were like concrete. Each step towards the bed was a miracle of will and effort. He began shaking and sweating and a hand made its way over his mouth. The sight, sounds, smell, and sensation were overwhelming. He forced himself to the nurse's chair and fell into the cushion, unable to take his eyes off the dormant form of his mother.

He knew she had fought. He knew she had tried in the face of futility, could see how she hung on now by a thread. The past week had been a battle beyond the scope of words or any pathetic attempt at description. When the body rejected itself, there was only one outcome. It was truly time to say goodbye.

Something snapped in Rob, then. He hadn't noticed it; it didn't register, for the circumstances were far too overwhelming to recognize an internal change. It would take months to eek its way out of his subconscious. But it would show itself, as sure as the rain fell that day, and when it did he would never be able to recover the man he was before that moment. His body held the seated position while his mind levitated and rattled.

The machines made noise. Time passed. . .

No one but Wilson or Amelia's nurses could say how long Rob was in the room. A matter of minutes? An hour? It couldn't have been that long, could it? Ask Rob today and he would simply shrug. It was time lost, omitted from his life as if it never truly happened.

Before Rob knew it, he was in his bedroom. The door slammed behind him and he flipped a lamp on to reveal his belongings in the exact state he left them. He hadn't bothered to take notice, but a zip-up jacket still hung over his desk chair, his closet door was ajar, and items above his dresser were still in a mixture of organized disarray. The hardcover novel on his bedside table was upside down, spread open and likely with a cracked spine. It had been too unwieldy to bring along on his trip.

His knees felt weak and his fists clenched. He could feel his nails digging into the palms of his hands as he shook in waves of full-body tremors. The leather desk chair invited him over, tilted with its seat towards the door. Rob approached and, succumbing to gravity's command, slumped into the chair with exhausting release, letting some tears rain emotion onto his lap. With blurry eyes he swiveled to face the computer and turned it on. The machine had been a birthday gift from his mother. They had researched and ordered every piece for him to build it himself, like a grownup version of the building block sets he loved as a child. Everywhere he looked were memories tied to her. Pictures, clothes, gifts. Even looking in the mirror, he saw their resemblance in one another. She was everywhere.

Without looking, he slid the bottom right-hand drawer of his desk open and retrieved a bottle of Blue Label. Another birthday gift, but this one was from Rose. He wondered if she knew what was happening. After the way he ended things, though, he doubted she cared.

A pass of the wrist smeared a wave of tears from his cheeks. The only thing that felt natural at that moment to avoid inflicting heavy, irreversible damage to himself or his room was to drink. Heavily. Perhaps sleep would come to take him away from this living nightmare.

Rob unscrewed the cap at the same time his desktop came to life. He grabbed a few collectable shot glasses that lined the top shelf above his computer monitor, 4 to be precise, and filled them, splashing some drops on the wooden surface.

One, down the hatch. Then two, three, and four. An empty stomach received the golden spirits and Rob's face formed a scowl as his throat argued with his mouth. It burned. Rob closed his eyes and leaned his head on the back of his chair while raindrops broke against the windows.

Soon four more shots were lined up on the desk and Rob tossed a much lighter bottle carelessly into the drawer from which it came. Like before, he made quick work of them. One, down the hatch. Then two, three, and four. The onset of a buzz took a wavy shape in his vision, amplified by glossy eyes and exhaustion. It forced him to acknowledge the fatigue, at long last. More importantly, it made him want to avoid the fight against it. A yearning for sleep overcame him. He chose a musical mix on his computer to help calm his nerves and reset his emotions. It was a classical list, music his mom had taught him to appreciate. The first measures of *Clair de Lune* began to softly coax his mind, pulling him from his chair and cradling him into his bed like a mother to a newborn child. The rain sheeted off his windows, an odd yet balanced duet. A throbbing warmth from within hummed along in harmony and lured his body, mind, and soul deeper into the embrace of his mattress. His breaths were heavy and stinging and he coughed to rid the burn from his throat. Closing his eyes was one last hope for solace, even if temporary, and before the piece reached its final measures, Rob was asleep.

Time passed. The rain ended. And somewhere along the way, the machines stopped making noise.

Chapter 3: Peaks and Valleys

Morning came as unwanted as the guests that were slowly filling the apartment. They came to mourn and pay their respects to Amelia and the remainder of her little family. They came overwhelmed with emotion and grief. They came with sympathy cards, flowers, and tears. They came all day and into the night.

Rob was helpless to feeling it rude having his space impeded upon by the guests. It was an irrational aggravation, he knew, but he couldn't seem to shake it. Some people crave presence when they're grieving, others seek solace. Rob fell largely into the second group, allowing room for only a few people in whom he would confide - none of whom would be there that morning, for his family was now as good as a memory and his friends were scattered about amidst their tangential lives.

After listening to the third wave of foot-traffic spew from the elevator, he was finally agitated enough to rise from bed. Through glassy eyes, the alarm clock resting on his desk told him it was 8:01 a.m. *First day of the rest of my life,* he thought as he sat up and ran a hand through his hair. Feeling its slickness, he supposed it would be appropriate to shower if he was to face the crowd. So he gathered himself and made for his bathroom, wincing as his bare feet met the cold marble floor. He took a look in the mirror and smelled himself. He was, in a word, ripe. After all, his last shower had been two nerve-wracking days earlier in the Rhineland. Since then, hygiene hadn't been something he had prioritized.

He hadn't thought it possible, but the memory of Germany made him feel even less at home. The place seemed out of reach, like some faraway fantasy. That window to his past was foggy. The door to his future was locked. He felt trapped between the two, inside a terrible, uncertain situation. A thin layer of misery coated his blossoming depression as Rob stood in the shower, searching for some way - any way at all - to prepare for the proceedings, the forced exchanges, and whatever else lay ahead. . . He found none.

Freshly washed, he walked into his closet and browsed its offerings. The suit he chose fit him like a glove, even though he hadn't worn it in nearly a year. As he tightened the knot on his black necktie, a glance in the mirror made him smirk. *At least I clean up nice.* It was the first hint at a smile he'd had in about 48 hours. *Let's see if the act can hold.* With a deep breath, he mustered the courage to make for what was, judging by the commotion, surely a mess of people waiting.

Rob emerged from the hallway to find two dozen people in the living room carving out their territory for grief. Other voices could be heard from the kitchen and beyond in surround sound. Not Amelia, Wilson, nor Rob was religious. In lieu of a wake, Wilson had clearly felt it appropriate to honor Amelia's wishes to open the doors of their home to receive visitors who wished to pay their respects to the departed and the bereaved. It was commonplace for said visitors to bring food or flowers as a gesture of sympathy and mourning, which they had done in grand form as was evident by the favors atop the dining room table.

Good God, Rob thought at the sight. But frankly, he was relieved at this detail. He didn't have a desire to view his mother's dead body, let alone sit next to it for four hours straight. He made sure to make a mental note to thank Wilson for making the arrangements, however pushy he felt it to be.

His entrance was quiet and went mostly unnoticed as he sauntered a little deeper into the room to get a better feel for who had arrived. He quickly scanned the open expanse, recognizing a small percentage, and realized he hadn't the slightest idea of what to do. Should he approach people? Why? Maybe find someone to chat with? About what? His dead mother? Should he await hugs or condolences? How does one act in such a situation? Perhaps eat? No, he wasn't hungry. Perhaps drink? He wasn't thirsty either. . . Panic ensued.

Rob closed his eyes for a moment to slow his thoughts as anxiety fought to rule the day. If he didn't fight back, the day would be lost before it truly began. He squashed the grinding nervousness and decided the sensible thing would be to defer to Wilson. Figuring his stepfather to be in the living room or the kitchen, he began his walk, hoping no one had yet recognized him. But Rita had.

Rita Stockfield was a co-worker and dear friend of Amelia's. Their relationship dated back many years, having begun when Amelia first took work with the Hempstead Foundation, an upper-tier charitable organization focused on a range of medical research. Amelia had been loved for her overwhelming generosity and compassion for others, especially those in need. Although she hadn't practiced in many years, she was a nurse at heart, and when she and Wilson married, she devoted her newfound wealth and time to volunteering and supporting various charities with service and donations. Wilson's connections allowed Amelia to gain a position at the Foundation, where she flourished, reaching board membership within a decade.

While most of Rita's actions over the past twelve years had seemed genuine, there was always a hint of something else Rob picked up on. She was never publicly jealous or conniving, but it seemed like behind closed doors she would make sure no one usurped her position with Amelia. Maybe she was harmless, but, even barring any evidence to the contrary, he just didn't much care for the woman. She was about the last person he wanted to see in that moment.

"Rob, dear," Rita said between sniffles. Her left hand made its way to Rob's arm as her right was full of used tissues. "I'm so sorry. *Oh*," she whimpered, "we are all so devastated." Her makeup was running away from her eyes and her lipstick was smudged.

"I know," Rob sympathized, giving his most genuine try at sincerity. "Thank you for your thoughtfulness, Rita."

"This all happened so suddenly. We. . .just last month we were planning a trip together. What's the Foundation going to do?"

The poor Foundation. . . He stared blankly, nodding as if he shared her sorrow.

"This is such a tragedy," she wailed, and went in for the hug.

Rob considered the word 'tragedy' as she wrapped an arm around him. It felt frustratingly out of place.

"It'll be a tough road ahead," Rob answered lightly during the embrace.

When they parted he frowned and, to his relief, Rita disengaged, overcome by her emotions. He felt his feet begin to move on their own accord. Initially his path was directed toward the wide floor-to-ceiling window near Wilson's grand piano, but the scent of freshly brewed coffee curved his path into the kitchen. Inside were more visitors, mostly Wilson's associates, who had clearly segregated themselves to the kitchen and the study while the women from the Foundation, not coincidentally almost all wives of those businessmen, had congregated in the living room.

Wilson entered Rob's field of vision walking towards the study to join a circle of men whose faces and tones seemed quite upbeat considering the circumstances. *Let's avoid that ticking time bomb,* Rob thought as he poured himself a cup of coffee and took a sip.

"Rob," a shaky voice said from his rear.

He turned to find Cheyanne Madison a visible wreck. If there were two people that would identify themselves as Amelia's closest friends, Rita was one and Cheyanne the other.

Cheyanne was married to Wyatt Madison, Wilson's boss and the Chairman of the Board of Directors of Madison Corp., a powerhouse among the city's corporate institutions. The relationships between husbands led to a natural relationship between wives, having met in a similar fashion as Amelia and Rita had - through the Foundation.

Cheyanne may have considered herself a Philanthropist, though Rob had never seen evidence suggesting she was more than a check signer. Where she and not only Amelia, but other men and women, differed was in this: whereas most devoted time and ideas, she simply threw her husband's money in the mix. Amelia had understood that oftentimes care was more valuable than dollars, but had remained close with Cheyanne for many years. There had always been a small amount of tension between Cheyanne and Rob. Rob was an excellent student and athlete, outshining her son, Walter, in high school. Walter never held a grudge, actually he and Rob were friends, but Cheyanne couldn't seem to accept a boy who hadn't been born into wealth outdoing her son. At least that was Rob's guess.

"What's there to say?" Cheyanne cried as she rushed in for a hug. "Oh, I'm so sorry."

Rob did his best to comfort her. "Oh, thank you for your thoughtfulness," he responded, clicking the internal counter from 1 to 2 and wondering how many times he would repeat the phrase that morning.

"This is such a tragedy. It happened so suddenly. Just three weeks ago we were planning a major fundraiser in Denver."

'Tragedy'. . .'It all happened so suddenly'. . . Is there an echo in here?

Cheyanne continued, "We knew she was sick but. . .but not like this. How long have you been home?"

"Oh, not long. I–I found out too late."

Cheyanne pursed her lips and stared accusingly through her wet eyes. "I'm sure she wished you were there for her."

Rob showed an aggravated twitch. He ignored the shot and changed the subject. "How's Walter?"

"He's doing great." The smallest curl of a smile formed. "He graduated Cum Laude and was accepted to Mt. Hope Medical School. He'll be starting once he returns from London."

Walter was a year younger than Rob, so when Rob returned to college for a 5th year, the two were in the same class. He knew that behind her present sympathy, the woman was reveling in the fact that Rob had still not graduated.

"Oh, that's nice. His hockey buddies always said they could get him to cum loud. Would you excuse me?" Rob said, covering his glare with a sip of coffee and walked away, leaving Cheyenne flustered.

With each room getting fuller by the minute, Rob tried to find solitude on the balcony but it too was overrun with guests. His consolation was the floor-to-ceiling window near the piano which he found himself staring out habitually as the morning carried into the afternoon with repetitive blur. The city below and beyond bustled with activity. He had never felt more alone among such a mass of people. The apartment was packed, the city a madhouse as always, but his heart was empty. He wondered about the funeral arrangements, the amount of sleep he'd miss, and the ever-present guilt of being away in a time of need. He wondered about the future but no matter how hard he tried, every conceivable avenue led to a dead end. The paths were lonely beyond words.

Rob had, in one way or another, interacted with about everyone who visited. Presently, his count of "Thank you for your thoughtfulness" responses was at twenty-two, but his energy level was nearing zero. Yes, people were sad. Yes, people cried. No, it hadn't made him feel consoled or any less lonely. He felt trapped, like the floor and ceiling were closing jaws of some beast and the people were the teeth. Yet the entire maw of the beast was empty, a pretend vigil.

The arrival of lunch provided a break, and he was able to eat without disruption for a record-setting seven minutes. Ironically, the man who broke the silence was arguably the person who annoyed Rob the least out of the entire crowd.

Bronson Stalker was the youngest executive at Madison Corp. He worked closely with Wilson and, to Rob, was basically the only enjoyable person in this circle. All things considered, the small talk that ensued was less awkward than it would have been with a different guest. But after a few minutes even Bronson made Rob feel as if he was approaching a breaking point. He was tired of small talk, tired of the encroaching presence, and tired of this insincere charade. Bronson took Rob's cues and offered a compassionate closing remark.

As Bronson left, a caterer brought over a delivery of flowers and placed it on the dining room table. The bouquet was gorgeous, an arrangement of white roses in a clear vase with black ribbon tied around the neck. Rob stared at it inquisitively.

"From. . ." the caterer said while checking an attached note, "Mr. White." It was an obvious response to Rob's direct expression. She forced a solemn smile and spoke again before departing. "Roses."

The word made his ears perk up, and a sweet, lovely face entered his mind's eye, then, of a young woman who had held his heart for more than two years. She smiled at him, eyes sparkling, and blew him a kiss. The memory took him to a better time, if only for a moment, filled with love and companionship, when life was like a cool breeze. *Rose. God, it would be nice if she were here.*

Before Rob was aware of his actions he was standing in front of his desk, phone in hand, with Rose's number dialed, right thumb frozen over the rubber 'send' button.

She'd want to know. What if she doesn't want to see me? . . .Fuck it, just press the button.

His thumb clicked and the call connected. A rush of warmth overtook him as he waited for Rose to answer. It was the first time he had felt alive all day.

"Hello?" an elegant voice sounded from the other end of the call.

"Hi, Rose."

"Oh my God, Rob," Rose answered, unable to mask her shock. "Hey."

"How are you?" he blurted.

"I'm good. . ." she replied with some confusion. "What's going on? Are you calling me from Europe?"

"No, uh, actually I'm home right now," he said, struggling for a way to break the news. "My, uh, my mom got real sick so I had to come home."

"*Sick*? Is she alright?" If Rose still held any resentment toward Rob, she was concealing it well with genuine concern.

"No. She, uh. . .she died last night, Rose." It was the first time he had said the words out loud. The silence that followed felt terminal.

"*Oh* my *God*," Rose said. "I'm so sorry. Oh, I'm *so* sorry, Rob."

"I know, Rose. Um. . . Look, I was wondering. . ." He cleared his throat and tried again. "I know we didn't end things well but I was wondering if you had some time to meet up. I just–I just need to get out of the apartment."

"Aw, God, I'm sorry, Rob. I'm out of town right now at a conference for work. I–I'll be back on Thursday. I could meet you then. Does that work?"

"Oh, no that's okay."

"I'm sorry, I–"

"No, yeah," he shook his head, "maybe–maybe when you get back, then. Just–we'll just get in touch later. No worries. I know this was out of the blue."

"It's alright, Rob. I'm really sorry I'm not there. Just let me know about Thursday and I'll come see you. Just call me, alright?"

"Alright. I will. Thanks Rose."

When the call ended, he noticed he had, at some point in the conversation, sat down in his chair, perhaps to soften the blow of her potential refusal. In the quiet of his room, voices and commotion snuck under his door. A look at his watch showed 1:26 p.m. He exhaled sharply as the anxiety came back like a gust of wind. *I can't do this shit. I can't.* He hadn't realized how hard he held on to the short-lived hope of being able to see Rose. Without that outlet in sight, the prospect of an afternoon amongst the people felt like an eternity. He fought the sudden urge to duck out and waste the hours elsewhere - anywhere. But the urge was too great.

A little over an hour later, the apartment spinning in his vision, he snuck into the elevator, fleeing what would forever be an obscure, woeful memory of a day.

Rob watched the nitrogen bubbles of a freshly ordered stout cascade down the sides of his glass. It was his third pint and each view of the remarkable displacement of gas provided the most amusement he'd likely experience for a long time. A tan head sat atop the dark beer, so thick it could hold a dime without breaking surface tension. It was a trick Rob learned in Belgium of all places - the beer being from Ireland - and he looked forward to bringing the display back home. Today he only had bills on him, though. Maybe he'd show it off some other time.

A full draw left a thick foam moustache that he quickly removed with a curled lower lip. On average it took five draws for him to empty a pint. Today he had drunk the last two in four. It was bitter, slightly sweet, and held a mild twang at the back end. Either the tap lines were a little dirty or the beer had soured. Maybe it was an aspect of the style. How could he know? He had only learned lagers.

He sat at a modestly populated bar in the *Clover Leaf Pub*, wildly overdressed in his suit and tie and alone. People were chatting up and joking with the bartender. It was an ordinary spot, chosen at random after escaping the "afternoon rush" back at the apartment some thirty minutes earlier, and had been serving his current need to slam a few beers, but the mood was drowning. He craved something upbeat, maybe with some women around or better whiskey. Two gulps left his pint empty and he threw a fifty on the bar and headed for the door, indifferent to the change he was owed.

Rob's next stop was guided by chance once again. He supposed he was a few blocks south or maybe west by then. He hadn't cared to check the street signs. The name *The Nocked Arrow* caught his eye. It was a cheesy country-themed bar, trying to plant an outdoor vibe in the center of a metropolis, and Rob thought he could make the idea work. But in the end the place kind of sucked. Mostly dudes, no darts, and the Arcade-style hunting game at the rear was out of order. And he was looking to place bets, too. . .

Three more pints and a double shot had him riding a quick high. He felt pretty good, felt buzzed, but felt like getting *loaded*. This retreat from home was going to turn into a solo bar crawl until he got thrown out of somewhere or passed out. It was decided.

Rob stumbled out of *The Nocked Arrow* and into a sleek and upscale martini bar called *Apropos*. Outside of his attire, he didn't belong here either. He was a simple guy and this was an uppity place, white on white (not just the people), a stainless-steel bar, and probably 500 empty glass bottles lined up near the ceiling. Not liquor bottles, not soda bottles, not water bottles. . .just bottles. They were neat and tidy, but unbecoming of the setting. Rob ordered a gin martini to satisfy the status quo. Good thing it was ice cold or it would have been a chore to finish. He began to wonder why he was at this place. It was a date bar. Everyone was in pairs, engrossed in conversation, with him alone, merely an observer. *Rose would have liked this place*, he thought.

By the time he left he was full-on drunk with no intention of slowing down. He wandered the lamp-lit streets a bit longer, focused more on the cracks in the sidewalk than the traffic signs to guide his way. If he had to wait to cross a street, he simply turned and followed the walkway, content on chance's random assignment. It hadn't failed him yet.

Somewhere, sometime along the way, the sound of music grabbed his ear from amidst the dull hum of traffic. He halted his drunken stroll and looked towards its origin, a little sign above a maroon door that read *'Adrianna's Place. Live Blues music 7 days a week.'* Through the brick and wood exterior a saxophone could be heard wailing as hard as Rob's heart. He nodded at the sound, intrigued by this new venue for his sorrow.

Adrianna's Place was smoky inside and, although dark, soaked through with character. Photos, sayings, newspaper clippings, and concert posters lined the walls of the entryway and the hallway beyond, which opened onto a room - a theater of sorts - with a modest stage at the rear, some skinny tables hugged by small-backed chairs, and a bar lining the front wall, off to Rob's right. The room was backlit by neon bar signs and hidden wall sconces, a few meager spotlights the only thing distinguishing the performers. The bartenders' silhouettes could be seen crossing the beams of illuminated liquor shelves.

As Rob stumbled in, the place came alive with sound and movement. A few guys were well into a performance onstage, the guitarist mingling with a few dancing patrons in the crowd, and most tables were occupied. There was a *feel* here. Rob connected, could relate with the vibe. He had no doubt that this spot had lived through special nights and hosted special people.

Noticing a pretty waitress carrying a tray of drinks to a table, he decided to be waited on rather than beg for a drink at the bar. Standing was becoming a task anyway. He sat off to the left side and back a ways, not too far from the bar or the stage. Truthfully one couldn't sit far from anything in *Adrianna's Place*. It wasn't much bigger than a large classroom.

The waitress swooped over and Rob ordered expensive whiskey, uncaring of the price. The closing measures of the song sent the musicians offstage for an intermission, and in no time his waitress returned and delivered his drink. Noticing a painted wooden sign off to the left of the stage that read "illegitimus non carborundum," Rob chuckled. He admired the sentiment. *Cheers*, he thought, and raised his glass. But the fleeting excitement had waned after a few sips and his mind crawled back into a cave of sadness.

Some minutes later, two men appeared onstage and began the opening notes of a song. The music calmly rose and fell like the chest of a sleeping lover. Strings and horns caressed his ears, forming audible peaks and valleys of rhythmic form. At points in the piece he could literally feel the vibration in his body, like his buzz was coming alive with the music, leading him into the deeper, much darker reaches of his mind.

Then, her voice. An angel's voice. It snapped his misery and called him out of the depths of that depressed mental cave. Unique and entrancing, she sung with an attitude matching that of her audience. Mysterious yet honest, showing glimmers of feistiness within a bluesy sound, her voice emanated a sincerity that could only come from the heart. As her lyrics called his eyes upward he noticed a slight delay to the room, as if it took an extra half second to catch up to a turn of the head or shift of the eye. The fingers on his right hand were numbing from constant contact with his glass. His left was clenched, he realized. Rob looked down and loosened his grip. A mangled gold-lined paper napkin emerged from his left hand. He looked up again with the saddest eyes. Few times in his life had a voice stopped him in his tracks. And on the most unlikely of nights, here he had found a veritable siren's song calling to him.

She sang of love and loss. She sang and he listened, all the while forgetting the madness that was his life. Forgetting, if barely, the life that was taken from him. She was a beauty, he realized, this woman treating the room to her songs, with flowing dirty-blonde hair and a charcoal-colored hat. Even with the room practically spinning he could see her blue eyes. In another life, perhaps the one he had been living before today, he would have asked to meet her. He'd have kept that voice for himself and never let go. But that was done with now.

All too soon she left the stage and his break from sorrow expired, leaving him with a yearning for bed. He signaled for the check, which was delivered in record time. Opening the leather booklet revealed the damage of three glasses of top-shelf liquor.

His tab was $211. He laughed and paid the bill in cash, tipping generously.

He pushed the empty glass away and slid off the side of the chair. When he put his weight on his feet his knees shook like those of a newborn calf, fighting for the first few steps. He stumbled backwards and bumped into a body. Perhaps it was an inaudible mumble, perhaps it was a disingenuous excuse or a snide remark, but in Rob's mind, he apologized for the collision.

"*Yo.* What the fuck, faggot," the victim cursed. It was a man, short, stocky, and baldheaded. His figure was indistinct beyond a profile.

"Dude, I said, 'my bad.' Relax," Rob muttered, wobbling aside.

The man pulled Rob's coat to keep him in place. "I was relaxing, 'til you knocked my fuckin' drink over."

Rob shrugged, his hands upturned, to which the man straightened his stance.

"Nah, let's see what you got in that suit, boy. You owe me another one." The bald man reached into Rob's jacket then down to pat his pockets like a police officer.

Rob shifted. "Woah. And *I'm* the faggot."

Just as the victim was widening his eyes and clenching his fists, a broad, bearded man stepped between them.

"Ain't worth it, Marcus," the bearded man said with authority.

The bald man, apparently named Marcus, hesitated before walking back to the bar. The bearded man turned and looked Rob straight in the face. His breath was all whiskey and something sour.

"Little advice, kid: make sure your fists can back up your mouth. Now do yourself a favor and go home before my boys and I take you out back."

There was a slight pause that, for a sober person, would signify contemplation. For Rob, all it really indicated was diminished processing power.

"Done," he answered, already turning to stagger out of the bar.

Rob awoke the next morning feeling as if a rhinoceros were sitting on his head practicing rhythmic Kegels. His cheek was resting in a small puddle of drool, and the only part of his body that his brain seemed to be giving permission to move was his eyes. He groaned aloud, wondering where he was, until a kick met his right foot.

"*Rob.* Get off the floor," Wilson said with a tone of disgust.

He groaned again. "Wha-oh. Uh. . .oh, God." Downward-Facing-Dog was about all he could muster for the first few moments. "Fuck," he mumbled.

Wilson simply stood and observed as Rob sat back, turning the quasi-yoga movement into a temporary upright position before his state of torpor forced him to collapse forward, elbows on knees, eyes buried into palms.

"The funeral has been arranged for tomorrow at 10 a.m. Try to clean yourself up before then, please," Wilson said before exiting the living room with certainly more important things to take care of than a hungover stepson.

Although fearful that opening his eyes fully and letting in direct sunlight would cause his head to explode, Rob managed with effort to finally stand. He searched for the hallway that led to his bedroom in a Frankenstein walk, opening his eyes only enough to see through slits. The wall felt cold on his palm and he bumped into a frame along the way, leaving it crooked. He was still in his suit.

He hadn't felt a hangover so crushing since Amsterdam, where he and Julius had tested the limits of bodily consumption in what had been, though neither really remembered it, a night that would put any average human being in the hospital. For mornings such as this, there was only one method for recovery: water, ibuprofen, more water, a shower, a toothbrush, darkened blinds and submission to bed.

He finally awoke from his third, maybe fourth, nap around 2 a.m. the following morning, shaky but confident he could move about without having to pause for the pain. He rolled out of bed and made his way over to his desk chair. Mindlessly, he slid his bottom drawer open to expose the half-empty bottle of Blue Label. They stared at each other.

Don't do it. . . But this headache's gotta go. Hair of the dog will fix that. The bottle kept staring. He grabbed it, feeling it slosh in his hand, and set it on the desk. *Maybe one shot. This is to sip, asshole. Not rip shots of.* He settled on leaving it atop his desk for the time being, unsatisfied with the internal discussion, and leaned back down to close his drawer.

Then Rob froze. He must have missed it the previous night, a single white envelope resting in plain sight atop the neatly stacked notebooks within his drawer. Written neatly on the envelope was a name: Robin.

He squinted deeply. *Robin? Only mom calls me that.* A gentle swipe brought it before his face and he removed a folded piece of paper from within.

My dearest Robin,

If you are reading this, you've found out about my illness the hard way. I want you to know that I didn't keep this from you out of neglect, but out of love. It may take some time for my intentions to make sense to you, however, I know that one day you'll understand that even though your goodbye has been difficult, my motivations were always with your wellbeing in mind.

Did I ever tell you why I named you Robin? Before you came into my life I was in a dark place. It was like winter had fallen over my heart and there was no end to the cold bitterness in sight. A Robin is a symbol of spring, and like spring saving the Earth from winter, you opened your eyes and breathed fresh life into my heart. From that moment on, regardless of any troubles or pain, my winter never returned.

You saved me, Robin. You are the bravest, strongest person I know. Do not use my death as an excuse not to be great. You may have dark days that follow this time, but know that the warmth of spring is in your soul. You have a flame that can never be put out. Feed it. And let others find warmth in it too.

You have yet to make your mark on the world, but even though you may be saddened that I won't be able to share in your accomplishments, you have already left your mark on me – and that is the greatest joy I could have ever asked for.

Never be fearful to spread your wings, never be fearful of being daring, and never let <u>anyone</u> make your decisions for you. And of course, don't say I never did anything for you. ☺

Love,
Mom

Those who have lost someone dear to them know all too well about "the breakdown." For some, it may happen in the moments leading up to the death. For others, it happens immediately or shortly thereafter. And there are those who make it days or even months before breaking down. Sometimes there's a trigger and sometimes there isn't. Some are able to have one breakdown and move on while others have multiple. The point remains that it's inevitable, like the coming dawn. Rob had his immediately after reading his letter, and after close to an hour of emotional tears, and a few broken trinkets in his room, he finally settled.

By then it was a little after 3 a.m. Coming off of numerous lengthy naps and the surge of energy from his outburst, he knew sleep was not in his future. He showered, *again*, changed into exercise gear, and decided to go for a run to clear his head and sweat out some of the shame of the previous night. On his way from his bedroom to the elevator door he noticed a light in the kitchen. He went in for a quick drink of water and saw Wilson seated at the island reading a copy of yesterday's newspaper.

"Are we up early or are we up late?" Rob asked.

"Conference call with a client from India before the funeral," Wilson responded without taking his eyes off the paper.

"Aw, does that mean we can't have breakfast together?"

"It seems last night's escapade made you lose your sense of respect along with your dignity," Wilson said, making purposeful eye contact by way of accepting the challenge.

"Yeah, must have been while I was searching for your sense of humor," Rob answered, tiring of the back and forth.

Wilson dropped the newspaper. "Sit down for a second," he instructed.

"I'll stand."

"*Fine.* Let me give you a little piece of advice, because I think you need it. Instances such as the one in which we are both now involved are inevitabilities in life. I'm far older than you, therefore I've dealt with death a far greater number of times. In no way does that diminish your feelings or somehow make me superior, yet my experience allows me to shed some light for you onto that which follows these times.

"What I'm speaking about is coping. *Mourning.* We mourn in our own ways. I am private. Others, as was displayed Monday and will surely be displayed today, are public. It's a process. There is no *right* way - what is right depends on the individual - but there are certainly *wrong* ways. And I'm not talking about your little binge - I've been there. I'm speaking towards cause and effect for the long term. Holding pain inside works for a time. It really does. But the longer it's held inside, the greater the pressure you build up. It gets fed by other, less important things, until it either leaks out in a prolonged series of problems or explodes in one massive event. I've seen it happen both ways.

"The underlying point is as follows: make sure you find yourself an outlet. Something healthy to pour your emotion into. Mine is work, which, personally, I highly recommend."

The words left Rob contemplative and strangely at peace. It was the first time Wilson had spoken to him like a father. They shared a look for a moment's time, maybe for once having reached an understanding, albeit in the most unlikely of circumstances.

"That's all," Wilson concluded, presently noticing Rob's outfit. "But before you go wherever you're going, I'd like to remind you that you have the opportunity to speak at the funeral today if you wish. Think about it."

Rob nodded and said, "Alright. I'm going for a run."

Wilson returned his attention to his newspaper with a soft look Rob rarely saw in the man.

The run forced the last of the hangover out of Rob's system like a bilge pump. Back in the apartment, sweaty and panting, his hunger took reign, pulling him directly to the refrigerator. An abundance of leftovers from the gathering presented him with what seemed like an endless number of options. He grabbed a container of chicken salad and went for a round roll in a bag on the island. A sheet of paper placed before Wilson's earlier seat caught his attention. He pulled it over and read a short message scribbled in ink.

Meeting with the lawyers immediately after funeral. Do not miss it.

-W

Chapter 4: An Unknown Blow

The law firm of Wycroft & Schafer had represented Wilson for over two decades. It was a modest practice in size, yet boasted many clients of the upper echelon, offering a range of legal services from family law and estate planning to real estate law. The firm occupied a building registered in the Fort Dearborn Historical Society's list of Heritage Sites, dating back nearly two hundred years, which sat not in the hustle-and-bustle of Downtown Fort Dearborn, as one might expect for its clients, but just a stone's throw from the Inner District. The neighborhood was not quite touched by the Inner District's derelict atmosphere, yet was far too near for the particular societal ease of some. Wilson, however, cared not.

He straightened his tie and fluffed his blazer, steadying himself for the forthcoming conference. The leather seat of his chair was warm from the minutes spent idle. Rob was late for their meeting, causing Wilson to momentarily wonder whether or not his absence was due to traffic or because Rob knew the longer Wilson sat, the more money he'd spend. The thought left his mind as quickly as it arrived, merely a product of his aggravation. Rob had wanted some time alone at the cemetery after the service, and it was beyond Wilson to deny him it, regardless of the necessities to be discussed with the firm.

Gabe Schafer sat to Wilson's right. He was an annoying man, but did his job well. Wilson and Gabe's late father had been close, so out of respect Wilson remained a client of the firm. A lone seat, meant for Rob, was positioned across from the two men, the oversized wooden table creating a tangible partition between camps.

As the minutes passed, Wilson thought about the first time he met Rob, he a skeptical, somewhat rebellious youth unwelcoming of a stepfather. He'd grown well out of that pubescent pissant but Wilson hadn't seen him fulfill his potential in life. Instead, Rob had explored rather than focused. He had searched and searched to find some motivation, to find a direction to follow, but always managed to come up short. It had been an acceptable endeavor at first, but it was now showing no promise, only absence and childish hope.

Wilson felt some regret that the two had never meshed, never connected. He had loved Amelia dearly, but initially thought Rob to possess qualities unbecoming of a man. He later found that potential in him, only to wait for a flower that never quite bloomed, and his attempts to encourage the boy and find some middle ground to form a relationship had only dissipated in recent years.

Wilson often wondered if he was simply ill-equipped to be a father-figure. He had never wanted children and had it not been for his love of Amelia, he'd have been turned off at the addition of a stepson. It was burdensome. In truth, it had made him hesitate to propose. He had tried to parent, truly given it a shot, but was incessantly met with resistance of a groundless and immature kind. Presently, Wilson found himself content to be at odds, placing the two in unfortunate standing over the current situation.

Seven minutes elapsed before Gabe's office door opened with a creak and his secretary poked her head in to say that Rob had arrived. Gabe rose from his chair and asked her to send him in.

Rob entered quietly with a frozen expression of loss. He looked tired and his suit was unkempt with an open jacket and collar. He approached the table and Gabe began the formalities.

"Hello, Rob," he said kindly and extended a hand. "I'm Gabe Schafer."

"How ya doin'," Rob replied skeptically as he met Gabe's hand.

"I'd like you to know I'm very sorry for your loss. Your mother was a wonderful woman." Gabe paused and motioned to the open chair. "Have a seat."

Rob hesitated momentarily, glancing between both men, and complied. "What's this all about?" he asked while he and Gabe sat.

Wilson could see Rob's mind working as he inspected the scenario further. An intense expression overcame him when he realized the seating arrangement left him isolated. *Always sharp*, Wilson thought. *I'll give him that.*

"Well, I'll get right to it, as you both have been through quite enough. As incredibly unfortunate as it is, there is a legal side to your mother's passing. And that's what we're here for today."

Every sentence Gabe spoke started with a click of the tongue. It irritated the hell out of Wilson and made him eager to be done with this ordeal. He understood the business aspect of a loved one's death quite well, having lost both parents, his brother, and his first wife. And though he felt the procedures to be absolutely awful, he knew their necessity trumped that prodding emotion. All of life was a business arrangement, after all.

Gabe clicked. "Your stepfather is the Executor of Amelia's Will. He and I will be taking care of the appropriate paperwork and legal proceedings over the course of the next few weeks. Today, however, we're here to discuss your mother's assets," Gabe said as he pulled a manila folder from the surface of the desk. "I have prepared some documents for you to review and sign. They detail what has been left to you."

Wilson eyed Rob prudently. It had been a whirlwind of a week for the boy, and he knew it was about to get a bit more turbulent. For Rob's sake, he hoped he wouldn't lose his head. This was simply a matter of business, to be concluded promptly.

"Your mother's assets are few," Gabe continued, sliding the folder to Rob. "She didn't own property or vehicles, stocks, equity, or investments - assets of that nature were handled by Wilson and only in the event of his death would they be left unto her. As you'll see within the document, she held a checking account totaling $26,102 and had a rather minimal life insurance policy of $50,000. Both are left to you, however, I've reviewed the paperwork and due to a contestability clause the insurance policy's payout may take 6-12 months," he paused and breathed, "at which time a check will be mailed to you directly."

"*Al*right." Rob's tone told of caution as he skimmed the papers carefully.

It's a shame, what's coming, Wilson thought as he watched Rob's body language. *Necessary, but a shame.*

"Additionally," Gabe clicked, "you're the beneficiary of her personal items - mementos, things of that nature. Nothing in particular was listed in the Will, as it was structured in a rather. . .plain manner, but Amelia had wanted it clear that items of sentimental import were to be left to you. I would imagine there are some heirlooms, family items and such."

Rob glanced between the two men again, holding his gaze on Wilson for a moment. "I understand. . ."

Silence elapsed as Wilson prepared for the next part of the meeting. Rob, however, was growing uncomfortable, rolling a hand in the air as if to coax the proverbial elephant in the room to appear.

"Is this it? I feel like I'm in a principal's office or something. What else is this about?"

Wilson leaned forward and rested his clasped hands on the tabletop. *He's going to hate me for this. But in time he'll see the necessity in it.*

"The time has come for you and me to have a little discussion," Wilson stated firmly.

Over the years, he'd developed a manner of speech that he employed universally during business arrangements: enunciate each word, avoid grammatical shortcuts, and keep a steady, confident tone. To him, it was the only surefire way to get a point across.

"I have decided that it is fruitless to delay our circumstances any longer. To put it simply, you and I are at a crossroads in our relationship. What kept us together was our mutual bond with your mother. Her passing leaves us in a situation of uncertainty. . . Volatility, per se."

"I don't like the sound of this," Rob admitted.

Wilson could hear Gabe rustling beside him, preparing to chime in.

"You have two options today," Wilson continued. "One: you will enroll in classes once more and complete your education. Upon graduating you will accept a position that I will set up for you in your field of study - you will continue on with life, occupy yourself and spend your time valuably. I will not baby you. Your mother is dead. *You* are not. You will not mope; you will not drink yourself into oblivion or disappear to another country indefinitely. You will become a man." The sentence was like the sound of a door shutting. "That is the first option. Refusal leaves you with the second - which is less appealing, if I'm speaking truthfully."

Rob gave a disturbed squint. "And what might that be?" he asked.

Wilson hardened his expression. "The second is such: Today is where our paths separate."

"No," Rob blurted agitatedly. "Hold on a second, here. You're not just kicking me out, man."

Gabe clicked from off to the side. "Well, you're an adult, therefore, legally–"

"Gabe, I'm going to need you to shut the fuck up now," Wilson coolly remarked, staring the lawyer down for a tense three seconds before turning back to Rob. "Thank you. . . Today is where our paths separate," he repeated. "You will become independent, in every sense of the word. Your mother's money as well as your freedom - which you've held in such a high regard - will be yours entirely." He noticed Rob beginning to shake his head. "*Our* relationship ends. You will remove your things from the apartment and get situated elsewhere."

"What the fuck is wrong with you?" Rob asked painfully.

"It's tough love, Rob. I believe in it fully. My father forced it on me and while I thought it to be harsh at first, it made me who I am."

"What makes you think I've ever wanted to be like you?"

Wilson leaned in. "Childhood is *over*. You will grow up and end this nonsense you've been engaging in. I have never approved of your decisions."

"That doesn't make them wrong. Wha–"

"You will mature or you will maintain. The choice is yours. You will see no further sympathy from me regarding the current situation. In your shoes, I'd find it rather attractive."

Rob blinked. His lips were separated, moving ever so slightly as if forming a silent sentence. Finally, he spoke, quickening as he went. "*Attractive*. . . That's about the coldest thing I've ever had said to me." His hands went up. "What is this? Why is it such a problem to find my own path? Wha–" he stammered. "How is something like this going to help me? I–I don't get it."

Wilson ignored the pain in the boy's voice. "It is a push. And you need it."

"No, I don't," he laughed emptily.

"You *do*."

"*No*," Rob fired back. "I fucking *don't*."

Wilson held out an open hand. His expression remained. "Which will it be?"

"My mom dies and you think kicking me out will help?"

"That is simply one option."

"Nah, fuck that. You *want* me gone. There's no other explanation. Absolutely none."

Wilson could tell he was stalling through complaint. It showed his weakness and wasting potential. Truthfully, it made Wilson sad. He was trying to help the boy the only way he knew how.

"I do not wish to be rid of you, hence my offer. I know I am often a cold man but I will not tolerate your behavior like your mother did. If our familial relationship is to continue, you will abide by my rules. Elsewise. . ."

"You're serious?" The boy's chest was beginning to heave and his lips thinned.

A head nod was all Wilson gave. He saw the turmoil, the vicious dialogue taking place in the boy's head. His eyes shot about the room, then rested on the papers in front of him.

"Give me a pen," he ordered.

"Rob."

He looked up from the table and met Wilson's eyes. His voice was like ice. "Give me a *fucking* pen."

Wilson removed a slim item from his jacket pocket and slid it towards Rob. "Do not let your emotions cloud your rationale," he urged. "Think this through. It is irrevocable."

"I've given it about as much thought as you have," Rob snapped, and swirled his signature hastily, closing the folder. "Take your offer and choke on it, you prick." He pushed away from the table and stood.

"*Rob.*"

Rob's look showed no love lost, the moment a culmination of a long battle between opposites who in some ancient era of time would have settled the contention physically. Though a fist was clenched, he chose to use his words.

"Go fuck yourself, Wilson," he snarled, and left the office.

Rob's steps were furious and brusque. He stormed out of the firm and quickly found himself walking the city streets directionless again, guided by anger this time rather than chance. His mind was racing as fast as his heart and Wilson's cold ultimatum lingered painfully.

He hadn't realized it, but he had begun walking along Orange Ave., westward and slightly south towards an unfamiliar, forgotten portion of the city. The afternoon rush had commenced, yet these streets were less busy. Cross streets rolled by in a fog.

He felt like a boulder tumbling down a hill, gaining speed with each passing second, hoping nothing would get caught in his path. He begged for the slope to level out and let him come to a slow, peaceful stroll, for if a clash occurred it may bring irreversible damage.

He walked with unintentional blinders, deeper into the rugged neighborhood known as the Inner District. For an unknown amount of time he passed vacant lots, some abandoned rowhomes, a scrap yard, an industrial park, dim storefronts and brick apartment complexes. The sky was an overcast tribute to the abounding browns and greys below it. It looked like a storm was in the forecast.

Rob approached a shady corner bar and hesitated. The front door was open, inviting him in for an easy drink. The thought of another binge snuck through his rage, but he stifled it. Wilson's comments had infuriated him to no end, yet today he defied drink and continued walking. A path bolstered by alcohol would assuredly lead the boulder of emotions to a shattering halt. Still, before turning around and trekking the long distance home, his nerves had to settle. Avoiding Wilson for as long as possible would be best, lest a true fight break out. If he went back at all that day, it wouldn't be until evening.

The sidewalk grew fractured with tufts of grass stretching through towards the grey sky. Orange Ave. became skinnier as he went, like a chasm now splitting the taller, imposing buildings about him. Passing an alleyway between buildings, Rob was hit with an overwhelming stench of trash. The thin, short homeless man who became visible, with a bag over his shoulder, didn't so much as offer a glance. It was the first person he had noticed during the entire walk, having been oblivious to the myriad of stares that had fallen upon him before. It caused him to lift his head from the sidewalk and observe his foreign surroundings.

One block ahead to the left, a brick theater had the remainder of a slogan written on its exterior side wall. The colors were faded and the text was barely legible. It read: *The Future of City Living is Here.*

Rob recognized the phrase from a History class years back. There had been some failed transformation that took place in these parts, some Mayoral scam or city development project gone wrong. It could be seen in the buildings, the attempt at renewal. Here and there, patches of residential and commercial real estate, though worse for wear, seemed to be built of a more modern material. Aside from these units, the Inner District was dated, worn out like some miserable cloud had befallen the area. Most streets were narrow, some side roads were still cobbled, and though rotten or paint-stripped, Victorian accents curled and jutted from awnings, railings, windows, and rooftops.

He passed more brownstones and row homes until suddenly he came upon a vast opening in the dense District, where the southerly section of a rather large field stretched northward and out of sight. It was several blocks wide, overgrown with weeds and trees and seemingly abandoned. A waist-high stone wall fenced in the park's south end, and likely wrapping it in its entirety.

The opening among buildings offered a view of larger structures at points beyond the row of businesses bordering the park. Two large, unfinished towers stood out off in the distance. He wagered they were a good ten blocks farther west. He squinted. Were they the very same ones that had always caught his attention on rides to and from the airport? Though a dreary day, he wagered they were indeed, unchanged and unfinished as always.

At the end of the park, Rob had reached a crossroads where Orange Ave. ended and a new road, Atlantic Ave., which ran along the length of the park, began. He turned left, away from the park, and continued for several blocks without a thought as to what was to come until the cross above a church on his left made him crane his neck. As he slowed to examine the decaying structure, a deep voice announced itself.

"Hey, pal," the voice called out. "Makin' a sales call?"

Rob looked over his right shoulder and saw a behemoth of a man, easily six and a half feet tall with incredible bulk, moseying along the opposite sidewalk. His arms were folded, exposing thick sinewy forearms, and he wore boots and jeans. *Oh boy*, Rob thought. To the behemoth's right was a smaller man wearing baggy pants, a long-sleeve shirt, and a backwards hat. He had something in his right hand.

Rob turned, ignoring the provocation, and picked up his pace. Not five steps farther, something hard hit his head and landed on the ground. Rob recoiled, mumbled a curse, and fingered the impact site. He looked down to find a half-eaten apple rolling to a stop on the edge of the sidewalk.

"Yo, what the fuck's your problem?" Rob shouted as he spun around.

"You had a fly on your head – big one too. My buddy, here, got it off for you," the giant hollered. "Still didn't answer my question, though."

Their looks reflected what appeared to be a brutal initiative. Rob's adrenaline spiked at the prospect of an altercation.

"Don't fuck with me, man," he said, pointing. "I'm not in the mood to teach you a lesson."

"Didn't care much for school. Not sure we're gonna like that."

The two began to approach him. In a flash, Rob pulled his jacket off and dropped it to the ground. *This is what they want? Fuck it*, he thought. Rob was ready to unleash on someone. Why not these two? If he could land a punch to the throat of the monster, he would go down and Rob could let loose on the shorter one. If he got his ass kicked, so be it. *Just don't care anymore.*

Rob stuffed his tie in a space between buttons on his shirt. Suddenly, as the pair neared the double-yellow line in the road a voice rang out from Rob's rear.

"Boys! Stop right there." The voice was forceful, carrying an expectation of being obeyed.

The pair halted at the command.

"We were just going to introduce ourselves a little better to the visitor," the behemoth said as he turned back from the sound to make eye contact with Rob. "Ain't that right, pal?"

"Something like that," Rob muttered, meeting the stare.

"It appears he's has had enough interaction for the day," the voice hollered. "I think it's time for you two to move along."

Defeated, the pair turned to walk the way they came. Before they got out of earshot, though, the voice spoke again.

"Oh, and boys? I expect to see you bright and early tomorrow. You have promises to keep."

They exchanged a glance. The smaller man slouched dramatically. Then they disappeared down a side street away from Rob and his temporary savior.

Rob picked up his jacket and turned toward the man who had assuredly spared him from an overwhelming amount of pain and suffering. He was somewhat short, with a grey head of hair and a grey beard covering a pale face. A naturally furrowed brow gave the appearance that he was engaged in deep contemplation and his posture seemed to tell a tale of many miles traveled.

"They'll have to thank you one day," Rob said to the man. "You saved 'em from a hell of a medical bill."

With a playful frown the man responded. "Yes, well, good thing I protected them from you."

Rob glanced about as his nerves began to settle. He ran a hand through his hair and made to turn away.

"My name is Ernest. I'm the pastor here at St. Augustine's," the man said warmly, holding an open hand sideward towards the church.

Rob absorbed the building with his eyes, as if he was reviewing its history in the cracks and blemishes. He could tell the man expected a response, but he hesitated. Apprehension came about in his mind like a funky smell entering a room. What was this man's intention? This place was unfamiliar, rough, and the argument had him agitated. *Where the hell am I for that matter?*

As briefly as the uneasiness came, it faded as logic overrode the barrier of his emotions. The man was sincere. He decided to answer using his full name, one he hadn't enjoyed much less considered introducing himself by until just then.

"I'm Robin." The introduction, though new, comfortably rolled off of his tongue. He couldn't remember the last time he called himself that.

"It's a pleasure to meet you, Robin. I have some tea brewing, why don't you come inside for a cup?" Ernest asked. "Settle those nerves."

Robin considered the offer momentarily and looked down the road. If he kept walking he'd potentially run into trouble again. Or simply find himself even more lost. As he looked around, the setting felt more intimidating than he had thought earlier. Perhaps he'd gone as far as he needed to go that day.

"Or you're welcome to stand outside as long as you'd like, too," Ernest added drolly.

Robin softened his expression and smirked. He motioned to the door and began walking up the steps of the church. "After you."

If a passerby were to call St. Augustine's Church an eyesore, the locals would have a difficult time arguing. Decades of seasonal weather had expanded and contracted the cement veranda, creating a web of cracks, dips, and jagged peaks. It was such that one had to plot each step carefully as to not lose footing. The once ornately carved angels and cherubs on the wooden entryway doors were now smooth, faceless gestures towards their original shapes, like shores that had weathered the assault of a million tides. Through the doors was the church's sanctuary, where a center aisle leading to the sanctuary's altar divided two rows of pews. The pews were few, unable to hold more than 200 people at maximum capacity. Above the altar was a large crucifix that reached towards a vaulted ceiling. Immediately after entering, Ernest noticed that Robin's footsteps had stopped.

"Is something the matter?" Ernest asked.

Robin's eyes were skyward and scanning. He had the same look as when he inspected the exterior just a minute past and spoke without moving his attention from the ceiling.

"This is the first time I've really looked at the inside of a church," Robin answered, glancing finally down from the stained-glass windows.

"Take all the time you need. There is a hallway behind the altar and to the right. My study is the last door on your left. The tea will be there if you'd like to join me."

Ernest turned and began towards his study, leaving Robin by his lonesome. It was a path he had walked countless times over the past thirty years, sometimes fueled by anger, other times by doubt or restlessness. Today, though, he walked with confidence. A poised feeling, perhaps his faith, told him Robin would eventually make his way to the study and grant him the chance to learn more about this odd traveler.

The carpet beneath him was flattened from decades of foot traffic, and the floorboards greeted him with a creak each step of the way. It bothered him not, for he found the creaking to be a part of the building's character. Repairing the carpet, however, was near the top of the renovations list, just as soon as a new coat of paint was applied to the walls.

The hallway was dim, lit only by wall sconces, and had several doors which connected to the old Sunday school and nursery, a former choir room, vacant office space, and a restroom. Where the hallway terminated lay the kitchen, dining room, and a door that led to the rear parking lot.

Inside his study, Ernest poured a cup of tea and sat down at his desk. Neatly packed bookshelves lined the perimeter of the room, and orderly papers sat stacked on the desk's surface. At times, it reminded Ernest of a former professor's office he had seen in college. It had impressed him, how the man had created his own library within a confined and tidy space.

He tilted his head and took a soothing sip from his mug. Ernest's love of the beverage was less for the taste and more for the comfort that washed over him as he held the warm cup in his hands and succumbed to the aromas. Even in the summer he would enjoy a cup or two each day. Today he had brewed a white tea for its subtle floral notes and sweetness. In winter he preferred the earthiness and spice of black tea.

The silence of his office had him wondering about his new guest. The situation intrigued him, feeling as he did as if he and Robin had once met. It was all the more reason to want to learn this man's story, be it familiar or novel. He had an air about him, and try as Ernest might, he could not shake an uncanny feeling. Presently, there was nothing to do but mull over the feeling and sip away.

A minute or so passed and Ernest's thoughts were brought to an abrupt end as Robin strolled into his office, hands in his pockets. His suit jacket was missing. Ernest watched as Robin eased into the chair opposite him and breathed a sigh of relief. He looked as if he hadn't sat down for days.

"Would you like some tea?"

Robin raised a hand in dismissal and let his eyes wander the room. Though his body language was subdued his eyes squinted and traced about as if his mind was making an unknown judgement. Finally, they rested on Ernest.

"So, Robin," Ernest started cheerily, "what brings you here?"

Robin burst out laughing. Ernest smiled, letting the boy have his laugh, whatever it was directed towards. He had a thought, then.

"That bad, hm?"

Robin's head shook slightly as if recalling some turn of events. "*Yeah.* A lot has brought me here, now that you ask."

"Like what?"

"Well, so far this week, I've travelled 4,000 miles, basically watched my mother die, drank myself half to death, then buried her, then got kicked out of my house and cut off by my stepfather, all on about a dozen hours of sleep."

"You've had quite the week."

"Shit, the week isn't even over. Could have added 'getting my ass kicked' to the list if it wasn't for you."

"Hmm," Ernest sounded. "That may have happened, yes. And I do apologize for that unpleasant run in. The boys do that out of protection for me and for others - even though I instruct them not to. Sometimes people come here, dressed like you are, and try to take advantage of the less fortunate. I think the boys are trying to keep that element away. You have my apologies and one on their behalf as well."

The traveler watched Ernest as he spoke, as if each sentence revealed a surprise to him. "No, it's fine," he said lightly. "Couldn't care less at this point."

Ernest knew this was a lie, though an unintentional one. Ernest understood all too well how indifference was a mere defense mechanism against pain.

"I am very sorry to hear of your mother's passing."

"Thanks for your thoughtfulness," Robin answered. The statement sounded mechanical.

"How are you doing?"

Robin looked at Ernest intently. "You know, you're the first person to ask me that."

Ernest frowned. "I'm sorry for that as well. It's hard enough to sort through the death of a loved one, let alone find yourself at odds in your own home."

"At odds, yeah. . . I don't have anybody, now. . . I don't have *any*body."

"You have yourself," Ernest said encouragingly. "And you have God."

"Look, I'm not religious so if you wouldn't mind, maybe we could talk without reflecting things back on God. It's just going to bounce right off."

"I understand. That's fair." Ernest accepted the man's wishes. Far be it from him to presume that the stranger was a person of faith. That aspect was irrelevant in this time of need. "Do you want to talk about what happened?"

"Not really. It was fucking horrible," he added quickly. "It was like I had to console everyone *else*. I couldn't stand being around it all. These people in my mom and stepdad's social circle publicize their grief like they don't know how to deal with it themselves. The display is pathetic. I wanted to grab them and say, 'Grow the fuck up. Get a hold of yourselves.' I must've heard the word 'tragedy' ten times." He breathed a hollow laugh. "Was it? Really? Tragedies are catastrophes. Disasters. Yeah, it's eternally sad but was it a tragedy? *No*. . . Not at all. She wasn't murdered. She didn't drop dead or fall victim to some horrible accident. Fuck. It all just felt so fake to me for some reason."

"Well, one thing I'll say is that just because their grieving makes you uncomfortable, it does not make it pathetic. Some people cannot reign in their emotions. It isn't wrong for them to be expressive. It's simply an aspect of having people pay their respects."

"I'd like to agree with you there, but I just feel so detached."

Ernest nodded and interlocked his fingers. Robin's black suit made it pretty clear from where he had just come. "Were you able to speak at the funeral?"

Robin shook his head. "No."

"Why not?"

"I–I tried writing something this morning and I just didn't think it was good enough. I was afraid I'd break down or something. I guess I just wasn't ready. . .I could tell people were looking to me to say something, like I was obligated."

"Mm. I've had a similar experience with my son, Jack. He fell victim to an unfortunate situation many years ago. What I learned then is that what's expected of us is not always what is necessary. Expectations are the wishes of others that creep into our thoughts. *And* our circumstances. If you were ready, you would have spoken. And if there were others that expected you to do so, well, an experience such as your mother's burial is highly personal. I would imagine that the individuals who displayed such outward grief are the same who would have expected you to speak. Perhaps they should empathize more with the ways in which others grieve."

Robin eyed him for a moment, and began to nod. "Thanks."

Ernest sympathized with Robin. He knew all too well what it was like to feel lost and without purpose. The young man couldn't have been older than twenty-four, a largely transitional time in many people's lives. If Ernest was to reflect personally on the changes of that decade in his own life, it would be evening before his recollection concluded.

Robin checked his watch and shifted in the chair. "I think I should probably get going."

"I have an idea. How about you come by tomorrow and help with some repairs. Maybe it will help take your mind off things. This can be a very peaceful place once you get used to it."

That uncanny feeling lingered still in Ernest, and he was sorting through a way to have the man return. Perhaps Ernest could be a mentor or source of guidance in Robin's troubled time.

"Um. . .I have some things to take care of unfortunately," Robin said as he rose from his seat. "Thank you for the tea," he added.

"All are welcome at all times," Ernest replied. "It was a pleasure to meet you."

As the creaks of Robin's footsteps lessened, Ernest hoped the chance to meet would once again present itself. He could hear it in his head, the rote response he would offer to another with this wish. *Your paths will cross if the Lord wishes.* It almost made him laugh out loud.

Later that evening, Ernest was making his way to the front of the church to retrieve the day's mail when he discovered a black suit jacket draped neatly over the last pew. He lifted it off the pew and folded it, smiling to himself, and his gaze involuntarily turned to the crucifix hanging above the altar. *As you wish.* He looked to the ceiling, as Robin had earlier that day, curious of how long it would be until he saw that odd traveler again.

Chapter 5: The Odd Traveler

A rotten plastic tarp hung off the side of the overhead balcony, flapping chaotically in the wind like the flag of a defeated country. Early light poked through the tarp's many holes and trailed across the man sitting on the balcony below, creating a kaleidoscope of the eastern sun on his face as he took in the meager view of his complex's courtyard and the tops of buildings from neighboring city blocks. The fifth-floor vantage had its limitations, yet the man cherished his morning routine. He envied the upper levels of the building - those with views stretching for miles - but settled for his elevated perch; it was better than the ground floor, after all.

Jon was a rather simple man who found himself living in a rather complicated place. He was brought to the Rockport Apartment Complex in the Inner District some 20 years ago when he was a young child. He had been abandoned by parents he didn't remember and fostered by parents he'd rather forget. They had moved in during the *Future of City Living* scandal, having bought into the failed promise of a fresh start, modern housing, and new career opportunities. They, like so many others, were left with only remnants of the dreams and savings stolen from them. And they, like so many others, tried to mitigate their losses by fostering children to supplement their minimal income.

In those early years, when he felt like he was being kept for the government check rather than for love, he would sneak onto the metal balcony to watch the sunlight dance on the concrete entrance to the apartment complex. When he realized quite early that he was indeed only being kept for the check, the act evolved into a daily ritual. He found enjoyment and blissful solitude in sitting and contemplating the past, present, or future, a mere spectator to what seemed to be a choreographed light show.

Even though Jon had a history with the law, the local people knew him to be kind and helpful, especially to children and the elderly. Those who liked to cause problems, however, knew him for his sheer physicality. He stood over six and a half feet tall, weighed nearly three-hundred pounds, and if he wanted to, could leave you disabled merely by shaking your hand. The weight he carried was anything but excessive. He was as agile as men half his size, and if he had to choose, he would rather be gentle than overwhelming. Oftentimes he'd offer to play the role of pick-up truck or crane for those less capable in the apartment complex. Such generosity raised him to the status of a minor celebrity. Many would thank him for helping to move a couch or fix a light when they passed him in the neighborhood or the hallway. Even though he was always gracious, he personally did not respond well to the attention. He was a quiet and shy person who would have rather avoided the spotlight, but could not help the fact that he felt a duty to use his size to help others.

On this mild morning, he was peeling an orange and contemplating life. Jon often dreamt of living somewhere else, somewhere far away. Somewhere peaceful. He read about farming and raising animals like hens and goats and had seen photos of green pastures and huge, breathtaking blue skies. He thought it would be a fulfilling life to own land, grow things, and work with his hands. A farm looked like the best place on earth to raise a family. The colors were so vivid and alive, a marvelous opposite to this drab landscape of browns and greys, concrete and metal that he called home.

He thought he could adapt fairly well to that dream life. He was pretty good with his hands, but nothing like his friend Wil. Wil was quick-witted and an even quicker learner. He was strong for his size and knew his way around cars and construction as well as he knew his way around women. Even though he and Wil did the repair work at St. Augustine's as a favor to Ernest, it was quite a pleasant job. It allowed Jon some time to fine tune his skills and learn by Wil's example. Over months of renovations, they had fixed a lengthy list of problems like leaks in the roof, cracks in the rear foundation, and faulty circuits in the sanctuary. It was slow going, but they didn't have much better to do. Plus, it kept them out of trouble.

He thought of the man he and Wil encountered yesterday evening. He hoped Ernest had been able to handle him well enough. Jon hated when people came through the District with a scam or scheme. He felt a duty to run those types out of town – and forcefully. While Jon had no memory of the collapse that had beset the District, he felt he knew it as well as anyone based on his surroundings and the stories shared by those who lived it. He had a responsibility to stand up for those who couldn't do so on their own.

After a while the tarp stopped flapping and sunlight came to brighten his entire view. He had begun wondering what repairs needed to be done that day, when suddenly a small rock hit him in the side of the head and broke his concentration. He cursed, through shaggy hair checking the stinging point of contact with the tips of his fingers. No blood, thankfully.

When he regained his composure, he leaned over the balcony and saw his friend Wil staring back at him with a devious look, bouncing another rock in his hand.

"Hey, *dick*, that almost hit my face," Jon hollered.

"No shit. That's what I was aimin' for," Wil yelled up. "Figured a scar or lazy eye might make the girls pity you, y'know?"

Jon stood and flipped him the middle finger.

"C'mon," Wil pressed. "We're gonna be late if you spend any more time pickin' daisies in your mind."

"Comin' down," said Jon, rubbing his head.

Jon met Wil in the courtyard and they made their way out of the complex and onto the avenue. Jon's apartment was along Wil's path to St. Augustine's, and each morning they worked, the pair would take the five-minute trip together, recapping their previous evening or planning future exploits.

If Jon knew one thing about Wil, it was that he loved to talk. And further, he loved to joke around. He, like Jon, had dropped out of high school midway through, and though on paper they'd be lumped in with uneducated simpletons, he liked to think that they both were smarter than they led on. Commonplace banter held commonplace topics, but on occasion – typically over a few beers – they'd find themselves deep in a philosophical debate or situational examination of their condition. Walks such as these rarely held those gems, however.

"Here," Wil said, tossing a foil-wrapped sandwich to Jon.

"Only one?" Jon joked.

"Yes. Only one. Consider it a snack, you big bastard."

Jon tore the sandwich from its wrapper and went to work on it. One bite lopped off nearly a quarter of its mass. He spoke between chews, muffling his words with a bolus of egg, cheese, and bread.

"You end up taking Nora home last night?" he asked.

"*Oh* yeah," answered Wil happily.

"What's that, like, the tenth time now?"

"Somethin' like that."

"I thought you weren't even attracted to her."

"Dude it's like fucking a closed fist. Plus, it was a Wednesday."

"So?"

"So I'm gonna get a Wednesday type of girl," he said matter-of-factly.

"Meaning what?"

"Meaning that on Saturday I'm gonna go for a Saturday type of girl."

Jon motioned for him to elaborate.

"Meaning that as the week progresses, bar-going girls get hotter. Middle of the week, middle of the road. Know what I mean?"

Wil was an animated speaker, always emphasizing his words with accompanying body language. It made engaging with him interactive and even fun in a way, but it also made his hands dangerous around a bar or table. The number of drinks he had spilled in his lifetime would keep the two of them drunk for a week straight. And these boys could drink.

"Can't argue with that," Jon nodded.

"But! Today is *Thursday*. Which means we need to find us some *Thursday* girls. Which also means the weekend is upon us – and so too are. . ." He trailed off, raising an eyebrow to Jon as if to lead him into finishing the sentiment.

"Weekend girls," Jon nodded back and the two shared a laugh. He took the last of his sandwich in a massive bite.

Jon and Wil had been best friends since elementary school, and balanced each other out in a way that only best friends could. Where Jon was laidback, reserved, and even shy, Wil was outgoing, social, and oftentimes abrasive. Generally speaking, Wil was the type of guy Jon usually loathed being around, and Jon was the type of guy Wil usually picked on. Yet in their unique relationship, their opposite qualities complimented each other like oil and vinegar. And as many times as they'd been at each other's throats over the years, their bond had never weakened. They understood each other on a level most friends never reached and most importantly, no matter the circumstances, they never abandoned each other.

"Which leads us to our next topic of conversation," Wil continued. "What are we doin' tonight?"

"I dunno," said Jon halfheartedly as he rolled the foil into a ball. "Wanna hit McGrady's or somethin'?"

The pair ducked under a low-hanging powerline without missing a beat, Jon bending a bit lower than his buddy.

"Fuck that. That place is always dead. Thursday girls, remember? Let's do Michigan Rick's," Wil suggested. "I wanna fuck that waitress."

Jon grunted and twisted his mouth at the recommendation.

"What? What's wrong with that?"

"I don't wanna run into the old girlfriend again, that's all."

"Dude," Wil huffed. "I'm not just gonna avoid every good spot 'til this blows over - whenever that might be."

"I'll think about it."

"Well let's see then. . . Chance's and Keystone are out since you, oh I dunno–"

Jon shook his head. "Don't even say it."

"–decided to *bounce* the bouncer."

"Relax, alright? I said *I'll* think about it," he pressed.

"Bah," Wil cried. "At your speed, by the time you answer my Thursday question it'll be Monday morning."

The pair approached the halfway mark in their short journey and Wil swooped down to grab a stone from a gravel driveway. Each day, he made it a point to use one of the old *Future of City Living* billboards as quick target practice. He scooped up a stone, and whipped it at the *'C'*, marginally enlarging a softball-sized hole there. He'd been working on knocking out the *'C'* for two weeks since empty spaces remained where the *'F'* and *'o'* had once been.

Continuing apace past the sign, they sidestepped a fallen awning and crossed under another low wire, a cable feed this time, as if they were scheduled parts of the walk. Neither was necessarily desensitized to the condition about them, but had rather adapted to their environment as a means of ensuring their hopeful sense of being survived. It was simply where they lived.

Jon and Wil finished their trek in two short minutes, deciding on one of Wil's bar suggestions and arriving at the church some twenty minutes late. Jon tried his best not to let it show that the single sandwich had done nothing to quell the bottomless pit that was his stomach. He was already counting the minutes until lunch.

St. Augustine's was quiet when the pair entered. The sanctuary glowed with natural morning light and the atmosphere was ever peaceful. Sometimes, it felt to Jon like the eye of the storm, tranquil in the center of a turbulent, rough, and unforgiving city. In the first few years of foster care, Jon was raised to be religious. But he, like most everyone else he knew, had rebelled as an adolescent, avoiding this place like 8th period math class. To find himself returning regularly, especially later in life, was ironic. Yet he rather enjoyed the aesthetics and energy now. This quiet, open space was a calming work environment and Ernest was always welcoming and good to him and Wil. He also never pressured them about religion, which helped bolster the feeling of acceptance.

Wil took the lead, walking through the newly lacquered pews and rounding the altar towards the rear hallway. He entered and suddenly pulled up, causing Jon to walk into him from behind and nearly knock him forward. They focused their eyes on a man standing on a ladder at the end of the wide hallway, removing an old ballast from a ceiling light fixture. He was dressed modestly in jeans, a white t-shirt, and boots, but his face was unmistakable.

This guy again? You've gotta be kidding me. Before either had a chance to speak Ernest had appeared from behind and engaged them.

"Jon. Wil. Better late than never, I suppose," he said brightly, trying to pull their attention away from the end of the hallway. "Behind you are some more spackle and painting supplies I picked up this morning. I'd like you two to patch the holes in the hallway and each vacant room, and then begin repainting the walls once the spackle dries. And don't mind the carpet. The new one should be delivered early next week." He patted Wil on the shoulder. "Hopefully you can make some good progress today, yes?"

Both men eyed the newcomer as Ernest delivered his orders. Their body language expressed suspicion, but neither raised alarm. Ernest noticed.

"Ah. You boys met our traveler friend yesterday?" he said, using a subtle hand gesture to motion to the man on the ladder. "He's offered his help on our project. I trust you will all get along."

A huff from Wil showed his growing suspicion of their new circumstances. Jon quickly decided to speak and satisfy Ernest's concern.

"Sure thing," said Jon.

Contently, Ernest turned and departed, releasing Wil and Jon to their work.

"What the fuck is he doing here?" Wil whispered.

"I dunno," Jon murmured back. "Let's just get our work done."

Even though the guy had been within earshot of their conversation with Ernest, he hadn't yet reacted to their presence. To Jon, he looked unconcerned by the two men, even though they had threatened his wellbeing not a day earlier.

Jon was curious. Who was this guy to Ernest and why was he here? What had transpired between them yesterday? *He said he's helping on the project. Meaning the remainder? That's a good couple of weeks.* He shook his head, sensing something was afoot. . .

He couldn't speak for his friend, but judging by his silence Wil shared in Jon's discomfort. It was nothing shy of awkward. An unknown feeling of trepidation filled his body, unsure if some sort of residual fallout would occur.

He looked at the man again, sizing him up briefly. He was clean-cut and well-built, like an athlete. Him being on a ladder made it not fair to say, but he appeared to be around six feet tall.

With a lengthy exhale, Jon shrugged and grabbed a spackle knife and some material and began patching the damaged sheetrock. Reluctantly, Wil followed. They worked quietly for a time, spackling, patching, and prepping for an afternoon paintjob. Some holes would have to rest until the following day in order for the spackle to dry, but mostly they made quick work of the entryway. The hallway itself was wide. It had two rows of recessed fluorescent light fixtures and several wall sconces for variable lighting options. Admittedly, Jon thought it nice to see the fixtures being worked on. Each had burnt out over the course of the past few months until only the wall sconces were available, offering mood-lighting at best. And the stranger was replacing the drop-ceiling tiles as he went along as well, some being stained brown and so droopy they were ready to fall apart. Inwardly, Jon approved of the man's work.

Like clockwork, every fifteen minutes or so the man would finish a fixture, stroll past him and Wil to the entrance of the hall, and flip the switch, flashing the lights on/off as he checked his work. Each time, Wil would look over his shoulder at him, growing more and more agitated by the routine, and shake his head, mumbling to himself about how the guy was going to get himself electrocuted by not turning off the breaker.

The parties continued through the morning and into the early afternoon without any interaction. As both progressed, though, their respective work brought them closer and closer to each other. Eventually, the trio met in the center of the hallway beside the doorway to a vacant office. Jon was about finished patching a hole next to the office doorway when he heard a faint whistle in the air. He recognized the tune but couldn't quite place it.

Without warning, Wil piped up and delivered his first words to the man since their initial meeting. His tone hadn't improved despite the hours in between.

"Yo, you're gonna have cut that whistling out, man. You're makin' my ears hurt."

"Sorry about that. The silence was getting to me," the traveler replied.

"Silence sounds better than that shit," Wil said bitterly.

"Oh, come on. That's one of my favorite pieces."

"Of what? Shit?"

"Music," the traveler replied. The answer sounded more like a question.

"Pieces-of-music," Wil annunciated. "A song, you mean?"

"Sure. A song. It's called *Claire de Lune* by Debussy," the man offered.

"Oh cool. I think I've met his brother, *De Pussy*," Wil replied mockingly. "Either stop whistling or pick something by someone a little less gay."

The remark caused the traveler to stop his work and look directly at Wil. Jon patched onward but listened intently.

"Debussy was quite the playboy, actually. He had many affairs over his lifetime."

Wil flashed his eyes briefly. "Wow, no way." His sarcasm was blatant.

"*Way*. . . Hey, I could whistle Chopin for ya. Maybe more. . ." He paused and raised a limp wrist, wagging his hand toward Wil. ". . .your style?"

The line elicited a chuckle from Jon. Wil shot a look back at him.

"What? Who the fuck is *Show Pan*?" Wil questioned, the insult going clear over his head.

"Chopin was a composer from the 1800s. He was thought to be gay," Jon answered as he grinned at Wil.

"How the fuck do you know that?"

Jon could hear Wil's discomfort in his voice and knew he'd take his amusement as siding with the newcomer. "Janelle listens to it all the time. Drives me nuts. Part of the reason I hang out with you so much."

"Fuck you both," Wil snapped.

He'd never tell Wil, but Jon had taken some pleasure in the brief back and forth. Wil was normally the one dishing out the insults and trash talk, reveling in besting others. Jon savored the few moments it was dealt to Wil, because he was never able to handle it coming toward him very well. In Wil's own words, 'That's what you get when you grab a skunk by the ass.'

"You actually look a bit like him," the man added. "You wouldn't happen to be Polish, would you?"

Jon tried to stifle a laugh but it was no good.

"Keep it up. Both of you. I'm fixin' to make two head-shaped holes in this wall," Wil threatened.

It was a bluff, of course. Empty threats and the like were common banter between them, but Jon was surprised at the lack of apology, or any reaction at all, from the traveler. But before the scene progressed, Ernest appeared and convinced the disjointed trio to take a lunchbreak. Jon's stomach rumbled a cheer of support.

Jon and Wil took a walk around the corner to the El Salvadorian kitchen. Rice, beans, stewed chicken, and fried plantains filled them up well for the forthcoming afternoon workload. Jon ordered two pupusas to-go for an afternoon snack. On the way, he tried to have Wil promise not to try to get any more rises out of the traveler, but the harder he pressed, the more enthusiasm Wil showed for it. Jon's previous trepidation then turned into legitimate concern.

By the time they returned to work the traveler was already on his ladder installing another ballast. After only a few minutes, Wil turned to Jon unprompted to whisper.

"I'm gonna go hit the bathroom," he said, and gave him a quick pat on the back.

His tone, however, suggested something quite different. Jon raised an eyebrow. *This ain't gonna be good.* He frowned as he eyed Wil's path past the ladder, which he passed without so much as a glance and slowly made his way to the restroom. Just as he was about to enter, though, he stopped and spun on the balls of his feet, peeking at the man on the ladder. A mischievous look came over him and his eyebrows jumped as he walked two steps over to an additional light switch just inside the entrance to the kitchen. Jon watched as Wil waited until the man grabbed his pliers and made to cut the existing connections off the wires.

The moment the plier's jaws clenched - the very instant the man applied pressure - Wil flipped the switch and sent electric current straight to the fixture. A pop and a flash emitted a spray of sparks and the lights went out as fast as they appeared.

"Yo!" the traveler wailed, recoiling suddenly and dropping the pliers to the carpet. He froze in shock at the sudden flare. When his shock subsided, he searched down the corridor towards the entranceway light switch. Wil's booming laughter snapped his attention back towards the kitchen.

"Next time shut the breaker off, numb-nuts," Wil teased.

"What the *fuck* is wrong with you?" the man yelled as he descended the ladder. He began striding towards Wil, who was still laughing at the pyrotechnics.

In no time, Jon was down the hallway to intervene. He passed the man and stretched a hand out, stopping him in his tracks. He then grabbed Wil, who had begun approaching quickly.

"Woah, woah, woah. You're not doin' this," Jon said to Wil.

"Fuck that. Let him through," Wil replied with a pompous smile.

"He apologizes, he just doesn't know it yet," Jon pressed, looking over his shoulder.

"No I don't," Wil argued.

"Shut the fuck up." Jon threw him down the hallway and turned to the man. "He does. I'm sorry about that."

The man kept his eyes glued to Wil, who was flashing his middle finger.

"Don't forget to wipe his ass when you're done babying him," the man said.

Jon turned and pointed. "Mouthin' off to me ain't your best decision today, pal. Leave it at this or I'll leave you on the floor. Tell Ernest we had to take care of some things and we'll be back tomorrow."

Jon moved without waiting for a response to meet Wil and escorted him towards the rear exit through the kitchen. Curbside, Wil squirmed away from Jon's grasp.

"Ok, *mom*. Let go of me," he said.

"What's wrong with you? Did you have to fuck with the guy? Ernest is gonna think we just bailed on him."

Wil's demeanor was lighthearted. "Scared the shit out of him, huh? Ha-ha-ha."

"No, actually, you didn't," Jon snapped. "You made us look like assholes." He hid his embarrassment as well as possible, but he feared a bit was slipping out in his tone.

"So what?"

"So I'm fucking tired of it. Why do you always gotta make it an ordeal?"

"Don't even start with that."

"Just shut up for the rest of the walk. We'll talk about this later."

"You're really pissed?"

"Yes," Jon said emphatically.

Wil rolled his eyes. "Whatever. Fuck that guy."

"No, not 'fuck that guy.' Yesterday, sure, but today all we had to do was keep to ourselves and you couldn't even do that. That place ain't our playground. It ain't our *house*. We ain't out here in the neighborhood for you to go off like that. It's Ernest's call and he asked us to get along."

"But the guy–"

"I don't fucking care, Wil."

Wil threw his hands up. "Great. Now I got all three of you pissed at me. Tomorrow oughta be *real* interesting."

"That's one way to put it. Awkward is another."

"Whatever. We'll probably never see that guy again, anyway. I bet he's just traveling through."

Jon let out a sigh in response, yearning for his balcony. He wondered whether Wil was right. *If only I were just traveling through. . .*

Chapter 6: Tabula Rasa

The following morning, Jon walked to St. Augustine's alone. He had waited fifteen extra minutes for Wil to arrive but, unsurprisingly, he was a no-show. Jon had been awfully hard on him the previous afternoon, venting his embarrassment over Wil's actions and essentially telling him to grow the fuck up. Admittedly, embarrassment wasn't an emotion Jon handled well - and neither did Wil for that matter - but Wil deserved a reaming for his stunt.

Even early in their relationship, Jon always felt like those around him questioned why he was so close with Wil. He understood the skepticism, and never disputed that they were different kinds of people when asked about it point blank. What bothered him, though, was that the question was always empty, devoid of the true desire to understand the answer. No one seemed to actually care *why* they were close, only that it was strange or different, like glancing at a funny cover of a magazine without reading the articles inside. In the end, Jon knew Wil would be over to his apartment later that night, as if the argument had never happened. So he begrudgingly accepted the day's circumstances: solo work at St. Augustine's, open to awkward silence and probably awkward contact in the hallway with the traveler. At least their jobs would be separate, he supposed.

The concrete courtyard of his complex vanished as he rounded a corner and a rumbling announced itself from his belly. His foster mother, Janelle, had eaten the last of his egg salad, leaving his stomach as empty as his walk. *I hope Mr. Hawkins has the deli open or I'm gonna have to raid Ernest's fridge*, Jon thought, trying to ignore the anxious digestive beckoning.

The morning was calm and bright. Low, puffy clouds floated against the blue sky overhead, as if following him on his route. Pavement and sidewalk filled his view, better sights than some of the dilapidated spaces further up in his field of vision. Often, he imagined the storefronts and rowhomes in a refurbished state, colorful and alive, bustling with people. The dripping gutters were cleared of leaves, sticks, and what-not, the eroded brick and mortar was repaired, rotten porches had their boards replaced, some even painted white or tawny. Most of all, the people would smile more. That day, though, Jon only looked at the sidewalk and the grasses that split each slab, crying to the sky for freedom.

By the grace of the hunger gods, the deli was open. Mr. Hawkins was old - very old - and rarely had a scheduled opening time. The griddle hadn't yet been fired up so Jon was left with cold options beyond the glass of the refrigerated counter. He checked his pocket and only found fourteen dollars. Upon wagering what would need to be saved for lunch, he ordered two egg salad sandwiches with lettuce and hot sauce on round rolls and a bag of chips. The order cost half of his money.

When Jon entered the church it was Ernest he saw first.

"Hello, Jon," Ernest began, looking up to meet the hulking man's eyes. "Were you able to take care of the things you needed to?"

"Uh, yeah. Sorry for bailing yesterday."

"You're forgiven," answered Ernest lightly. "Where's Wil?"

"Oh, he wasn't feeling well last night. I don't think he's gonna make it."

There was a pause before Ernest responded and a small smile came to his face. *I know that smile. What's up his sleeve this time?*

"Well, I assure you, you will not have to work alone today."

"What? You gonna spot me on the ladder?"

"Ah, no. God saw to it that I lost the strength for that years ago." He motioned to Jon. "Follow me."

Aw, Christ. . .

Their walk took them back to the hallway, and as they turned the corner, Jon knew precisely what Ernest had meant. Ahead, the traveler was bent down, removing a piece of baseboard molding from the far wall. Immediately, Jon got the sense that this day would be a memorable one, for better or for worse.

Great. Fucking Wil. He won't get away with leaving me alone with this guy.

"Robin," Ernest called out while continuing to walk Jon down the hallway.

Hearing his name, Robin paused to look over. In the back of his mind, Jon worried there would be a falling out. It wasn't that Jon would have trouble handling the guy, but he was getting tired of the aggressive charade following him from teenage years into adulthood. Perhaps it was the tingling feeling of growing up. And perhaps today, when the time was right, he would step up and be the bigger man for once - figuratively speaking. Perhaps not, though. What did he owe this guy? Surprisingly, the man didn't recoil from Jon looming over him, but simply looked back and forth between the two as if his work had been unjustly interrupted.

"Robin, in case you weren't introduced yesterday, this is Jon," Ernest said.

Robin offered a subtle nod, his emotions encased in a stoic expression.

"Jon," was all Jon managed.

"Robin ended up finishing the patchwork yesterday," Ernest reported. "Today, I'd like to remove all of the molding and pull the carpet. I received a call that the new one may arrive a day earlier than expected and I want to install it as soon as possible."

"Sounds like a one-person job, you need anything else?" The last thing Jon wanted was to work with this guy all day long.

"I think you two can work together. If you finish early, that's all for today. Deal?"

Ernest's indifference was curious. Either he was ignorant of the tension or making decisions because of it. Jon felt like it was the latter.

"Fine by me," Robin responded directly to Ernest.

"Fine," Jon echoed.

Upon Ernest's departure, Jon grabbed his tools and purposely began work on the opposite side of the hallway. It was a quick job and after about an hour all of the molding was removed and loaded in the dumpster out back. Next, the pair began working on pulling the carpeting. Though Jon removed the molding easily the carpet was providing much more of a challenge. His demolition experience was limited to walls and ceilings, leaving him a greenhorn in this situation. He snuck a look at Robin to see if he could acquire an observable tip, but the traveler's body was blocking his view.

After a few failed attempts he was about stumped. It was obvious the person who installed the carpet made sure to secure the corners in case anyone had the idea of undoing all of his hard work, but Jon was determined to succeed in front of his new associate. His last-ditch effort was to rely on his strength and give the carpet no choice but to separate from the floor. He dug his claws in and yanked.

"You'll never make progress that way."

Jon's struggle was interrupted when he turned around and saw Robin peering over his shoulder. Past him, Jon noticed his corner was already undone. He turned back to his work and got a better grip.

"Havin' too much fun," Jon responded, trying to mask his frustration.

He gave it a healthy jerk but came up with only a few strands. He sat on his heels with the frayed ends in his hand, looking like a kid with a fistful of grass, and exhaled a deep breath that more closely resembled a growl than anything else.

"You get any closer you'll be munchin' on that carpet for lunch."

"Yeah, yeah."

"You want some tartar sauce with that bearded clam?"

"Fuck you," Jon said, twisting just enough to make eye contact. *Who the fuck does this kid think he is?* He turned back to work on the carpet, trying to control his emotions.

"Nah, you–" Robin said while watching, unwilling to give up on his advice, "you gotta pull out before up."

Jon let go of the carpet momentarily and took a breath. "I don't pull out 'til I'm finished," he joked.

That got a good laugh out of Robin and Jon smirked. He had stolen the joke from Wil but hadn't been able to resist. Before he knew it Robin had slid across the carpet and was kneeling next to him.

"The carpet's held down by strips of nails on the edges," he said, raising a crowbar off the floor. "Shit's miserable to remove. Thankfully, we don't need to salvage any of it."

Robin took the crowbar and leveraged it under the edge of the carpet. With a few forceful jerks the nail strip was off the floor and the corner of the carpet came free.

"Thanks for the tip," Jon said hesitantly.

"No problem. Gonna get a water, you want one?"

"Sure."

When the pair broke for lunch they had finished about half of the hallway in mostly silence. Jon was unsure if their brief dialogue from the morning was a fluke or there was the possibility for more during the afternoon. What he was sure of, however, was that he wanted to learn more about this 'Robin' guy. He just didn't know exactly how to approach it. Wil was always better with icebreakers or funny stories to get a conversation going.

The routine carried on through the early afternoon until just about the entire carpet was freed from the floor. As they were working on removing the last section, Robin broke the silence.

"So, how'd you and Mr. Happy become friends?"

"Who, Wil? He's harmless."

The remark made Robin pause, drop the carpet, and smirk. "Is he now?"

"Well, actually, he can do a lot of harm, hah. He's misunderstood, that's all," Jon corrected.

"And how is that?"

"Let's just say neither of us had the best childhood."

"What do you mean?" Robin asked.

"Umm. We were both abandoned at a young age. In terms of abandoned kids, I got lucky. I got a foster family that tolerates me but more importantly gives me a bed to sleep in at night. At least when I don't fuck it up. Wil, well, Wil's mom just up and left him when he was a kid. Father was already gone by then. Pretty much dropped him off out front - like, meaning here, at St. Augustine's. Told him she was running an errand or somethin' and just bailed. He's been surviving the best he can, but I know he's still got a lotta built up hate. Sometimes it comes out at the wrong times and in the wrong ways."

Robin hadn't yet picked the rug back up. He seemed to be digesting the information. "Everyone has their demons."

"You ain't wrong on that. We met in 5th grade - a couple blocks from here. This kid was giving me shit 'cuz I was bigger than everyone else."

"That sounds like a stupid move."

Jon laughed. "It was." He looked away briefly, as a memory came to him. "Ricky Denton - I hate that fucker. Anyway, I ended up knockin' him out, and when the principal came to get me in trouble Wil took the fall. Told me the kid got what he deserved and he'd take care of it. All the other kids were too scared to correct him - even Ricky. On top of that he somehow talked them outta kicking him outta school."

"Damn."

"I know. From then on we've had each other's backs. When 11th grade came around we both decided school wasn't for us, so we never went back."

"To each his own, I guess."

After a brief pause, Jon decided to try to keep the conversation going. "What about you? You definitely didn't grow up around here."

"Yeah. . . You could say I was abandoned by my family as well."

Jon waited for more, but never got it. Family appeared to be a sore subject for Robin, and Jon was never one to pry because he hated when it was done to him. Instead, he decided to just leave it be.

They made easy work of the remainder of the carpet, cutting it into manageable pieces and dragging it outside with the rest of the trash, all the while chatting about sports, cars and other superficial topics to pass the time. The final trip back to the hallway found Ernest standing square with a furrowed brow. Whether he was analyzing the work they had done or what seemed like their new, budding friendship, Jon couldn't initially tell.

"I must say, boys. Nice work," Ernest said, rubbing his chin. "I didn't think you would progress so far. How about we call it for today?"

"Couldn't agree more," Jon answered with relief.

"Jon, will you be joining us for dinner?"

Jon was taken aback by the question. *The kid's staying here with Ernest?* It took a moment to register, but once it did, some pieces fell into place and the puzzle of this man became a fraction clearer. He shook off the desire to know more, as to not appear rude.

"Uh, no. I got other plans. Thanks for the offer, though."

"My pleasure, Jon. Good work today," Ernest said, and disappeared.

Ernest's exit left the pair frozen in the hallway for a time as an idea formulated itself in Jon's mind. He had really enjoyed the company and conversation that day, and was bummed to see it end. Truth be told, it was a nice change of pace from the typical banter with Wil.

"Hey, it was nice meeting you, man," Robin offered with an outstretched hand.

"You too, bud," Jon said, shaking his hand. "Listen," he blurted, "uh, a few friends are getting together tonight at my apartment - my mom's workin' the night shift. You're welcome to come by and hang if you want. Around 10."

Robin put on a contemplative face, "I might just do that," he responded.

"Ernest'll give you the directions if you wanna stop by."

"Cool."

"Either way, I'll see ya."

A few hours later, Robin sat down after setting the table for two, weary from the second straight day of manual labor. His hands were tender and flush like sunburned skin, but he didn't mind. The work was a welcome distraction from the other, more difficult topics in his life. Why he decided to stay with Ernest, he couldn't quite explain. It just happened. He left his jacket after their chance encounter not by accident but for a reason to return. Something about the old man enticed him, and Robin fled his apartment the following morning while Wilson was at work, carrying a pack filled with essentials and personal mementos taken from the life he knew he was never returning to. The departure locked Wilson away in the vault of the past, and Robin meant to keep it that way. His inheritance combined with his leftover bank account was enough to either rent a new place or stay at a cheap motel for a few months until he figured out what the hell he was going to do. He thought about returning to Germany or moving to another city, even priced out plane tickets, but some vague pull kept him local. He hadn't the slightest idea what the pull was, and at that point he didn't care as long as he could avoid his painful past.

The moment Ernest saw the pack he offered up a vacant room behind his study and Robin accepted graciously. Robin made it a point to volunteer his services around the church as payment since Ernest refused any monetary compensation. And so, there he was on day three of his new life, in surprisingly good spirits and with an appetite like the old days.

Dinner that evening was modest, reminiscent of his meals in Germany: butternut squash soup with toasted pine nuts and buttered, crusty bread. To Robin's surprise, Ernest was one hell of a cook. The soup was rustic, smooth and seasoned perfectly. And even more, Ernest appeared to have made enough for a second serving or, hopefully, a third.

Robin hadn't yet learned much about the man he was staying with, having worked all day and into the night the previous day. It eerily seemed like Ernest was a survivor of some personal calamity or mishap. He had an air about him that told of both triumphs and tribulations, as if he'd seen it all and lived to tell the proverbial tale. Robin thought he might be able to learn a thing or two from this man, despite his religiousness, and decided to explore that opportunity amid their somewhat private dinner.

"So, how long have you been a pastor here?" Robin asked comfortably as the pair began their meal. The round dinner table was big enough to seat four or five but still allowed for a close dining experience when seated across from one another. Dusk and a few modest kitchen lights offered mood lighting which Robin had accepted as the norm at St. Augustine's outside of the newly florescent hallway.

"Just over thirty years," Ernest responded between spoonfuls.

"You waited thirty years to start renovating?" Robin said with a grin.

The question drew a low rumble of laughter from across the table. "It was in much better condition when I started here. It was quite lovely, actually."

"I can tell. When did it turn to–uh, what was the turning point?"

"Ah, when the scandal with Mayor Xavier happened it really damaged our District. Most businesses and buildings, this one included, still have not recovered. I am sure you've noticed the landscape here."

"Yeah. I studied that debacle briefly in school," Robin said as he poured a glass of water.

"That's good to hear. At least education is trying to help us to avoid repeating history."

"Well, I don't know about that. I hate to say it but I don't think that type of education will make a difference."

"If we don't educate, then how might we avoid history repeating?"

Robin paused with the spoon halfway to his mouth. *Be careful with this,* he thought. "Mm, you probably won't like my answer," he said, and lightly placed the spoon in his mouth.

"Try me," Ernest replied. His intrigue had caused him to stop eating for the moment.

Robin paused again to put his utensil down and contemplate the decision in front of him. Answer lightly or speak his mind?

He quickly resigned himself to the fact that he would not be able to filter his response.

"The wrong man was voted into office. The warning signs were all over – it was ridiculous, really. He only won because the other candidate flubbed the 'Do you believe in God' question and Xavier was 'a good Christian man.' Classic issue in politics that if not shifted away from, collectively, will prove to play out over and over."

"And what is that classic issue?"

Robin searched for sarcasm in the question but found none. "Well, a majority of the voting population still thinks the characteristic most enabling a candidate's political success is a devout belief in God."

"And they are wrong?"

"Yes."

"How so?"

"In politics, or leadership, belief in God is completely irrelevant. Y'know, formulating and implementing a budget, or developing a fair and expedient judicial system, or, for instance, making executive wartime decisions on a national level has nothing to do with faith and everything to do with reason and rationality."

The point furrowed Ernest's brow. "Go on," he encouraged, sensing that Robin wasn't finished.

"Critical thinking skills," he continued, "the ability to analyze data and evidence and make a calculated prediction or decision are characteristics of a good leader. Not whether they read the Bible or go to church on Sunday."

"And those characteristics cannot be achieved by a religious man?" Ernest questioned, speaking with his spoon to add emphasis.

Robin cleared his throat, preparing to drop the hammer yet hoping not to insult Ernest. "Those skills are the antithesis of the foundation of religion, of faith. Faith, by definition and practice," he continued, "is to believe without corroborating evidence. To have blind trust. You cannot make rational decisions, especially for the betterment of a society, blindly."

"Hmm," Ernest voiced softly. He sat blinking, clearly in thought.

"So, no. I don't think those characteristics can be achieved by a religious man. Separation of Church and State has a specific purpose, but unfortunately it only seems to be practiced in the classroom. Where it's really necessary is public office. Anytime a public official would rather defer to religion before the constitution, you know they're not making decisions for the betterment of country, state, or city. I mean, the establishment clause of the 14th amendment says that government can't establish a religion, yet no candidate has ever been voted into office without aligning themselves with a religious majority. It's so ass-backwards. If elections, and governments for that matter, were sanitized of religious undertones, the world would be a better place and that scandal would've never happened."

A few seconds ticked by without a change in Ernest's expression. Robin worried he'd taken the answer too far, and couldn't help but start to feel like an apology was necessary. After all, he had practically just met the man. "I-I'm sorry if that came across as offensive or crass. I just feel strongly about the topic."

"Not at all. Your opinions do not bother me. You're allowed to feel however you would like. Remember, I've been having discussions like this for a long time."

"Understood," Robin replied with a deep nod. "I just, you know, hoped it didn't seem like a personal attack."

"No, no," Ernest urged. "You can consider this table an open forum. In fact, I admire your levelheadedness. You speak clearly and have at least thought about your position on this topic before blurting out an opinion, like many others do. In my years most discussions turn to an argument because emotions seep into the subject matter - sometimes from both sides."

Ernest raised a suggestive eyebrow. Robin understood the hint and nodded so.

"But I wonder of your ideal leader's morality," Ernest continued, raising a finger. "Or their conscience. You had said - in so many words - that the characteristics engendered by faith are the antithesis of those of a great leader, correct?"

"I did."

"I fear that you are missing an essential element of faith that most all uneducated individuals - in the context of faith, mind you - tend to miss."

"And what would that be?"

"That faith and morality are directly related. That, further, faith in God builds moral fiber."

"Moral fiber based on faith does not translate into the ability to make decisions in a time of crisis or balance a budget, or, really, anything remotely involved in leadership."

"Oh but I think it does."

"N–no. Reasoning skills, education, and experience. . . Those are the necessary qualities."

"When lives are considered, it's always a matter of morality. There is no issue in politics in which human lives are unaffected. Therefore, decisions must always be considered from a moral standpoint in order to act in a manner of goodness. The points you're touching upon are a very important piece of this. . .*puzzle*, so to speak. But they are limited to facets of mental operation, of processing power, and decisiveness."

"Exactly. That's precisely what it should be limited to."

"It appears to me that you're essentially describing a machine, void of human qualities – such as compassion. Rationality is not absolute. We must consider our emotional faculties as well. But I most certainly agree that we must be responsible about it, lest we face circumstances such as the ones in this District."

"Yeah, but the issue with that is that emotion clouds judgement. You said it yourself, just now, in reference to discussions like this. Insert passions, preconceptions, urges, or opinions and you're left with a mess."

"Emotions grounded in faith sing with goodness and morality. Love – not simply passion. True faith – not some advantageous representation of faith that individuals, such as Xavier, abuse for personal gain."

"There's really no other way to put this other than this: faith is irrational. It is a copout. There is no evidence, no proof, not even a whiff of a shred of tangibility. Enter something as unfounded as faith into politics – into issues concerning *human* lives – and you're already down a road of unjust representation. I mean, to tout God's will or defer control of your thoughts to pure, baseless feeling is illogical. It has no place in the betterment of society."

"Faith may challenge our rationality, but it does not disqualify us as rational beings. I think it balances us, humanizes us. . . Consider this. Assume you are a good person. With reason, you have options. Choice. 'I had to make a decision and, using logic, my reason for deciding is X.' With morality there is no choice, there is simply the *right* thing to do, which is always predicated upon empathy, compassion, and humanity. Reason may subvert those qualities in favor of a particular outcome. In other words, decisions based on pure reason are exposed to the curse of the context in which the decisions must be made. That, I fear, is the shortcoming in what you describe—that reason does not equate to goodness, it relates to intelligence. Balanced with reason, however, a decision backed by morality is one that never changes."

"The problem with what you're saying is its relation to faith. If you removed the facet of faith from your argument I'd agree with it completely."

"Oh no," Ernest smiled. "That's the *foundation* of what I'm saying - the morality-faith link. That true moral depth comes from faith in God. If voters identify with God, it is not faith that is to be blamed if the candidate abuses that fact. Perhaps what the voters are looking for is an individual with similar morals, grounded in faith, as they possess."

"Then the voters are wrong. Their moral basis, being faith in God, is unfounded."

"You may argue that religion is unfounded but. . .perhaps faith in God is a theory that is constantly tested by the moral and the righteous."

Robin tried to stifle a laugh. "The only theories that exist are scientific ones."

"Faith is also a search, like science is. While we may not see the tangible results that science offers, it allows us to search our minds - hopefully together, as a congregation or community - for other evidence of energy and power."

"There's no evidence to find. You cannot experiment, you cannot research, you cannot provide results. That search is fruitless and quite honestly, an insult to our intelligence as human beings," Robin finished. His tone had a touch of sympathy. "An experiment through faith will yield results that are impossible to reproduce unilaterally, meaning any resulting 'theories' cannot be accepted as truth by a community. Science *only* accepts theories when results are reproduced unilaterally. It's a *way* stronger validator."

Ernest inhaled deeply, causing him to smile thinly. He spoke, then, gently and reverently. "You will probably call them electrical signals in the brain, but what of deep emotion, like love? Or soulmates? Or what of what many people call 'coincidence'? What of miracles, hmm, these emotions we feel - quite literally - in our heart? Science is but the exploration of our physical environment. What of our consciousness or the metaphysical nature of us as beings and our reality around us? Our minds are more powerful than anything conceivable by science, or any idea that can be written on paper. There are higher facets to existence than categorizing us as simply an anomaly of nature or some scientific byproduct. There are deeper foundations of our identity." Ernest smiled, then. "There are answers elsewhere."

"And where might that be?" Robin asked.

Ernest smiled wider at the rhetoric. "God."

Robin shook his head with amusement, and decided to hold off on his thoughts, accepting instead the stalemate. "I have a feeling this may be an ongoing discussion."

"Well then I welcome that opportunity."

Robin mulled over the discussion momentarily, a strange conclusion coming to his mind. "What kind of pastor are you?" he asked in a bemused fashion.

Ernest couldn't contain his laughter at the question.

"Someone who preaches the Bible doesn't talk like this, I mean, not once did you reference a biblical lesson or figure or something. Just feels strange to me for some reason. I don't understand - is this some other sort church I haven't realized yet?"

"No. I most certainly follow the Bible and teach its lessons. It is the most important part of my life. What I'm doing is offering you an alternate route to having faith in God. Jamming the Bible down your throat with quotes or stories would be insulting, quite honestly - to both of us. True counsel comes from guidance, among other things. You reject the Bible, but perhaps there is another path for you towards God, if you were only to be shown it."

The two men shared a look that could only be described as one of understanding. "Well, though I *strongly* doubt that that will be the case, I do respect and appreciate your arguments. To be honest," Robin admitted, "I haven't thought of it that way before."

"Then this was a worthwhile discussion."

By the time they finished the conversation - put it on hold, truthfully - the soup was tepid at best. The men realized they had let their meal turn almost cold with how long they'd been at it, and shared a laugh. Dinner and chit-chat ensued with a content look on each of their faces.

When dinner concluded, Robin checked his watch. "I, uh, told Jon I'd meet up with him in a little while. I–I'm not sure if you lock the door, or what, so–"

"Oh," Ernest remarked, "I'll leave you with the key."

"You're sure?"

"It's not a problem at all." He stood from his seat and placed his napkin on the table. "I'm glad to see you've become friendly with them."

"Well, that's still to-be-determined with his friend, Wil, but I'll let you know how it goes."

"Wil is a good kid if you can break through his walls. They're both good kids, for that matter," he said, "but be advised. They have tendency to. . .*over*indulge."

The cool, late summer wind rose up from the street to Jon's balcony, drying his damp brow like steam off a mirror. Presently, he was alone, enjoying a moment's peace from the night's festivities swinging into full motion inside. He could hear the muffled sounds of music and voices beyond the sliding glass door as if from underwater. Occasionally, one of his friends would come out for a quick smoke or a chat only to quickly burrow back into the social milieu. Jon never intentionally ignored his company, but he could only spend so much time cramped indoors. Each time there was a gathering at his place, he would make his way onto the balcony at some point to sort out his thoughts. Tonight, they were consumed by his new acquaintance, Robin, and if he would manage to show up.

There was something unique about the kid, something elusive that Jon couldn't quite place. There had been an unnaturally natural ease between them while working. Rare are the instances where someone leaves a mark on you after only a minor exchange or chance meeting. He knew that if the circumstances allowed, Robin had potential to be an addition to his small circle of close friends. Jon simply liked him.

Jon was pulled from his thoughts when he noticed an eerie diminishment of sound in the formerly buzzing apartment. He quickly left the balcony, and upon entering saw Robin, dressed in brown boots, jeans, and a solid, pale green t-shirt, standing in the doorway. Most everyone had their eyes on the clean-cut guest that dropped in, the oddball, the man out of his element among such a tightknit crowd. Jon had to chuckle inside. He was still amazed at how this guy could control his emotions in tense or foreign situations. Had Jon been the one with this type of focus turned upon him, he'd likely have fainted.

Jon immediately noticed Wil take on a defensive pose. He had told Wil a few hours earlier that the guy might be stopping by, but hadn't been sure Wil had really heard him through his cackling laughter at discovering the traveler's name was Robin. He hoped Wil wouldn't make it a source of entertainment for the night, or convince others to lay into him for the androgynous name.

"Wil, I told you Robin might stop by," Jon said.

"Oh yeah." Wil turned to Robin and pointed down the hallway beside the living room. "The blown circuit's in the bedroom."

"Shut up," Jon said and nodded his head to Robin. "Beer's in the fridge, man. Make yourself at home."

"Thanks," Robin replied, brushing off the insult.

Jon's other guests began mingling again as Robin made his way to the kitchen, somehow navigating past the penetrating stare of Wil. Once Robin had turned the corner out of sight, Jon immediately grabbed Wil's arm and met him face to face.

"I need to talk to you on the balcony," Jon said sternly.

"Fuck that. Get off me," Wil answered, temporarily escaping Jon's grasp.

"I wasn't asking."

Wil tried to remain free but Jon was like a grizzly bear toying with a salmon. When they made it outside, Wil seemed outwardly amused Robin actually showed up, but Jon was upset.

"Still can't believe his name," Wil said between laughs as he cracked open a fresh beer.

"Don't make this a thing tonight."

"Why not?" Wil turned to Jon with a wave of his hand. "I don't care what we talked about. Fuck that guy. Nothing good can come of this. I–I mean, look at him."

They turned and leaned back on the iron railing to face the interior of Jon's living room through the sliding glass door. Robin had already managed to intertwine himself with Perry, one of the better looking girls at the gathering, leaving a smirk on Jon's face and a grimace on Wil's.

"That guy's trouble, man, mark my words. Just look at him. He's a dream chaser."

"You say that like it's a bad thing."

"A guy looking like that, hitting on girls around here – his face would look like Ernest's wall in a week. I ain't getting hit 'cause that guy's gonna move on someone else's girl."

"Oh and you haven't?" Jon asked.

Wil frowned and turned his head away as if to deflect the question.

"Stop judging him," Jon added.

"Why are you defending him so much?"

"Because I don't know him yet. And maybe he's misunderstood. You of all people should cut him a little slack."

"Fine," Wil answered, giving up the fight. "Just tonight, though. After that I make no promises."

Jon accepted Wil's offer with only a nod. Frankly, it was a victory to back him down at all, so the terms would have to do. The silence blanketing the balcony was disturbed when Robin slid the door open and took a timid step onto the metal grate.

"Hey guys. Thanks for the invite again." He raised his can. "And the beer."

"No problem, man," Jon answered while trying to draw out a response from Wil with his eyes. There was a brief moment before Wil succumbed to the pressure and chimed in.

"Hey, man, about yesterday. . ." Wil began.

"No worries. I'm already over it," Robin said. To Jon it sounded genuine. "So how often do you guys hang out like this?"

"Just about every weekend. Don't last here very long most nights, but if it's cold or shitty out it could be an all-nighter," Jon responded.

"We're almost done here though," Wil added.

"Cool. What's on the agenda?"

"Same thing as always," said Wil cheerfully.

Robin raised an eyebrow. "Which is?"

"We go chase the dream, man. You ready?" Wil said, slapping Robin's back.

"Chase the dream?" he asked, glancing between the two. "I don't get it."

Jon and Wil both smiled. Jon grabbed Robin and turned him gently back to the living room. He hovered over and pointed to Perry, the laughing beauty through the glass. "You were chasing it the second you got here. Bigger fish to catch out there, though."

Robin gave a brief laugh. "Let's go throw some lines out, then."

The party left Jon's apartment some forty-five minutes later and made their way to a local bar, *Stonewall's*, to start off the night. There was Jon, Wil, Perry, their buddy Chucky, the Mills brothers, Fox, who lived down the hall from Jon, Jesse Ferguson, who was Wil's older second cousin, Pat Gallagher, Martina Montoya, who dated Wil back in high school, and her stepsister Daisy. And then there was Robin. Robin walked quietly, laughing at jokes here and there or chatting with Perry or Jon, content to be apart among the established group of friends. Jon thought he'd likely act the same way had he been in Robin's shoes, and admired him for it. Others might've acted overbearing in order to make an impression. The guy was cool and casual.

Stonewall's was a large rectangular space, and held its typical bustling Friday night crowd. Jon and Wil knew the bouncer, Dennis, well and the group filed in without being hassled for I.D. All save Robin had been there countless times, and since most people who grew up in the District never left town, Jon expected to see many people he knew. It was an element that was as comforting as it was irritating. Every so often he wished he could meet new people or have a different nightly adventure, yet found himself stuck in the re-run of nightlife around the neighborhood. Robin, however, seemed impressed.

"Man, this place is jumpin'," he offhandedly remarked over the commotion.

To Jon's surprise, Wil answered, "Only one thing to do with your money here, man," he laughed, patting him on the back. *"Drink."*

Jon smiled inwardly. He supposed this was indeed one of the better spots to take an out-of-towner. Among other bars, *Stonewall's* was a great escape within the District. Despite abounding hardship, the youth still knew how to have a good time.

The space was made entirely of wood, from floor to bar to ceiling. The walls were painted off-white where bare, but were mostly covered in beer signs, dart boards, or, on one wall, a large mirror. Behind the bar there was a portrait of a man, who Jon had learned after a few years as a regular was Stonewall Jackson, the old Civil War General. Apparently, the original owner was a distant relative of the man and named his bar in homage to old Stonewall's exploits. Under the painting was a quote that read, "Let us cross over the river, and rest under the shade of trees." It always made Jon smile, thinking of a journey to somewhere better, but Wil seemed to think it referred to death.

As the group made their way to the back of the bar to overrun a few open booths, Jon used his height to count the faces he recognized—some old classmates of his, two younger troublemakers from his building, and a group of firemen he had met a few months back.

The one person - the *only* person - in the District he hoped he wouldn't see was Jade. It had been three weeks since they broke up, and their first run-in thereafter had been anything but amicable. Jon had been taken by surprise and may have been a few beers deeper than he should have. Unfortunately, the guy she had been talking to had taken the brunt of his anger. Jon vowed to apologize when the doctors removed the wires from the guy's jaw.

They made their way into the booths as Wil ducked off to grab the first round of pitchers. Just as Jon was finishing his scan of the room, like being drawn to a beam of light penetrating darkness, his eyes fell on a beautiful girl laughing with her friends, seemingly without a care in the world. It was Jade. As hard as he tried, he couldn't take his eyes off of her. To him, she was the most beautiful girl he ever knew, and it twisted the dagger in his heart every time he saw her showing the world she was okay with the break up.

Eight months ago she swept him off his feet, gave him something he never thought he deserved, and as fast as she came into his life she was gone, without ever offering an explanation he was able to accept. "I just need some space to figure things out," was how she started the talk. Jon couldn't remember the rest of it, having tuned her out when he realized the inevitable hammer would fall. The conversation held little closure for him because her true motivation was hidden behind a posturing façade. Sometimes it's better to get punched with the truth, just to be able to end a chapter of your life and start a new one.

Jon did not want to admit it but he knew the night had been ruined for him. It was simply a matter of time before he exploded, internally or externally, and went home. Not wanting to embarrass himself in front of Robin, he decided to run to the bathroom while his friends enjoyed the first round, hoping to delay the unavoidable for just a short while. He dawdled there in a stall for a few short minutes, trying miserably to snap out of the suffocating dejection closing in on him. He just wished he could have a night out without being plagued by her presence or the longing thereof. The limbo was enough to drive him reclusive. With a deep breath, he left the bathroom to face the certain downfall waiting beyond.

When Jon returned, Robin, Perry, Wil, and their friend Chucky were in the corner booth, seemingly involved in a heated argument. The others had dispersed throughout the crowd, amidst their social endeavors.

"Fuck you. I can do it," Wil said aggressively towards Robin, who had his right hand on the back of the booth around where Perry was sitting.

"I told you. I'll give you 100 dollars if you can. Man up," he said calmly.

"What if he can't do it?" Chucky said, leaning on his elbows toward Robin with the anxiousness of a dog awaiting a treat.

Wil closed his eyes. "*Chucky*, shut the fuck up. What if I can't do it?" he repeated, as if Chucky hadn't asked the same question five seconds earlier.

"Aw, what happened? Second guessing ourselves already?" Robin joked.

"Don't start, alright. What if I can't?"

"I've always wondered how much I would enjoy someone literally kissing my ass."

The group laughed and Jon took his seat silently and halfheartedly tried to figure out what the conversation was about.

"Just gimme the fuckin' thing," Wil said, snatching a red napkin out of Robin's hand.

Robin had evidently bet Wil he couldn't fold a napkin more than seven times, and after the sixth fold Wil had an immovable knot of paper. He dropped it to the table, losing his gusto with his breath. Laughter and shit-talking ensued, but Robin and Wil continued challenging each other to various competitions.

Jon may have been there in body, but his mind was in the dirt. By the time they had concluded the chugging contest, Perry and Chucky needed to make their way to the bathroom, leaving the trio alone in the booth.

"What's up with you? You've been quiet since we got here," Robin said to Jon when Perry and Chucky were out of earshot.

"He's sulking about the dream he can't have anymore. See that girl in the blue vest with the grey long-sleeve shirt? Long blonde hair?" Wil asked as he turned around and pointed at Jade. "She broke his heart a couple weeks ago. Surprisingly he's only destroyed one dude's jaw over it."

"You knew she was here?" Jon asked with surprise. Wil rarely showed restraint in this regard.

"Dude, I knew the second we got in here," Wil said with a knowing smiling. "You tripped like that fifteen-amp breaker Robin almost blew up."

They shared a retrospective laugh, the other two more heartily than Jon.

"I figured you'd have said somethin'."

"Eh. I thought you could use a night off. Plus I was too busy beating this shithead in a chugging contest."

"Hey, it feels good to know you let things down your throat easier than I do," Robin jabbed.

Wil smirked and flipped a middle finger towards Robin.

"Why'd she break up with you?" Robin said as he returned the focus to Jon's problem.

It made Jon a little uncomfortable to talk about it since he rarely presented his feelings for discussion. "She never really said," he started cautiously. "Said she needed space or some bullshit. Can't really figure it out."

"She cheat on you?"

"Nah, I don't think so. We were great for like eight months. Just kind of came out of nowhere. She acts like it ain't a big deal."

"He's been fucked up over it since," Wil said in resignation. He seemed to know Jon's departure was rapidly approaching.

The three remained silent for a minute, trying to find the words to continue the conversation. Jon began to think this would be a good time for him to bail and go home, before things got worse.

"Well fuck her then," Robin said with moxie. "Let's fade outta here and chase the dream somewhere else."

Jon raised an eyebrow. *"Now?"* he said unconfidently.

Robin sighed in frustration. "Is she the girl you're gonna marry?"

"I mean, obviously not."

"Alright, well, when you were together is that what you planned?"

Jon could feel the pulse in his neck. He was only twenty-three and had never thought that hard on a relationship in his life - even with Jade. How could he answer a question like that?

"I dunno," was all he managed, which Robin pounced on.

"Then that's a 'no'," he began confidently. "Look, it's easy to get lost in a relationship and then crave it when it's gone, when in reality you should just appreciate the good memories and that phase of your life. You can't harp on potential, or else we'd all be destroyed from the ones that didn't pan out. Move on and move up, you know?"

"Easier said than done, dude."

"We all know what it's like, man," Robin continued softly. "Being single sucks most of the time. The highs are high, sure, but the lows can be *incredibly* low. . . It can hurt. But the most important thing to remember is that anything can happen."

Jon twisted his mouth, considering the sentiment, and put on a hard face.

"I got a good place we can go. Not too far from here - maybe a twenty-minute walk. It'll take your mind off everything and we'll see if we can ride that high."

Jon noticed Wil observing with caution, understanding far better than Robin the danger of being candid about a topic such as Jade. Wil's focus oscillated nervously between the two, appearing to some degree relieved someone was telling Jon what he needed to hear. Robin hadn't appeared to notice. He just sipped his beer.

It took a solid ten seconds of the trio holding that pose before Jon mustered up a response. *What's the worst that could happen?* Jon wondered. *Just go with it.*

"Aright, my man. Fuck it. Lead the way."

"Let's do it," Robin said.

The trio dipped out of the bar before Chucky and Perry returned and without so much as a mention to their other friends. The minute Jon filled his lungs with the sweet summer air he felt invigorated. The feeling of depression was lifted and his body pumped freely with excitement. All it took was a little 'real talk' to break him, even temporarily, out of his indolence.

The bar Robin led them to was a place called *The Drunken Huntsman*. It lay outside the Inner District, in Old City, somewhat foreign territory for Wil and Jon, who knew the area well enough, but not the bar scene. Robin ordered six shots for them when they approached the bar and took out a fifty-dollar bill.

"How do you know about this place, moneybags?" Wil asked over the bar banter, surprised at the ambitious order.

"Went to FDU. Spent some time down here barhopping."

"You went to Fort Dearborn University?" Jon asked in puzzlement. *This guy gets more interesting every minute.*

"Yeah. I finished up my senior year last year. Didn't graduate, though." The comment made Robin drift into his own thoughts until the shots arrived. Wil was the first to pick up his pair.

"All three of us didn't finish school? I'll drink to that."

The trio shared a smile and down the hatch the shots went.

They drank, joked, and made friends with the bartender, a cute redhead with an infectious laugh and sense of humor to match. Robin even convinced her to give Jon her number, which he shyly accepted but deep down knew he'd never act upon. The night grew raucous the later they stayed and after striking out with a couple sets of ladies, the trio decided to begin their serpentine trek home.

They walked aimlessly, intermittent streetlamps revealing parallel-parked cars along the long, flat roads. It seemed like a pocket of quietness followed them, cars passing only on distant intersections. Jon reflected on the night while Robin and Wil talked. It was the first night since the break-up he'd had a genuinely good time, free of the weight on his heart. He knew he had Robin to thank for that. Eventually they made their way to Orange Ave., which would take them directly back to the Inner District, from which they could hit both the church and Jon's apartment complex.

Turning left onto Orange Ave., Jon and Wil stopped after a few steps when they noticed Robin's absence. He was frozen in the quiet intersection, fixated on an old building. Before Jon could call to him, Robin began walking across the intersection. Jon and Wil turned toward each other and, after a confused non-verbal exchange, decided to follow. When they caught up to Robin he was looking up at the business's name above the building's glass door. Wycroft & Shafer, it read. It was some sort of law office.

"Yo, Robin. Let's go," Jon hollered.

"Hold on," Robin answered sharply before lowering his voice. "I've got a debt to settle here." It wasn't clear to Jon whether the thought was meant to be verbalized.

"Well, they're closed, my man. Settle it tomorrow," Wil said scanning the intersection for cars.

Robin was unresponsive. Instead, he nonchalantly walked over to the small garden beside the entryway, grabbed an edge stone, and hurled it through the second-story window. The glass shattered with a crash, some skating down the stone exterior. Jon and Wil flinched in unison and looked around for witnesses. Before they could make sense of the action Robin was climbing the bars guarding the first floor window. He hopped inside and disappeared.

"Dude. . .*what* the *fuck*," Wil said absently. "This kid's nuts. Let's get the fuck out of here."

Jon didn't answer. Instead, he stood like a statue, trying to stare through the wall next to the second story window, wondering what could provoke a seemingly levelheaded man to do something so impulsive. Wil hopped three steps toward the

District and then returned quickly to stand in front of Jon when he noticed he was not being followed.

“Um, are you too drunk to process the urgency here? Do you know where we’re at? If we get caught here we’re *fucked*.”

It didn’t take Jon long to respond. “I’m stayin’,” he said, eyes glued to the window.

Just as Jon made up his mind a computer monitor and tower flew out of the window followed by a torrent of papers and folders, flapping through the air like a flock of injured birds.

“I hate you, Jon,” Wil breathed.

Before they knew it Robin had climbed down as quickly as he’d gone up. The instant his feet hit the ground he began to sprint down Orange Ave. towards the Inner District.

“Debt settled!” he shouted as he brushed past.

Chapter 7: Gross Excess

A beautiful, dark-haired young woman stood at a floor-to-ceiling window atop a highrise in the heart of the city. She admired the darkened landscape below as the brightly trafficked streets stretched across town and traced the lines through the glass with the tip of her finger, navigating the giant luminescent maze. Behind her a lavish party continued. With the thumb and forefinger of her left hand she unconciously spun an unadorned platinum necklace. As her finger traced into the farther, much older reaches of the city she stopped and found herself wondering about how little she knew of the area, just a short subway ride away. Unexpectedly a hand rested on her waist that made her flinch and abruptly concluded her thoughts. She turned to find her boyfriend standing behind her with an inviting smile on his face.

Dalton was a tall, skinny man with short blond hair and pale skin. Being the son of a wealthy developer gave him an air of entitlement that he carried with him both in public and in private. He could be a prick, really, but Marian wasn't often subjected to that side of him. His father owned one of the largest property development companies in the region and in short time, dear Dalton would take the reigns.

Partly joking he said, "I pay all this money for the highest view of the city and you decide to look out of *this* window."

She gave him a crooked smile, and squinted playfully before turning to peer out the window once more.

"It's much prettier on the other side. I think it's clear enough to see the cargo ships docked on the bay. Come on, I'll show you."

He gently took Marian's hand away from the glass and pulled her toward him. She acquiesced, her subtle perfume lingering in the space left by her body. Her cream-colored dress softly rippled in the air as the couple walked arm in arm across the elegant loft. Her long, barely curled, dark hair bounced quietly off her shoulderblades with each step. Having just turned twenty-six, her youthful figure was one that turned heads. She had a beatifully symmetrical face, accentuated by the slightest dimple that appeared on her left cheek when she smiled. One look into her hazel eyes left men desiring much more. If one looked closely enough at the guests tonight, they'd find a woman or three glancing her way with envy or, perhaps, a look of distaste. She noticed these things, made it a point to meet each stare, if only briefly. These weren't the first looks and they wouldn't be the last. She knew them. They were her closest friends at the party.

This particular event was a step above most others she'd attended during the three months she'd been dating Dalton. Their brief trip across the room saw intricate ice sculptures, lavish flower arrangements, and delicacies from around the world. A heavyset man and his wife were decorating their tiny plates with an impressive amount of food from the raw bar while a surprisingly young couple next to them was having their champagne flutes topped off by a passing waiter. You'd never know by the look of it, but this celebration was in the name of charity.

When the pair reached the opposing side of the loft, Dalton guided Marian to the window and said matter of factly, "See? Much prettier from this side."

"Yeah," she whispered.

"If it wasn't too windy we could've gone to the rooftop." He embraced her from behind. "Some October this is. Fucking weather." He broke a momentary pause with, "You know, when I was a child my father used to tell me there were old shipwrecks at the bottom of the bay. Centuries-old ships filled with more riches than you could imagine, sunken with their priceless treasure and forgotten by all." He curled the ends of her hair around a finger. "I used to bug him all the time, 'Why doesn't anyone rescue the treasure? Can't someone dive and save all that gold and all those jewels? We should do it, dad,' I said."

"And what did he tell you?" asked Marian.

"He said, 'We make our own riches, son.'"

The sound of breaking glass caused him to pause and turn. A waiter had dropped an empty champagne glass and was being reamed out by an elderly man. With a half grin he turned back and checked his watch. It was the third time he had made an excuse to look in the direction of one table in particular since they arrived, and the third time he had followed it with a look at his watch, Marian noticed. And each time, there was a very particular blonde who happened to fall into his line of vision.

"What is it?" Marian asked suspiciously.

With a slight shake of his head he said, "Nothing, sweetheart. So, would you like to see the real reason I brought you to this vantage?

"Ok. . ." She nodded with a deepening look in her eyes.

He pointed to an unassuming building on the corner of a busy intersection towards the Waterfront. "We just signed the deal today. By this time next year we'll be well on our way towards building the tallest luxury apartment building in the metropolitan area. The first of four towers. *And*. . .we'll have the top two floors as our own apartment. What do you think?" He beamed a smile.

Her words became stuck for a moment. "It sounds like so much. I. . .I don't know what to say."

Marian had never gotten used to the wealth seeping from this community. She tried to convince herself that after a little more time she would adjust, but in her heart she knew it to be a lie. She forced herself to appear comfortable.

"Say *yes*," he said with surprising intensity, tightening his embrace. But before she could respond he continued, "Although it wont be my father's crowning achievement, it is his pride and joy."

"Will he finally retire after this?" asked Marian, intentionally turning the subject away from living together.

Dalton let out an obnoxious laugh. "The day my father retires is the day he's buried."

"What could he possibly plan to do after a project like that?" she wondered aloud.

"We've got plenty of plans. Once this project nears completion and enough units are sold, we'll start buying up the slums little by little and turn them into parks or something. He mentioned a stadium, but its all speculative at this point."

She turned to him stunned. "You're going to tear down the Inner District?"

"After we buy it, yes," Dalton responded matter-of-factly.

"Where will all those people go?"

"Hopefully some place else. I'm not too concerned," he said smiling.

"You realize you'll be forcing thousands of people from their homes, from their livelihoods, right?"

"So what? It's a pathetic livelihood anyway."

She took his arms off her waist and turned to face him. ". . .So what?"

"Yeah, so what? I love this city, Marian. I think it's the greatest place on earth. But like every city of this size there's flaws. That shithole," he pointed with his thumb towards the far window at his rear, "is one of them."

"What the fuck is wrong with you?"

Dalton rolled his eyes like a teenager. "The city is cheapened by their presence. The buildings are run-down and old. Living so near to that decreases property value. It's business. Every deal we execute, it's a step closer to my family's dream."

"This is more than property value and more than your 'dream.' People's futures, their lives, will be in jeopardy."

"Their *lives*? Marian, come on. Let's not start this shit. You're stretching again."

"Its not a stretch at all. Where do you suppose they'll go once you buy their neighborhoods and tear them down? They can't buy anything else or I'm sure they'd live somewhere nicer. Whether you choose to look at it this way or not, the fact is that they'll be homeless."

"You're getting ahead of yourself. They'll be given plenty of notice to make the proper adjustments. We're talking years from now, I mean, relax."

"You're acting like an asshole and I'll never agree with that mindset."

"And what's your alternative? Build them a better place to live? Please don't tell me you believe that."

"Yes. You *could* use your good fortune and wealth to help those in need rather than. . .*displace* them. They're partially in that 'shithole' because of what the city did to them."

"They did that to themselves. I will not assume someone else's problem and I don't give handouts."

"You know plenty of people that could make a groundbreaking effort to restore the Inner District. It could be a model for other cities to follow. A message to others in your position to give back. What you're talking about doesn't help people. It's not an answer to our problems here."

"You wanna know why I love my job?"

She waited.

"Because I decide the answers."

That he was still trying to impress her with his "power" was repulsive. As smart as he was, he had continued to fail in understanding what she found attractive. She knew that his pompous side only really came out at events like this, but her tolerance had dried up. Marian had been assertive her entire life. But as her workload increased, flashes of real aggression had been making an appearance every now and again. Yet she was finding a surprising amount of self-control tonight. Continuing to argue this point, this night, would do nothing but make her feel more distant in this crowd of strangers.

Her silence was stark in contrast to the night's environment as well as the bustling city below. It invited questions.

"What's going on with you tonight, M?"

"Nothing. I'm fine. Just been a long week."

The sound of skin slapping skin would have been audible in the adjacent motel rooms, had there been anyone there to hear it. The metronomic clap reverberating on the walls resembled a meat tenderizer hitting veal. A droning news anchor on the television drowned out little of the sound. He was balding and wore a tweed jacket. Above the bed a ten dollar painting of a sunset in some faraway paradise gently skipped off the smoke-stained wall with each drive. It was now crooked.

His belt was strung around her neck. With the excess wrapped around his fist, it might as well have been a giant zip-tie. Just such a zip-tie was holding her wrists together behind her back. Her bleached-blonde hair was disheveled, separated into four clumps at the dark roots where it was being held against the bed in his clenched left hand. He pushed with his left and pulled with his right. Harder as he approached climax. If her screams could have escaped her pinched windpipe, the panties stuffed in her mouth would've muffled them anyway. The duct tape over her lips, though, let through only a mild grunting vibrato. Her mascara was inexpensive. It ran a bit from her tears. The man watched himself in the oversized mirror hanging on a nearby wall. A crack ran diagonally through the top half of the mirror, etching a line through his bearded face. He refocused on his work and pounded harder.

The recoil of thigh skin moved in waves from each thrust, rippling across her legs and cheeks. Her skin was pink from friction. Reddening. He finished inside her and lay over her back with one hand holding himself up from the bed and the other gripping her breast. Winded, the broad, bearded man composed himself, pulled out, and pulled his pants up from around his ankles. He fished a cigarette out of the pack in his pocket and lit it while the girl was still incapacitated – a tribute to the event's meaninglessness. She was panting harder than he was. After some time he eventually pulled his belt off her neck and tore the tape off her mouth with disregard. She spit her panties out on the comforter. It was paisley. They were black. The girl caught enough breath to speak.

"Fuck. . .fuck. . .you fucking asshole. . .you fucking. . ." she gasped. "Why the fuck did you tape my mouth?"

The man took a drag and replied, "You had nothing to say earlier, so I figured you had nothing to say now."

"Fuck you. . .I was working. I couldn't talk. Fuck. . .fuck you. . ." Air eluded her. She rolled over onto her side, hands still bound behind her. "And you *fucking* came inside me. You know I don't allow that."

"That's for not answering. When I call you next time what'll happen?"

The girl glared at him.

"What. . .will happen?"

"I'll answer you, damn it. . .I'll *answer*."

"Make me look for you again and next time I'll bring friends."

"You can't. . . I have limits. . .you can't," she huffed, "you can't do this shit to me."

"Funny. I just did."

With her groaning and heaving breaths, the man entered the facilities attached to the room. The bathroom was in worse shape than the bedroom. A shower with no curtain and rust-stained porcelain, a broken toilet seat, and another cracked mirror. Drab colors, the whole place drab. The sink water maxed-out at lukewarm and the soap appeared used from the previous "tenant." He exhaled audibly and threw his cigarette in the toilet.

"Fuckin' shithole. Fuck it."

The man splashed running water on his face, but it did little to rinse away the night's buzz. He leaned on the edge of the sink and stared at himself in the mirror. Water dripped from his black beard, where a scowl slowly formed. His nostrils flared, just slightly. He pushed down on the sink harder, still unblinking. The sound of caulk cracking was what finally snapped him out of his stare. He released the downward pressure, relieved himself in toilet, and left without flushing.

She followed him with her eyes as he walked across the room towards the remainder of his clothes, squirming a bit in her restraints. She seemed to have unwound.

"This place is disgusting," she complained and coughed a smoker's cough. "Take me somewhere nicer next time."

"It's a shithole. I think it suits you. And I'll take you wherever I feel like."

"You're a pig."

"Oh, is that right?" She looked away from him as he spoke. "If I'm a pig, what does that make you?"

She cast her eyes down in defeat. The bearded man reached in his pocket and threw a baggy of coke at her.

"For your effort," he said, and made his way towards the door, giving her less of a glance than he would a package of expired meat. Her neck was red now. The bag bounced off the mattress and rolled to her stomach. Her wet eyes lit up and a small smile curled her lips, showing crooked teeth.

"Where d'you get this shit? It's so pure."

"Nicaragua," he joked.

". . .Where?" she asked perplexedly, still looking at the bag.

"It's Downtown."

"Oh."

And with that, the man left, shutting the door with a crash behind him.

Adorned with delicate orchid displays, the tables were set with fine silver utensils and crystal stemware. White linen napkins, cold salad forks and mother of pearl spoons were set in place, the latter in anticipation of the forthcoming caviar plate. Marian's theory was that some illusion of doing well for others helped these people justify getting together to enjoy such nights of inordinate extravagance. For dinner there were four entrees to choose from. Thinking he was being gentlemanly, Dalton had already ordered her steak cooked medium. In Marian's opinion choosing what a woman will have for dinner was an amateur move. She had wanted the duck.

She was beginning to hate eating so late, too. They rarely sat down before 9 p.m., which left her stomach rumbling loud enough to hear at times. It was 9:04. *Stop ruminating, God damn it.* Marian sat upright and composed herself for the impending social onslaught. From what she had been told nights like this became practically a weekly affair as the warmer months tapered.

Being October, she supposed high season was just around the bend.

The dinner that night was being hosted by Dalton's parents, Jackson and Felicia, "in an effort to raise funds for spinal cord research." A clinic in Houston was widely regarded as the leading research center for such efforts and, therefore, would be the blessed beneficiaries of the evening's endowment. At the head table tonight were the regulars: Dalton's Aunt Jane and Uncle Fred, his parents, an elderly couple introduced to her as the Montefiore's, and Mayor Crowley and his wife. The Mayor, Marian reasoned, would of course need to be convinced somehow to ease his grip on the regulatory limitations the city zoning board was notorious for enforcing. That the Mayor's youngest brother had been paralyzed at an early age might well have explained the evening's charitable cause.

The conversation was outrageous, oftentimes comical. The dialogue and subjects themselves were earnest, of course, but the manner in which they were said was so offhandedly frank and overtly distasteful that Marian found herself not only awestruck that people actually lived in such a way but genuinely amused that she appeared to be the only one laughing on the inside. They discussed money and properties, stocks and investments, new construction, and toys. They complained about a recent tuna shortage, the poor forecast for skiing conditions in Chamonix that winter, and the threat of a coup in Tanzania that had forced them to cancel their safari the next month. Marian remembered how her first dinner with this group had left her head spinning, conversation that night having been about the various options in selecting a new company jet. Lease or buy? Turbine or propeller? Decisions, decisions.

A decaying middle-aged woman interrupted Marian's train of thought with a piercing voice. "So, *Marian*, tell us how you've been faring at work these days."

Here we go. Dalton's Aunt Jane was a probing, rather nasty bitch to be around. Without fail Jane would prod at Marian, searching for a point of attack. Before Marian could respond she was interrupted.

"What is it she's doing again?" asked Jane's husband in a strikingly disrepectful manner. His eyes never left his plate while speaking. *Don't address me. It's fine.*

"She's working in the DA's office, you asked last time," Jane replied in a hushed voice, feigning irritation.

Marian piped in. "I'm an Assistant District Attorney for–"

"Ah, yes," he nodded, and took another bite of his dinner.

Marian blinked and redirected her attention back to Jane. "It's quite busy, Jane, but I enjoy public service. Beyond the stresses of each case and, well, the pressures of real consequence if I perform poorly, I truly enjoy my work. I–"

"*Real* consequence? What do you mean by that, honey?" Jane asked with a raised eyebrow.

"Oh, I just meant that in my field people's lives can be at stake. We work off taxpayer's money – if I make a mistake I see the effects firsthand, versus someone, who may work elsewhere."

"Elsewhere being. . .where? Are our consequences at work less *real*?"

"Oh, I'm sorry. I think you're misunderstanding me."

"*Am* I?" Jane fired back.

After a pause, Marian contiuned. "I simply meant that this type of work has a reailty to it. . .a tangibility if you will. Crime is real and if I make a mistake, the wrong people can benefit. In my opinion, other professions are more forgiving."

"Hm. Interesting opinion." Jane's eyebrows flashed upward and she looked down at her plate. She had been pushing a pearl onion around with her fork for the past minute. "Well, honey, I think what you're doing is wonderful, but there's such *money* in corporate law, don't you think? You can't be making much more than a school teacher's salary." She glanced at Dalton's mother, Felicia, who had been quietly following along while Dalton and his father socialized with the Mayor, and now was visibly amused.

"Sure, theres more money if I go corporate, but to be truthful I feel richer knowing I've helped the city than I would having a larger paycheck. My salary doesn't affect my sense of accomplishment."

"Aw, well that's admirable."

Marian met her gaze and smiled without showing teeth. *Condescending bitch. What have you done with yourself but suck money and life out of every man you've met?*

"In this circle, honey, your salary won't mean much anyway. But as long as you feel accomplished." Janet pierced the tiny onion and popped it in her mouth with a smile.

Outside the motel, the October wind blew fiercely. After two failed attempts to strike a match, the bearded man managed to light a fresh cigarette. He surveyed the parking lot quickly, with the intent of not being noticed. A deep drag gently relieved the mild headache that was forming behind his eyeballs, but the effects of liquor were waning. His untied boots thumped along the parking lot pavement with each step towards his dark blue car, ambiguous and of American make. The windows were tinted to an illegal shade. He slid into the driver's seat and opened his phone. Out of his opposite jacket pocket came a roll of cash collected, forcibly, from a bookie earlier in the day. Scrolling through the contacts list, he simultaneously opened the glove box and slid a dented metal flask from the dim opening. A shake revealed that it was empty.

"Motherfucker," he grunted.

He threw it back in the glove box and shut the door with frustration. Tendrils of smoke explored the car's interior. He glanced through the haze and out the windshield again. An empty lot looked back at him. Before he could scroll to the contact he sought, the phone rang in his hand.

"I'll be God damned. If it isn't Mr. Aksakov," he answered. "What's wrong, Teddy? You out of pierogis? . . .Not at all. Stay there, I'll swing by right now."

Jackson stood at the podium like a President addressing the nation. His suit was custom, likely worth more than most people's cars. He cleared his throat with a grunt. Words came shortly thereafter.

"Ladies and gentlemen, I will keep this quite brief," Jackson began. From what Marian could see, he was without speech papers. "Firstly, let me take this moment to thank you all for joining us this evening. We deeply value your generosity towards such an important and oftentimes overlooked cause, and without your support, this evening would simply have remained a thought in my mind. We also want to thank our dear Mayor for attending tonight, as most of us know of he and his wife's personal connection to this cause. Surely, your schedule is rife with pressing political issues, so for you to favor us with your presence is a true honor. Not only will this money aid in the search for a cure, it will also help the overall quality of life for the injurred and their families. I truly believe in this effort and may this money be used to see my vision for it become a reality. At this time I would like to personally present the Houston Clinic with a check for $750,000. May this endowment springboard your efforts in hopes to one day cure all those affected by spinal cord injuries."

In a clatter of applause, Jackson dismounted the podium and presented an oversized check to a grateful-looking man in a navy blue suit. His departure from the spotlight concluded the formalities and the party returned to its indulgences and conversation. Marian noticed Jackson linger around the numerous benefactors that gathered to meet him after his speech. Inquisitive by nature, she eyed the body language between the three men who approached Mr. White. Two were subdued, while one was overdoing his liveliness.

"Who are those men your father's talking with?" she asked Dalton.

"Which? Oh, a few of them are involved in the new project I told you about. The one who's underdressed is my father's lead architect. He's an ace, but socially he's a little awkward. If you watch you'll notice him trying too hard to fit in. I think he's a fag."

"Wha–" Marian stopped to stifle an urge to lash out. "What do the other two do?" she asked plainly.

Dalton sighed. "Um. . .they're–"

Just then a couple approached and interrupted Dalton, asking him to meet another family. Marian awaited an introduction that never came. Dalton stood and followed the two over to the adjacent table, leaving Marian behind. *Hi, I'm Marian. What a fucking honor to meet you. Oh, really? No, my asshole boyfriend never mentioned that. . .*

". . .well with her weight issues she's been such a burden on the family." Janet's piercing voice had interrupted Marian's thoughts once more. "Not only socially but finacially. My God I can't imagine what it takes to *feed* that girl."

"She's a *cow*, Jane." Felicia had no intention of disguising her disgust.

"She should just get surgery for God's sake. Her father's a *doctor*. He *knows* better." The two were several glasses deep at this point. Likely a fine champagne.

"She shouldn't have gotten to where she is in the first place. It's a disgrace to her family and I have *no* sympathy."

"These dinners aren't helping *my* cause these days either. Ugh, I've put on at *least* twelve pounds this year."

"That makes two of us. So much for resolutions. My trainer Antoine is at wit's end."

"So is mine," Jane cried. "I had to get a second wardrobe for this season just in case I keep gaining weight. How *embarrassing*."

"And the desserts haven't even come out. Anything coffee is just too much to resist."

Jane looked across the table to find Marian eavesdropping on the conversation. She nudged Felicia with her leg. "Oh you'll find out one day, sweetheart," Jane spat Marian's way. "You don't think that figure of yours will last, do you?"

The pair chuckled knowingly.

"Just wait until you and Dalt have a few children," Felicia added.

Yeah, no. Better chance of seeing Jesus. "Oh, I don't plan on children for a long time," Marian said.

"We'll change that. In this family, we intend to carry on the name. Besides. Children or not, we're women. Our bodies never stay the same."

"I mean no disrespect, but speak for yourselves."

Felicia disregarded her with a drunken wave of the hand, and Jane finished the jab. "Don't worry, honey, in our younger years we'd have given you a run for your money. You're not the only one who's turned heads in this room. Just remember, youth doesn't last forever. "

Dalton returned to his seat, but Marian's mind at this point was finally made up. Interestingly, he didn't put up an argument when she informed him of her intention to leave early. He just smiled and nodded. Several of the guests at their table noticed Marian getting her belongings together.

"Marian, sweetheart, are you leaving us so soon?" asked Felicia.

"Oh, honey, but you haven't had dessert," chimed Jane.

"Please forgive me Mrs. White, I have to be going. I think they still consider me a new employee at the office," she said with a laugh. "My week ended with a fresh stack of paperwork to tend to. Thank you all for such a lovely evening. Enjoy your desserts. They look delicious."

Dalton rose as she did and kissed her farewell. Marian walked slowly enough as to not appear in a rush, but with the purpose to get the fuck out of there. *Through the grinder again,* she thought. This time she wasn't so sure she had made it out unscathed. She knew she wouldn't feel at ease until she was back in her apartment.

It was half past one when the bearded man made his way into his office. He often slept there to appear as if he had spent the night working - one of many ruses he employed. Thirty minutes later he was in the guest chair, his feet propped on his desk, sipping on a second glass of whiskey.

His old office as Staff Sergeant had been much nicer, with a mahogany desk. In general, though, the department needed to upgrade these cabinets they worked in. How was he supposed to rid the city of corruption and vice with such derisory and outdated accommodations? The streets were his office, now, not this ant farm of useless automatons. *Not even one piece of ass in the building. I should have been a lawyer.*

The man found himself in a staring contest with the placard atop his desk. It read 'Senior Investigator Mervin Hamstead.' *Senior Investigator. If the Captain only knew the freedom demotion permits.* Merv smiled. *Ah, the perks of a plainclothes detective.* He downed the last finger of whiskey in his glass and poured three more. He continued staring at the nameplate. Moonlight split the blinds of his office window into silver bars. Merv's look deepened and his thoughts wandered to his younger, glory-filled days.

"Oh, how the mighty have fallen," he misquoted with a raised glass and a nod to the placard. "And the fallen will show his might once again." Merv emptied the glass and exhaled fire. ". . .God damn right I will."

Chapter 8: Between the Lines

Four weeks had passed since the trio's night carousing at *Stonewall's*. It had been four weeks of laborious renovations, excessive nights out, and story-filled bonding. Four weeks of mutual respect and dream chasing. Four weeks of novel friendship and fun. Four weeks of fresh faces, church visitors, and new lunch spots. In those four weeks, Robin had the opportunity to better familiarize himself with the District's layout and feel, gaining a truer sense of the place. One night, he and Perry even managed to hook up. It was four weeks of time that felt fluid and transparent, like twenty-eight compounding versions of the same day, yet each with its own accent, spice, or surprise. Indeed, Robin had spent nearly the entirety of every day with his new friends, and in doing so, felt closer to them than most any friend he'd had in his life. It was as if their initial conflict removed certain inevitabilities, such as drama, that may continue through less circumstantial relationships. It built rapport early on, subsequently bolstered by a high concentration of contact time. Such was a recipe for friendship.

The present evening marked the completion of the renovations at St. Augustine's. Materials were exhausted and so too was the budget. The issues atop Ernest's list were either addressed, corrected, or prevented, and the interior space was a marked improvement from its former condition. While the final improvements were modest—replacing a roof panel and fixing some shingles to prevent further leakage, painting part of the church interior, troubleshooting a few kitchen circuits, additional interior aesthetical work, etc.—the improvements to their psyche and emotional wellbeing were great. True accomplishment was a feeling seldom visited by anyone in the party and their collective attitude reflected such.

To celebrate the occasion, the four men sat down to a banquet - Robin's treat. Ernest had been reluctant to allow Robin to supply the meal, but after some coaxing, he gave in. He settled on feeling grateful for the company as well as the food, which was indeed quite lavish to the tastes of all save Robin. The past few hours had been spent braising beef short ribs, roasting fingerling potatoes and Brussels sprouts, and lastly, butter-poaching lobster meat to top off the surf-and-turf menu. Neither Jon nor Wil had had lobster in their lifetime, and it proved to be a delight.

Fulfillment at having provided such a great meal for everyone had Robin on a high, surely, but his thoughts leading up to dinner were of a larger affair. His temporary plan to stay at St. Augustine's had transitioned from asking himself how long he should be there into questioning why he should leave. Further, his desire to stay was met by the problem of how to stay. Should he strike a deal with Ernest? Should he find his own place? If so, then what? The issue would need to be addressed, and rather soon, else his discomfort would drive him to anxiety.

He had taken the opportunity to take a lengthy walk through the Inner District with Jon several times in the past month, yielding, among other things, a chance to connect with some locals. It was a journey of mixed feelings, seeing people among such deterioration. A sense of community was present in particular areas, evident through Jon's connections, though also fragmented by certain negative elements, like drugs, and even vacancies on some blocks. Initially, he knew that the news and his History classes did him a disservice in their muddled descriptions of the *Future of City Living* scandal and the resulting conditions in this forgotten District. He immediately realized that any previous interpretations, especially from schooling, were absolutely foolish. No book or teacher could do this place justice. He remembered Jon calling the Downtown skyline a "fortress" as they walked along Baker's Memorial Park. Truthfully, from his new vantage, he happened to agree. He hadn't vocalized his frustrations quite yet, as to not offend his new friends, but internally the feelings had mounted. After that first walk, he had quickly come to see his new surroundings as a perfect image of neglect.

Jon set plates and silverware while Ernest finished at the stove. Wil stood to the side, in conversation.

"Well," Robin overheard Ernest saying to Wil, "if it wasn't for you three I'd be a little less of spirits and a little colder come this winter."

"I dunno," Wil said. "I was looking at the forecast this morning. The rest of October's gonna be balmy at worst. Shit, it was almost eighty degrees today. They're predicting it'll carry into November too."

"Is that right?" Ernest asked, intrigued. "Well you won't hear me complaining. Many winters I could see my breath in the sanctuary. I welcome the change."

Ernest grabbed a tray of beautifully browned sprouts out of the oven and placed it on the stovetop beside a shallow, steaming pot of lobster. He then sprinkled the sprouts with salt and a light dose of pepper before returning to the pot to begin fishing out pieces of claw and tail meat, in all their butter-soaked glory.

"The smells in this kitchen are outrageous," Wil remarked. "My mouth's been watering for forty-five minutes."

As he removed the last few pieces of lobster, Ernest said, "Robin, our thanks will never be enough. This will surely be a meal to remember."

"Glad to do it, guys," he replied with a gratified smile.

"Shall we start, then?" Ernest asked expectantly.

"Hold up," Wil announced as he turned to the refrigerator. "Before we start, how about a toast?"

Wil pulled out a six pack of pounders, or tallboys as Wil called them, from the fridge. Robin and Jon each eagerly grabbed a dangling can and tore it out of the plastic yoke. Wil pulled a can and placed it beside his empty plate, setting the remainder in the middle of the table where they would meet their inevitable demise.

Robin momentarily pondered the white *Bearport* can. Jon and Wil had recently turned him on to the regional lager, which they drank religiously. The label read in pink graffiti-style bubble letters and the logo was a cartoon, sleepy-eyed, fluffy brown bear straddling an airplane while holding an overflowing stein. A dotted line trailing from the rear of the plane implied to the imbiber that the aircraft had just executed an in-flight backflip. Robin thought it was quite the feat for the bear to keep his stein full after such a maneuver. Apparently a few other styles of beer in the series showcased this bear, or ones identical to him, performing various airport duties. An airport run by bears. . . A Bearport. Apparently the brewers were advocates of drinking and flying.

Wil offered one to Ernest, who sneered, chuckled, and refused with a simple "no thank you." His answer brought Robin and Jon to a halt, who had both assumed he'd ask them to put the drinks away.

"You don't mind, do you?" Wil clarified.

"No, it's quite alright," Ernest said dryly. "Enjoy yourselves."

"I didn't even think to ask. This ain't part of your pastor thing, is it?"

"Pastor thing?" Robin questioned.

"You know what I mean. Your job."

"No, no. It is not uncommon to find a man in my position who enjoys a drink or two at the end of the night. But a long time ago I was given a choice: this," he motioned to the can, "or my life. I chose my life."

Wil sat down with a thud and cracked his beer. "What happened?"

Jon shook his head and huffed at the intrusiveness of the question.

"It's alright. It's alright," Ernest said. "Let's have a toast first, serve ourselves before the meal gets cold, and then I'll tell you about it."

"Fair enough."

Wil raised his can above the circular table to be met by Robin and Jon. Ernest dunked his teabag in the black mug he frequently drank from and joined in.

"What should we cheers to?" Wil asked.

Robin looked each man in the eyes and took advantage of the pause. "Foundations," he offered.

"To foundations," the group echoed.

They sipped as one, and lined up at the stove and countertop to serve themselves. Robin had made it a point to purchase enough food to feed nearly double their number, what with the major appetites present and all. Jon's plate had a literal pile of food, while Ernest chose meagerly - one piece of short rib, a few potatoes and sprouts, and one half of a lobster tail. Robin hoped his modesty wasn't at the expense of his hunger, as he and Wil were showing no less restraint than Jon. They sat and indulged Ernest in a quick prayer over their food. A minute passed by, filled with satisfied groans of palate pleasure.

Robin glanced about as he ate, curiously observing Jon and Wil with their first lobster pieces. Rare did he have the opportunity to observe an adult experiencing a flavor for the first time. He felt validated in providing for their enjoyment, and feeling it for the first time since Germany, he actively locked the sensation away in his memory.

"So," Wil said to Ernest between bites, "what happened?"

"Ah, yes." Ernest put his fork and knife beside his plate and clasped his hands together. "Three decades ago, in what seems like a different life, I walked through the front doors of this very church - not unlike you did, Robin, just weeks ago. But that man was much different than the one you see before you."

"I imagine he had more hair," Wil joked.

Ernest chuckled. "Not much more, believe it or not. No, the difference is that man was a slave to addiction. . . Oftentimes, soldiers take pride in the values dearest to their heart. 'God, country, family,' they may say. If my younger self was asked, he would have said, 'Beer, whiskey, and gin.' And he'd have meant it.

"This body looks old now, I know, but I used to be like you boys. Young, strong, and energetic. My problem was that my energy was directed towards rather immoral outlets. And my strength was sapped by that same liquid burden you have in your hands. Alcohol replaced everything in my life that I cared for. Family, career, sense of self. . . People rarely refer to it as a drug, but make no mistake about it - it is. It lures you to sleep with promises of comfort and solace, only for you to find yourself stripped of any such things when you wake, left empty and bare. Certain circumstances led me here, one being the death of my son," he paused and his eyes widened, as if he was staring into a dream, "another of which, perhaps I'll tell at a different time. . . But I walked into this very church and met with the pastor. I was resurfacing after a deep dive into that sleep, and was beginning to think clearly again. We spoke for hours, he and I. Life, loss, future, past, but mostly, the present. He was a wise man, which you all would have benefitted from meeting, but more importantly, he was honest. He never softened or coated honesty with sweetness. It was delivered purposefully, with the onus placed thereupon the recipient to determine a course of action. He gave me a choice that day: walk out the door the same man I was, and die, or stay here to become the man I want to be, and live. And so I spent the next thirty years trying to give to others what he gave back to me: life."

Ernest put a close to the story with a sip of tea. The three men stared intently at the pastor, reliving a part of his life unknown to them until that time.

"I woulda never guessed that about you," Wil remarked with curiosity.

Jon was silent.

Robin squinted. "You said you walked in here like me. What did you mean?"

"Well, addiction certainly didn't bring you here, but we were coming from somewhat similar places on the days we walked into this sanctuary."

Robin nodded after a moment's consideration, a knowing look passing between him and Ernest.

Jon leaned forward, unsatisfied with the statement. "What brought you here, anyway?" he asked. "You've still never told us."

Oddly, Robin smiled at the question. "I suppose it's my turn for a story," he said, to which Ernest chuckled and grabbed his silverware once more. "Remember that day you and Wil tried to jump me?"

Jon and Wil momentarily looked towards each other, betraying the slightest air of embarrassment. All knew Robin had avoided baiting them for an apology, but perhaps now they felt compelled to offer one anyway, considering their friendship.

Jon spoke for them both. "We remember it. Probably not the best introduction, but it is what it is," he said, raising the can to his lips.

Robin's head shook in dismissal as he spoke, physically steering the conversation away from that minute plot detail. "No, no. That's not what I'm getting at. That morning was my mother's funeral."

Jon gulped his beer and set it down on the table. He blinked a few times, processing the unexpected information delivered to him, and held what would have otherwise been a loud burp in so as to offer Robin his sincere attention. Wil had his arms folded and sat expressionless as Robin told them about his mother's death and his legal break with Wilson. The silence was broken only softly by Ernest's slow eating. He had heard the story before and understood the importance of the moment between friends.

"So you just took a stroll over here and found yourself with Ernest? Just like that?" Wil said after a time.

"Pretty much. None of that would matter much if I wasn't an only child, or if I had blood relatives that were at all decent human beings. Sadly, my stepdad's, like, my closest family at this point. We argued and at the end of the meeting I told him to go fuck himself and haven't been back besides a trip to pick up some clothes and things."

"Fuck, man. That's pretty hardcore."

"Yep. So that's that. I was left with a little bit of money but. . .obviously I would trade that for my Mom in a heartbeat."

"Obviously."

"How much were you left with?" Jon asked.

Robin eyed him to see if any greed had slipped into his expression, but all he was met with was a concerned face. "Twenty-six grand," he replied simply.

Jon snorted and Wil nearly spit his beer out. "Ain't *that* small."

Robin grabbed and opened a second beer, smiling across the table. "There's a much different world out there, my man."

The comment left Jon in silence. His demeanor tightened.

Wil stirred. "Not to downplay your situation, but you did have a solid amount of time with your mom," he said with an edge to his voice. "And while it sounds like your stepdad has issues of his own, he did provide for you, right?"

"Yes and yes."

"At least you had that time with them, y'know? I got exactly zero minutes of memory with my parents. There's a pair of cocksuckers for you."

"Do you know anything about them?"

"Not really. I heard stories when I was a kid, but who knows. From what I do know they'd have made Ernest look like a Catholic school girl."

Ernest shook his head at the remark and continued eating.

"Big druggies apparently," Wil continued. "It's a miracle I didn't end up some crack baby, or braindead with half a skull or somethin'. I don't think back on childhood often so my memories aren't that clear, but I bounced around from foster home to foster home. At one point, early on, I spent some time with two of my parent's 'friends.'" He emphasized this last word with air-quotes. "I doubt they were ever really that close, but I'll never know. They mentioned that my father used to draw portraits on the street or something. Like that's all they ever said about him. It was weird. Not what he was like, not where he was from or anything pertinent about him personally. It used to frustrate the hell out of me when I'd think about it, but it's nothing I fuss over anymore. As for my mom. . . Fuck if I know. I've been made to understand that they're both dead."

"His parents left him with the talent, though," Jon added.

"At least I got that, I guess. Art's always been an outlet for me."

"Huh. I didn't know that about you. What do you like to do mostly?"

"Anything I want, really. I do–" Wil shot a look at Ernest. "I *did* graffiti a lot when I was younger. That was my favorite. But it ain't worth it anymore. I'd just end up getting arrested." Wil grinned and turned to Jon. "Ain't that right, Jon?"

"Uh oh." Robin smiled. "Looks like were making the rounds with stories tonight."

"Ain't happenin'," Jon said shortly.

"What did you do?"

Jon shook his head.

"C'mon."

"It's a long story."

"Well, let me refill that plate for you, big boy, while you start," Robin encouraged.

He stood, grabbed Jon's plate, and walked over to the stovetop. Ernest quietly excused himself and began toiling away at some dirty bowls, dishes, pots, and pans. A resigned look came over Jon and he took a moment to reflect on the experience before beginning. Robin returned his plate and sat in his seat, painted with anticipation.

"Alright, God damn it," Jon huffed, causing Ernest to shake his head at the blasphemy. "The short of it is this: when I was nineteen I used to hit the bars pretty hard with this girl I was seeing. We were out one night and every time I'd go take a piss or chat with someone I knew - y'know just mingling about the bar and shit - I'd look over and this dude had her pinned, like arm against the wall talking *at* her. So I'd go over to check it out and each time she'd blow it off like it wasn't a big deal or the guy was just hitting on her or whatever. I mean, it happened like three or four times over a few hours, and as the drinks came, so'd my aggravation. So eventually I walked over and basically told him to fuck off, which he did, and I figured my girl and I would hit another spot - try to be rid of this dude before I went off on him. Not thirty seconds later, he comes back with his buddies and starts talkin' all kinds of shit. I'm trying my best to blow it off, so I grab my girl and walk outside. They follow us out to the street and start getting physical with me. So I turn to meet them and the dude spits in my face."

"Yikes."

"At that point I'm pretty much in war-mode. I freaked. I'm just fuckin' these guys up. There must have been like five or six of 'em, I dunno. I couldn't feel anything, I mean, I'm pullin' one off me while throwing another into a windshield. It escalated pretty quickly. I'm about done with them when all of the sudden, from behind, I feel someone wrap their arm around my neck and try to restrain my left arm. So I turn to grab the guy's collar, and without thinking - y'know, war-mode and everything - I cock back-"

"Oh no," Robin lamented.

"-and, thank God I stopped myself, because - sure enough - it was one of Fort Dearborn's finest."

"Fuck."

"I remember making eye contact and seeing that fear, that dread in his eyes, like he's about to have his face destroyed. And when I held off there was this split second of relief." Jon paused and shook his head. "Anyway, before you know it I'm on the ground in cuffs and the rest is basically self-explanatory."

"Well did you go to jail or what?"

"Charges ended up being 'Misdemeanor Assault' - pegged me for cocking back on an officer. A 'Resisting Arrest' charge was dropped because I had a pretty clean record. Worst part was that they fucked with me while I was at the station. Kept screamin' at me that I hit a cop, that they were gonna put me in jail for a few years. Wouldn't let me use the bathroom, wouldn't let me call Janelle, wouldn't give me anything to drink or eat, wouldn't let me shower, packed me in with drunks and junkies overnight in a holding cell. Those guys I fought, though. . .sent them home within the hour. Why? They weren't from the District. It was obvious. Just another set of assholes that came through looking for trouble. They found it, that's for damn sure, but without consequence. The cops knew where I was from. I could tell. They knew it. All these motherfuckers from the suburbs, like, Varsity Joe and his football buddies or somethin', that figured out they could get paid to be dickheads after school ended. It's a fucking force full of 'em. Simpleminded bulls, fuckin' meatheads that think they can get away with anything 'cause they got a badge on." Robin could see Jon getting flustered as he went, his shoulders tensing up. "You know me by now. I'm not aggressive. People just push and push and I know I shouldn't get physical but I can't handle being overwhelmed like that. I *cannot* handle it. I just fuckin' *need* space when that happens. And if you're in my way, I'm taking you out of it. Of course, I'd fight anyone back then because I didn't really care, but the point is that it takes a lot to get me to that point. All that being said, even with the charges and all the shit I had to do because of it, I consider myself lucky."

"Why's that?" Robin asked after a sip.

"Coulda been that Harrison kid," Wil chimed in. "Cops fuckin' shot him in a situation just like Jon's. Hit an officer by accident during a brawl one night and they opened fire."

"For real?"

Jon nodded.

"Dead." Wil added.

"They killed him," Robin said disbelievingly.

"Dead," Wil repeated with emphasis.

"Jesus Christ."

"Or Christie Tavington's older brother - what's his name. . ." Wil snapped his fingers, "Tommy. Dude was 'uncooperative' during a traffic stop - whatever that means - and got *whacked* with a *baton.* Now he can't turn his head to the right. Or left. Or some shit."

"Damaged vertebrae," Jon corrected between bites.

Robin blinked twice and leaned in. "Okay, humor me here. Is this, like, a regular thing? Stories like these?"

"You have no idea," Jon replied.

"What do you consider regular?" Wil asked. "'Cause I could go on. You don't wanna get me started on this topic. Shit, I got ten more stories without even thinking on it."

"It's every couple of months," Jon said.

"Have you ever had anything like that happen to you, Wil?" Robin asked.

"Nah. I always outrun 'em."

Robin waited for a smile or any other sign of jest, but none came. "Wait - seriously?"

"Yeah. They can't catch me."

"Kid's like the fucking wind," Jon said simply. He dropped his fork, which clanged on the ceramic plate, Jon having made quick work of the potato pile.

"I mean, I've been lucky too. I've only had run-ins while doing graffiti and stuff, so I'm not the best - what d'you call it - barometer. It's not like I get in bar fights and when the cops show up, I take off. Just sayin' based off my experience."

Jon leaned back and folded his arms, flexing a matrix of sinew and banded tendons through his skin as he locked eyes with Robin.

"It's a much different world *in here*, my man," Jon mimicked.

Such a revelation left Robin pensive for the remainder of the meal. He hadn't understood the reality of things lying underneath the crumbling façade of the District. What he once viewed simply as neglect seemed to actually tell tales of abuse and exploitation - and not simply at the hands of police. That seemed to be the tip of the iceberg. Ernest, of all people, joined in and told tales of corruption and victimization of locals at the hands of insurers, contractors, ill-favored judges, and city officials. It was enough to make Robin's head spin.

After a time, Wil batted the table with his palms and said, "I'm gonna make like fetus and head out."

Jon followed suit, bidding his farewell to Robin and Ernest with plans to stop by the following afternoon to hang.

By then, Ernest had about every pan, tray, pot, plate, and utensil cleaned, and asked Robin to take the larger items back to the storage room where they came from. Robin gladly obliged. Upon entering, he came across some curious items. At first glance, the room appeared to hold catering equipment, however, Robin soon deduced the items to have a more particular use.

When he returned, Ernest was wiping down the countertop.

"Hey," Robin said, jerking a thumb over his shoulder, "I, uh, noticed a bunch of hotboxes and coolers and a chest freezer in your storage room. What's all that equipment for?"

"That was for a weekly Soup Kitchen we used to host. I think we ended about. . .oh, seven years or so ago. My former understudy, Kevin, moved across the river to New Orange to take over at another church and I didn't have enough help to carry it on."

Robin leaned back on the countertop. "What would it take to get that started again?"

Chapter 9: Maple Bacon Glazed Donuts

"On Monday we should do a dinner service," Jon suggested as he and Robin walked the final blocks to Jon's apartment in the beaming midday sun. Jon had invited Robin over for a bite to eat before they met up with Wil for an afternoon game of pick-up basketball.

"Maybe just a longer lunch instead," Robin replied disinterestedly. "Can't leave people hungry like yesterday."

"True. Dinner could be a goal for the future, then. What'll it take to get a larger order?"

"Just a phone call. I'll go over the numbers with Ernest. Shouldn't be an issue to have it in time for Monday." Robin skipped over a missing sidewalk tile and continued his stride.

In the past three weeks, the Soup Kitchen had been held five times, beginning with a post-mass food service the Sunday following the idea's reinstating. Many of Ernest's old contacts were still in business and even held a history of his order forms, making for quite an easy startup. Robin had gladly fronted a few hundred dollars as seed money, which had been nearly recouped already. Shockingly, the monetary turnaround was proving the system self-sustainable, if allocating only for food, plates/bowls, and utensils. Volunteer work had made that possible.

Each lunch service featured a rotating dish from Ernest's many recipes, from chili, to soups, to stews, and more, all of which had been constructed for maximum flavor and minimum expenditure. Following the first service, word spread quickly, and increased attendance was recorded each subsequent day; so much so that yesterday's posole had ran out before each customer was served. It was an unexpected issue, remedied quite simply by larger orders and production.

Jon and Wil had been invaluable to the task, completing the service line, cleanup, and early morning prep work. Their public do-gooding had garnered recognition and respect in a way Robin was unaccustomed to. People had been stopping him, Jon, and Wil on the street with compliments, thanks, and support as if their work somehow called for gratitude. The way the trio saw it, they were simply keeping busy. Nevertheless, those benefitting from the Kitchen made it a point for them to know so.

On this very walk, he and Jon had been stopped three times. A number of waves, nods, and shouts were sent their way as well from distant groups, shop owners, and passing vehicles. Through the Kitchen, people were becoming familiar with Robin's name and face, along with his association with the guys. He had always been good at remembering people's names, but the sheer number of new faces was enough to drown his confidence. Robin would have some work ahead of him if he wanted to reciprocate the now-hundreds of acknowledgements he was receiving.

Meeting so many new people was wonderful, but the attention felt awkward. The people acted like his actions were redeeming them from some burden, as if the people couldn't do so themselves. Being thanked for a small church-based Soup Kitchen? It felt wrong. It felt uncomfortable. Perhaps he was being uncouth - he truthfully wasn't sure. Whatever the reason, whatever the origin of the feelings, he decided to push them away even as they surfaced more and more each day for the past week.

Up in Jon's apartment, the pair sat on the only two chairs at his family's kitchen table. They had been greeted with a surprise upon entering: Janelle, Jon's foster mother, was home early from work. The moment Jon walked in the door and laid eyes on her, Robin could sense his regret. Jon never much spoke of Janelle. Their relationship was strained, more businesslike than familial. He seemingly avoided her, taking advantage of the apartment's vacancy when she was at work or elsewhere.

Janelle had, resentfully, instructed them to sit upon learning of their business. She said, as more of an order than an offer, that she'd cook them lunch. By the look and tone of the woman, Robin didn't dare refuse. She was ragged, maybe in her mid-fifties, and didn't seem to take kindly to staring. Robin did his best to look at ease.

The stove had one working burner, from which, Robin noticed, she habitually lit her cigarettes. It was as if the smoke hovered around her. She batted at it, waved it away from her sight, yet it hung gently in defiance. Ashtrays beside the stove and on the kitchen table overflowed with piles of the butts. Janelle served up the meal in less than five minutes, dropping a plate in front of Robin like it was a letter in the mail, and walked back to the stovetop to cook for herself.

Jon kept busy reading *The Friendly Farmer*, a weekly magazine about farming techniques with news and spotlight articles. This installment was dubbed 'The Year of the Goat,' and featured articles on boutique goat's milk cheeses and yogurts, grazing benefits, breeding, and a pastoral recipe for southwestern goat tacos from a chef out of New Mexico.

"Not much of a talker huh," Janelle spat in the table's direction.

"Your food probably made him sick," Jon said without looking away from his magazine.

"Oh yeah? Cook your own fuckin' food then," Janelle responded before proceeding to hack up decades of tar and smoking residue.

This was their first encounter, Robin and Janelle, and he could tell the woman had a shell of granite encasing her heart. What he could not tell was whether she had been born with it or one had been cultivated over the past few decades of life's struggles.

"The food is fine," Robin said in an attempt to diffuse the situation.

"Ain't much, but you get used to it. I just pretend it's something fancy, like lobster."

"Well your cooking tastes like lobster to me," Robin said in an obvious attempt to butter her up.

Jon rolled his eyes from behind the magazine.

"Won't do no good to flatter me, boy," she said, perking up then, "but maybe Little Jon over here could learn a lesson from you. All he does around here is eat, sleep, shit, repeat. Ain't that right, Little Jon?"

She looked away from her cooking and turned to catch Jon's glare out of the side of her eye. Her smirk revealed yellowed, rotten teeth. Robin swore this woman had been a wicked grandmother in her past life, spending her days convincing innocent children to enter her confectionary house, never to return to daylight.

"Well either way, thank you," Robin said, trying to hide his discomfort.

"Holy shit. I'll be God damned. A thank you, too. Hear that Little Jon? Keep this boy comin' round," Janelle said.

Jon dropped his magazine on the tabletop and stood slowly, drawing the wooden chair's screech along the weathered linoleum floor. "Robin and I have to go."

Robin looked up at his towering friend. Even now he was surprised he hadn't succumbed to fear the first time he saw him. As on that day, however, something told him that though they might argue from time to time, they would never truly fight one another.

He knew Jon was uncomfortable, but something was beckoning him to stay and talk to Janelle. His recent reflections on the people in the District had brought his own actions into question. Perhaps this unlikely woman could shed some light on his growing restlessness. He also hadn't wanted to be rude and leave food on the table.

"Let me just finish eating real quick, then we can go."

Jon's look was one of restraint. "I'll be outside."

Robin picked away at his plate as Jon dismissed himself. Baked beans with a sorry excuse for corn bread and a slab of dry maple-glazed ham that he'd rather use to patch a hole in a truck tire than eat. Before Robin could think of a way to break the ice, Janelle did it for him.

"Always been his solution to problems." She pointed a thumb towards their balcony door. "Runnin' away."

"Maybe he thinks he'd cause less damage that way considering his size, even if you still think he's *little,*" Robin said.

"Ah, so the flattering was temporary. Speak on it, son."

"Nah, it just seems like you guys don't get a lot out of having each other around, especially since he's an adult now. Either you both enjoy the punishment or. . ."

"Or we need each other more than we let on," Janelle finished his sentence. "When we all got fucked here I needed money," Janelle continued. "Wasn't much per kid, but enough to keep our heads above water. I got paid for taking care of him and in exchange I gave him a bed and meals. I like to be clear about the relationship so there's no misunderstanding."

"Guess it's better than pretending. It's always just been for the money?"

"Yep. And that's all there is to it. Had some other kids years back. Some were adopted. Others with my Ex. Jon's too old now for me to see any money from the government, so he pays me rent to stay."

"I understand. Must have been a tough spot to be in back then."

"Tough is too kind of a word. Yeah, we ate up all those promises. Made us blind."

"Blind to what?"

"We were convinced to dig our own grave, and right before we were done we were kicked into it and forgotten. Never once offered a way out."

"You don't see a way to get your*self* out?"

"They're the ones who should give us a way out. None of this was our fault, we just got so caught up in a new beginning, committed everything we had. Oooo-weee they played us good too. I gave up my job, apartment. . .went all-in."

"What exactly happened? In your experience."

Janelle looked him over with piercing, accusatory eyes. "I ain't gettin' started on all that, boy."

Robin backpedaled. "Oh, I'm sorry. I–I'm not from here, I didn't mean to pry."

"Relax, I ain't angry. Just don't feel like taking a stroll down that road."

"You're not angry?" Robin asked after a moment.

"Not no more. To be honest, I couldn't give a fuck. This is life. And it'll always be. No one helped then. And ain't no one gonna help now."

"Didn't anyone try to fight back or–"

"Ah, don't start with that shit. It ain't no use. Your ideas or theories and what have you ain't gonna save us. You ain't got the answer." She laughed. "That's for damn sure."

Robin paused to truly look at Janelle for the first time. He wouldn't be surprised if her hands were scraped of their finger prints. If she walked past a tannery she might be kidnapped for her hide. Based on her relentless hacking, her lungs most likely resembled marshmallows left over a campfire for too long. But though her outer appearance screamed mistreatment, her words spoke not of ignorance but of something deeper. Of a carpenter without a saw, a potter without clay, or a painter without a canvas. She used to be a fighter, but she was caged. Like all she needed was a push or a helping hand and she could break the disastrous cycle. Yet the hand to help or the hand to push seemed to keep taking instead.

To Robin, she seemed like a metaphor for the District. Overworked, neglected, hopeless, helpless, and tired. She was defeated, plain and simple, just like everyone else. *That's it*, he realized. *They've given up. Like the fight's over.* He couldn't say why, but he rejected that answer. It wasn't good enough. *There's gotta be some fight left around here.*

"Can I ask you one more thing?" Robin asked.

"Yeah."

"Do you think it's beyond repair? This place?"

"For me? Probably. I like to think not, though. It could get better for the younger ones who were born here. Especially someone like Jon."

"You think others feel the same way?"

"Depends. Some are like me, others are too far gone into drugs or debt or just plain old age. Won't see me gettin' my hopes up on seein' changes."

"Why are people okay with it?"

"Because there ain't no use feelin' otherwise. It was adapt or die. So most of us adapted."

Robin considered her words momentarily and finished the last bit of food on the plate, combining each item to make the individual pieces more palatable. *That's not adaptation,* he thought. *It's submission. And it's fucking infuriating.* He decided it was time to be leaving, lest he provoke her a bit too far.

"Hey, thanks for lunch. It was nice to meet you," he said as kindly as he could.

"Don't make it a habit. Never got no check in the mail for you."

They traded uncomfortable laughter and Robin exited the room, the sound of Janelle hacking up her lungs faded from his senses. He found Jon on the balcony and nudged him in the shoulder to bring him back to the earth.

"You alright?"

Jon took a while to come to and finally turned toward Robin. "Yep."

"Let's go then. Wil's probably waiting, and eventually I've gotta make it back to Ernest's for dinner before we hang tonight."

A nod was all he got from Jon. On the way out of the building Robin decided to try to break the newly formed shell around his massive friend.

"So. Why's she call you Little Jon?"

Dinner was simple and well-prepared as usual, oxtail stew so savory and robust it challenged one's preconceptions of what should be delicious and what shouldn't. After all, they were eating an animal's tail. Ernest and Robin sat across from one another at the round table, lit mostly by the overhanging fixture and a shallow glow coming off the lights above the stovetop. Intermittent silences were broken by the buzz and whirl of the old refrigerator's motor like distant background music. Robin's off-mood was palpable and caused Ernest some perplexity. Nonetheless, he tried to keep the struggling conversation going in hopes of easing the tense atmosphere.

"I suppose we'll be receiving our shipment of canned goods on Sunday?" Ernest asked, getting up once they were through to brew some coffee.

"Yeah, everything should be delivered by the afternoon so we can prep for the week. Cans, meat, bulk seasonings, more to-go boxes, and plastic utensils. We're about out of spoons. We'll need to increase the order to feed twenty-five more people or so after the shortage the other day."

Ernest nodded as he returned to his seat, cup freshly steaming with an acrid roasted aroma. "I've said it before but it really is a bit surreal to see the Kitchen up and running again. It brings a lot of joy to those in need. And even an old pastor."

Robin huffed. "Look, if you're trying to thank me, there's no need. You shouldn't have been put in this situation in the first place."

"Well, the Kitchen simply couldn't continue without help, so–"

"That's not what I'm saying," Robin interrupted. "I'm saying you shouldn't have been put into *this* situation. The District. The fact that a Soup Kitchen is at all necessary."

"Mm," Ernest voiced mid-sip. He clicked his tongue after pulling the mug away. "Fretting over 'should have' or 'should not have' is a bit of a futile exercise."

"It's pissing me off, Ernest. A lot."

The remark commanded Ernest's attention. He met Robin's eyes across the table as the younger man spoke.

"Things are beginning to normalize and the novelty is wearing off."

"Well, that was bound to happen," Ernest returned. "But what you've experienced isn't disingenuous."

"No, it's completely genuine. And it's enough to infuriate me. Two miles, two fucking *miles* away from here are some of the most expensive places to live in the entire *world*. Yet you'd think we were in some post-war town, like a fucking bomb went off down the street."

"Examining the disparity or dichotomy in our city is an exhausting exercise. The fact is that we all come across times in our lives where things don't quite work out as planned, Robin. You know that. Those obstacles do not warrant resentment or anger, though."

"Why aren't you at all mad about what happened here?"

"Of course I get mad," Ernest replied penitently.

"Doesn't seem like it," Robin challenged. "You just said the obstacles don't warrant that feeling. All you ever say on the matter is 'it is what it is' or 'take the good with the bad.' 'God's will' and all that happy shit. Come on, we're not at mass."

"I encourage you to try to realize that there are alternate ways to sort through anger. Because I display what you might call passivity doesn't mean I'm content with this situation. Don't mistake me. I lost a great deal." Ernest's voice intensified. "A *great* deal."

"Got me fooled. You're a very smart man. Which is why I have trouble understanding your acceptance."

"As a religious man I do refrain from questioning God's will, but I do not blindly accept it. I deal with it as a faithful human being does. I acknowledge the challenge that is presented to me, and through dealing with it I grow spiritually and as a man."

"*Come on*, man, that's bullshit," Robin cried.

Ernest cocked his head. "Is it? Because I've seen what festering hate can do to those around me. I've lived it. It leads to dark actions and darker results. Piety is the answer for me and for many others. Not hatred and violence. Watch neighbors, friends, people you trust riot and loot and I think you'll change you tune, Robin."

"Violence isn't always bad. Whether you want to hear that or not, it's the truth. I say you and everyone else has a right to feel anger. If you dilute it with 'God's will' and 'God's challenge,' you're taking the air right out of your sail. You call it piety, I call it apathy. You're giving them exactly what they want."

"Do I give the impression that I feel resigned to defeat?"

Robin dropped his fork with a clank. "Man, look around you. Everyone here is resigned to defeat. This District is nothing but solid footing for the rest of the city to step upon. And no one seems to mind the shoeprints on their backs."

"And you've learned all of this in the month that you've been here?"

"I learned it in one day. It's practically written on the walls."

"So we're the reason, then?" Ernest chuckled emptily. "This is a new theory."

"You're not acting like the solution, that's for damn sure."

Ernest flared his nostrils and rolled his lips. "So then. Whom should we direct this anger towards? Whom should we fight and how? You seem to have a good versus evil mentality here. Are we the good? Are all others the evil? Haves vs. the have nots?"

"I don't know who to fight. I. . ." he huffed, seeming to deflate. "All I know is that churches, homes, and businesses shouldn't have to wait twenty-five years for half-ass renovations. There shouldn't be a line of people looking to be fed every afternoon like a fucking refugee camp. There's something terribly wrong with that."

"Perhaps everyone should live a week in our world, then, to appreciate the disparity? That ought to show them."

"You know, your stoicism towards this is infuriating."

"Son, I have lived *this* life," he motioned about, "longer than you've been alive. The city has done a fantastic job forgetting the atrocious acts levied against this District. I cannot change the past, but what I can do is help others deal with the present and the future. That is my role. I give people a reason. I give people a hope. I give them a pedestal to lay their hate upon and have it absolved so they can wake up the next day with the cloud above their heads a little lighter. This heals far better than destruction or fighting a losing battle."

Robin gritted his teeth. "You're one of the few people I've met in life that I truly respect. And I'm going to say this because I respect you. You're not helping these people the way they need to be helped. You're cheating them. They don't need to hear your voice. They need their own. And if it's a voice of anger, then I say let it soar. It's okay to fight a losing battle. Fighting is better than nothing at all."

"Maybe we've reached a point where you and I simply differ," Ernest concluded.

"Maybe. But I'm not going to hold my anger in." Robin scooped his bowl off the table and marched to the sink, dropping it against the steel well with a thud.

"Robin. . ."

Robin stopped at the back door but refused to meet Ernest's eyes.

"Think before you direct your anger towards someone or something. You can't help anybody if you're in jail."

Without a reply, Robin left.

Holier Than Thou Donut Shop was arguably the best around. Despite being in the District, it was a destination for foodies "in the know" and local lovers of things fried, garnering something of a cult-like following in Fort Dearborn and neighboring New Orange. Their glazed donuts were particularly coveted, often selling out within an hour or two of opening. The size of the operation only permitted a limited amount of batter to be made each day, adding mystique and demand to the already legendary establishment.

As the trio passed the shop, long closed at that time of the evening, a delicious smell still lingered in the air, as if it were seeping from the pores of the building's brick exterior. It was enough to tickle Jon's sweet tooth.

"You gotta try this place, Robin," he said, pointing as they passed. "They make the best donuts there."

"Hmm?" He looked over at the brick storefront. "Oh, yeah, definitely. There was a place I used to go to that closed down last year. Shame," Robin responded shortly.

"What? They went out of business?"

"Owner died."

"Probably ate too many donuts," said Wil.

"Actually, yeah, he did. But that place was still the best in town in my opinion."

"What was it called?" Jon asked.

"Glazed Over."

"Never heard of it," Jon said.

"It was Downtown. You think you know glazed donuts."

"Believe me. I do. That place we just passed may as well have invented the donut. All others are imitators in my book."

"Dude," Wil said. "They're crullers are fuckin' sick."

"Well. . .looks like I know what I'm doing tomorrow morning," Robin decided aloud.

"Get there early," Jon advised automatically.

Wil grew a sly smile at a thought. "You guys know how donuts got their shape, right?"

"I dunno. After the bagel?" Robin guessed.

"It was the same night that the glazed donut was invented, actually."

"Here we go. . ." Jon said.

"No, for real," Wil insisted. "Okay, so originally they were a solid round circle. Think of, like, an unfilled Boston Cream. So the guy that first made them - right here in Fort Dearborn - made. . .let's say a baker's dozen, right? Fried them up and ate the first one of the batch, fresh. It was *so good* that after finishing it in three bites, he popped a woody and *literally* took the second one and fucked it. That's how they got the hole in the center. He stacked every one of them up and fucked them. When his wife got home she found him passed out on the couch and two or three of 'em left over on the kitchen counter, all with a hole in the middle. Not knowing what it was, she ate one and obviously fell in love. She got to the last one of the batch and realized it was different. It had some sort of coating on it. That last one. . .that's how the glazed donut came to be. In the end he didn't have the heart to tell her he cheated on her with a pastry so he forever kept the hole in the center. Minus the semen."

"I wouldn't doubt if that's how it happened," Jon said. Robin merely shook his head at the story.

"It is, I'm tellin' you," Wil said, feigning seriousness.

"Alright, enough already," Jon said.

"Alright, Alright. I'll give it a rest. Let's change the topic. Hmm. Okay. 'Would you rather'. . ." Wil said, incapable of maintaining silence.

"No, no, no," Jon appealed. "Don't do it."

"Don't even start this shit," Robin warned.

"Would you rather. . .would you rather. . .okay would you rather fuck your mom or get fucked by your dad?"

"You're an idiot," Jon said.

"Jesus Christ, man."

"What? Alright, fine. Different one. Would you rather. . . would you rather. . ."

"You know what I'd rather?" Robin snapped. "I'd rather you shut the fuck up. For five seconds." He shook his head and huffed. "Fuckin' A, dude. You're like a child."

The affront quieted the group and Jon and Wil exchanged sidelong, squinting glances.

"Alright," Wil voiced feebly. "Relax."

An awkward minute passed by as the sidewalk rolled by underfoot. Though it was Friday night, fatigue beckoned the trio to keep the evening low-key, forgoing the usual bar scene in favor of a few *Bearport* pounders and some welcomed rest. They rounded a corner and were presented with the west side of the massive park Robin had passed when he first walked into the

District weeks back. He hadn't come to learn much more about it other than its name: Baker's Memorial Park. They walked a block south and reached their destination, Harper's Corner Store on the intersection of Atlantic Ave. and Front St. Jon and Wil were to go inside for some *Bearports* while Robin waited outside.

"Yo! Speaking of donuts, grab me a bear claw!" Robin yelled to them as they entered the convenience store.

"Alright," he heard Wil holler.

The guys spoke about this place like it was a beloved old-timey institution, but the store was nearly dilapidated. The second 'R' was missing off the large neon sign making the name look at first glance to Robin like it said *Herpe's*. The honest mistake was good for a laugh, but the blemishes didn't stop there. A look through the window revealed that the store had more shelves than items, and was in need of serious electrical, tile, and drywall overhaul. Robin walked a couple steps over to the side of the store and leaned against its maroon outer wall, propping his head against the brick with the brim of his backwards hat, a camouflage number his uncle had given him years back, now worn with love. The fluorescent overhead lights were dim from every other bulb having burnt out at some point, lighting his left side brighter than his right.

The breeze that night was tolerable in jeans and long sleeve shirt. It had been a peculiar autumn weather-wise, with nightly temperatures rarely dipping below sixty degrees; an oddity all recognized, but about which none complained. Back against the wall, legs crossed, he peered across the street towards a cluster of skyscrapers protruding into the night above the park's shallow treetop horizon. The buildings he eyed were distant not only in perspective but in feeling. A disconnect, he realized, that for him existed for real now. How long he'd stay here in the city was up in the air, but one thing was certain: he'd move away before living among those hollow pillars again.

Farther upward, silvery moonlight made silhouettes of the puffy evening clouds. It oddly reminded him of the classic black and white films his mother loved so much. *If she could see me now, what would she say?* She would've told him to be careful. . . He pursed his lips together and looked down for a moment. Her smile came to view in his mind. When his eyes returned to the sky a second later, he exhaled and buried the feelings. The wind gusted. Suddenly, a strained voice broke his concentration.

"Excuse me?" said the voice.

Robin looked over to find an elderly woman holding a grocery bag in her left hand and a cane in her right. Beady eyes stared at him through glasses as thick as two poker chips stacked together.

"Hello," he said.

"Are you the man who helps out at St. Augustine's?" she asked expectantly.

"One of them, yeah." He stood, nodded his head, and extended a hand from out of his pocket to greet her. "I'm Robin. Nice to meet you."

With all due respect to the lady, Robin had repeated that response to the identical question innumerable times in the past week. It came out in a practiced tone and he anticipated a usual exchange to follow.

"Why are you here?"

Maybe not so usual. He figured it was obvious by then that if one went so far as to ask if he worked at the Soup Kitchen, they also knew he wasn't local. Word travelled around this place quicker than college.

"Chance, I suppose," he answered honestly.

"Hmm. Perhaps," she said. "Maybe there's a better reason than that."

"What's wrong with chance?" Robin asked in amusement.

"My husband used to say, 'Being random is boring.'"

Robin blinked. "Fair enough."

"I suppose you're expecting me to thank you for the food service, huh?"

"Oh, no. It's nothing, we're just volunteering that's all. Hoping to make some sort of a difference."

"That wasn't a compliment," she said with a tired laugh.

". . .I don't understand."

"A soup kitchen's nice and all, but it doesn't go nowhere. A young man like you can do something better with your time."

"I'm sorry, ma'am, I–"

"Don't ma'am me, boy. If you want to help, better make it stick. That's all."

"Alright." He put his hands up in what could be interpreted as surrender. "I'll keep that in mind."

"You'd do well to do just that." With a precise nod the lady turned to leave.

"Hey, before you go. You've lived here your whole life, right?"

"You tryin' to ask me my age, boy?" she joked.

Robin smiled. "Never."

"My whole life. That's right," she replied proudly.

"What's the one thing you'd like to see change around here?"

"I'm too old to worry about the future, son. All I think about is the past. There's some things I miss more than others, but there's one thing I miss more than anything." She cracked a sideways smile, turned slightly, and pointed with her cane. "See that park across the street?"

Robin glanced and nodded calmly. "I see it."

"They call it Baker's now, but it used to be called Greenwood Park years ago. And each year, on the first day of May, a festival was held there. People from all over the city would come to celebrate spring. It's where I met my husband. It's where I fell in love. It's where a lot of people fell in love. . . If I miss one thing, I miss the festivals. They were the best days of my life."

They maintained eye contact for a moment. Then without anything more the lady made her way into the dimness. Robin watched her mosey along down the street until she was lost from sight.

He turned his head to the park, at what appeared to be more of a thicket. Beyond the waist-high rock wall, tall weeds and shrubs filled the gaps between trees like an impenetrable fence of brush. There was a sizable gap, however, a ways towards the north end which Robin figured was a field or even a pond. It was dark and spooky inside. Whatever joy frolicked in that space, the park hadn't seen the like in many, many years. *I wonder if the guys know anything about this festival. Ernest probably knows.*

Unconsciously, he slid the inside tray of his tiny box of matches in and out repeatedly with his fingers. He decided it a proper time for a smoke to clear his head, relax, and try to make some enjoyment of the night. Robin shifted, stood a little straighter, and propped one foot up against the wall, knee bent at a 45 degree angle.

Just as he took the matches out of his pocket and reached for a cigar, two striking, dolled-up girls emerged from the store and rounded the corner towards him. The shorter brunette closest to Robin beamed at him. The dirty-blonde next to her gave him the slightest of glances and placed a lollipop suggestively in her mouth. Each wore a skirt and heels.

Robin knew these two a bit. He'd never formally met them, but recognized them from the bars. *Nice girls. And sexy as hell*, he thought. *Fuck, what are their names?*

"What are you two gettin' into?" Robin asked openly after taking them in.

"Oh, I dunno. To be honest, I thought it was the other way around," said the brunette.

"Maybe someone will help us out. . ." the blonde giggled, flashing her eyes in Robin's direction.

A laugh burst from Robin. "I doubt you'll have trouble with that one."

"Oh, I thought you were smarter than that," she flirted.

"Hey, I'm always up for some fun. I just don't think you could handle me."

"Handle you?" The two looked at each other and giggled confidently. "Pretty sure we'd own you."

"Well these goods ain't for sale."

"Maybe we'll have to take it from you, then."

Robin laughed again. "Looks like I'm outnumbered. Be gentle with me, alright?"

"No promises, cowboy."

He shook his head and smiled. "Uh oh. What's that supposed to mean?"

"It's simple, Robin. It means we do exactly what we want," said the blonde. She quickly raised her eyebrows before the pair continued down the sidewalk holding hands.

Jesus Christ. Does anyone not *know my name around here?* With one more glance and a slight shake of his head he pinched the cigar in his teeth and struck the side of the little black box, hands cupped to block the wind. Just as the flame consumed the match's green tip, the red shine of brake lights followed by a commotion grabbed his attention off to his right. He paused and held the lit match an inch away from the cigar, slowly guiding his concentration down the street. A vehicle, seemingly an unmarked police car, was creeping down the street next to the girls at a tempo matching theirs. The passenger had his window down and was motioning for them to come closer. Rob pulled the cigar out of his mouth and turned slightly. He couldn't quite make out what was being said, but he clearly heard one of them being addressed as 'baby.'

You've gotta be fucking kidding me. In the time it took for the flame to reach his fingers, his decision was made. He dropped the match, pocketed the box and cigar, turned his hat forward, low on his brow, and took a stroll towards the commotion.

Commands became clearer as he approached. Within seconds, the voice was distinct. The man had an arm and bald head leaning out the window.

". . .didn't offer to pay so you won't get in trouble. Trust me. C'mon, get in," the man ordered.

"Fuck off already," one of the girls cried.

"*C'mon*. . . It wouldn't be either of your first time. I'll treat you like a princess. C'mon."

"Why don't you treat her like a human being and respect her answer?"

"See, that was rude. We're nice guys if you give us a chance, but I'm losing my patience."

"Take a hint, pig, we're not getting in."

"Oh baby. That's the fuckin' spirit. Talk dirty to me."

"Get fucked!" she snapped.

"It's you who'll be getting fucked if you keep this cat and mouse game up. Now get in the *fucking* car."

The sound of Robin's footsteps caused the girls to peer over their shoulders. The eyes he saw were like those of cornered animals, frantic and afraid. The man leaning out of the passenger window turned on Robin like he was interrupting a business meeting and the car came to a halt. The thick, round head held eyes heavy with a buzz of some sort. Robin pointed with his left thumb down the road from which they came.

"Donut shop's back that way, boys."

The balding man rearranged his expression into one of intimidation. "Then you better head that way if you wanna keep your teeth."

"That's weird. My dentist always told me to stay away from sugar," Robin fired back. He redirected his attention on the girls, "You two alright?"

The cop interjected. "That's none of your concern."

"Oh, I think it is, my friend."

"Okay, you got two options here, son. First–"

"You know my *stepdad* called me 'son.' And I fucking *hate* my stepdad." He turned back. "You girls alright?"

"Alright," the man mumbled as he and the driver opened their doors and stepped out of the vehicle.

"Now would be the time to leave," Robin warned to the girls under his breath.

They heeded and began backpedaling along the sidewalk as the goon slammed his door and stood erect, taking steps towards Rob with practiced swagger. The driver rounded the rear of the vehicle, stocky with a wide chest, short legs, and what appeared to be just a head on shoulders. Both wore plain clothes.

"Got something to say now?" he asked as he got closer.

Robin inhaled. "Nope."

Without warning, Robin stepped towards the bald man and kicked him square in the testicles. With a cry of agony the big man's knees buckled and he went down. A lighter man would have quite possibly been lifted off the ground. Quickly, much quicker than the driver excepted, Robin was on him. He threw his fist towards the driver's stomach, ducking under a slow punch, and connected with a loose abdomen. The man doubled over in a painful and fruitless attempt at breathing. Robin stood tall and grabbed the man's neck, wrapping his fingers together behind it like a vice, and drove his knee into the man's face. After three or four hits, Robin backed off and let the driver fall. The bald cop writhed alongside him, clawing at the pavement with one hand and clenching his manhood with the other. He may have even puked. Whether the pair was screaming, silent, or yelling specific obscenities to Robin, he'd never know. His heartbeat was too loud. Time to assess the aftermath was cut short by extraneous voices as Jon and Wil finally appeared on the scene.

"No way!" Wil exclaimed.

"*Dude*, what the *fuck*?!" Jon yelled.

Robin snapped out of his trance as he realized the two had shown up. His attention shot from the scene to his friends.

Between heaving breaths, with a voice like iron, he said, "We have to go."

"You still want your bear claw?" Wil asked with an astonished smile on his face.

"Now!" Robin shouted and took off down the road in rapid strides.

Chapter 10: Whiskey Shivers

At 10 a.m., laughter was filling Merv Hamstead's office with a thunderous rumble. It could be heard in the hallway, escaping through the thin slivers of space between the oak door and its rigid frame. Across from him were two of his former trainees, Officer Marcus Telman and Officer Rodney Puglisi. They had been assigned as deputies to Merv roughly two and a half years ago through a detective program. Seated, Rodney watched Merv's laughter through two bruised, swollen eye sockets, while Marcus's injuries forced him to lean against the far office wall nursing his groin with a bag of ice. Sitting was still a touch too excruciating on his unmentionables, so with a wide stance he waited until the current round of embarrassment came to a lull.

Merv had granted their request of audience with him and for the past minute had heard their recount of an "incident" that had transpired less than twelve hours prior. His chuckles started immediately when they entered the office and turned into full on laughter by the conclusion of their narrative. He stood against a half-open window thirteen stories above the city, smoking a cigarette while he listened. His tie was loose around an unbuttoned collar and the wife-beater he wore was visible through his transparent white button-down shirt. Wisps of smoke curled in the air, a dance that lasted but a few moments before the outside atmosphere claimed them with its invisible pull. Smoking was prohibited in the office, he was told.

"What really happened? 'Cuz there's no way you two were had. Tell me you got drunk and fought each other again," Merv asked between a chuckle and puff. "You try to arrest each other by mistake? . . .Fuck each other's wives?"

The two were silent.

"Wait! I got it!" he exclaimed with a raised finger. "You head-butted his dick!" Merv waited with feigned expectation for the two to confess to the absurd supposition. Instead they held steadfast to their story.

"We told you. Guy came out of nowhere."

"In the *Inner* District? Doubt it," Merv said with penetrating eyes.

"Well it happened."

"The old 'Raucous Brothers' shown a little roughness of their own, huh?"

"Does any of that matter, God damn it? Let's get to business," burst Marcus, tending to his jewels. It was clear he'd rather a swollen face than a swollen package.

"Yeah it fucking matters, Marcus, look at you," Merv snapped. "You're a piss poor reflection on me. You know how *useless* you two look? Like fuckin' children crying to their daddy because they got sand thrown at them on the playground." Merv shook his head in aggravation. "'Does it matter,'" he mimicked.

Merv knew their story was mostly bullshit, fabricated out of embarrassment and shame. He had taught these men everything they knew, but always judged them to be a couple of fuck-ups. Degenerates, really. Just the way Merv liked it. He genuinely valued them for their usefulness in certain specialized instances; however, on the whole they were less than skilled policemen. Any chance he had to reinforce their inferiority, he jumped on, and by his judgment he expected they probably got tanked, drove around, tried to pick up some sluts, caught more resistance than they expected, and got their asses handed to them.

But the fact was: they had been disrespected. Though comical, the longer that fact simmered in Merv's head the more he wanted to solve this predicament for them. This was a matter of defending his men, and Merv protected his men like family. They were products of him. If they failed, he failed. He kept those thoughts inside and let Rodney and Marcus suffer through the meeting, a small price to pay on top of a beating for their greater mistake - the mistake of letting themselves be dominated. No loss is as grave as the loss of control.

"So you're banged up. . .with a questionable, albeit pitiful, story. Now what?" Merv waited expectantly.

Rodney glanced over at Marcus and spoke for the two of them, as Marcus's anger seemed to be clouding his ability to make any valuable additions to the conversation and only seemed to draw further disgust from Merv.

"You know why we're here. We want this guy. And that's that."

"I bet you do."

"What's it going to take to make this happen?" Rodney offered.

"You'll owe me. You can be damn sure of that."

Rodney nodded. "We know. But what do you need from us to find him?"

"Gee, Rod, y-you could tell me what he fuckin' looks like. There's a start," Merv said with bewilderment.

"I *know*. I-I meant do you need us to *do* anything," he asked regretfully.

"Like I need you two fuck-ups fumbling around on the street," Merv said, then pointed to Marcus. "Maybe you can have him waddle down the block with his nuts out putting up reward signs. What do you think of that? Or how-"

Captain Hogan burst through the door speaking in his signature booming voice. "Hammer, my office-" The Captain paused in surprise when he saw the two officers. After a look at them, then a glance at Merv and his cigarette, then back to them, he demanded, "What's this bullshit?"

"Car accident," said Merv, after a slight stretch of silence.

"In one of *my* fucking cars?" he asked with a raised eyebrow.

"Off duty, Captain," said Rodney.

"Better have been. I'll fuck you both if it wasn't. Hammer, finish up. My office. Five minutes." Without more the Captain shut the door and left the three to their business. He seemingly had missed the bag of ice over Marcus's balls or there would have been a few more questions, Merv wagered.

"Be careful out there. He wants to fuck you. . . Useless faggot," Merv snarled. "Anyway."

Shifting in his seat, Rodney took it upon himself to commence the limited description he had on hand. "The girls were locals. No doubt in my mind. Seen 'em before. One blonde, one brunette, pale and olive skinned respectively. Young, probably eighteen to twenty. Tight bodies. Shouldn't be too hard to find, the way they were dressed. Find one, you'll find the other. The punk. . .I-I dunno. He didn't seem like he was from around there. Not the way he spoke," Rodney recalled.

"If that's the case, I'll have to move quickly. What else?"

"About six feet flat. White, athletic build. Boots, jeans, dark shirt. . . Umm, he was wearing a hat so I didn't get a good look at his face. Little growth of facial hair, brown."

"Wouldn't happen to have a name, would you?" Merv asked jokingly.

"No," Rodney said, missing the quip. "Like I said, he spoke differently. Little more refined. I–I can't quite say but it was noticeable."

"What did you do? Discuss politics? I thought he jumped you."

Rodney shrugged with a look of discomfiture.

"How old was he? And why am I pulling this information out of you?"

"Sorry. He couldn't have been older than 25. That's all I got on him. Happened quickly."

"What the fuck happened to you two? I sharpened you two like fucking swords. Now look at you. You don't even know how to defend yourselves, let alone return a beating. You've lost your edge."

Merv stared at the floor in repulsion for a moment while his mind took a brief respite to figure out the day's route and which liquor store was most convenient to stop at. A tremor suddenly came about in his right hand, causing ash to fall from the short cigarette. It shook autonomously, only at the wrist, like some electrical motor was planted within. It was something that had been afflicting him for a year, now. He ignored it.

"I'm going to kill that piece of shit," Marcus said, his voice trembling in rage. "And those fucking *cunts*, I swear they–"

"No, you ain't. You ain't killing anybody this time, you understand me?"

"Motherfucker kicked me in the nuts!"

"Yeah? What's that say about you? A better cop wouldn't have let that happen. Next time give the beating instead of taking it. You find him, you do what you want. But if we do this my way, it's my rules. That's it."

Marcus's facial expression evolved from disagreement to acquiescence, and an air of stiffness filled the room.

"Umm. . ." Rodney hummed.

"'Umm' what?"

"The three of them knew we were cops."

"*Jesus Christ*. . .why didn't you fucking tell me that?"

Another embarrassing silence followed the remark.

"How many times do I have to beat it into your fucking heads? When we take extras on the side, we have to be invisible. Complacency breeds laziness. Laziness is just sloppiness without action. And when you're sloppy, we find ourselves here. Now *I* have to fix it. . ." Merv lit another cigarette and continued, "Go home. I'll take some time to gather more information and I'll get a name. Once I do, we'll make contact and we'll take care of it. Until then, I don't want to see you. The way you two look will draw questions, *obviously*," he said in reference to the Captain with a nod to the door, "and I won't be involved. Take a day or two of leave. Make up whatever you want."

The two deputies began to gather their things and made to leave the tense office with as much haste as they could muster. Before they reached the door, Merv spoke.

"Hey," he said softly, in a tone heretofore unseen during the meeting. "You've killed for me and I won't forget that. You're fucking warriors. But don't ever let this happen again. . . Wait for my call."

"We won't. Thank you, sir."

"And Rodney," Merv said, staring at the tile floor once more.

Rod turned, halfway out the door.

"Fix your fucking face before you come back."

"Yes, sir," Rodney said with conviction and shut the door quietly.

A well-trained dog will never bite the hand that feeds. And that hand is mine. These dogs are old, though. They're running out of tricks. Wide eyed, Merv remained glued in a staring contest with the tile. Plans rolled through the spatial fabric of his mind like a snowball collecting mass. *Find the girls, find him. They'll know. Going to have to move on this soon. I'll start with the District bars, somewhere shitty. See what I can drag up from the bottom feeders there. Chances are if cops caught a beating it's turned into a rumor by now. Find the girls, find him. Patience, tonight. It has to be tonight. Start early. 9 p.m. I'll change clothes and lift first.*

Merv extinguished his cigarette butt on the window sill and stood, making for the Captain's office. He clenched his hand into a fist to settle its shivering. The tremors had been lasting longer than usual recently, well into the mornings. He opened his office door with force.

Find the girls.

". . .It's an excellent school. We don't usually see applicants with such impressive resumes."

Merv opened Captain Hogan's office door as if it were his own. Inside, two men were seated across from the Captain in plain clothes with clean shaven faces. He squinted, casing the scene before him. The Captain wore his shoulder holster daily, a transparent symbol of authority that he struggled to convey. The other two in the meeting appeared young, perhaps new transfers for the department. Inwardly, Merv cursed the Captain for calling on him only to stumble upon an ongoing meeting.

"Gentlemen, let me introduce you to the legend himself, Merv 'The Hammer' Hamstead. A 17-year veteran of the New Orange and Fort Dearborn Police Departments. A man with more career arrests than any two active detectives in the metropolitan area. A man that at one time held the most convictions in a five year stretch in the country, leading to his inevitable and *auspicious* nickname, 'Hammer'. Every time he cuffed you, it was as if the judge's gavel already hit the sounding block. . . A man that's saved my life and is responsible for the downfall of some heavy hitters in both his time undercover and. . .well, during overt operations. Along with his Senior Investigative role he's taken a mentorship position in recent years that dominates his time these days but make no mistake, you won't find a more seasoned officer in the city."

Merv watched Captain Hogan make his prideful speech, sounding as if Merv was somehow a product of him. Upon its conclusion Merv met the eyes of the two men who'd turned half around in their seats to gaze upon his alleged holiness.

He held a legendary status among those in the force due to his career's earlier glories like his raids on crime lords and drug rings. The mixture of veterans and young guns in the precinct saw men that knew his former height and men that merely heard tales. Both viewpoints made Merv out to be fabled and his independent nature over the past few years only advanced his reputation.

"Different times back then," Merv said with vigilance.

"Bullshit. Hammer, let me introduce you to your new deputies, Eric Mancuso and Brian Taylor," the Captain presented with an open hand. "Consider yourselves privileged to be under his direction for the next twelve months."

Oh fuck. That's right. New pups today. Merv hid his surprise like a poker player that just flopped the nut flush. He had forgotten about the assignment papers he'd signed earlier in the month accepting their addition to his group. The two men stood in unison and introduced themselves. The one called Brian eagerly took the lead.

"Mr. Hamstead, sir, pleasure to be working with you," he urged. Merv sized him up immediately and nearly rolled his eyes. This "Taylor" guy had a pathetic, weak presence. Merv could tell he wasn't city-born by the plain inflection. *This oughta be a letdown.*

"Alright, how ya doing," Merv replied lazily.

"We studied you're tactics from the early nineties when you guys took down the Santoro Family. Just brilliant," Taylor said with animation.

Jesus fucking Christ, here we go. "Oh y'know, just had to break out the tomato sauce and those wops came running. No big deal."

"Uh, Eric Mancuso. Nice to meet you, sir," the other one said and extended a hand. Merv clasped it strongly. A strong grip met him back. The two met eyes and Merv nodded to him. *Here's a guy I can use. There's talent in those eyes.*

"Merv Hamstead. Good to meet you." He glanced between the two. "I'm going to teach you boys how to be a cop." *And just when I thought I was short on ability, I get to forge my own. Let's see if these rocks polish into gems.*

"Hammer, do you have time to sit down and discuss some details of the upcoming program?" the Captain begged.

"Got some business to tend to, unfortunately. I'm on my way out the door in ten. Sorry about that, boys. Wasn't expecting you this early."

"Well, no matter, I just wanted to get you all acquainted. I had them brought in informally today but Monday we'll commence the program."

"Monday it is."

Chapter 11: Trimming the Fat

The Corked Apple sat halfway between Broad & Heron St. within view of the north end of Baker's Memorial Park, known by all for its loose ID policy and even looser female patrons. Residents of the adjacent neighborhoods often traveled to the Inner District well before the legal drinking age to have a taste of sin, and their stops almost always included *The Corked Apple.* Locals didn't shy away from the bar's wares either, joking that "an apple a day keeps the doctor away".

Merv Hamstead entered the bar inconspicuously, glad to be out of the drizzling evening weather. Dressed in boot-cut jeans, high-top work boots, a black long-sleeve shirt and a dark brown zip-up hooded jacket, he looked convincingly a man who worked with his hands for a living. Name a trade, it'd probably fit. It wasn't as obvious these days, but ten years ago his wide, athletic build had brought many a male stare of jealousy and female gawks of fantasy. While the bulk of his physique remained, its definition was now hidden by layers of drinking, smoking, and dietary neglect, despite his exercise regimen.

Earlier in the day, after Hogan slapped him with two new deputy recruits, he had hit the gym with his standard Saturday routine. He had opted not to shower in an effort to fit the mold of tradesman, and in support of his theory that attraction was based on several animalistic factors—one of them being pheromones. The potential that he'd have to test that theory by using attraction to question a woman or two tonight was high enough. His jet-black, five-day-old beard conveniently supplemented the front he'd built to aide in the hunt that evening.

Merv set out with but one goal in mind: information. The night wouldn't end, he vowed, without a name, whereabouts, and accurate description of the man responsible for the beating, as the account given to him by Rodney and Marcus was about as generic as could be. Not only did this bar look like a place to obtain that type of information after buying someone a round or three, it happened to be less than a quarter mile from where his two deputies had met their match the night prior. He made his way to the bar with what seemed like blinders on, acting as any other patron determined to drink his way to numbness. The bar made an L-shape to the right, with the longer section perpendicular to the pathway from the door. The perfect seat was in the corner of the bar, just past the L, enabling one to act like they were engrossed in a drink while being able to easily observe the surrounding environment.

As Merv took his seat, a haggard barkeep made her way over with little haste. The dim lighting concealed what twenty years of bartending had done to both her looks and her stature. On her chest, above her right breast, was a faded tattoo that read "Love" in basic script. *Hopeful or longing?* Its smudged lettering appeared as if someone had written it in ink and then tried to remove it with a pencil eraser. *Must be tough to tattoo leather*, Merv thought. She silently made eye contact with him and waited.

"Whiskey and a Bud heavy," Merv ordered with the comfort of repetition. It had been his standard order since he started drinking heavily his rookie year on the force. He had never killed someone until then. . . The barkeep nodded and took off with melancholy motivation.

Merv was an extraordinary drinker, but an even better investigator. Out of the corner of his eye he was able to case the bar with ease. Two townies sat in the back left booth several rounds deep, likely reminiscing about the same dross they had the day earlier. Three blue-collar workers, dressed similarly to Merv, sat on the end of the bar arguing over what to do with the lottery money they were destined to win after the weekend's MegaBall drawing. Two young women sat immediately to the right of the entrance holding artificial conversation while swirling their long untouched drinks. Too old and far too unattractive to be his marks, he quickly determined. *Hookers. . . Probably sucking on a Midori sour and some Rumple Minze. I'm sure it'll be a cock later tonight. Fucking whores.*

His concentration soon returned to his line of sight when the whiskey and beer arrived. “Eight even,” the bartender remarked with a soulless voice.

Merv slid a $50 bill across the bar. “Round one never tastes as good as round two, and round three tastes best of all,” he said with a subtle grin.

“Still 26 over.”

“Take one with me, and then let’s see how the night goes,” Merv rebutted as he raised the shot to the bartender.

Surprisingly, the gesture seemed to crack her onyx demeanor as a momentary smirk formed on her face. She removed the $50 bill from the bar and poured herself a shot from the same bottle.

“Let’s,” she said, staring into Merv’s eyes. Unblinking, she downed the shot and her smile grew ever so faintly. *Not as soulless as she seems. All she needed was a little attention, the ugly bitch.*

The healthy shot left Merv’s lip curled, even after all the years and all the drinks. “Cheap well shit,” he said softly to himself as he pushed the empty shot glass towards the inside rail.

“I could squeeze the bar rag out for you next time. . .or are we staying with the well?” she jabbed.

“Ah, so the barmaid not only serves but she entertains! The well it is, my dear,” Merv returned with a nod. A quick stare from the bartender ended the dialogue and the pair returned to silence as she washed some dirty glasses.

Merv tolerated the droll atmosphere for longer than most would have, his determination dominating a lightly budding frustration within. After pretending to drink for about thirty minutes, the two women left the bar out of boredom only to be replaced by another set that, unsurprisingly, fell into the same routine: simulate casual drinking and search for prey. A few metalworkers came in after their shift and consumed the front left portion of the establishment. For the most part, they kept the noise level down.

After a little more than an hour, Merv had honed attention on the two townies in the back left-hand corner. As the night wore on and the beers flowed, their noise level rose and their conversation moved from barely discernable to clearly audible. Additionally, their conversation shifted from irrelevant (how Drunk 1 tried to convince Drunk 2 that the moon landing was a conspiracy) to potentially informative (whether or not they could take two men at once in a fight). It quickly turned into both a verbal and physical recap. *That's it, boys. Keep it coming. I'll kiss your bare asses if you give me a name this early in the night.*

"You'd think they were on a stage," he commented when the bartender brought him round five. At that point, Merv began to feel the calming effects that set in with a good buzz. The same amount of alcohol in the same amount of time would have most casual drinkers close to swaying and slurring, but Merv was seasoned. Knowing how to play he had been making his speech progressively slower since his arrival.

"They just got a hard-on about the fight last night. Not much excitement around here. And when there *is* it never involves someone from here coming out a winner," she said emphatically.

"Ain't that the truth? Something like that could make someone famous around here."

"The girls were in last night, guys linin' up to buy 'em drinks. 'Bout as famous as it gets 'round here, y'know? Girls probably deserved it though. Liv worked here a while back 'fore I had to can her for drinkin' more than she sold. Was surprised to see her in here last night 'cause of it. She wasn't done braggin' when she left here neither. Won't be the last time she plays the damsel."

"Who's the hero?"

"Couldn't tell ya."

Motherfucker. Why would you. "Well, whoever it was, they're lucky. Might not get saved next time," Merv replied with contrived disinterest.

"Like I said, probably deserved it," she said.

Merv spoke as he raised the bottle to his lips, his voice softly muffled by the glass opening. "Glad they ain't here tonight. I might get star struck."

"Better avoid *Bootlegger's* then. If they ain't here, they'll be there. . . Wouldn't want ya to get. . .*star struck*," she finished with a measure of sarcasm.

Jackpot. With a smile on his face, Merv easily dispatched round five. For good measure, he made sure to add a loose sway of the head and upper body through the drink. He kept the smile, content with the development as well as his perseverance, and ordered round six. Leaving now would do nothing but cause suspicion. He knew where they were, and, knowing they liked to party, had no reason to rush. After round six he made his way off the barstool, adding a notable stumble.

"If you make it to round seven you might be tasting the floor," the bartender remarked.

Merv's hooded jacket, which was draped over the stool next to him, presented quite a challenge. His acting was so believable it even earned a chuckle from one of the closer patrons.

"Not sure that would be a good end to the night. Think I'll be taking myself home instead," Merv said absentmindedly. With his left arm in the right arm of his jacket, his wallet somehow fell to the floor. He took a while to realize and made it a chore to bend down and retrieve it. He finally did and fumbled for some more cash for the bartender.

"You're more than covered. Don't puke in my bar or I'll make you eat it."

Seems like I've overstayed my welcome. Time to be moving on. The false-drunk offered the bartender a silent, wobbly head nod before making his way out of the establishment.

Merv stumbled onto the dimly lit street and, like a snake shedding old skin for new, abandoned the clumsy routine by the time he reached the next intersection. The ruse did its job, giving him a justifiable reason to leave the bar without making enough of a scene for anyone to remember him as more than a drunk fool. Luckily for Merv, *Bootlegger's* was only two avenues east, easily walkable from his current location.

The next chapter of his investigation began with a cigarette. Puffs, flicks of ash, and footsteps all worked in sync along the lonely four-minute walk, void of pedestrians and with minimal car traffic. *Seems like the type of place a street altercation might go unnoticed. That may come in handy. . .*

As if on cue, the noise emanating from *Bootlegger's* became audible at the same time his cigarette reached the end of its life. *Hmm. Much different crowd here, I'll have to alter my persona.* A flick of the cigarette butt and a crack of the neck preceded his entrance into the saloon.

As he opened the door, a rush of external stimuli intensified. He worked quickly to adjust. Sounds, smells, and actions came at him with rapidity compared to the previous bar, but due to the commotion he was able to pause at the door and case the place. Identifying the girls was offensively easy. It was clear they had only used about seven and a half minutes of their fifteen minutes of fame. The crowd obstructed any chance of a clear view, but by that point, it mattered not. The targets were in his sights and his confidence was through the roof.

He continued his scan and noticed four smaller groups located opposite the girls and company. *Either unimpressed, over it, jealous, or enemies.* One group was composed of three younger girls who currently had the attention of zero potential courters. *Jealous, maybe that's the angle.* Another consisted of two men and two women who looked like they would fit in better at *The Corked Apple. Unimpressed, useless for now.*

Merv made his way toward the perimeter of the small crowd surrounding the two targets. His presence would be loosely felt, he judged, or perhaps acknowledged but not found to be encroaching. He was able to take a good look at the final two groups of people during the walk to the bar. One seemed completely engaged in a game of cards. The other held two young couples so uncomfortable that all four were completely oblivious of the commotion, exerting way too much effort as they were to making small talk.

Perhaps the play is to be aggressive? I could force my way into the crowd, get into a dick-measuring contest with the other men, win, and we three could go along our merry way. . . But seems impossible to recover from if it's unsuccessful, not to mention I would red-flag myself for future incursions. His thought process was interrupted by the bartender who, by comparison to the last, seemed overly bubbly.

"Can I get you somethin', hon?" she asked warmly, with confidence that anything he ordered she'd know how to make and make well.

"Whiskey and a Bud heavy," he ordered and leaned on the bar.

"Comin' up."

Attention whores, obviously. If I gave attention to someone else, like the set of three hopeless girls, I wonder if they would take the bait. Would I even have to flirt with them? Waiting it out right here might make them interested enough to make a move. They've gotta be riding high with all the unwarranted attention. I bet they won't be able to stand it if I hang out this close to them as if they don't exist. Maybe start a positive commotion of my own?

As his order arrived, Merv decided the decision he faced, for now, was an easy one considering the risk and recovery factor. Sit, ignore, wait. Patience, now, kept all doors unlocked. In an effort to eavesdrop, he diverted his attention from his libations to the girls and the crowd surrounding them, hoping for some clues.

"Another round for the ladies, Sharon, would ya?" a burly man in a button-up mechanic's shirt shouted to the bartender.

"You got it, Al," Sharon called back.

He's a regular. It would be best not to piss off the patrons or the bartender, then. That would probably bring the night to a quick close. And I haven't even had fun yet. . .

The evening continued until eventually the audience around the girls began to calm and diminish. Over the past hour Merv had heard a range of conversational topics but only vague mentions of "the story." Each time he thought they'd go for the full tale some asshole would interrupt or stall it. It became a frustrating bit, and Merv had to take trouble to hide his vexation. Luckily, for his sanity's sake, every once in a while the circle broke and Merv was able to make eye contact with the brunette. He found out through eavesdropping that her name was Tammy and from the way she flashed her eyes, the looks his way were clearly intentional. She was radiating the signs for him to approach her but Merv kept it casual.

No more than ten minutes later, her friend, who Merv decided must be named Liv, broke away to go to the bathroom. On the way back from the facilities, Liv stopped right next to Merv and pretended to order a drink, but Merv remained steadfast. Liv's patience had a shorter fuse.

"So you gonna order me a drink, cowboy, or what? It's your turn," Liv said, turning her attention to Merv.

He glanced at her briefly and returned his gaze forward. She wasn't nearly as good looking up close as he once wagered. Plain-faced, but her body was undeniable.

"Depends. I only buy drinks for people who fit into two categories: those I lose a bet to and those who give me something in return," he replied confidently, using a grin as an exclamation point as he glanced back at her. The response from Liv was a smile as well. *That's it sweetheart.*

"Well, I've been known to gamble, so I'm game," Liv answered with intrigue and raised an eyebrow.

This one likes a challenge. Merv turned and looked her directly in the eyes. "I have a bet for you. . .but. . .I don't think you'd want to take it."

"Why's that? What is it?"

"Mm, I dunno if I wanna tell you. You might laugh and hurt my feelings."

She chuckled. "Try me."

Merv inhaled and paused for effect. "I bet I can beat you in a thumb war."

Liv was caught off guard, but recovered and with a squint. "Wasn't expecting *that*, but I guess we have to start somewhere."

The way Merv figured, one must never underestimate how much can be conveyed through physical contact, even if it's just grasping hands. With this move he was able to break the touch barrier and display that he was assertive and strong, two qualities that always seemed to tickle the fancy of his marks.

The grasp was important to Merv. Her hand was firm but controlled, evidence that she'd be able to handle herself in an altercation. If apprehension was necessary it would be best not to underestimate this one. His grasp on her, however, was stronger and forceful. He pulled her hand toward him to exert his dominance. She responded with a squeak.

"Firm handshake. . ." Liv paused for a name.

"Patrick," Merv answered.

"I'm Liv." *I know.* "Good luck, Patrick."

The game ended as quickly as it began with Merv dominating the entire go. He faked a struggle briefly, just to toy around, and then overpowered her for the win.

"Luck had nothing to do with it," he said as their grasp parted.

Silence followed the game and Merv realized the moment's monumental import. Losing her now could end the night and shame his every calculated step. He took a quick sip of his beer and spoke hurriedly before the loss set in.

"How about this," Merv began. "That wasn't entirely fair, so let's go double or nothing." He sent her a seductive look. "This time, I have a different idea."

"Now we're talkin', cowboy," Liv replied, holding her hand out for another round.

He grabbed her wrist gently and brought her hand back to her side. "A *different* idea. Just wait."

Merv took his wallet out and removed two twenty-dollar bills. He fanned them out face up on his right palm. At a quick glance, they both appeared identical. As his eyes traced back to her, he noticed a small butterfly tattoo in the sliver of skin between her top and skirt.

"Okay. Do you notice a difference between the two?" Merv asked.

After a moment of analyzing, Liv smirked. "The top one looks skinnier and a little shorter."

Luckily for Merv, there had been a bust on a counterfeit currency ring a few weeks back. Hundreds of thousands of phony bills were confiscated, and Merv may or may not have taken some for. . .closer inspection.

"Nicely done, Liv! *Really.* Good eye," Merv said, genuinely impressed. *So. She's not as dumb as bricks.*

"Looks like you owe me two drinks now," she said, smiling with one eyebrow raised.

Smiling back, Merv raised a finger, bringing her eagerness to a halt. "Not so fast. You didn't listen. That wasn't the bet. The *reason* there is a difference is because the top one is counterfeit. You see, the blade used to separate the sheet of bills into individual bills was misaligned. It made all the ones on that run a little smaller. There's other errors but this is the most obvious."

"And how do we know that, *cowboy*?" Liv asked, easing her way closer to standing between Merv's legs.

"Because I made it," he said with a smile, spreading his legs a little more. "So the bet is this: I can buy you a drink, here, with the counterfeit bill and get away with it."

"So what category do I fall into since you're buying me a drink?" she questioned.

"Well if I win, you get a drink and I didn't really pay for it since the bill's fake. If I lose, you won and I'll have to figure out a way to buy you two drinks with the real twenty."

"Deal," Liv responded, enjoying the back and forth.

The deal with the bartender went over smoothly. Whiskey, Bud heavy, and a gin and tonic were easily covered by the twenty. Bubbly Sharon didn't look twice.

"Impressive. Guess you get double," Liv said as she slid in between Merv's legs.

"Seems like it. Wonder if you could handle giving me double yourself. . .or you need a friend?" Merv suggested, his hand sliding gently up and down Liv's thigh.

The look she returned was one of lust. "Be right back, cowboy," Liv said, squeezing Merv's inner thigh.

Merv swiveled his stool back toward the bar and downed his shot. Liv returned moments later with Tammy. After close inspection, Merv found that Tammy's beauty was about equal to Liv's. Faces aside, Liv was more athletic, whereas Tammy had tits and half an ass. Merv inwardly adored the dichotomy. *Best of both worlds.*

"*So.* Liv says she lost double or nothin'," Tammy said flirtatiously. "Let's see how you do against me."

Merv sat shirtless on a foldable steel chair in the middle of a musty, rundown motel room. His broad, hairy chest was damp with sweat, glistening in the remote light. A rickety laminated table stood beside him, holding an overflowing, smoking ashtray, a Glock 911, and thirteen upright bullets dotted beside it. An 8" horn-handled hunting knife was in his lap. He groomed a fingernail here and there with its tip. The air in the room was dense and smoke-filled. A single chest-high standing lamp glowed next to the table and background music played softly, at a volume loud enough to drown out whispering yet soft enough as to not disturb his thoughts. It was his favorite radio station. It spoke to him, then.

Yeah, c'mon

The song was in its early psychedelic measures as Merv melted into the chair, leaned his head back and blissfully blew two smoke rings toward the deactivated detector dangling from the ceiling. Before him sat a queen-sized bed. Atop the bed lay the bound, gagged, and sleeping bodies of Liv and Tammy. It screamed to him, then.

YEAH!

Their high heels and light jackets had been removed and their wrists had been tied together above their heads and secured to the bars of the bedframe so that their upper bodies and heads were propped up. Their ankles were bound as well and tied with a length of rope to the frame at the foot of the bed, positioned in such a way that their legs were spread wide enough to make them question, upon waking, whether or not Merv could see anything precious from his vantage. He could.

Chloroform was a wholly underestimated chemical in Merv's opinion. One simply had to employ proper dosage to achieve desired results. Too strong of a concentration applied to one's face could cause redness, irritation, or even sores, and further, inhaling too strong of a concentration could cause liver damage and even death. Too little of a concentration merely made a victim woozy. While the recovery time, when unconsciousness was achieved, was a matter of minutes, mild hallucinogenic aftereffects were typical and disorientation lingered after waking, making repeated smothering possible without much struggle. The music called for him to turn out the lights. To turn out the lights. To turn out the lights. *Not yet,* he answered.

When he lured them out of *Bootlegger's* to hit another bar, he intentionally led them past his cruiser. A quick bathroom stop before they left had allowed him to soak two rags in Chloroform in preparation. Had he used ether, the odor would have spooked them, he was sure, but the beauty of Chloroform is that it has an intensely sweet smell. Walking with an arm around each girl, he merely reached in his pockets, grabbed the rags, and locked their heads in his jaw-like grip, holding them to his chest and dragging their torpid bodies to his cruiser. He only needed to reapply once during the drive and once before dragging them into the motel room, the very same to which he took most of his hookers and which he had rented earlier in the day.

The gentle song in the room uttered words like a voice in his head, so special and remote.

For the music is your special friend
Dance on fire as it intends
Music is your only friend

So special, so remote.

Until the end

In that very moment, Merv was calmer than he had been all evening. The girls, while decent looking, had been beginning to drive him nuts in the bar with general immaturity and lack of depth. He had a finite tolerance for women beyond the purpose of fucking, but these two had tested his patience. Merv was enjoying their silent company now more than ever. But he had work to do. Mumbling, he and the music beckoned for them to wake. Then, a body stirred.

It was Tammy, on the left, who groaned first as the chemicals wore off. His money had been on the other one, but it mattered not. He watched her eyes roll around slowly, struggling to orient herself to the material nature of her growing nightmare. Merv sang along to the song lightly, a cigarette bobbing in his mouth and his head swaying, feeling the verse eclipse his eardrums.

Cancel my subscription to the Resurrection
Send my credentials to the House of Detention
I've got some friends inside

He pulled on his cigarette as her eyes opened and blinked sluggishly again and again. She writhed around and her eyes grew wider as the stained plaster ceiling took on focus for her. Some moments passed as she shifted and realized her bound condition. The music welcomed her to the party.

A feast of friends

It was almost visible, the horror of her realization.

"Alive!" she cried

Wrists wiggled, arms pulled, then legs kicked and ankles rolled.

Waitin' for me

Finally, the gag in her mouth emitted a muted, pained scream. The music screamed back.

Outside!

"Shhhhhh. . ." Merv said, a finger over his lips. He hadn't wanted to miss the melodic strings and tapping of drums under her guttural, humming sounds.

Before I sink
Into the big sleep

He sang again, then, with the lyricist,

I want to hear
I want to hear
The scream of the butterfly

He closed his eyes and absorbed the mixture of sounds, a tingling feeling creeping up his spine. Softly, oh so gently, then, lovely Liv's legs began to shift. Merv crooned along with a smile.

Come back baby
Back into my arm

His singing stopped as he pulled on his cigarette and looked downward at his lap.

We're gettin' tired of hangin' around
Waitin' around with our heads to the ground

A whimper came, then. And Merv's head reared and focused on the body.

I hear a very gentle sound

Then her arms pulled, oh so gently.

Very near yet very far

He'd never have heard it or noticed the motion had he not been before her petite figure.

Very soft, yeah, very clear

Then, a moan. Her eyes fluttered, beckoning for power to open from the deep darkness that claimed her.

Come today, come today

Her eyes batted and blinked, rolled and focused.

What have they done to the earth?

She wriggled, becoming aware of her restraints.

What have they done to our fair sister?

She became aware of Merv. And of a body lying next to her. Darkness coated the walls of the room. But not everywhere.

Ravaged and plundered and ripped her and bit her

Still coming to, her head plopped to its side and like a jolt from a nightmare, she became conscious. Tammy shivered and cried beside her.

Stuck her with knives in the side of the dawn

The development made her pull and squirm against the restraints.

And tied her with fences and dragged her down

And then she cried into the gag. The music narrated, gladly.

I hear a very gentle sound

The music mocked them, mocked their wants.

With your ear down to the ground
We want the world and we want it...
We want the world and we want it...
Now

But they'd never have it.

Now?

She howled at the top of her lungs.

NOW!

Merv relished in the beauty of the moment. Such control was unattainable. It was perfect.

The darkness was confusing.

Persian night, babe

The light offered hope.

See the light, babe

She cried to be saved.

Save us!

She begged for God.

Jesus!

She cried to be saved.

Save us!

But there was only him. And the music. Time vanished, then reappeared with lyrics.

So when the music's over
When the music's over, yeah
When the music's over
Turn out the lights
Turn out the lights
Turn out the lights

Merv swayed his head, eyes heavy and unfocused. Smoke swirled.

Well the music is your special friend
Dance on fire as it intends
Music is your only friend
Until the end
Until the end

The music screamed for the end. And so did they.

Until the END!

But the end didn't come yet. Only the beginning. The music faded. Then it was over. The pair flailed together, praying, searching for a way out of captivity, away from this madman. It angered Merv, such disrespect of his work. His bicep tightened as he gripped his hunting knife and slammed it into the table beside him with explosive power. The bullets jumped, tumbled over, and rolled onto the ground. It stood erect, the knife; its tip buried two inches into the wood. The pair settled and Merv inhaled.

"Now I want you to know," Merv began calmly, his speech cutting into the silent room, "that it is not my intention to hurt you even though your situation suggests otherwise. I ensure you that no further harm will come to you if you only *help* me. I'm here for one thing."

His pause was intentional, as was his seemingly unconscious grab onto his manhood with his right hand. *To inspire truth from the weak, you must make them fear the unknown,* he thought.

"Information," he declared finally, easing some of the terror on his victims' faces.

Merv stood, walked to the foot of the bed, and climbed on, positioning himself on his hands and knees. He straddled Tammy, and held her gaze briefly. She was refusing to blink, perhaps still clinging to the slim hope that a chance for release or escape would arise, and a blink might make her miss it. He then put himself on top of her suggestively, precisely where she'd be able to feel his manhood, and leaned over her. He breathed heavily, knowing very well the distinct odor of man and whiskey seeping out of his pores. His left hand made its way to the back of her head, supporting it gently, while the right moved a tuft of hair out of her teary eyes with a careful caress. The girl cowered.

"The police are looking for both of you. They're very, *very* upset. They think you're directly involved with the assault on those cops last night. They think *you're* responsible." His eyes darted back and forth between both girls. "I'm concerned for your safety and the safety of the man involved. That's why I brought you here. To protect you. Tell me your friend's name so I can protect him too."

Tammy's face remained horrified, cringing each time she inhaled his scent. Liv pleaded to an unknown entity.

"Now, I'm going to remove your gag so you can answer the question. Okay?" Merv told her in a comforting tone.

Untying the gag slowly betrayed Tammy's intent as her demeanor changed from terror to defiance. Perhaps she thought the moment of escape was upon her. As the gag left her mouth, she inhaled deeply and prepared for a belting scream. And she did scream, if only briefly. Like a lightning strike, Merv grabbed her hair in his cradling hand, cocked his arm back, and backhanded her across the jaw, knocking her out cold. Her remaining breath came out weakly as her head plopped sideways towards Liv. Merv sat back in shame and defeat, mortified that he'd been disobeyed. He thought of smashing her skull to pieces with his bare hands, but held back, calmed by Liv's frantic cries, a rising lullaby about him now replacing the absent music.

Merv dismounted and walked to the table. "I do not deal with disobedience well. . . I don't feel my requests are outlandish." He spun towards her and gripped the handle of his hunting knife. "When they're not met, I get. . ." he yanked it out of the wood with an eerie ping, "impulsive."

He returned to the bed, quicker this time, to straddle her. He carried the knife carelessly, sliding over her and placing it flat on her chest, between her breasts, point towards her throat. Liv writhed beneath him in vain. Again, Merv's tender touch froze the girl in place.

"Perhaps I began too quickly. Let us start with some simpler questions, alright? I'm going to remove your gag. And when I do, you're going to answer me. . . You are the master of your own fate." As he finished speaking, he slowly turned Liv's head to see Tammy's bleeding, unconscious face. With a jerk, Merv twisted her head forward and removed the gag.

"Now, let's start easy. What is your name?" Merv asked kindly, inching her out of her terror.

"Liv," she whimpered in response.

"Good. Where are you from, Liv?"

"Here."

"Good. And do you work, Liv?"

"N-No. Not right now."

"That's too bad. I bet–"

Merv was interrupted by a newfound courage. "I don't know anything, I swear!" she claimed with a cry. "I swear. I swear."

His demeanor changed from comforting to stern. "Liv, *Liv.* You were doing so well."

Before he finished speaking, he had forced the gag back into her mouth. She screamed and cried. Merv moved his face closer, letting his stink shed over her. His grip clenched her fragile throat and squeezed. The pressure was not enough to kill, but to send a message of ownership. Suddenly, his eyes softened as he began to stroke the side of her face with his left hand. He caressed her skin, trailing his fingers slowly down her cheek to her shoulder, and nudged the U-shaped collar of her shirt, hooking her bra strap with a passing finger and exposing her collarbone and shoulder. She began to tremble, watching his eyes gleam with fascination and fantasy. Further his hand moved, over her left breast, past the knife, and to her waist. Her stretched position exposed a sliver of soft skin between her navel and the waist of her skirt, where her little butterfly tattoo rested calmly. Merv rubbed it, and his hand was met with a squirm. He then reached his fingers under the fabric of her skirt, stopping at knuckle's depth. Liv's eyes squeezed shut, creating creases of skin beside her eyes.

"So soft. And pure." He pulled his knuckles out and made circles around her navel. "You have so much to offer. . ." his eyes shot back to her mouth, "yet so little." Again he undressed her with his eyes, focusing on her breasts, then. "So much to enjoy. . ." and back to her face, "or not at all."

Liv's tears flowed like a river as fearful possibility set in. Merv leaned over and positioned his mouth beside her left ear.

"I'm going to grant you one more chance. If you try to take advantage of it again, I will take advantage of you."

Liv had blinked out most of the tears, and she nodded rapidly. Her gag came out tenderly.

"*Who* was the *man* who *saved you* from the *cops*?"

"His name is Robin," she blurted through quivering lips.

"And if I wanted to talk to 'Robin,' where would I find him?"

"H-He works at this Soup Kitchen thing sometimes. At a church - St. Augustine's. I think it happens every Tuesday and Thursday. And Sundays," she sputtered.

"And what does he look like?"

"He's young. White. Handsome," she gasped, her eyes shooting about. "Tan a little and built. Wears a dark green hat sometimes."

Liv's voice had regained some strength at the prospect of pleasing her captor. Perhaps he would be satisfied and let the two of them go, harmed but unbroken. Merv mimicked her hopes with a cruel expression. He smiled gleefully and bent down, placing a light and lovely kiss on her forehead. In an instant, his expression grew more sinister and he placed his forehead against hers. Eye to eye he spoke.

"Thank you, dear."

Suddenly, the gag was rammed into Liv's mouth with a jolting amount of strength. The mattress bounced from the action and Liv wailed inside. Sadistic joy overwhelmed the man on top of her and somehow, his eyes seemed to light up red. He was about to take much more than just his promised information.

Merv leaned over the bathroom sink with his elbows locked and his palms on the porcelain, letting gravity pull rinse-water through the maze of his beard and off his face. The dripping sound broke the silence inside the room and he raised his head to face the mirror, fogged up still from his recent shower. He first examined his physique. His white undershirt struggled to hold his deltoids, biceps, and triceps. No matter his neglect, his mass never lessened. He was a bull.

Just for an instant, just for a split second, he questioned the tactics he had used to gather that necessary information. But as quickly as it came, that uncertainty receded into the darkness. *It is a war. There are no innocent, no abstainers. Choose a side and fight. No remorse. No regrets.*

Merv stood, dried his hands and pulled his cellular phone from his pocket. He dialed a familiar number and was answered by a familiar accented voice.

"Teddy. . .got a job for you and Marty. Need it handled immediately. Two packages. Usual spot. Make sure you trim the fat when you're done."

Chapter 12: Fruit of the Poisonous Tree

Marian's heel caught a chipped edge of the city seal in the center of the main foyer of the Fort Dearborn County District Attorney's Office. Her ankle rolled briefly, causing her to nearly drop the dollar coffee bought from the food cart outside. A roasted aroma wafted in the movement, and after settling herself she found a few tan droplets trickling down her navy blazer. She cursed and rushed by the security desk, where Rosco and Hal greeted her daily with overdone kindness and a not-so-subtle eye-fuck. It had bothered her for a few months, but after two years on the job, she hardly noticed anymore. Inside, a quick pat with a paper towel erased any evidence of the spill. Thankfully the season commanded darker dress - despite the weather - else she'd have likely ruined a piece of her lighter summer wardrobe. Marian sighed and straightened her jacket in the bathroom mirror. *Great start to the week. Can't imagine how it'll finish.* Aside from being Monday, she knew full well that the week's workload would again carry into the weekend. It seemed relentless at times, yet the work of a lawyer never stopped. She pulled a thread of dark hair out of her face and considered her looks momentarily. The hint of summer tan she clung to was fading, bringing with it an inevitable seven month span of paleness. Her hair needed a trim and the slightest swell of bags showed beneath her eyes. She didn't feel pretty today.

It had been a rapid three weeks since the uncomfortable charity dinner hosted by Dalton's parents. Surprisingly, in those three weeks she'd only seen him a handful of times. Their work schedules conflicted more often than not, and since she hadn't remotely made herself available, only weekend dates had been feasible. Her fear of confronting him about the look that passed between him and the blonde that night compounded each day. Her imagination had reached points of wild assumption, but she was mostly able to tell herself it was nothing and worked overtime to bury the less palatable inklings that came about. Similarly, he kept busier than normal with the recent land deal in place. Neither one of them, she realized, was trying to fix their relationship. They had reached an impasse. More and more she wondered why she hung around with him at all.

When Marian stepped off the elevator onto the 7th floor, she was met with typical morning buzz and banter. Like the pair of men at the security desk, she received a daily stare in the office as well, only this was one look she'd never grow accustomed to. Randi, the haggard receptionist, burned a hole through her as Marian passed by. A "good morning" followed by a shallow smile was all Marian ever found herself able to muster. It was a standard frizzy hair day for Randi, and it appeared the weekend had done something malevolent to her as well. Or the other way around. She sometimes wondered if the woman had trouble at home.

Moments later Marian was upon her office, floating by the brass nameplate adorning her door that read, 'Assistant District Attorney Marian Fitzwalter.' Marian's office was newly renovated and immaculately maintained. Plush beige carpets, a fresh coat of white paint, a shiny Cherrywood desk and credenza, a state-of-the-art, and quite thin, computer, and floor-to-ceiling windows were among the improvements. In the main office's open floorplan, new half-height cubical walls had been installed to give the space more freedom, replacement ceiling tiles eliminated evidence of the formerly leaky ceiling, and a lengthened conference room was constructed near the new bathrooms and lunchroom. To better reflect the workload, she'd have much rather seen a pay increase for her and her colleagues in lieu of office-wide renovations, but among the other luxuries, the new chair and desk height had cured her once chronic back aches. That was better than nothing at all.

Marian placed her coffee on her desk, dropped her briefcase, and sank into her chair, immediately flipping her high-heels off her little feet. She hated having to wear them all day. A press of her finger turned her computer monitor on and she waited a moment for the screen to waken and come into focus. In that time she glanced up at her diploma from the prestigious New Orange Law School on the wall beside her. It was a daily ritual she did to motivate herself, offering longer reflection on the days that needed greater enthusiasm for her to give her best effort. Today was such a day.

It was a pretty piece of paper, but she wondered if it truly was anything more than that. The past two years had been quite the eye-opening experience, and sometimes her diploma felt cheaper than it had cost. A once-naïve crusader for justice and righting wrongs, these days Marian mostly felt reduced to settling for the best option, letting little fish go in efforts to chase the big, or simply bullied out of a position of control. All-around, she felt rundown and exhausted of a previously coveted line of work now shown to be littered with corruption, greed, and the infinite grip of money. She just wanted to do *good* in the city, but the bureaucratic powers that be left her cynical and searching for an idea of what the word 'good' even meant anymore.

When she was feeling particularly insecure she'd fall into the trap of considering a switch to the private sector, especially with the growing pressure Dalton's family was putting upon her. Sure, a much better paycheck would be had, but Marian knew there was no salary that justified voluntarily defending the guilty. Profiting from and inheriting those demons was beyond her moral capabilities.

And so an uneventful morning of reading briefs transitioned into an uneventful lunch, and at 2:30 in the afternoon Marian returned to her office ready to work on "the Judge" as she called it, a rather despicable case presented against a local District Judge named Fulson. When she entered, she noticed a stack of briefs missing from the right side of her desk, exactly where the Fulson briefs she had been working on earlier had been resting. Right away, she thought Micah, her paralegal, had taken them to pull information for the DA, Herbert Hanser. He had a bad habit of acting without first getting Marian's consent. She raised an eyebrow and quickly walked five cubicles down to Micah's desk, across from Herb's office.

"Micah, did you pull the Fulson briefs from my office?"

"Yeah, Herb said he needed them immediately," Micah replied with minimal acknowledgement of Marian's presence.

Ah, what a talent you are, Micah. Thanks for asking me. Marian turned and strode to Herb's wide office, knocking as she entered. He had his typical afternoon face on, one of boredom and distraction.

"Herb, did you have Micah pull the Fulson files from my office?" Marian asked impatiently.

"Yeah," Herb answered quietly. Even though his computer screen was blocked from the doorway she could see the game of solitaire reflecting off the lenses of his horn-rimmed glasses.

"If you're finished, could I have that back, please? I need to get-"

"No."

Marian blinked. "No what?"

"You can't have it back," he replied and squinted at the screen.

". . .Why?"

"Uh, as of an hour ago we've officially dropped the case."

"What?"

"Yeah, we had a major problem today."

"We're going to trial in three weeks! This was a slam dunk. What in the hell happened?" Marian pried.

Herb searched his screen while he answered. "Some detective fucked us big time with the search warrant."

"And?" Marian asked, trying to hide her simmering anger.

"*And* it makes our evidence exclusionary. Anything else we had on him is therefore inadmissible. Unless a new witness or a *videotape* comes out, we're shit outta luck."

"We can't argue good faith?"

"If it was good faith I wouldn't have thrown it out."

"Oh, you've got to be kidding me," she said in disbelief.

Herb looked up then, an image of frustration. "Marian, do I look like I'm kidding?"

"I put twenty hours into it this weekend."

Herb overdid a shrug. "What do you what from me?"

"That's it? It's out of our hands?"

"For Christ's sake," he huffed, "our key piece of evidence, hell *all* of our evidence now, is inadmissible. I'm dropping it. It's over. I will not waste the resources."

"Would you mind if I looked at the files again?" Her question came out sounding more like a demand. She searched Herb's eyes, giving off more suspicion then she realized.

Herb noticed her tone and put on an authoritative face, pointing at her with his index finger. "When I say the case is being dropped your answer shouldn't be 'Why?' or 'But I put in so much time.' Your answer should be 'Ok sir,' and then you turn and wiggle your way back to your office. That might help you out."

The comment and the look boiled Marian's blood. *Fucking prick.* She flushed, bit her lower lip and decided not to give him a piece of her mind.

"Ok sir," she said with false kindness. She began to turn away but paused. "Oh, by the way, you may want to wiggle that seven of clubs over to the eight of hearts. Might help you out," she said and slammed his office door.

Later that night, Marian sat alone at her desk browsing paperwork and reviewing a list of necessary phones calls for Tuesday morning. Usually, something calming came about in her when night fell. Her concentration elevated as the contrast of fluorescent light against dark window panes set in. The droning office settled in the late hours, too, leaving her solitary and quite productive. Sure, she'd always rather be at the City Library, but the office made do on occasion. Tonight, though, her typical calm had been disturbed.

She couldn't shake her uneasiness over the Fulson case. Something sat awfully wrong, something was askew here. She knew it in her heart. She'd been over the briefs numerous times and found nothing wrong with the procedural details, nor evidence collection. And Herb's explanation had been so evasive and curt. Perhaps a little peek in his office would provide some insight into why her files had disappeared or, more precisely, what had caused the case itself to be squashed.

It was past 8 when her curiosity got the best of her. Cy, the janitor, had made his rounds already, clearing the trash bins and replacing the old bags with new. All was quiet on the 7th floor and a mischievous voice from deep within called to her. *Just go take a look,* it said. *Check it out. No one will ever know, and if you don't find anything...oh well.*

Leaving her high heels behind, Marian stood and walked to her door to casually peek out, scanning the reaches of the office unseen from her desk. Curiously, the light was still on in Herb's office, though he had been nowhere to be found since four or five in the afternoon. *It's a little too quiet,* she thought as she listened to a mass of computer cooling fans and the faint ticking of a wall clock. *Like someone is waiting for me to move. . . Oh, stop it.*

A stride took her into the main area between a maze of cubicle walls and bordering offices. It was a medium-sized workplace, not too tight but sometimes cramped when crunch time came around. To be safe, she trotted past Herb's office to the water fountain. If he had somehow managed to return without her knowing, and was sitting in his office, it would be best to have a reason for passing before barging in. *Don't be obvious.* A sideways glance exposed an empty chair and a messy desk, just as he had left it. She hurried a drink at the fountain.

Then, just as she rose, a commotion spooked her. Herb's voice echoed in the empty space, growing in volume as it traveled down the hallway. Marian panicked, hustled in the direction she came, and ducked into Micah's cubicle. The new walls were so shallow she needed to drop to the floor to hide herself from view. *Just pretend you're searching for something if he looks in. . . Yeah, on my hands and knees?* she argued internally. *Why didn't you just go to your fucking office? There was no time!* she argued back.

Herb's voice was accompanied by footsteps as he approached, his presence becoming imposing in the vacant area. He hovered outside his door, on a cellular phone call of some sort, presumably with his wife. *You're so stupid. Should have just walked calmly back to your office like nothing happened. Stupid. Stupid. Look at yourself.* Some rustling sounded, like papers being shuffled or folders being stacked, and Herb hung up after an "Okay, dear. Bye." *If he finds me like this I'll look like such a fool. You* are *a fool for getting yourself in this spot. For once, I've got to stop trying to be sneaky. It never works. . .*

Two impossibly long minutes ticked by before suddenly a desk phone rang. Herb answered on the first ring and Marian's ears perked up.

"District Attorney Hanser," he said. ". . .Oh, yes, yes. . . No, not at all, put him through. . . Yes, how are you? . . .Y–Yes, it all went through this afternoon. Right. No, I handled it personally. I spoke with Gene and it's all taken care of. . ."

Gene? From Defense?

"Glad to help out in any way, Mr. Mayor."

Mayor? What exactly went through today, Herb? There's only one thing I can think of.

". . .No. . .no not at all. . .Well, listen. Between. . . Right. . . Between me and you, I know we haven't seen eye to eye on certain things in the past, but I haven't forgotten who endorsed me when I ran for this position. On a personal level, those, uh, *details* didn't go unseen. So when I'm called upon, I have no qualms about setting things straight. . . *Yes. . .*"

A lengthy paused elapsed. Marian grew livid. *Oh I cannot fucking believe what I'm hearing.*

"No, *I* appreciate it. . . I understand. A–. . .Alright. Alright. Take care."

A rattle signaled the phone had landed back on its receiver. Marian heard a huff, a mumble, the click of Herb's office light shutting off, and footsteps down the hall.

She stood slowly and eyed Herb as he walked towards the elevators. A sour, penetrating look came over her. *Fruit of the Poisonous Tree, they'll call it. . . Is it the evidence that's poisonous in this case, or is it the system? Based off the fruit I've picked I think I have my answer. And it's more poisonous than I ever imagined.*

Chapter 13: Hammerfall

To anyone with an eye for it, the unmarked police cruiser blended in poorly with the decrepit vehicles it was parallel-parked between a block away from St. Augustine's Church. But then again, missing hubcaps and rust spots were commonplace to most vehicles in this area, a reflection to Merv of how the owners most certainly rode through life with apathy and neglect. The cruiser itself was dated and showed some minor wear, evidence of its time "on assignment." Its tinted windows prevented casual passersby from noticing its three occupants. Inside, Merv sat with his new deputies, Mancuso and Taylor. This would constitute their first ride-along and lessons taught today would be paramount to their development as officers in his specialized unit.

In a briefing that morning, Merv had informed his deputies of a vague agenda and recited a witness's description of the man they were looking for. He told them that they would "simply observe" and the day would develop from there onward. Taylor and Mancuso had, at that point, nearly the same information he did. It would be their task to properly identify the suspect while Merv did his own reconnaissance and maneuvering. The only fact Merv had left out of his briefing was that this "Robin" *worked* at the food bank. His intent was to offer just enough information for the new deputies to observe properly, but not spoon-feed them an assured I.D.

Following his weekend encounter, a shred of doubt had crept in the back of Merv's mind concerning the validity of the information collected from the two dames. He had to. . .*press* them to ascertain the pitiful amount of knowledge they had on the man they called Robin. Besides a name and a likely location on a likely day, he hadn't much more to work with to bring this issue to a resolution. The accuracy of their information was most vital, for if they were misinformed his search would come to a crashing halt. Fortunately his concern was put to rest, as the man he sought presented himself not ten minutes after they arrived.

The food operation drew dozens of people and seemingly employed a half-dozen of its own. Even after waiting in line and being fed, people loitered in the lot at length which added to the difficulty one might have had in making the I.D. But Merv's talent shined wonderfully in these situations. He had the uncanny ability to read people as well as situations, an innate talent harnessed over his career into an aptitude valued over even his physical prowess. From studying one's movements he could peek into their nature, expanding their characteristics into more than mere statistics. Merv, therefore, spotted Robin with ease, but held his delight inside, deciding to commence his men's assignment while he causally worked out the details of the forthcoming encounter.

"Alright. Based on the information I briefed you with, I want you to determine the identity of the individual I seek. You'll be partners when this program comes to a close, so I want you two to work together to identify the perpetrator properly." He took a sip of his fourth cup of coffee, which was fighting gallantly to cover the smell of several shots of Sambuca he had poured in the cup before they departed from the precinct, and added a final anecdote to establish the reality of the circumstances. "The truth, men, is that this man tuned up two of my officers on the level of hospitalization. You haven't met them, but take my word for it, 'fucked up' is an understatement. Your task, now, is to observe. *I* see him. . . Can you? I'll give you a few minutes and you'll report your observations. Consider this an exercise in deductive reasoning, but be warned. . .use your time wisely." Without more, he left them to their assignment and lit a cigarette.

Until the man appeared, Merv spent most of the stakeout recounting his overtime work, as he liked to call it, as well as smothering his creeping hangover. He often replayed the scenarios in his mind. Merv lived a life where deceit, corruption, violence, and depravity were commonplace. The only way a life full of those vices could continue without self-destruction was to remove any sign of regret; to alienate himself from empathy.

Such emotions are the poisons that kill those living their lives on the dark side of morality. He purposefully recalled these situations to learn and improve for the future. Out of this particularly successful encounter he reinforced the notion that within the confines of the human mind lay the most treacherous and horrifying scenarios possible. At times it was more effective to provoke the uninhibited exploration of that dreadful possibility in someone than actually inflicting terror upon them. That fact had garnered Merv information in this particular case, and he would make sure to reinforce that knowledge for future encounters.

What consumed Merv currently, however, was the task of making contact with Robin without endangering himself, his new men, or their cover. Doing so during the church event would reduce the chance of a physical encounter, but he would forfeit the information and retribution he sought. Furthermore, it would expose them to dozens of individuals. The confrontation, he decided, would have to be in another location or, in the worst case, after the crowd died down. What concerned him most was the emergence of a behemoth that worked by Robin's side. If they didn't separate at some point later in the day, he would have to alter his plans considerably. Merv could easily handle himself against any average person, even a few at a time, but a wildcard like that was not something he wanted to chance. *Is he a dough boy or a goliath?* Sizing him up from this distance was reckless and during a fight was not when he wanted that question definitively answered. He could sacrifice his pawns to distract the giant, but he hadn't trained them to blindly follow orders, especially an order that would likely cause excessive physical harm. Weapons, though obvious, were out of the question. Merv took pride in solving issues with his bare hands. Besides, this situation didn't warrant the use of weapons. A beating was more personal.

Merv resolved that the encounter must materialize that evening in a location with limited interference from the general public. *Perhaps a side street or a parking lot near the church while under the cover of darkness. We'll have to case the area.* Handshakes and hugs made it clear that this Robin character was well respected. Some sort of figurehead, possibly. *You keep making this more complicated than it has to be, kid.*

The most effective solution was often the simplest. Using one of Robin's weaknesses against him, he'd lure him into a trap with another chance for the man to prove his capabilities at dealing with cops that had less than perfect moral compasses. *His character will make it irresistible. If it happened once, it'll happen again. We're all creatures of habit.* He would have to press his luck and hope to find Robin alone or potentially postpone the confrontation.

He considered his new men momentarily. Including them on a matter that was technically "extracurricular" posed minimal concern. In his experience they would adapt accordingly, as was the standard in his unit. If not, he would deal with them later.

Merv yawned. The hangover was showing. Last night's binge was particularly excessive in the booze and coke department, leaving him a tad rough around the edges that morning. His outward detachment may have shown stupor but his wit was sharp as a tack. He didn't doubt a tinge of underestimation in his abilities had rooted itself in his inferiors, but that perception meant nothing. His words and his actions would squash any doubts that arose, sure as the sun would set that afternoon. He checked his watch. It was 2:17 p.m.

"Alright, you've had plenty of time by now. Tell me what you see," Merv commanded, lighting another cigarette and waiting in relaxed anticipation for their report.

Mancuso and Taylor shared a quick look and with a nod directed at him, Taylor took the lead.

"Well, based off the witness reports I've narrowed it down to two men. There was an individual in line that piqued my interest for a moment but I decided to dismiss him. By my judgment it's one of the individuals working the bags. From this distance I can only estimate heights but I'm confident that the three range as such: left roughly six or six-one, middle more like five-nine. The one beside them is too large. Six-five-plus. . . A big boy. The report didn't indicate someone that large so that leaves the other two. Potentially a toss-up between them, but I have an inkling. Eric?"

There's a useless description if I've ever heard one, Merv thought. *Jesus Christ this guy is dead weight.*

"Yeah, agreed, but I'd say it's pretty clearly between the two. The man on the left is wearing a hat, which lines up. Seems the other men are deferring to him as well. It's subtle, but I'd peg him as the organizer. That doesn't necessarily coincide with the report, but it's something to keep in mind."

That's what I like to hear, Mancuso. There's that talent. Good eye.

"Good point," Taylor admitted.

Mancuso continued, "If we're looking to arrest, the implication of violence may make it safer to close in at another location, perhaps with backup. The situation here seems docile but it wouldn't be worth the risk with such a large crowd. *Or* we could wait it out. Nonetheless, that's our guy."

"Yeah, that's him," Taylor concluded arrogantly. "If we're questioning, we can initiate at will."

"Mm," Merv grunted.

"Do you share our conclusion, sir?" queried Taylor.

Merv exhaled sharply before speaking. "You ever shoot your load too soon, Taylor?"

". . .What?" he asked in bafflement.

Merv glanced over at him expectantly.

"Uh, I-I mean. . .I-I dunno, I mean who hasn't, right?" he responded with an uncomfortable chuckle.

Merv returned his gaze towards the church function. "Figured. Maybe you can tell me what that's like one day. . .but based off what I just heard I think I got the gist of it. Do I share your conclusion? In a word. . . No. No, I don't share your conclusion."

"I'm not sure I understand, sir," Mancuso said, trying to ease the tension. "Not to simplify, but with the minimal information we've been given and a man in front of us very clearly matching the description from the witnesses, it can only be him. I'm confident. That's our man. The church, the food bank, the date, his size, age, dress, the hat. . .it's him."

"I respect your confidence. What I have issues with is your thoughtlessness."

Merv sat in contemplation for a moment's time. His demeanor for the entirety of the stakeout had been classic calm, cool, and collected. He did not falter now, as arising was a brilliant opportunity for the day's lesson. He spoke slowly as not to lose the fresh minds in his often cryptic prose.

"What is in identification? Is it simply descriptive details a witness provides, to be taken at their very word? Is recognition itself just a confirmation of reports based on your own scrutiny, or do we but put together pieces of a puzzle others have laid on the table for us like some glorified masons, building our cases with blocks of other's perceptions?

"Identification, such as the one we're presently engaged in, is nothing without recognition and recognition is nothing without observation. Observation, therefore, is the skeleton key of Detection, unlocking the door to every truth imaginable. It is the only true arbiter, unveiling the facts of our environment. How are we to use such a powerful agent? You, rightly, do not know.

"So I ask again: what is in identification? It's a collection of feeling, sights, and intuition. Unquantifiable. Visually discernable features implore our deeper senses to reveal the true 'identity' that lies behind that facial mask, that bodily figure. Beneath the glowing irises we peer into the bowels of one's individuality. It's a duality of purpose, this identification we employ, evident in physicality and unearthed through surveillance of nature. When we observe the nature of our subjects, we observe their mind's expression in physical form.

"Robin is the man in the hat, yes. You're both correct. But, contain your fervor, for you did not *observe* correctly. He is Robin not simply because of what he looks like. It's his unspoken language of being; of verve, of bluster ever so faint. Observe his ways and you observe his mind. Always remember that the body is but an avatar of the mind. Actions reveal intent, sure, but more so they reveal secrets buried in the psyche. Learn to observe and you'll learn to unlock those secrets. Nothing is more valuable in our line of work."

Dead silence and slow nods followed his words, as if the vehicle had entered a vacuum.

"There! He's laughing. . . He smiles, therefore he feels; he feels, therefore he hurts; he hurts, therefore he bleeds; and he bleeds, therefore he dies. He is but a man, but a man he is much more than. Observe, now. Look about yourselves. He doesn't live this life of gloom and decay you witness. At least not yet. The others, these feeders. . .these parasitic consumers, have a way about them. . .a lack of presence. A nonexistence. *His* attitude, though, is tangible. His brightness is contagious and his posture is commanding. It insults his place in the order of things. This festering cyst, this quagmire of a town. . .this place. . .it's not his."

Twisting fronds of cigarette smoke wound through the cruiser, kissing fabric and skin as they explored. Merv took a healthy drag, exhaling forcibly through the cabin towards a crack in the driver's side window and continued.

"Closer, I look at this scene. The order, the organization we see in front of us, though elementary and fragile, is indicative of standards and of acknowledgment of directive, of command. When one is open to command, one is open to dominance. And dominance over another, as you will soon learn, is the single greatest glory an individual can achieve. It is the epitome of our evolution as humans. The dominant do not merely survive; *they thrive. We* are the dominant. All others are the exposed, the insubstantial," he turned and locked eyes with Taylor, breaking his concentration on the church for the first time during his speech, "and they must be controlled."

A cautious look passed between the two deputies at the close of the monologue. Merv opened the driver's-side window from a crack to half-open, downed the remainder of coffee in his paper cup, and tossed the trash onto the pavement. He nodded to himself, focused again on the man in the hat.

"What do we do now?" a voice uttered.

"We wait until sundown. . . Then we have a trap to set."

Chocobo Joe's was the sandwich stand Robin, Wil, and Jon were known to frequent on the nights after they held the Soup Kitchen. It was a place the trio liked to hit not only to engorge themselves but more importantly to discuss what good, if any, came out of the work they were doing. Their discussions were occasionally broken up by those who passed by to offer up their thanks and even some bids to volunteer in the future. While the thanks were always accepted, and the offers appreciated, the trio knew from the onset that extra help was unnecessary. The willingness they saw was promising, if they could but decipher the direction in which to guide it. For now, they simply told the appreciative supporters that when the time came, they'd take them up on the offer.

Robin found it ironic that they regularly ate out after serving food all day. They could have easily saved portions for themselves if they had chosen, but the change in scenery and flip in provider-consumer relation proved useful for their morale. It made them feel regular.

Wil ate loudly, squirting a pool of barbeque sauce on each bite of his brisket sandwich. The bag of potato chips he ordered crinkled as he reached in, following every soft bite with a crunchy chip or three. Sometimes he even opened the sandwich and added his chips on top. "Adds texture," he claimed.

Jon bought three sandwiches. Standard practice. He ate much quieter than Wil, usually averaging about four bites per sandwich to finish one. The man's appetite was unmatched by anyone Robin had met in life. It was no wonder Jon never bought anything but food. The man hadn't the money to.

Robin sat quietly, pondering things. The evening's dialogue was subdued. Running the Soup Kitchen was turning into a fulltime operation. The larger the undertaking, the greater the people served, the earlier their mornings were and the later the nights. As a matter of fact, the guys were wholly exhausted. Though inexpensive, many of their dishes require hours of prep-time and cooking. Add that to setup and teardown and it was turning into what felt like a full-time job.

The minutes passed without much conversation. Eventually, Robin remembered something he wanted to bring up the other day but had been cut short by his unplanned altercation outside *Harper's*.

"Oh," he said. "So I never asked you guys. Do you know anything about the festival they used to hold in that park down the road?"

"Baker's? Nah, not really," Wil said.

"Before our time I think," Jon said without much thought. "It used to be a big deal, like the District would shut down for the day, school schedules were shortened, stuff like that."

"Why do you ask?" Wil asked, squirting sauce on his last bite.

"Ran into an old woman the other day. She described it to me briefly, but I didn't have a chance to find out more. Made me curious about it."

"Ernest would know," said Jon.

Robin nodded. "I thought of asking him but I haven't gotten around to it yet. I'm going to do some more research on it. Might be a nice project for us."

"What was the lady's name?" Wil asked, shuffling through his bag of chips.

"She didn't say." Robin paused, and then smiled to himself. "She did make it a point to criticize the Soup Kitchen though."

Wil squinted. "What the fuck? Why?"

"Well. . .the more I think about it," Robin admitted, "she's not entirely wrong."

Jon began on his third sandwich, content to observe for the moment. Wil, however, became agitated.

"You'll have to explain this one to me."

"We're spending a great deal of effort on something that's not really improving quality of life," Robin said matter-of-factly.

"I mean. . .we're practically giving away food. How is that not improving quality of life?" Wil asked.

"Honestly, that's a good question. I've asked myself the same thing for a few days, because on the surface, yeah, it looks that way. But I think that if we were to stop, the people here would be worse off, not better."

"It's making their *now* better. What's the future got to do with it?" Wil argued.

Robin put his sandwich down and twisted his mouth. He inhaled, "I see it like this: let's say you have a pet. . .like a dog."

"Rottweiler," Wil interrupted with intensity in his voice.

"You have a Rottweiler. You feed it every day at noon, right on cue, to the point that it sits by its bowl in anticipation. It'll grow, sure, and it might seem like the dog's doing great. But if you stopped feeding it just *one* day, the dog would sit there staring at you like. . .um. . .what the fuck, man? I need some food. Feed me. Maybe it even thinks that day was a fluke so it comes back the next day, hungrier. And again, it doesn't get fed. . . Eventually the dog might try to seek out its own food, but that would only be after it's already been weakened by hunger 'cuz it waited around for you to feed it for so fucking long. *And* it probably won't find much when it looks since it hasn't ever fended for itself. Sure it has instincts, whatever. That's not the point. The point is you've fed it all this time without making it work or learn to appreciate where its food comes from, and therefore you've essentially made it a useless being that can't function on its own. It's like clockwork at that point.

"That's what I see us doing in a nutshell," Robin continued. "I mean, obviously people are different than dogs, but all we're doing is making it okay to exist. . .to take without earning it. We're allowing people to maintain, we're not giving any means of growth. That in and of itself makes you weaker in the long run."

"There's no such thing as a free lunch," Jon quoted softly. Robin looked over and nodded deeply.

"Hmm," Wil grunted and detached.

"The Soup Kitchen has a purpose. So do our motivations. . .but this isn't enough. It shouldn't be a fulltime endeavor. The more I think about it, the more it feels like we shouldn't even be involved. I think our time's best spent on bigger things."

"Maybe we'll just hold them on the weekends," Jon offered, still missing the point.

"Somethin' like that. . ." Robin mumbled. Suddenly, his aggravation swelled. He threw up his hands. "What are we even doing? This is so empty, isn't it? It's so temporary. It's just like. . .a fuckin' band-aid or something. 'Oh, you're slowly dying?

Here, I'll put a stitch in it!' We're capable of *way* more than this."

"Well what do you have in mind?"

Robin laughed. "I have *no* idea."

"I'm with you, Robin," Jon said. "But we can't make people grow. There's a difference between people wanting to change and people being ready to change."

"I'm just frustrated."

The group silenced momentarily until Wil grew a smile. "You ain't gonna beat the shit out of us if we wanna keep doin' the Soup Kitchen, are you?" Wil joked. "I don't wanna end up lookin' like those two goons the other night."

"Lay off that already." Robin waved a hand.

Wil ignored him. "I mean, I'd like to keep my nuts."

Jon laughed and Robin cracked a smile.

"They're pretty high on my priority list of 'necessary appendages.' Like, next to my brain. I know you guys don't use yours very often but. . .I kinda like mine." Wil raised a finger. "Now that I think of it, a black eye does help play the pity card but. . .nah, I kinda like my face too. So if you're gonna go *Harper's* on me, stick to my ribs or somethin' unseen."

"I'm seriously going to hit you if you keep it up," Robin threatened emptily.

Wil exaggerated a flinch. "*Woah*, alright man," he ducked. "Meant nothin' by it, sir."

If the guys were anywhere near letting up on their jokes about Robin's fight, they didn't show it. The jokes had been coming in every way, shape, and form since that night. He supposed the jabs were an expression of relief that there had not been harder consequences.

Well past dusk, the guys bid one another farewell. Robin adjusted his hat forward and made towards St. Augustine's. The walk was lengthy, but he welcomed it. Robin needed to let his mind wander over this vacancy of purpose plaguing them. Something bold was on the tip of his tongue; something important which couldn't yet be seen, like a glimpse of a path. The guys were capable, hardworking, and followed Robin's lead naturally. If he could only steer the energy somewhere positive. . .

About four blocks from St. Augustine's, he noticed a single vehicle parked ahead of him in front of an alleyway. The car was clearly maintained, baring minimal scratches or dents, and the streetlights above illuminated dark window tint and a push bar on the front bumper. *Undercover car.* Immediately, Robin's senses shot toward a level of heightened awareness. As he walked past the car, a muffled noise came from the alleyway. Up close he could see one uniformed cop and another man in plain clothes teeing up on someone behind a dumpster in the alley.

Robin quickly unzipped his jacket and dropped it at the entrance to the alley. He clenched both fists, took a deep breath, and sprinted down the alley toward the three men.

"HEY!" Robin shouted as he advanced, startling the two aggressors.

Without hesitation, they dashed off towards the far end of the alleyway. Robin pulled up abruptly just past the dumpster, surprised at their immediate flight. His boots skidded on loose gravel as he turned his attention on the victim, squirming and groaning on the ground. With purpose, Robin moved toward him and offered a hand to help the disheveled man to his feet. To his shock, the man looked odd for a vagrant, like an ex-athlete, with thick shoulders, a firm grip, and stocky legs. Wobbling and weak, the man required a steady hold of one of his arms to stand entirely.

"You alright, man?"

He spit on the gravel and after a wheeze said, "Thanks a lot, son. Not sure how much more of that I could've taken."

Once he was finally able to gain his composure, Robin allowed him to stand on his own. Standing straight, the man was easily two or three inches taller and a good twenty-to-thirty pounds heavier than Robin.

"Not a problem. Too bad they didn't stick around to get what they deserved," Robin said, shifting his focus in the direction the assailants had fled. He felt sneaking suspicion about just what had provoked them to run away so quickly, in the opposite direction of their car.

"Yeah, too bad," the man said with a short laugh, quickly recoiling at pain in his side. "What's your name, son?"

"Robin," Robin answered, still focused down the alley.

"*Robin*? Shit, that name's about as queer as a three-dollar bill," the man said with uncharacteristic strength to his voice.

Huh? Robin thought. Just as he turned to question the insult the man stepped forward and sent a low, powerful hook to his abdomen. The blow caught Robin completely off guard, sending him back a few paces with a loud grunt. He doubled over in agony and slumped down to the wet pavement, gasping intermittently between spikes of pain. Writhing slightly, he held his stomach in a feeble effort at protection and comfort. He turned his head to look at the man who had betrayed him and out of the corner of his eye saw the two initial assailants walking nonchalantly toward him from the front of the alleyway, where he had entered but a minute ago. Panic flooded Robin's mind. The bearded man squatted down on the balls of his feet and knocked Robin's hat off his head, exposing his face for the first time. He grabbed his hair from its roots, forcing him to meet his gaze. By then the two men were visible over the man's shoulders, towering figures in the shadowy tunnel.

"Well, Robin. *My* name is Merv Hamstead. And I'm here on behalf of my associates to return a very brutal, very *bloody* favor."

Chapter 14: To Whom It May Concern

A beaten man fell slowly into an old bench in Baker's Memorial Park. The wooden slats pinched at his bruises as he shuffled around in a useless attempt to find comfort. A quick wince upward revealed a gorgeous afternoon sky. Cotton-ball clouds drifted overhead, reflecting gently on the surface of a nebulous pond before him, bordered with high weeds and lily pads along the shoreline. It was deceptively large, with a number of arms and skinny sections that opened deeper into the parkland. This was the first true look Robin had taken inside the grounds, which had confirmed his initial views that it was too grossly overgrown and neglected to be thought of as a city park. The environmental microcosm that existed here was something of an anomaly. Not for miles, he wagered, was there an ecosystem as diverse with greenery and wildlife. In its abandonment, it had become awfully beautiful. He tried again and again to picture this place cleared-out and bustling with a festival, but again and again he failed to see it.

Robin had spent nine days in the hospital. Nine days. Not for the concussion, not the deep bone bruises in his legs, the swollen jaw, or the broken ribs. Not for the eye and not for the staples in his head - surprisingly, those would all heal on their own (the jaw with a little encouragement). It had been for his collapsed lung. Ironically, he had been lucky. They told him his broken eye socket could've needed surgery and that his lung was only barely punctured by his cracked rib, that it would be healed in a week's time. His doctor made him promise he'd be back in three days to have the staples in his head removed. Robin decided to, instead, give that task to Wil. It was nothing a pair of pliers couldn't fix.

Apparently, a homeless man had discovered his body an hour or so after the attack and flagged someone down to call for help. Robin wished he could find the man and thank him, repay him somehow. He very well may have saved his life.

Ernest had visited the morning following the beating, teary and frantic. So too had the guys, but Robin only allowed it the once. Assurances from his doctors and commands from Robin himself were enough to keep them at bay. He felt like a spectacle and couldn't bear the attention. Ernest promised he'd pray for a fast recovery and wanted to alert the authorities immediately. Wil vowed to scour the city for the offender(s). What happened? Who had done it? What did Robin know? They all pried but he hadn't the constitution to talk about it. He feigned a lapse in memory and gave bland details. Jon's face, however, knew the true story. Robin noticed his conclusive eyes and that scowl that formed, those fists clenching in rage. Before it went further, Robin pleaded to table to discussion until he was out. They obliged, if only out of respect.

They had wanted to keep him another night to be safe, but the moment he was cleared he left that place like a bat out of hell. He hated hospitals, hated being around the sick and the dying. He hated feeling helpless and dependent. The place only brought feelings of death, not healing. Robin touched his swollen, purple cheek and pressed at it gently. He flinched as a torrent of pain shot across his face. He had taken plenty of hits in sports, had broken a few bones, and even fought a kid or two back when he was a teenager. This, though, this changed everything.

Physical wounds heal. Cuts become scabs which become skin anew. Broken bones fuse together, stronger than they once were. Bruises disappear without a trace and healthy color returns. Scars are dermal stories, nothing more. In short time, you'd never know Robin was attacked. He'd be walking normally, talking normally, breathing normally, and the swelled mass around his bloodshot left eye would recede. But inside, he would feel it *every single day*. You read about it in books, see it on television, and hear about it on the news. But only a tragic few know the feeling of a full-force kick to the face, of someone slamming your head into a rusted metal dumpster, of feeling coarse, wet gravel scrape your ear and neck as someone grinds your head into the pavement with a hammer-like fist, again, and again. Only a tragic few know the hurt of intent.

Thereafter he spent each day in solitude. He attempted thought, yet thinking hadn't come easy. His emotions peaked and troughed hourly from hurt, depression, guilt, mortification, rage, and everything in between. As often as he felt angry and motivated, he felt reduced and tiny. The pain medication made it hard to focus. Robin remembered having an irrational fear that someone he knew from his old life would find him there. He feared that Wilson would somehow be alerted, even though Robin claimed he didn't have any family. Having Wilson see him in that condition would have been too much to bear. The bastard would have lectured him again, he would have claimed he was right all along and that Robin should have listened to him. Perhaps he would have been kind instead, but Robin didn't want to find out. Days came and went like they were being rattled off at an auction.

Ahead, a duck squawked and landed gracefully in the center of the pond. A cone of ripples trailed behind like a zipper was being pulled over the once still surface. Robin shifted again on the park bench and winced in pain. A lost feeling came about inside him, then, and his mind grew wracked with uncertainty. Where should he go? What should he do? What was the next move? What the fuck was he even doing there? Desperate options flooded his mind.

In twelve hours he could be on a plane headed back to Germany, as if this stint had never happened, as if these people he had met didn't exist. He could forget about this pathetic chapter of life. He could abandon everything. He could escape.

Or a trip to the nearest bank would put thousands in his pocket. He could buy a car, drive away, find a new life, a new town, a new city, and start over.

Or, in an hour he could be a few miles from there. He could crawl back to Wilson and return to the swaddle of money, the embrace of the glittering monster Downtown. He could assume that fixed course. He could surrender.

Or he could stay. He could fight. He could heal and in healing, he could become stronger. That's what Jon had done. That's what Wil had done. Hell, Ernest had done it too. He was one of them now. His upbringing, his entitled experiences, his old life didn't matter anymore. He'd always be able to relate to this place. He'd always be associated. His scars made him fit in.

Robin sat gingerly for the better part of an hour, weighing his options and reflecting on his time in the hospital. Gradually, his mind drifted to thoughts of his mother. Seeing her son this way would have crushed her, a thought which instead crushed *him*. He began to cry there, on that bench, alone and broken. Doing so physically hurt. His fractured face, his ruined jaw, his crippled lung, all pleaded for him to stop, but the tears flowed onward, making rivers down his cheeks. Only the serenity of the park could eventually calm him. The wind shushed his cries.

When the worry and shame settled, he was left with a rebellious, defiant urge. Wild ideas took his mind by storm and his heart rate spiked. He had visions and experienced a moment of clarity, seeing an image of the city in a way he never had before. The District became clearer, the struggle and disparity simpler. The opulence nearby became fragile. Now the wind brought laughter and songs, and when he closed his eyes he could finally imagine that fabled festival of the past. It was so colorful, so wondrous, and bright. Smiling faces told of a forgotten dream. They told him that the only way to follow a dream was to open one's eyes and try.

So he opened them.

Rich crimson clouds floated along the few patches of visible sky beyond the courtyard outside Jon's sliding glass door. From the living room, it looked like a storm was approaching from off in the distance. For now, the sunset's colors commanded the clouds as if in a painting. Jon would've been on the balcony if he hadn't spent the last three hours there. After long, he'd grow agitated by the concrete and iron framing nature's beauty. Trees would have helped him relax a little better in light of recent events.

Jon sat in his recliner, flipping carelessly through his *Friendly Farmer* magazine and pulling the occasional mouthful of beer from his *Bearport* pounder on the coffee table. Across from him, sprawled on the couch, Wil stared at the ceiling. Jon hadn't seen Wil this upset in years. He brooded in furor, day in and day out. It took half of the week to calm him to a level beneath shaking rage. He kept repeating, "This changes things, man. It's gone too far." Jon hadn't an argument against him, and feared him exploding. They were missing their friend.

The pair had been lounging uncomfortably for a good while when, unexpectedly, a gentle knock caught their attention. Jon sprung out of his chair and closed the distance to the door in three strides. Swinging the door wide presented Robin's battered form leaning on the jamb, out of breath. He looked awful, yet lively at the same time.

"You're out!" Jon blurted, grabbing him in a hug.

Robin grunted.

Wil looked up from the couch. *"Robin?"*

Jon released him and met his icicle eyes.

"I'm out. We need to talk," Robin said.

Wil sat tall and scooted across the couch, making room for Robin in a space closest to the door. Gently, Robin fell into the cushion, giving a groan as his flesh landed. He took a deep breath and ran a hand through his hair, avoiding his wound, while Jon situated himself on the edge of his recliner. Wil inspected his injuries.

"I don't even know where to begin, man," Jon confessed. "I'd ask 'how are you' but that'd almost be laughable."

Robin chuckled anyway. "I'll be alright."

"Have you gone to see Ernest?"

"Nah. Not yet."

"Those staples look gnarly," Wil said, lifting his head.

"Yeah, I'm gonna need your expertise on these. They need to come out in a few days."

"No problem."

Jon held back a skeptical comment and switched gears. "Want something to drink? Pounder?"

Robin shook his head. "Not right now. We need to talk."

"Anything you want," Jon encouraged.

"Can I ask you somethin' first?" Wil interrupted. He was unable to bear the question any longer.

Robin took his time turning his head to face Wil. He was met with penetrating eyes. "What."

"Is Jon right? Was it cops?"

"Oh yeah. It was cops. Wasn't the same ones, though."

"Any ideas who they were?"

Robin bit his tongue as a bearded man's face came into his mind's eye. He knew the face and the name. He'd remember it forever.

"That's not important," he answered instead.

"The fuck it ain't," Wil said. "This ain't over."

"Forget the cops for a minute. Fuck 'em. . .but forget them for right now. This is bigger than them."

"No it ain't," Wil protested.

"It *is*. This isn't about Police."

"How could you possibly say that? Look at what they fuckin' did to you."

Aggravated, Robin spoke quickly. "It's not, dude. Like, I get it - I'm fucked up. But there's bigger issues here."

"You've got to be fucking kidding–"

"Let me explain something, okay? If cops come to this neighborhood and exploit their power it's not because Police are inherently evil, it's because when you give average, sometimes questionable human beings an extraordinary amount of power, eventually it'll show itself in abusive ways. All it takes is one act that gets swept under the rug. From there it evolves into a problem of not 'if', but 'when' and 'how often'. They can run wild because it's *allowed*. No one speaks up! No one says anything - on either side. Oh, wait–" Robin diverted sarcastically. "I guess I could have filed a formal complaint. Yeah. Or better yet I could've sued. Right, that would have solved things. They'd never even *try* this shit again. That'd show 'em. . .What are you fucking kidding me?"

"I *know*," Wil said. "That's what I'm sayin'."

"What happened to me is a tiny example of the problem. It pales in comparison to the bigger issue, man. Okay, I stepped into a situation and beat the shit out of two cops. Somehow, they found a way to return the favor. Some would say that's justice. And honestly, I'm lucky I didn't get seriously fucked up or end up dead. But forget those instances and realize the bigger issue at hand - the *fact* that either of those two instances happened in the first place. They're products of a major problem. On one hand, immorality and abuse of power. On the other, having no other way to combat the problem other than violence. Because the only other option to fighting them is submission. . . Letting the dominance roll over me. Those girls I helped out? Where would they have gone? If those cocksuckers pulled a gun out and forced them into the car what would they have done? Who would they go to after they were taken advantage of? Or raped? Or God knows what?"

Wil repeated himself, with anger growing in his tone. "That's what I'm sayin'. It's not gonna happen anymore."

"But, again, you need to understand the bigger problem."

Jon butted in unexpectedly. "Yo, settle the fuck down and let's think on this a little more rationally."

Wil huffed. "No. You sound like Ernest, man."

"Fuck you, I'm not wrong."

"No, he's not wrong," Robin agreed.

"Yeah he is! Fuck all that! We're not *settling* down! I'm not calming down, God damn it! Look at you," Wil motioned. "You're *fucked* up. For what?"

"It's not about me."

"The fuck it's not!"

"It *isn't*. It's much bigger than me or you or Jon. *This*," Robin motioned to his face, "will go away. *That*," he moved his hand towards the window, "won't. Not unless someone does something about it. And I'm saying it's *us* who's gonna make it change."

"Woah, woah, woah. Let's back up to what you were gonna say earlier. This isn't even on topic. What exactly did you wanna talk about, Robin?"

Robin cleared his throat and flinched. "I made a decision today. And it involves both of you."

"Okay," Jon pushed.

"I decided I wanna get serious. I want. . .I decided I want to change things here. I want to do things. Illegal things. I want to hurt people. I want to ruin people. Not how you might think. I'm not talking about assault or violence. I'm talking about. . .shame and ridicule. Deep hurt. I have an idea and I need both of your help to make it happen. I'm prepared to do anything to convince you. Us three must be the ones to get things started around here, and today is the day where it either begins or the opportunity slips away entirely."

"I don't think I'm understanding what you mean," Jon said regretfully, if not skeptically.

"I know what he means." Wil scowled, nodding to himself as the idea clicked. "Fuck yeah I do. We're gonna rebel. We're gonna revolt."

"C'mon," Jon dismissed. "Seriously guys?"

"I mean it," Wil maintained.

"Look. I know we're all upset here, but you're being dramatic."

"No, he's not," Robin interjected. "That's how this has to happen."

"Okay, you're *both* being dramatic. What does that even mean, 'revolt'?"

"It's simple," Wil said. "It means fight back."

Jon laughed, then. "Fight who? How?"

"Jon, think about it. What other way is there?" Wil lobbied.

"If I knew, I'd say. But I was in school long enough to know just about every revolution in history failed, though. And failed hard." Jon responded, still unconvinced.

"At least they tried," said Wil.

"No, that's bullshit. Trying is overrated. Like it makes everything ok just because you're hearts in the right place or you gave it your best shot. I hate hearing that. It's unrealistic. It's a way to make failure hurt less. It makes you soft."

"It's about effort, not failure," Robin said. "People use the sentiment in the wrong way. They only use it after someone has failed. Never before. In our case, failure doesn't matter compared to the effort."

"I think you're talkin' crazy. Both of you."

"God fucking damn it!" Wil pointed his finger across the coffee table. "I won't have this negativity from you. If you wanna laugh about it or dissent all day long, then. . .go fuck yourself." He threw his hands up. "I dunno what else to say."

"Fuck you," Jon spat back.

"No, fuck you. It's like you've got this attitude burned into you that nothing can ever change and we're destined to be insignificant. Like we don't matter. You're literally speaking *their* words. You're squashing any hope of change or doing right by us, by everyone here. Think for yourself, God damn it."

"I am, dick. Talk is cheap. What the fuck are *we* gonna do about all of this, huh? Rally the troops?" Jon said mockingly. "Arm them with weapons and storm City Hall? What's the war plan, huh? I'll make a few phone calls. We could be there by eight."

"Typical ways aren't going to work," Robin chimed. "Forget everything you've ever learned and everything you've ever known about revolutions. It doesn't apply. This isn't the 1700s. Life nowadays is easy compared to that. It's fuckin' *cake* for most people now. People are content, understand? Even here. A new environment, a new context, calls for new tactics - a new way to approach the word. Fuck, forget the word if you want. This needs to be like nothing anyone's ever seen before."

Jon shook his head, unsatisfied. "I don't see this working. What on earth could we possibly do?"

Robin grew intense. "Don't say it won't work just because you're being a pussy. If you say it won't work it should be because you don't care. *If* you care, and I know you do, *and* you're not a pussy, which I know you're not, then you will be on board. So which is it? You don't care? Or you're a being a pussy?"

Jon was sorting through words with which to answer, but Robin didn't give him the luxury of time.

"I'm *dead* fucking serious, here. We can *do* this. We can *change* things. The people here will gain confidence if they're shown how fragile the beast of opulence truly is. That 'fortress,' as I've heard you call it, is full of complacent, weak, selfish individuals. They're not ready for what we're about to bring."

"They have the law on their side! Cops, money, power, numbers, you name it - fuckin' government!"

"None of that is an advantage this time. Trust me. They're weak spots that we can exploit."

Jon rolled his eyes. "Jesus Christ. That's insane."

"Those groups over there, they're not one. They're not unified. They don't know the meaning of the word. All they know is how to mutually profit from each other. That's it. They exert their dominance because they're afraid of the minority. Think about it: a major crime was committed here, in this neighborhood, and no one with the power to do so has done anything to right the wrong. *All because it's easier to ignore a problem than it is to fix it,"* Robin emphasized. "We will not be ignored any longer. This place has been filed away and forgotten about. It's time to open the file again.

"I know what you're thinking. But this isn't about revenge. This isn't about money or fame or the Police or anything like that. It's about being heard and in doing so, giving confidence to those who have been taught to accept defeat like it's a place they belong. Like defeat is their birthright. You ask 'how.' The actions won't be easy, but the concept is. If you take a symbol, and you shame it publicly, it loses a degree of power. Cheapen respect of and cheapen fear of these symbols and each gross pillar of our city gets weaker. Confidence is strengthened by support. The people will see that their voice is as loud as anyone's. And it matters all the same. Jon, the neighborhood you were born in doesn't make you less of a human being. Even if it feels that way."

Jon remained silent, on the defensive, as if Wil and Robin were overwhelming him with words.

"This is how it has to happen," Robin added. "It's the only way."

"My mind's made up," Wil declared.

"I'm sorry, but mine's not," Jon answered. "We're gonna end up in jail or making things worse. Or both."

Wil made a face of disgust. "*Man*. . .You're *un*believable. All those times we've struggled - *really* struggled - all those times we've been on the verge of madness and *now* you're afraid."

"I'm not afraid." Jon leaned in. "I'm being rational."

"*No*. You're afraid," Wil insisted defiantly. "You've always been afraid. Your whole fuckin' life."

"Fuck you, you're not? Where was this big talk '*all those times*'?"

"This is different now."

"How?" Jon seemed flabbergasted.

"Because of him," Wil pointed.

Jon's eyes moved to Robin, unable to skip an inspection of his visible wounds. He thought of the recent months since that man appeared out of the blue; all the changes it brought about in him and Wil's attitude and the content of their days.

"You wanna know what I *am* afraid of?" Wil continued, drawing Jon's attention back. "I'm afraid of one thing: being a waste. And right now, that's what I am. I'm the epitome of wasted potential. I've got nothin'. I *do* nothin'. Many of my poor choices are my own, and that's fine, but I'm not equipped to deal with struggles like this. No one is! I've been hungry for twenty-three years straight. Every morning I wake up wondering why I keep at it. Why I'm still here. I've wanted to die more mornings than I've wanted to live. I've got *no* purpose, I've got *no* reasons, I've got *nothin'* in front of me, *no* path to happiness. I observe. I exist. I cut my own hair. I pulled my own tooth when it rotted out of my mouth. I barter for shit 'cuz I can't pay. My feet hurt 'cuz the secondhand shoes I wear are three years old. I've got the same shirts on from high school. Every winter I wonder if I'm gonna freeze. I'm gettin' worn down, man. *This isn't me inside*. I am more than this. But this is all I'll ever be unless something changes. And I ain't waitin' on someone else to do it for me. I'm ready to get serious. I'm ready to get *fuckin' crazy*. I don't give a *fuck* anymore. I'm changin' things or I'll die tryin'. Nothing else matters. Not me, not you, not him. This is our life, and I say we're aloud to dictate how it turns out."

Jon blinked furiously and slowly shook his head.

Wil snatched the can off the table and whipped it against the wall with a crack. He screamed, "Don't shake your fuckin' head, Jon! Man up! I'm tired of this shit, God damn it! Better to die than rot here forever!"

Jon spoke quietly. "Wil."

"NO! FUCK 'EM ALL!"

The room grew quiet as Wil settled his shaking fury. As close as Wil and Jon were, it was clear they hadn't spoken so deeply in front of one another in a long while. Robin admired Wil's tenacity.

"I'm in," Wil added, still an image of ferocity. "Hundred percent."

Robin spoke gently. "It's happening, Jon. It has to."

Jon was red in the face. Robin couldn't be sure from his angle, but his eyes looked glassy. This afternoon was more than a spurt of anger. It was their whole lives compounded into a conversation.

"We can't do this by ourselves, can we?" Jon asked. "Don't we need support? Numbers? I mean, we're so few. . .and they're so many."

Robin smiled. "We already have numbers. They just don't know they're a part of it yet."

Friday mornings were Jordan Fontano's favorite time of the week. As Assistant Editor for the *Fort Dearborn Ledger*, he had the luxury of looking through the weekly Op-Ed submissions. Friday morning's pile was always the largest, in anticipation of the Sunday edition, and he took pride in being able to have some control over the content of the paper. From the hours of eight to eleven he'd sit with his pimply, red-headed intern and submerge himself into other people's truths, lies, and solutions to the city's problems. This was his third year on the job and he couldn't imagine doing anything else. Someday, he hoped to become the Editor in Chief.

Today's stack had started off slow, but his mood was still positive, even after reading a senile old woman's complaints about the speed of cars in the city and an animal activist with fourth-grade literacy levels relating the increase in albino pigeons to the stress they endure from pedestrians. While pieces like these were not at all worthy of print, sometimes he would try to slip a few by his boss just to imagine the reader's reactions, and maybe give the generic reader the motivation to submit their own work.

Just then Samuel, his intern, returned from a coffee run.

"There was another one in our mailbox today. Separate from the usual delivery. Someone must have brought it themselves," Sam said, out of breath for reasons unbeknownst to Jordan.

“Must be one anxious opinion. Let’s see what has them so riled up,” Jordan said, motioning to Sam to pass him the envelope. Jordan admired the handwriting on the front, trying to get a bead on the person submitting the piece. *You can tell a lot about a person by their handwriting,* he thought. Inside the folder was a single page with neatly written text:

To Whom It May Concern,

The crime was to forget
The atrocities that beset
Those who live in the Inner District
So now all must bear witness.

The corrupt and evil are put on notice
And on us falls the onus
To embark on our mission of vengeance
To share our verdict and carry out the sentence
Of exposing truth and restoring order.

Against the corrupt, a marauder,
For the weak, a succor,
Against the evil, a slaughter,
For the good, a protector.

Regardless of where you fall,
Enlightenment awaits you all.

You’ve been warned.

The Few Against Many (F.A.M.)

PART 2: ANY MEANS NECESSARY

"Every normal man must be tempted, at times, to spit on his hands, hoist the black flag, and begin slitting throats."

- H.L. Mencken

Chapter 15: Failure is the Best Medicine

There are more than 43 quintillion possible combinations for a standard 3x3x3 Rubik's cube. That's a number greater than the number of seconds that have elapsed since the Big Bang, greater than the number of cells in each human being in the country of Jamaica, and enough combinations that each person on earth could own a unique set of six billion cubes. If there were individual cubes with each possible combination exhibited, they would stack from the earth to the sun and back over 17,000 times. Since its invention, people from across the globe have tested their mettle against others in speed competitions that have evolved over time into incredible variety. There's blindfolded competitions, one-handed competitions, and even blindfolded one-handed competitions. Allegedly, a kid solved the cube in less than thirty seconds using only his feet.

With just one side completed to his credit, Robin had a ways to go. He sank into the middle cushion of the couch in Wil's studio like he was sitting on a toilet bowl with the seat up. His hips broke parallel and his lumbar curve was non-existent, but despite the discomfort, Robin's concentration on the Rubik's cube in his hand was firm. The first rule he learned was that the center pieces never move, a common misconception among first-time cubers. An almost equally interesting fact to Robin was the self-proclaimed title "cuber." He supposed he was a cuber now? . . .Probably best to keep that to himself. The first rule was relevant, though, as most try to move the colors absentmindedly, ignoring the fact that the center pieces serve as a reference point from which all moves should be based.

The softened noise coming from the television was the closing minutes of a sitcom rerun well past its prime. But the episode, though nostalgic, was not the purpose of his sedentary entertainment session. In the coming minutes, the 4 p.m. news report would air. Tonight was the second night in a row Robin, Jon and Wil had gathered together to watch the news in hopes of some public recognition of their work over the weekend. Last night's newscast had awarded them no acclaim, but they returned this evening with high hopes.

Robin started with the green side of the cube, because, why not? It had all four corners and two edge pieces already in place. The previous night he had been able to finish the entire side, but arrived that afternoon to find it scrambled again. He kept his suspicion of Wil's tampering to himself because, after all, the cube was his and completing one side wasn't exactly noteworthy. The exercise was filler, and the motions kept Robin occupied to ease his anticipation of the night's broadcast.

Jon and Wil cackled from the corner of the studio. It was Wil's apartment they now occupied these days, not because it was in the best shape or the most spacious—it was actually the worst of their options in both categories—but because it was occupied solely by Wil. Each of their other options came with baggage: the church came with Ernest, and Jon's apartment came with Janelle. Wil's was the only spot the trio could exist without any threat of disruption or eavesdropping or judgement. For Robin, it reminded him of those teenage years when a friend's parents were away on vacation. Only here that vacation existed all the time.

How Wil secured the apartment, or was even in good standing with rent payments, eluded Robin. He claimed the landlord just didn't care enough to kick him out, but Robin supposed something else was afoot. In the end, it wasn't his business.

The apartment was a five-hundred square foot rectangle that housed a bed, couch, television, a wall of minimal kitchen appliances and a storage closet. Thankfully, the builders had enough material to separate the toilet and shower from the rest of the apartment with a wall. The only possible attraction would be the sliding glass door that led to a small concrete balcony, a common theme for apartments in the area, as Robin had come to learn. At least from the balcony you could see the other parts of the District, and the sprawling, flourishing city-center beyond, like seeing heaven from the open door of purgatory, even hearing the joyous noise emanating from afar.

In the corner of the bedroom/living room/kitchen area, beyond pizza boxes stacked high, Jon and Wil were playing what had become their usual game of Cricket on an old dart board Wil had stolen from *Peepers* two months ago. It was a token, for lack of a better word, taken with him after they got kicked out for their "fireman's carry" routine. Wil was currently on a tear, having closed sections seventeen and eighteen on consecutive triple throws, and was moving to section nineteen just as the classic Channel 3 news jingle came on.

"Guys, it's on," Robin announced as he placed the cube on the wooden coffee table, its green face missing only one edge piece.

Wil knocked the darts out of Jon's hand and jumped the L-section of the couch perpendicular to Robin, claiming the entire leg as his territory. Smiling, Jon lumbered to the edge of the couch and rolled over the side in slow motion like an elephant seal tumbling back into the water after a nap. With a painful grunt, Wil disappeared squirming for dear life under his friend's mass. Muffled commotion ensued from within the innards of the couch that could hardly be recognized as Wil's cries.

"Come on!" Robin yelled in frustration. "I can't hear."

Jon finally offered Wil reprieve after much stifled begging, and Wil conceded the section of the couch, moving next to Robin as the jingle for the news ended and the co-anchors began their choreographed charade.

Ten minutes and three stories into the broadcast, Wil snatched the Rubik's cube off the coffee table and began to fool with it, rotating the sides with ease that went unnoticed. He spun it casually, looking up at the broadcast for most of the program and back down at the cube intermittently. Because Robin had first found the cube at Wil's in an unsolved state, he had never once thought to ask Wil for pointers. The thing practically had dust on it anyway.

"Don't fuck my cube up," Robin snapped in jest.

"You already fucked your cube up," Wil replied.

"What? You're gonna solve it?" he pressed.

"I never said that."

Some forty-five minutes later, Robin glanced down at the coffee table and discovered the Rubik's cube completely solved form. He pointed at it.

". . .What?" Wil asked.

"You solved it?"

"Yeah?"

"What the fuck. I've been working on this thing for two days. I didn't know you could do it."

"Sure I can," Wil said with a smile.

"I thought you were messing with it because you were bored. What was your time?"

"I dunno. I solved it a bunch of times during the show."

"A bunch? You were playing with it for like thirty minutes."

"Yeah, I know. I'd solve it, scramble it; solve it, scramble it; solve it, scramble it."

"Jesus. How many times?"

"I dunno. Like fourteen or fifteen."

"Seriously? Why haven't you helped me with it?"

"You never asked," he fired back. "Plus, you've only been cubing for two days. Still haven't put real effort into it, man."

"Cubing?" Jon asked, having kept and ear on their conversation.

"Yeah, Jon, cubing." Robin defended.

"There's a name for you nerds?"

"Been cubing for years, bitch," Wil said. "Used to be able to do it without looking."

"You've gotta be kidding me," Robin muttered.

The first hour of news was utterly fruitless. The day's topics were mostly fluff—uninteresting tales of theft, animal abilities, a minor Listeria outbreak and acts of police heroism. "Major" headlines like Fort Dearborn's 250th birthday and dropped charges on some judge named Fulson dominated the newscast in an anticlimactic fashion. Another hour of news down and a jittery, unwelcome feeling snuck up on Robin.

At 4:59 p.m. he flipped to the Channel five's 5 o'clock news, which began on cue with choreography offensively similar to Channel three's 4 p.m. show. Changing the anchors and backdrop did little to alter the content being delivered. It seemed like the news was form-pressed and sent to each station at the beginning of the evening to be regurgitated back by talking heads in tweed and colored suede.

"Do they issue names to these people when they get hired? There's no fucking way they're born with those names," Wil scoffed. "Maybe it's part of the job requirements. 'Must have: outlandish name or be willing to assume one, on-camera presence, fair features and complexion, impeccable hair. . .and no soul.' I swear to you they've probably figured out that if you have a bizarre name people will listen more closely."

He wasn't entirely wrong, Robin thought. Names like Rosalie Flowers, Aloysius Von Rahn, and Bill Billings. Brett Prendergast, the stunning Alexandra Sky (Meteorologist, of course), Bob Ball. . .

"It's like making your own porn name," Wil added. The comment received a chuckle from the group, a welcomed lightness to what was otherwise developing into a tense room.

The second hour of news was everything but news. Topics remained the same and the delivery animatedly repetitive. Jon grabbed three *Bearport* pounders from the fridge and divvied them out. A simultaneous *tssk* and *crack* ensued as they hunkered down for the remainder of the broadcast, hopeful and anticipating. As time went on and topics transitioned, though, the group began losing their faith. A mild shake of the head here, an aggravated sigh there, or a tightening of the brow were the only outward signs of frustration, that last faint hope of mention lingering in them all. But of mention, there was none.

The past weekend they researched a list of thirteen news corporations to which to deliver a clearly written copy of their declaration. The list included the four highest-rated news stations, the four highest-rated newspaper and magazine publishers, and five other local or free papers—the ones handed out ad nauseum at subway stops and such. They figured the newspapers might take a little longer to print something about their delivery, but they still collected them each day expecting a story. The pile in the corner of the apartment between the television and the sliding glass door was already about twenty newspapers deep. Had any of them actually read the newspaper rather than skimmed the headlines, they'd have recognized a missing person's report about a set of young girls that disappeared from a local bar. The man they left with was known only by the name "Patrick."

The broadcast was nearly through when Robin let the remote fall out of his hands. Jon and Wil eyed him as he rose from the couch and walked over to the pile, staring longingly, seeming to lose himself in thought as he ran his hands through his hair. A stir ensued behind him, neither Jon nor Will wishing to first offer his comments to Robin. None of them was ready to address the issue aloud nor attempt to formulate a redeeming plan.

Truth be told they had entered this as green as a blade of grass. They weren't criminals, they weren't politicians, and they weren't revolutionaries. So what did they know? Mentally they found the idea sound, but that was just a result of rationalization. Only recognition could dictate their next action and therefore progress. Once a "shout out" on television was achieved, a progressive move could be made with confidence; they would be legitimized.

Background noise penetrated the silent atmosphere with a sardonic tone. While the three were temporarily speechless, the television blared on. A sting that was the fear of failure crawled up Robin's spine. Wil, visibly exhausted of patience, finally addressed the elephant in the room.

"So. . .what does this mean?" Wil asked.

Silence.

". . .Fuck. . ." Robin breathed after a time.

Jon offered, "Maybe they're just figuring out what to do with it."

"I think they're ignoring it on purpose," Robin said. "I *know* they got it."

Wil shifted in the depths of the couch. "What about those free papers? They'll print anything. They've gotta do something with it."

"I dunno. I'm not sure about those. We'll have to check tomorrow morning. There might be a delay with printing. I dunno." Robin's response was less than enthusiastic.

"So what now?" Jon asked.

"I, for one, feel kinda stupid for getting so excited," Wil said with a laugh.

"Hey, I got excited too. . ." Robin said. "We're in a spot here, though."

"Listen, maybe this was a good thing," Jon proposed.

Wil and Robin looked over at him inquisitively.

"How so?"

"Think about it, why would they take us seriously? We didn't really do anything yet except draft a declaration. To be honest, I don't even know if *I* take us seriously right now."

"Thanks for the vote of confidence," Robin said with a touch of attitude and a thumbs up.

"Listen. I think you need to get off your pedestal for a second here and take a look at this from my view. All we did so far was write a fuckin' letter, okay? These days. . .I'm not sure how much weight words hold."

"A formal declaration is often the most important step in a revolution," Robin shot back.

"Yeah, I agree, but it's not useful if the people who are supposed to revolt don't know about it," Jon said. "We went about it the wrong way."

The comment held weight. Robin pursed his lips and exhaled sharply. *". . .Fuck."*

"Alright," Jon continued, trying to curb Robin's mood. "Why did we send this to the news organizations and papers in the first place?"

"Airplay. Recognition. Show it off to the city," Robin said absently.

"I think that, more precisely, we expected them to do the heavy lifting for us," chimed in Wil.

"Exactly," Jon agreed. "We used a middle man. That always makes things more complicated."

"Okay. That was inadvertently lazy on our part. That was a misstep," Robin decided.

"Time to cut out the middle man," Jon encouraged, "that's all."

"I like it. How're we gonna do it?" Wil asked.

"I dunno. . ."

The conversation paused. Wil watched Jon while Jon watched Robin while Robin stared away in thought. A defeated silence cloaked the apartment as a question crept into each of their minds. Was their revolution over before it had even started? They had failed to discuss how to deal with the potential failure of their actions, and now instead of being able to bask in the notoriety, they were being forced to face the true reasons behind their actions and whether to continue to pursue this dream. They had undoubtedly been plagued by their own arrogance. But when arrogance and overconfidence threaten to sicken, oftentimes failure is the best medicine.

Robin continued to curse himself inwardly as he scanned the upwards of fifty or sixty signatures and quotes oddly inscribed on Wil's "kitchen" wall. They littered the paint in a range of colored inks. One name was even carved into the wall. It was something he'd seen several times but never once asked about.

"I never asked you, where'd all these signatures come from?" he asked.

The question pulled Wil from his mind. With a chuckle he said, "Kinda started off as a joke. We were playing Quarters one night, and Chucky - you know him - he won the tournament and in a drunken stupor went over and signed his name as the champion. He decided he wanted a 'Wall of Fame,' so now it's a thing. I sure as hell didn't protest."

"It's been a while since we've added some names up there, actually," Jon remarked.

"Yeah well, maybe Robin will get to sign it if he gets his Cricket game in order. He's gotta fix that T-Rex throw of his," Wil jabbed.

Robin kept his eyes on the wall, but allowed a gentle smile to form on his lips.

"Who did that one up there?" he asked, pointing to an intricately detailed skyline of the city that lined the top of the wall like a wallpaper border.

"I did," Wil said.

Robin turned to him with a raised eyebrow. "For real?" he asked incredulously.

"I like to draw things sometimes. I told you that. So what?"

"No, no. I like it," Robin said. "I forgot."

When a laugh track on the television started indicating that the 6 p.m. sitcoms had begun, the trio moved out to the balcony. Jon slid the glass door shut with a thud. They cracked pounder cans in unison, the change in scenery welcome, but that little bear showing his carefree contentment in defiance of the trio's somber demeanor. After a healthy gulp, Robin initiated the discussion.

"God damn that's good. Alright, we need to talk this out. The question is: how do we better reach our target audience? We know the who, we know the what, we know the when (now), and the where and the why. Let's discuss the how."

Collectively they began crossing things off the list. They couldn't go on television themselves and calling a radio station lacked replay value. Plus, Wil was adamant that no one listened to the radio anyway. Nor could they hand the declaration out, as that would identify them too easily. And moreover, the approach was taboo. Handing someone a written manifesto would classify you as illegitimate and, likely, a fucking lunatic. It was an amateur move, they decided, and though they *were* amateurs, they needed to start thinking outside the box.

Delivery, they reinforced, was key. Sure, recognition on television would have been quite a start, but perhaps that even took some critical control out of their hands. A message holds weight in how, when, and under what circumstances one receives it.

The evening breeze at the height of Wil's balcony was mild for November. Ripples in Robin's long-sleeve t-shirt moved like a flag calmly rolling in the wind as he leaned on the railing, his eyes examining the nearby landscape like a hawk would from its perch. Apartment buildings Alpha and Omega, as Wil had surreptitiously named them, towered off to the right a ways. The unfinished towers stood solidly in spite of the history of their shortcomings, and defined the majority of the horizon in that direction. The parks at the base of the towers bore months-worth of scribbled graffiti on the outer walls and concrete, maybe longer. He read over some of the larger words and names that stood out from the mishmash of color. It was a mess.

"You do that artwork in your free time, Wil?"

"Which?" he followed Robin's finger to the parks. "Tagging? Nah, I'm not into that."

"He just sticks to inside walls where he can hide," Jon joked.

"Eh, inside's just for fun. Like, it has context, y'know? I do like to do scenes or lettering, but I never saw the point in just writing your name somewhere in public."

"Yeah, I don't get it either, man. Quite a narcissistic hobby," Robin agreed.

"I guess. . ." Wil replied ambiguously.

"It's like they're just feeding an ego. It's selfish."

"I mean, sometimes it's a territory thing too," Jon interjected. "Shows where they've been, what they can tag. I knew two guys that would collaborate on stuff."

"Still, must be fulfilling, even if most people look upon it as a crime."

"It only matters if that one group of people sees it as a crime. Just like everything else," said Wil.

"Yeah. . .and they do. Dudes are in jail now," Jon added.

"For spray-painting an abandoned building?" Robin asked.

"That would be defacing public property and vandalism. Multiple offenses," Jon informed.

"Seems a little excessive," Robin thought aloud.

"I guess they wanted to keep it in pristine dilapidation," Wil said sarcastically.

"That's not necessarily what gets you jail time, but what do you think happens when you're charged and can't pay thousands of dollars in fines?"

“They always collect, man. One way or another,” Wil added.

“Yeah they do.” The comment made Robin think of his beating. He moved his jaw from side to side and flirted with the residual pain that lingered. A close inspection in a mirror would still show a bloodshot corner of his eye and a puffy cheek. “So what’s the difference between vandalism and art?” he propositioned.

“Whatever their law states, man,” Wil said.

“Permission,” was Jon’s vote.

“Yeah, I guess,” Robin answered, pausing. “But just because graffiti isn’t allowed, or it isn’t legal, doesn’t mean it *shouldn’t* qualify as art. Art is creative self-expression. Context *does* determine who sees it, and how they see it, but it doesn’t wholly qualify or disqualify art. If someone painted the Mona Lisa on, like, the fucking White House, they’d remove it in a heartbeat and set out on a manhunt for whoever did it. But that painting wouldn’t be any less artistic or beautiful. You might say it isn’t art because someone didn’t ask for it or a certain individual, or group of individuals, sees it as destructive. But I think it is.”

The guys considered his words for a moment, not quite convinced yet thoughtful.

“I realize that not everyone agrees with that, but. . .it’s the truth. That point doesn’t even matter,” he said dismissively. “What matters is if the right people see it as art. And not art in the traditional sense. Art in the functional sense. Purposeful.”

“Just seems to me that no one cares until they can make money off of it,” Wil said.

“The people that would care are the exact people we’re trying to reach,” Robin replied.

“I dunno,” Jon said. “I think we’re getting off topic.”

“We’re not, though,” Robin replied. “I brought it up because I’ve only known of one artist like that that’s garnered some sort of recognition and following. And there’s a major difference between him and the people who do that shit.” He pointed at the tagged retaining wall.

“Which is?”

“Two things actually: he never got caught, and his artwork was thought provoking, first and foremost. Each piece sent a message or gave the public something to consider. Oftentimes, it was like juxtaposition. Like anything else, it usually got removed or painted over but you’d be surprised at how many followers he had.”

“What’re you gettin’ at? You wanna paint walls?” Wil asked.

“Think about it like this: At its core, the purpose of art is communication. How many people do you think see those tags a day?” Robin asked.

“Depends on where it is,” Jon rejoined. “And there’s a difference between how many people pass it, how many people see it, and how many people remember it.”

“Exactly,” Robin said as he held up a finger. “Okay, so what if it was in a location that everyone could see? And not only that, what if it was something they *wanted* to see?”

The two silently acknowledged the direction Robin was taking them.

“Who gives a fuck what the police think, or any landowners for that matter? Who gives a *fuck* if they think it’s destructive? You know what? If they do. . .*good.* They’ll cover it up to make people to forget about it, but it won’t matter *as long as it has airplay.* We have a message we want people to see. . . Put it out there and recognition will follow. It’s time to think big here.”

Wil smirked in understanding. “You’re fucking nuts, you know that?”

Robin assumed a serious demeanor and looked Wil in the eyes. “Fuck ‘em all,” he said.

Nodding along, Wil met his gaze. “Fuck ‘em all.”

Jon remained glued to the cityscape until slowly he began to nod too. “. . .Fuck ‘em all.”

A ‘fuck you’ not to the world, but to those who’d condemn their actions. A ‘fuck you’ to the controllers and censors, the policing nature of their city and the detached population at large. It was a ‘fuck you’ to everyone and everything that put their District in straits and actively kept it there. The three met eyes and gently raised their cans in a humble cheers.

“It’s just too bad none of us can draw. . .” Jon said.

Robin smiled. “Shame. . .”

The two eyed Wil with raised eyebrows. He glanced back and forth as a smile drew itself on his face.

“*Pfft.* Just give me a paint can and call me, fuckin’, Wilcasso, bro.” He smiled emphatically.

“All we need to do now is find our canvas.”

Robin turned his head to face the city again and Wil and Jon joined him. Leaning on the balcony, they watched the setting sun fall toward the horizon between apartment buildings Alpha and Omega like a field goal splitting the uprights. When they saw the sun glisten off the two large goalposts, they looked at each other and smiled.

Chapter 16: Curtains Up

Beginning at the nineteenth floor, apartment building Alpha was a bare, unfinished work, looking from afar as if all construction had halted suddenly on a single day. Columns held up concrete floors layered on top of one another in a way that more closely resembled skeletal remains than an apartment building. It was a playground of exposed rebar, unprotected ledges, open elevator shafts, and stairwells littered with graffiti that housed the occasional squatter from time to time. A few years back a teenager fell to his death from the upper reaches of the building while skateboarding. It was an 'enter at your own risk' scenario, with an unpatrolled fence bordering the property that had more loose openings than a five-dollar hooker. Needless to say Robin and Jon had been overly careful navigating it tonight, just after midnight when the streets were calming and most people were asleep. One by one they had carried the tapestries and additional equipment from Wil's to the fortieth floor, and minute by minute time had been running away with the night. They underestimated how long three trips would take, and by the time they were through, a faint light was present in the east. Within an hour the morning sun would pass above the horizon, and by then they'd have overstayed their welcome in these vacant towers. Luckily, they had not needed to travel very far from the stairwell they chose to find the edge of the building that faced Omega.

When the third and final roll of tapestry landed with a thud at the setup spot, both men took a moment to catch their breath.

The tapestries were the result of five long days and late nights spent working in Wil's apartment stenciling, painting, and drying. The latter had cost them many hours, as the size of his space was so small, and the tapestries were so large, that they could only paint one tapestry at a time, one section at a time, making the drying process awfully time consuming. Additionally, Wil reinforced from the get-go how crucial of a task stenciling was to ensure that the three pieces lined up correctly. Their patience endured, though; the trio had created a banner worthy of their message.

What made the tapestries so heavy was not just their monstrous length, but the fact that the very bottom of each roll had weights sewn into the fabric to help keep the banner taut and combat wind gusts. The last thing the trio wanted was to have their hard work foiled by a mere breeze. What good was a message if the sentences never once line up? Each tapestry was rolled tightly and laid out in proper order on the concrete floor along with the rest of their supplies, which Wil had carried up on the first trip. Jon had set up a dim battery-powered light to not only aid them in their task but to avoid the abrupt movement of flashlights that could draw unwanted attention to their operation.

The idea was simple: The top side of each tapestry was rigged with metal rings to be used as both the ultimate support from which the banner would hang and as a means to pull the three lengths across the span of open air between buildings Alpha and Omega. In building Alpha, Robin and Jon would thread the rings of each tapestry through a rope/wire combo. Once threaded, they would then tie the rope/wire combo to the end of a generous length of fishing line. Next, Robin would shoot an arrow tied with the opposite end of fishing line across the span, to Wil, who would secure the line in building Omega. Using the fishing line, Wil would then pull the rope and wire across. Once the rope/wire combo was across the span, Wil would separate the rope from the wire, fasten the rope as tight as possible to a specific beam and allow Jon and Robin to do the same, making it taut on both ends. In Alpha, the wire would be cut and fastened over the first ring in line, stringing the entire tapestry along the rope as Wil pulled the wire. Being in three pieces, the two gaps in fabric would have their first and last rings tied together with spare wire, making the total rings of the tapestry one unit, like a shower curtain moving along a rod. The bottom corners of each tapestry had rings attached as well that would be connected as they reached the edge of the building – a simple measure to maintain unity.

While Robin opened his bow case and began assembling his gear, Jon stood near the edge of the building, a look of uncertainty growing on his face. The wind was gusting and Wil's little circle of light shone on the floor of building Omega across what seemed a farther distance than he recollected. On paper, the idea was straightforward. However, the reality of spanning the gap had him questioning Robin's judgement.

"This looks kinda far, man," he called out.

"I paced it out," Robin replied. "It's seventy-seven yards between buildings."

"You sure you can make it?"

"My sight has a fifty-yard pin. I'll use that."

"So. . .no?"

"No what?"

"You're not sure you can make it?"

"No-*yes*. I just have to aim high."

"Guess, you mean?"

"*Estimate* I think is a better word but, fine. Yeah. I'm guessing."

Jon ran a hand over his face and exhaled in exasperation. "I didn't realize that."

Robin looked up from his case. "Stop worrying. You're freaking me out. This isn't that big of a deal."

"You're shooting a fucking arrow directly at Wil. It's a *little* bit of a deal. I mean, we're forty stories high."

"He's gonna move out of the way for Christ's sake. I'm not just gonna shoot the thing." He had an arrow in hand and was loosening the plastic knock from the arrow shaft in a twisting motion. "Remember the signs we went over?"

Jon was less than satisfied as he observed the swirling breeze. "What about the wind, though?"

"I'm not worried about left to right. I need to make sure it lands on the same floor as Wil or else I gotta shoot again. I want this to be one-and-done." He held out the reel of fishing line. "Come here. Take this."

Jon grabbed the reel and took a look at the equipment in the bow case. Robin's bow had a camouflage pattern on the limbs and body. The dim light they had set up caused four pins to glow in the bow's sight housing—yellow, red, green, and orange—from top to bottom indicating different range settings. There were four additional arrows in his quiver, a black sheathed hunting knife, a release aid, a small spray bottle, four years' worth of expired hunting permits, and a spare mesh facemask stuffed in the corner of the case. Jon looked to have a few curiosities about the gear, but he held his tongue.

"Alright," Robin announced. "Tie this to the rope and uncoil fifty arm's-lengths of line into the bucket, how I showed you. That should be well over a hundred yards, which'll be plenty for the shot."

He walked over to the building's edge and set his bow lightly on the concrete floor while Jon began stripping the reel. He took a quick glance at the upcoming shot and focused on Wil's flashlight that marked the floor, arrow still in hand.

"Lay it out right," he cautioned Jon. "If there's a snag or if it gets caught on itself, it'll make the arrow fall."

"I'm doing it how you showed me!" Jon snapped, extending his arms to full length and back somewhat hastily, unraveling the line.

Unsatisfied, Robin went over to take a look at his progress.

"I got it," Jon said defensively.

"Relax. I'm checking the bucket." Despite Jon's speed the line was coiling onto itself properly for a controlled unwinding. After a minute Jon finished and cut the line, handing the end to Robin.

"That's fifty," he said and watched Robin wrap some line around the rear of the arrow. "How's that going to hold?"

"This is the knock," Robin said, pointing to a plastic piece on the end of the arrow. "It's how you clip the arrow to the string. They're interchangeable, see?" He removed the piece from the shaft and returned it to its place. "So I'm just loosening it enough to tie a knot and then I'll jam it back in. Crimp it, so to speak." He did so and then reached in his pocket. "Tape just to be safe," he said as he tore a short piece of black electrical tape off of a roll and wrapped the end of the arrow.

Robin left Jon and returned to the edge, eying Wil's position in building Omega. Across the span, Wil's flashlight had remained motionless since he and Jon began their setup, forming a tight circle of light on the concrete floor at his feet. Robin motioned three quick waves over the beam of his flashlight, signaling to Wil that he was ready to shoot. Ten seconds went by without a reply signal. Robin mumbled and signaled again, and again Wil's light remained still. An ironic smile formed on his face.

"Motherfucker's sleeping," Robin laughed.

“No he’s not,” said Jon, looking up from the bucket and line. His hulking figure was a partial shadow with dark, indistinct pillars about him that seemed to go on forever. He sounded as if he was trying to convince himself by the tone of his voice.

Robin whistled into the span. The wind picked up and whistled back as the only unwelcome response. Next he yelled an abrupt “Yo!” to no avail. He looked to Jon, who shrugged, then looked back at the building.

“Do I go get him?” Jon asked. “Like wha–”

“No. We don’t have time for this shit. It’s getting light out.”

“Is he seriously asleep?”

Robin froze for a moment and blinked. “Get ready.”

“What are you doing?”

“Just get ready,” he repeated. “Bring the bucket over. And the rope.”

With one hand, Robin removed his hat and ran his fingers through his hair. He returned the hat backwards on his head and took a stance to pull his bow to full draw.

“Dude, no. . .”

Robin knocked the arrow, allowing the fishing line to drape over his wrist unobstructed, and raised the bow.

“I can’t watch this,” cried Jon.

Yet he did watch the bottom cam rollover as Robin pulled, the bow’s limbs bending like two trees in a storm. Robin inhaled as his cheek met his string.

“Oh I really can’t watch this,” Jon whined.

Robin tuned him out. The circle of Wil’s flashlight was a good enough target at which to aim. The wind howled and gusted as Robin judged the amount of drop his arrow might experience in flight. He decided to place his pin on what would be the ceiling of Wil’s floor, which would (hopefully) allow for just enough drop.

A strong, taunting gust came through the funnel between the buildings as if daring Robin to shoot. He held steady, ready to wait out the wind for the perfect shot opportunity. His bow had significant let-off in its pull, but to be at full draw for too long would compromise even the best archer’s abilities. After nearly a minute he began to waver.

“Don’t do it,” Jon chirped, watching between the fingers of the left hand he had placed on his face.

Finally, the wind settled to a breeze and with a thrum, Robin loosed. The pair immediately lost sight of the arrow in the darkness beyond. The air was silent, and for a bare moment, the only movement was the thin line streaming out of the bucket. Both men focused on the small circle of light in the other building, Jon praying under his breath and Robin intent on spotting the arrow's impact.

"I lost it," Rob began.

Just then, the glimmer of Wil's flashlight shook violently and fell to the ground, winking out into darkness.

". . .Jesus Christ," Jon lamented.

"Uh. . ."

"Jesus Christ, you fuckin' hit him. Please tell me you didn't hit him." He started pacing behind Robin, pulling on his hair so his hands didn't go in for a chokehold.

"Oh boy. . ." Robin piped. "Hah."

"Are you *fucking kidding me*? I *told* you–" Jon growled, stomping over towards Robin.

"Wait, wait!"

Across the way, light began to flicker until it was again a full beam. Wil made a frantic signal and screamed an obscenity across the gap. Though distant, it was clear that he was then turning around to go search for the arrow and secure the line. He scanned the ground behind him. It was too much for Robin to hold his laughter. Jon, on the other hand, squatted down to the floor to collect himself, breathing a sigh of relief.

"Oh he's gonna be pissed," he said, rubbing his eyes.

"Ah, let him."

"You're fucked up. Oh, you are – you're just. . ."

Robin smiled, composing himself. "Let's do this."

He made a second signal to Wil, waving the flashlight twice above his head. Then the process began. The trio worked steadily but quickly as daylight peeked its head over the distant horizon. Within a minute, Wil had the rope/wire combo in his hands. After a fine knot job, Wil signaled for Jon to fasten his end of the rope, which he yanked as taut as a powerline. While Jon finished securing the knot on their end, Robin unrolled as much of the fabric as possible to reduce the stress on the rope as each piece unraveled and submitted to gravity. It didn't do much to stop the tension, but it was something.

The rope bounced and swayed each time the weighted tapestries were dropped. By the third, it was sagging slightly. Altogether, though, the banner was hung without a hitch and the trio made to escape with haste. The only supplies left to carry were Robin's bow case, a small roll of fishing line, and their lighting equipment.

Their descent was a blur. They raced down the forty flights and found Wil waiting for them at the building's exit, eyes skyward. A soft ripple greeted them as they reunited and Robin and Jon turned to look upon their project. High above, their banner swayed and wiggled in a delayed motion. The sections caught the breeze and used it in tandem, connecting the seams as if it were one piece, separating at times but never more than a few feet apart. The message was completely legible, the sky around it like a watercolor painting, brushed in hues of pink, yellow, and orange.

"Let's see the news ignore that one," Robin said.

Chapter 17: Photobomb

With her right hand, Marian reached for the event programs in the perfectly halved geode centered on the cloth "Welcome" table before her, exposing the fair skin of her bicep between her shawl and her black satin elbow-length glove. The reach required her to bend a little at the hip toward the shimmering purple crystals, creating a momentary space between her low-cut gown and her cleavage, drawing the attention of two young men on the other side of the table like a magnet. When she turned away, she wondered if the two men had requested that particular station for its robust view. She couldn't blame them, she supposed. To them it was probably the best position in the house.

Even though it was just her and Dalton that evening, she made sure to grab a third program. She had taken an extra program at every ball, show, or sporting event since she was seven, when her father starting bringing her to baseball games. It had been a boring sport to Marian, even at that age, but her father had loved it, and baseball became a tradition of theirs for most of her childhood. They would always sit in one of the luxury boxes, with whomever her father had targeted as a business interest that month. If said target had a child, his or her presence would make the games tolerable for Marian. When it was just her and a group of grown men, however, boredom crept in; especially between innings or during pitching changes. First, her father tried to keep her occupied with souvenirs. When that failed, he sought to entertain her with food. When she thereafter threw up a hot dog and two boxes of Cracker Jacks on a potential client, he all but gave up. At that point it was full-count. She was on the verge of refusing to go any longer and he was willing to oblige. Just before all hope was lost, though, he saw Marian perk up while watching a paper glider slowly spiraling towards one of the lower decks of the stadium. She'd never seen anything like it, and wondered how something so small and delicate could fly with such ease. Noticing her awe he called her over to the ledge. "Want to make your own?" he had asked. Marian still remembered the excitement of the first glider she made out of the cover of the game's program, how her father had told her to keep it as flat as possible in order to make it float, how the little plane had left her grip, causing her to light up as bright as the stadium scoreboard, overwhelmed with a new sense of exhilaration. When she had voiced her concern that the glider might crash into someone in the rows below them, her father had chuckled. "It's just paper, my dear," he said. "Besides, even if they get mad, they're way down there and we're all the way up here." From that game on, she always made it a point to collect an extra program, just in case she had the opportunity to make a quick glider or two. It struck her, just then, that no matter how hard she tried, she never once could make one reach the field.

Programs in hand, Marian glided a few paces across the marble floor, through a two-story stone archway that led into the main corridor ahead of her. Her black dress was made of the same material as her gloves and fit in a similar fashion. *Tight.* Almost too tight. She had a feeling it would become increasingly constricting as the night went on, but so be it. As she crossed the threshold into the sprawling expanse she was met with an overload of the senses and a visual clash of tastes nothing short of epic in proportion.

Outlandish, peculiar, uncanny and *stunning* were among the adjectives she'd have used to describe the emotions that came over her. To see a place she had visited over one hundred times in her life transformed in such a way took more than a moment to process. Before she could manage a mere assessment of the atrium, a white-gloved attendant entered her field of vision with an outstretched hand, inviting her in the direction of seating assignment. He was wearing a lovely pressed tuxedo with a lapel pin celebrating the Sestercentennial event.

"Your seating card is just that way, ma'am," the man said with an elegant accent.

"Oh, yes. Thank you."

"Enjoy your evening," he concluded before returning several steps back to his post, a smiled glued to his freshly shaven face.

To her left, she realized, was an absolutely colossal 'table' holding the miniature seating arrangement cards for the evening's proceedings. In order to determine the table to which she and Dalton had been assigned as well as discover what the mysterious shape was, she approached the massive, round, thigh-high object. The three well-dressed guards positioned around the upper portion of the table only piqued her interest further. Only when she was upon the construct did she realize the breadth of her social destiny that night.

Before her rested the largest horizontal cross-section of a tree in the entire world. The diameter was such that she had to literally turn her head in order to see from end to end. A little placard standing next to the specimen dated it as ~2400 years old. Taking a closer look, she noticed little flags marking specific concentric rings with major historical events that had taken place throughout the span of the tree's life. Evidently, the tree started its life around the same time as Aristotle, in 384 B.C. *Unbelievable!*

Utter fascination enveloped Marian as she followed the timeline through the tree's life, reading some twenty-five notations of major events in human history. Each flag indicated how wide the tree would have been, from its center, at the year of the listed event. She noted some:

126: Pantheon completed in Rome
868: Earliest known printed book with a date. China.
1001: Leif Ericson lands on American coast
1050: The astrolabe is first used in Europe
1117: The University of Oxford is founded
1215: The Magna Carta is sealed by John of England
1325: The Aztecs found the city of Tenochtitlan
1665: Robert Hook discovers the cell

The dates were curious to her. She'd have imagined typically petty inclusions such as "Columbus sailed the ocean blue," "the Pilgrim Landings," or basic religious references. To her, the listed events reflected more truly the progress of humankind. The detail made her smile. Then she noticed a flag at the very edge of the tree.

1776: The Declaration of Independence is adopted by the Continental Congress.

She laughed at seeing how close to the edge the signing of the Declaration of Independence lay. *We're so young, yet screwed up already beyond recognition. Hopefully this is just our society's rebellious adolescence. The cheap tattoos and piercings, however, are permanent. Those stains can't be washed away; the holes can never be filled in. We'll all grow up one day, including me, or we'll go the way of tragedy. In the meantime. . .*

Marian bent down, squinting in the low light at the volume of choices in front of her while the guards got their looks in. Secretly she hoped someone would remark on her dress's homage to Audrey Hepburn, though she left a bit less to the imagination than Audrey had. Her necklace and hairstyle was quite simpler, too.

Alright where are you, card? M-Mariah. . .no. . .Marianne. . . not quite. . . Maria. . . When her name evaded her, she focused on finding Dalton's. She had to browse the cards for over a half-minute before she located the one with 'Mr. Dalton White & Guest' inscribed in hand-written calligraphy. *Guest...? 'Oh hi, I'm Dalton's girlfriend, Guest. Thrilled to be here.'. . . I guess my spot was up for question. Perhaps there were others in line?* She reached in and delicately plucked the card from the ancient arbor. With one last look she pondered it briefly. She supposed it was a Giant Sequoia or Redwood from out West. On its outer edge was a final flag. The tree had been cut down in 1888. Only God knows why.

She turned to face the gala, still focused on the card, and had her attention broken by cackles of laughter in the distance. The crowd in the atrium was widely subdued, making the source of the outburst easy to spot. She pinpointed Dalton amongst a group of other young men and their "guests" getting a laugh out of a likely inane reference. Rather than throw herself into that shit-show, she decided to snake her way through the aisles, for lack of a better word, to take in all the wonders before her. She glanced back at the card. *& Guest,* she wondered.

We belong to nobody, and nobody belongs to us. We don't even belong to each other.

Officer Brody Ortmann itched at his scalp and ear for the hundredth time. *Fucking assholes,* he thought as he rubbed a familiar path along his hairline. *Who puts itching powder in someone's hat?* Just two months ago he had been sworn in as a police officer, and the rookie hazing stories he had heard about were beginning to prove true. He was telling people he had been a police officer for eight months, even though six of those were spent at the academy. Since Brody had always been the type of man who needed third party approval, he indulged in minor inflations or exclusions when discussing personal accomplishments. No one had the heart to tell him those six months didn't count.

The alleyway Brody occupied was wet from afternoon rain showers. The weather of late had proven to be quite unpredictable for December, with hovering temperatures indicative of an incredibly late winter. Brody curled his nose as a whiff of the nearby dumpster tickled his nostrils. A soft stench of garbage lingered in the atmosphere. It was a sneaky smell, showing itself just as one forgot it was there. His frustrations about tonight's orders presented themselves in dejection and aloofness. *This isn't why I became a cop.* He huffed and leaned even deeper against the brick alleyway wall.

Brody had wanted to be a police officer because he wanted respect. He was never popular in high school and dropped out of college because he drank too much. To add in the misfortune he couldn't keep his job as an electrician's apprentice because he was scared of heights. Life in a lower-middle-class Irish neighborhood held less opportunity than a snowball fight in hell, according to Brody's father. And no one argued with Brody's father. He thought by joining the force he would be solving crimes, joining a fraternity, and gaining the respect of the citizens. Not to mention a better paycheck than his father ever brought home. Girls loved a man in uniform, didn't they? But instead of realizing his grandeurs, he'd been directing traffic, changing tires and, like today, pulling extended shifts of guard duty on the loading dock behind this glorified birthday party while those inside celebrated in excess. That's what you get when your uncle, a high-brass, places you in the silver-spoon precinct so you don't have to pay your dues running the midnight shift in the projects.

Brody was an example of a man slithering through life under the radar of those around him, searching halfheartedly for a meaningful existence. Despite his six-two, two-hundred-and-forty-five-pound stature, Brody was a person others bumped into on the sidewalk because they legitimately didn't notice him, then cursed at him for not watching where he was going.

"Hey officer, can you give us a hand over here?"

Brody's brooding session was cut short by a trio of bakers struggling to open a loading dock door for what looked like a rather large delivery. His self-reflection, along with the noise of late rush hour traffic on the nearby avenue, must have made him oblivious to the clunky white van parked at the entrance of the alleyway. *Snap out of it, Brody.* He quickly looked around to make sure there was no one else in the alley worth his attention, pushed off the brick wall with his left foot, and waddled over to the loading dock.

"How can I help you guys?" he asked, attempting to replicate the stern voice his captain used in the interrogation room.

"Can you hold the loading door open at the top of the ramp? This is the cake for the birthday celebration and we can't carry it in *and* hold the door. Our boss will mix us in with the next batch of batter if we mess up even one icing rose."

"Hey, this is off limits, guys. You should try the front entrance."

"*Please*, sir, we just came from there. We already tried asking the guys up front but they directed us here. It's supposed to be a surprise. My boss will *kill* me if it's blown. Please."

Overworked and stressed, the shorter man pleading his case looked like he could use a shower and a good night's sleep. Brody radioed to the officer at the entrance and confirmed their story. *Must've sent them here so I had to deal with it. Should have known something like this would happen.*

Brody wondered if this might be an opportunity for him to earn a little respect from someone in the city. Hell, the Mayor might even come to thank him for helping with the delivery. *Alright.* He hustled over and held the door open while trying to maintain a dominant pose. The trio struggled to safely walk the cake in, but managed to do so without damage or compromising the loose plastic cover. Once through the door the short man turned back to the cop while the other two continued to baby the cake down the hallway.

"Here, let me help you the rest of the way," Brody offered kindly.

"Nah, nah. You're good. We got it from here."

"Oh. . . Are you sure?" he asked.

"Thank you officer, I owe you one," the man said as he turned from the door to follow his colleagues.

"Oh, alright. Not a problem. Good luck in there." He let go of the door and returned to his post, aggravated at the missed opportunity. *Guess they didn't need me after all. So much for that.* He exhaled deeply and looked over at the van. His eyes weren't good enough to make out the full name, but he swore it said, "Le Petit Explosif."

The Wombach Institute of Art and Natural History occupied seven city blocks in east Fort Dearborn, and was known worldwide for its impressive and extensive collections in all disciplines, most notably from the Ancient Greek and Ancient Roman eras. While the museum had maintained a hefty price of admission for its first hundred years, presently it was the only free-to-the-public museum within the city limits courtesy of the Wombach family's endowment infusion. The Institute had become so revered that many allege the Louvre would loan the Venus di Milo if Alice Wombach, the current Chairwoman, batted her eyes and asked nicely.

Tonight marked the 250th Birthday of Fort Dearborn. On round number milestones, such as tonight, the city elite would gather at the Wombach Institute and congratulate themselves on a job well done, creating a city better today than it was yesterday, and looking ahead to future greatness. Politicians, business leaders, lobbyists, and customary representation from all well-known families were certainly in attendance. Businessmen were hatching mergers or takeovers, politicians schmoozing donors, and lobbyists kissing as much ass as possible, claiming they had the most logical stance on the current bills being discussed on the city's congressional floor. A giant chess match was occurring on this museum's grounds and not one player knew precisely which piece they were. In the end, though, they were all pawns to Marian.

Where she presently meandered was the epicenter of "Dinosaur Alley," as the wing had been dubbed. A massive open room, Dinosaur Alley acted as a focal point to the extensive geological, archeological, and paleontological exhibit. Its magnificent atrium had an arched and coffered ceiling, Corinthian columns on the perimeter, marble floors, and five exit points. Four of the exits (offshoots more or less) led into deeper sections of Dinosaur Alley, broken up by geological era: Pre-Paleozoic, Paleozoic, Mesozoic, and Cenozoic. The fifth exit was a doorway back to the entrance hall rotunda connecting to the main gates of the museum, the same direction from which Marian had come and the only way out of this wing other than a tributary from the Cenozoic exhibit to the cafeteria.

It was no secret that Marian was fascinated with museums. It had been her reputation as a child to linger behind her family at exhibits, trying to read each description, soaking up as much knowledge as she could, while her parents and older brothers took in the superficial sights to merely check them off the list. In her mind's eye, she saw herself as an archeologist in an alternate life, travelling to exotic locales and leading the most important digs of her time. In this life, though, law was her dig.

She wondered why, even in this museum, the lights were always dim. It was as if the curators were forcing you to become intimate with the artifacts, to approach them closely and absorb their story. Or maybe it subconsciously made the patrons quieter. Either way, she preferred the ambiance as she wandered, encountering displays littered between dinner tables highlighting the most popular exhibits within the museum. Her first stop was a second-century marble statue of Dionysus (or Bacchus). Sculptors of that era were famous for their contrapposto style of human form. The standing sculptures, such as this one, typically exhibited uneven weight distribution, creating a more dramatic, life-like feel. Most Roman sculptures, such as this, were copies of Greek sculptures with different names attributed to the Gods. Marian rarely praised her collegiate Art History professor, but her voice resonated within her in this instant. Very few original Ancient Greek sculptures remained, as most were Roman replicas. This was just such a copy.

She glided onward. The gemological exhibit was all about shock value. Somehow, the curators managed to obtain one of the largest columnar Selenite crystal formations ever mined, recently excavated out of a valley in Mexico. The cave from which it came was allegedly several hundred meters underground, and so hot that miners had to wear special suits in order to extract the specimen. Apparently this was the only sample that would ever make it out of that cave; it was to be flooded in the coming months, returning it back to its original state before humans ever stepped foot inside. A middle-aged man beside her remarked at how it reminded him of something out of Superman's Fortress of Solitude. She smiled and nodded, having no idea what he was talking about.

There were roughly half a dozen "exhibits" arranged for the evening's celebration, not to mention individual pieces on display towards the perimeter of the atrium. The only qualm she had with the curator's picks was the exemption of her very favorite exhibit in the museum: The Arms & Armor exhibit. Missing something as breathtaking as The Third Earl of Cumberland's suit of armor, for instance, was a misstep. Marian brushed off the thought and made her way through most of the remaining exhibits before she arrived at her table.

Among all of the wonders in this one room, it wasn't until she sat down that she noticed the regular inhabitants of the hall. The gigantic Braccheasorus "Darlene" on any other occasion would have dominated the scene, but it wasn't until she came to the farther reaches of the room that she noticed the silent warder. A superb string quartet was playing classical favorites nearby, under Darlene's jagged shadow, adding to the odd feeling Marian had previously registered that the whole setup was just eccentric. She looked upward and upward, past Darlene, and settled on the pterodactyls hanging from the ceiling. *Just shocks the senses. And they all love it. I guess it's useful being top banana in the shock department.*

Brody's right hand shot to his gun at the sound of a tremendously loud boom. *Shots?* With wide eyes he cautiously turned left, saw the same short baker strutting down the ramp angrily, and realized the heavy metal exit door slamming against a dumpster had been the source of the alarming noise. He recoiled without delay. A rush of heat overwhelmed him, fearful as he was that by some clairvoyance his fellow officers had witnessed the mistaken action and would exploit it in devising their next prank against him.

The baker huffed for a second, kicked a can, and then turned to find Brody. This brightened his demeanor. He put his hands in his pockets and strolled toward him with a newfound smile painted on his face. Brody pretended not to notice.

"Evenin', sir!" the man chirped.

"Evening," replied Brody plainly.

"Hey, thanks for helping us back there. How ya doin' tonight?"

"Fine," he offered with a nod.

The stranger fanned his shirt, showing signs of perspiration. He walked past Brody and leaned against the brick wall to his right. "Can't believe this weather we've been havin'. What's up with that?"

Brody paused. *The weather* is *pretty warm these days. . . No matter. Just focus on the job.* He continued his overt attempt to appear uninterested in chatting with the newcomer. "Eh. I'm not a weatherman."

"Indian summer they call it. I don't think that's politically correct anymore, though."

The cop shrugged and scanned the vacant alleyway.

"Can't say shit these days. . ." the man continued before raising his finger as if remembering an important incident. "Swear to God I saw a few dandelions this week. I heard on the radio it'll stay warm 'til spring, but that's bullshit. It's not even January yet. I'd bet my next load it'll snow before spring comes." The man fished a pack of cigarettes out of his breast pocket and extended the goods towards Brody. "Smoke?" he asked eagerly.

Brody peered over in acknowledgment and quickly dismissed him. "Can't on the job. Thanks though."

"No problem. Always offer our city's finest. Like I said before, I owe you one." The man finished the statement with a wink and placed a cigarette in his mouth before returning the pack to his pocket. "Hey, you wanna laugh?"

"Sure," Brody replied casually.

"It's always the firemen that join me, ha-ha-ha."

In spite of himself, the statement made Brody smirk.

"Even more ironic is they never have a light, ha-ha-ha-ha."

Brody joined in with a low chuckle and watched the guy take a Zippo out and light the cigarette. A heavy pull filled the man's lungs and brought an ecstasy-fueled quiver to his eyelids. He held. And held. And finally released both the pull and the tension in his body. Brody watched in envy. *Damn it. I should have joined him.*

"My brother was a fireman. Died in a six-alarm fire uptown a few years ago," the man said.

"That's an honorable way to go out."

"Not really. Had a thing for uniforms, but I'm sure you know what that's like. Hey," he added immediately, "you ever hear what the one pissed off tampon said to the other?"

"What."

"Nothing. They were both stuck-up cunts, ha-ha-ha-ha-ha!"

The pair shared a good laugh and Brody found himself feeling somewhat looser. *Got a joker on my hands.*

"C'mon, man, no one cares. Have a smoke with me," the man pressed.

"Alright, fuck it." *No one* does *care. Else I wouldn't be left out here.*

"Cool. My name's Bill," the man said, offering an outstretched hand.

"Officer Ortmann."

The two shook hands, Brody struck by the other's lifeless grip, which absolutely irritated him. *Weakling.*

"Yeah I read your tag, what's your wife call ya though?"

"Brody. And I'm not married."

"Oh, that must be lonely." Bill took another drag on his cigarette to seemingly let the comment sink in.

". . .Not quite," Brody managed, slightly confused and wholly aggravated by the remark. He had been finding the man tolerable, but the feeling slowly evaporated.

"No, I'm just sayin'. Seems like a demanding job. Can't really pull tail while you're working, am I right?"

"You'd be surprised," he bluffed.

Bill locked eyes with Brody with sudden intensity. "Surprise me."

With a long drag, Officer Ortmann cursed himself and weighed the options for a redeeming reply. Bill didn't give him time.

"'Cuz if you ask me, you couldn't get your dick wet if you stuck a hose down your pants."

Marian put her coat and her bag down on the seat next to her to save it for Dalton. She had called him this morning with every intention to end it "officially," but when he asked her to attend the event, for some reason she committed. *Maybe one last attempt. Maybe not.* While Dalton was surely looking to conduct voir dire with the politicians to see which one was most likely to take a bribe, Marian was stuck playing seat warmer, coat hanger, and basic arm candy. . .without the arm. With no one with whom to pass the time, she focused her attention on the third program she'd collected. She removed her satin gloves, a faux pas under these circumstances, but, considering her attitude towards the evening, she didn't much give a shit. Permitting her hands to breathe outweighed her interest in maintaining her intended look. *I think the gloves are going to stay off, Audrey. This may be where we part ways tonight, darling.*

Now, there were several keys to gliders most amateurs overlooked. Crisp folds and symmetry were the easy ones. She started working precisely with a middle crease, and then began to form the left wing and the right–

"Is this seat taken, Miss?"

Her concentration was broken by an elderly man and his wife who looked like they had just skipped the local early bird special and were regretting it. She decided to show some compassion.

"Not at all. I can move in so you two love birds can have the aisle seats." When the elderly man saw her smile she was worried his knees might buckle and cave in. Luckily he was holding on to his cane quite steadily.

"Thank you kindly, Miss," the man said and he and his wife began the drawn out, slow-motion dance of positioning themselves in their seats. *God forbid they have to use the bathroom.*

Even though the construction of a glider is a short process, she had to fend off 4 other vultures looking for seats. Each time her defense used a little more venom. *It's on your fucking place card,* she had wanted to say. She finally finished the miniature aircraft, sans the last step, which was to invert the nose. Most overlooked the fact that the conventional paper airplane was too large and caught too much air, like a parachute, losing velocity well before the target. Inverting the nose provided a better center of gravity, lower air resistance, and truer flight pattern. She smirked, imagining Dalton's reaction if she tried to explain that to him.

The thought brought a deeper, sneaky grin to her face as she skimmed the crowd, hoping to test him out as a target. He was to her two o'clock, across the orchestra section near the stage. At that distance, though, the throw was too far and the view too obstructed. She dropped the glider to her lap but kept her gaze. His lumbar curve was perfect, chest out, shoulders level and raised. He had spent thirty minutes that evening deciding to go stubble or no stubble and in the end, chose no. The opposite of what Marian was hoping for. She then played out the scenario if she were to throw the glider and manage to hit him. She would giggle and make a purposefully poor attempt at hiding. He would ignore it or play it off, or chastise her to his companions, all while his inner fire raged on, counting the minutes until he could confront her and tell her how she'd never understand business and should grow up. The thought brought a somber blanket over her in her seat and forced all possibility of excitement or enjoyment from the night right out of her body. *Maybe there will be a bacon cheeseburger on the menu.*

She scanned the audience closer, then, and noticed most all the wives and girlfriends obediently waiting for their men to return to them. They were walking, smiling, and breathing pieces of jewelry their husbands wore out on special occasions. It was like a museum within a museum or the night of the living dead. Her heart sunk at the thought of that future for her, and immediately knew how the night must end. Getting there, though, was a different beast.

It was quite ironic to Marian that an event such as this be held in a location such as this. If the dinner this evening had been informally held one day earlier, all in attendance, even the general public, could have come for free. Yet, in the company of "movers and shakers" such was not acceptable. Place a $2,500 price tag on the plated dinner, and a different "public" emerged. *I bet half the people here are here for their first time. I bet the other half are so old they don't even know where they are.* If Marian could snap her fingers and disintegrate all the people in the room who were full of shit, it would be a lonely and quiet night for her. She may as well go home.

A few minutes later, Dalton approached with a victorious grin indicating some strategic success on the battlefield, strutting along the floor like his own little battalion drum corps. His tuxedo was immaculate. Something you'd see in a Hollywood awards show. Next came a move Marian despised. Unbutton the jacket. Head slightly left, hips slightly right, flap the jacket out briefly and then a dramatic drop into the seat. It seemed a trademark assumption that everyone in the given assembly cared that he had decided to sit down. The worst part was that she would have to watch the same move in rewind when he stood up.

"Okay. Glad that's over," Dalton said out loud. "Thanks for coming tonight, M." He squeezed her leg right above her right knee gently, a move that months ago would have whet her appetite, but tonight dried her up like an apricot in the sun.

"Where else would I be?" she replied sarcastically, changing positions so his hand fell.

He appeared oblivious to the snide reaction, or was hiding his own to remain in control. Either way she was unsurprised. Back-and-forth countering had constituted a majority of their dialogues of late.

Marian watched him move his head back and forth as he looked towards the stage area. "Can you move down one?"

Her shoulders sank. "I've already moved down three."

"I want to have a better view of the speech."

"Selfish," she said with feigned sass and a head sway.

He shot her a look. "That's the third time you've said that to me today."

"Second. And I'm only half kidding."

"I don't read minds, Marian. I read tones. And you've had a tone all fucking week."

"I think you're tone deaf."

"I *think* I should have come by myself."

"*I* think you'll be getting rather used to that."

He gave her another sideways glance. In unison, the distant pair downed their champagne and had the flutes filled by a passing waiter.

The event was about to begin, with most all seated, but her thoughts were consumed with how she was going to break up with him. She wanted to have the satisfaction of doing so, not the other way around, and needed to plan the best method, with a little added "fuck you" on top.

Maybe she would just call him out about that blonde from dinner weeks back. She knew something had happened, but not how far it had gone. For that though, she would need some liquid courage. Luckily, the waiters seemed to be on conveyor belts.

Just walk away, right now. Leave the museum and move on. There's nothing here for you. But she couldn't do it. Was it fear? Uncertainty? Lack of confidence? Whatever it was shackled her feet together and bound her arms to the chair. The longer she thought of wanting to leave without leaving, the more the reigns tightened, blurring her vision with tears. Blinking, she realized there was already a whirr of conversation developing about the table. *Don't let them catch you.*

She didn't know any of the individuals at the table this time. Dalton's usual set of ringers were littered about the room and for that, Marian was grateful. She knew better, though, than to wish for something redeeming to emerge from this group.

"This is quite a lovely venue. I can't say I've visited before," some woman said.

"Indeed, they've truly made this elegant," replied a man.

"What a wondrous beast that is," a different, clone-like woman said.

Marian didn't care who the voices came from. She hadn't even taken a moment to look at the individuals at her table. *Nearly four months and the word love never crossed my mind, let alone my lips.*

"I'd like to return to this place, I rather enjoy it. Must we schedule an appointment?" remarked a middle-aged woman with a British accent.

"This isn't that type of place," replied Dalton.

"What's the fee, then?" she queried.

Marian recovered and looked up. "Actually, this museum is free to the general public," she declared.

"Is it?" the woman prayed.

"Yep–"

"Well," Dalton interrupted, "perhaps it is free to the *gen*eral public but. . ." He made a hand motion as if presenting the scene in front of them.

"Are we not part of the general public?" asked Marian quizzically.

Her statement was acknowledged with silence from the table. Dalton eyed Marian and then looked at each person at the table, and finally made a sweep of the room.

"Can't say I see any of the general public here," he said with a sneer. The observation brought laughter from the table. "Oh! Maybe those two," he exclaimed, pointing to two bakers in dirty white uniforms paired in a corner some distance away.

The joke brought a second, more raucous, round of laughter from the table. Except for Marian. She met the eyes of one of the bakers, who seemed to have noticed the joke made at their expense. He squinted in curiosity, and she turned back to the table, closing up to await the meal, a gloss of tears enveloping her eyes once again.

"In England they call this 'sucking down a fag.' Ha-ha, did you know that?"

Chuckling, Brody replied, "Can't say I did."

Brody felt satisfaction in making the man fall for his story a few minutes earlier. He wasn't going to let some pissant baker beat him in a verbal match. The alleyway had since grown awfully dark, lit only by a single light beside the loading dock door.

Bill, encased almost entirely in shadow, continued. "Too easy to make fun of that one. I could make a gay joke, butt fuck it."

The pun didn't register. Instead Brody took it in a different direction. "Can't stand 'em, between you and me," he said with a tinge of disgust.

"Englishmen?"

"No, fags."

Bill blinked twice and cracked the slightest of grins. "You probably think I'm a fag dressed like this. . .working at a bakery," he said, waiting intently for Brody to take the bait.

"Wasn't going to say anything. . .but I can think of a more manly job," Brody stated, looking Bill up and down for a brief moment.

"Yeah, well, don't be fooled. I slay pussy, man."

"I bet."

"I beat it up. I dunno if I can compete with your 'bus full cheerleaders' story, though."

The two met eyes, Bill's mocking tone telling all. Against Brody's better judgment, the story hadn't stuck as he once thought. *Time to finish this.*

"What's your job at that bakery? Fudge packer?" Inwardly, Brody rewarded himself for the satisfying jab. Bill, however, appeared outwardly irritated and turned to face the Officer.

"Used to be. I got promoted to cream filler."

"Oh, wow, look at you. From bitch to butch." Brody had recycled this jab from when it had been used on him at the academy.

"Yeah that's it. Was a Bottom for years but I prefer to be on top these days. Filling. You wouldn't know what that's like, though."

"No, I wouldn't. 'Cuz I'm not a *fag*."

"No, I meant you weigh so much you physically can't be on top, fag or not. Seriously, dude, what are you like 300lbs? Look at you. Looks like you visit the bakery more than I do. You'd have to be the Bottom if we were together."

"Keep your fantasies to yourself, kid. And if you think this is dead weight behind this vest you got another thing comin'."

"Yeah? How much you weigh?"

"Two-forty-five. Solid."

"That's cool bro. I'm one-sixty-six. Solid. And speaking of fantasies I think y'all are the ones living a fantasy each day. . . Uniforms, subordinates, emphasis on dominance and submission. . .restraints. Should I go on?"

"You should shut the fuck up if you wanna go home tonight."

"Maybe I'd rather see where you take me, *sir*."

"Time for you to go back inside before you regret it."

Deadlock ensued for a time. Watching his movements, Brody noticed Bill's physique a bit more closely. What appeared, at first, to be a meager man had proven to be an insufficient appraisal. Bill was of just about average height and of average build. His newly rolled sleeves showed veins running through his forearms like shattered glass. He had the hands of a tradesman. But it was Bill who stepped down to diffuse the situation before it hit a boiling point.

"Alright, alright. That got outta hand. I apologize. They won't let me back in anyway. I'm stuck out here. Sorry to get into it with you. That was disrespectful. Been up since yesterday morning planning all of this."

Brody remained on edge as he watched the man run a hand over his face.

"I think what you guys do is great, you know?" Bill added.

"Yeah, well, lotta people are giving us shit these days. You gimme shit, you'll get it back and worse. Just because some cops act one way doesn't mean we all do."

Bill's eyes thinned. "Yeah, nothing's worse than being lumped into a category just because of your job title."

"You said it."

The two returned to a purported stalemate.

The banal platitude of Mayor Crowley's speech dried Marian's tears like the sun does a puddle in the desert. "And may the next 250 years be just as prosperous" achieved quite the applause, enthralling the lemming-like audience. But not Marian. She was tired of high society celebrating each other's victories and ignoring the issues that really plagued the city. She was pleading with whatever higher power there may be to end this speech soon so she could get back to her life, since she was not brave enough to stand up and leave on her own.

While the Mayor was wrapping up his speech at the podium, on the left-hand side of the stage the audience's attention was drawn to an enormous cake being wheeled out by two worse-for-wear bakers. The "oohs" and "ahhs" disrupted the Mayor's flow, and caused him to turn to look at the cake with befuddlement, like an animal looking into a mirror at its own reflection for the first time. He walked over and was met by one of the bakers. A quick whispered exchange brought a smile to the Mayor's face. He skipped back to the podium.

"Ladies and gentlemen, a beautiful cake gifted to us from the *Fort Dearborn Ledger* to help celebrate this wonderful occasion! I would like to invite my cabinet to the stage so we can pose for a photo."

The crowd's noise level rose to that of an idling engine while the cabinet members excitedly gathered on the stage, proud to officially be a part of the occasion. Marian followed the two bakers as they walked offstage towards the corridor to a connecting Wing - the Cenozoic Wing in particular. She looked back to the cake as the mass of people began assembling and took in its features. To put it bluntly, the cake was fairly basic. Two-tiered, the only exception was how large it was. By her judgment it must have been four feet in diameter at its base and almost a foot tall per tier. The 250th signification rested against the second tier in a charming gold material.

Then Marian did a double take as she glanced again in the direction of the bakers. She'd imagined they would have left at that point, but some motion held her gaze for long enough to spot the two men huddled behind some lighting equipment against the wall just before the corridor. They seemed to be arguing over something with their backs to her.

What kept her attention was a move the man made. When the two turned around to face the cake, a floodlight illuminated the shorter one, just briefly, as he shifted his position. While the larger man kept his hat low on his brow, the other took his hat off, ran his hands through his hair, and placed it backwards on his head. His face, fully exposed for the first time, revealed him to be a shockingly handsome man. His arms were folded and he looked invigorated, in drastic contrast to his apparent exhaustion on stage a moment ago. When the light faded away from him several moments later, she pursed her lips together in acceptance and returned her focus on the upcoming photo op.

The Mayor and his cabinet, eleven in total, encircled the cake, all pointing gleefully at the bold "250th" on its front. Suddenly, just as the first flash from the photographer's camera went off, the cake exploded with an earsplitting *'pop,'* flinging debris in every direction. On instinct alone, Marian immediately clutched her jacket and purse, thinking her life was about to come to an end.

The blackness of night had descended upon the two men. Neither realized its presence, nor the lingering stench of trash creeping about the dock. Olfactory fatigue had taken root as a result of overexposure to the sweet-sharp organic decay, and the men stood casually in the rather unbefitting locale.

"You ever save anyone's life?"

This guy never stops. "Uh, about four months ago I delivered a baby in a supermarket. Ambulance got stuck in traffic."

"*Wow* that's great, man. Power to you. Need more cops like you around here."

The distant, adjacent avenue held a steady buzz of traffic. Rush hour had abated a while back, and the obligatory horns and sirens with it. Audibility had thenceforth been clarified.

"Just doin' my job," Brody shrugged.

"Ever have to. . .you know. . ." Bill made his hand into the form of a pistol, "do your job?"

Brody rested his hand on his holstered sidearm and spoke sternly. "Nah. Never."

"That's good. Man, I dunno if I could do it. I guess you only know in the heat of the moment."

"When duty calls. Part of the job."

"You ever, like. . ." Bill paused to think of a supposedly appropriate example, "run a red light? Or be in traffic and say 'fuck it' and just hit the sirens?"

"Never," replied Brody.

"C'mon," he prodded, "no harm in that. Look, if I was prairie doggin' it on the way home from work, I'd be tempted to hit the sirens so I didn't iceberg, y'know?"

"What?" asked Brody, confused by the slang.

"If I had to shit."

The tonal ebb and flow of this conversation as a whole caused Brody confusion. His tolerance was sincerely waning. *I cannot wait until this fuck-head leaves.*

"We do have privileges, but they're only used when needed."

"When I gotta shit it's a matter of *need,* my man."

"You have to get back to work or something?" he prayed.

"I got another minute," Bill said. "My associates are setting up the cake to be served to the distinguished guests."

. . .*Maybe the silent treatment will wor–*

"You said people give you shit for doin' you job. What do you mean? Do they, like, curse at you for giving them a ticket? Or. . .?"

Or not. Brody finally resigned himself to the chat. Frankly, it was easier than being a hard-ass. He huffed. "Bunch of shit. Was giving someone a speeding ticket the other day. Got real chippy. Ended poorly for him," replied Brody reconcilably.

"Woulda been different if they were cheerleaders, I bet. He try to run away or something?"

He noticed the jab, but, gritting his teeth, decided to ignore it. "Just a lotta lip."

"What if he ran? You would have chased him, right?"

"Of course, but that would have been worse for him. If you run, it's considered Evading Arrest and Willful Resistance. Creates risk for me, risk for others, most of all bad news for you."

"Bad news? Like getting shot?"

"I–I dunno. No. Depends on the situation."

"What happens if you're chasing someone that's faster than you?"

"You ain't outrunning the cops, you can be damn sure of that."

"I'm pretty fast. . . You think you can catch me?"

Brody turned, resuming his authoritative posture. "Is there a reason I should want to?"

"I'm just sayin'. I think I'm faster than you are." Bill stared straight ahead into the alleyway and puffed on his cigarette.

"I've been listening to your bullshit all night, kid. And you're treading a fine line here."

"There's no line. It's just a statement. I think I'm faster than you are. In fact, I think I'm faster than any cop you could find in this city." He finished his cigarette and flicked it into a nearby puddle.

"There's plenty of us who'd be willing to test that theory. Just give me a reason, kid. I'll end your week real quick," Brody said threateningly, his adrenaline on call.

Bill finally turned his head to meet the policeman's gaze and said, "I'll put it to you this way. I was an All-State sprinter in high school and I won Sectionals for cross-country and high jump. I bet if I slapped you in the face as hard as I could, then took off, there's not a fucking thing you could do about it you *fat, piggly, fuck.*"

In the two silent seconds that passed a conversation of ocular language transpired between the men. In a matter of moments, Bill had turned from an annoying episode of the evening's watch to a realistic and disconcerting threat. Brody placed his hand on his gun.

"Slowly turn and put your hands against that wall." No movement. A lull in traffic added to the tension. Brody positioned his hand over his mace and spoke again. "*Now!* I'm *not* going to repea–"

Before Brody could finish his command a crashing, startling boom caused both men to shutter and recoil in surprise. Bill's eyebrows shot up and his eyes widened. He was looking over Brody's shoulder towards the source of the bang.

"What the fu–" said Brody as he turned halfway around to face the source of the noise: the loading dock door.

The two men that had accompanied Bill at the beginning of the evening had burst out of the door and headed in a dead sprint towards their parked van. Laughter filled the alley. Why the sound was louder than expected, Brody hadn't the time to ponder. He needed Bill to stay where he was to pursue the suspicious men before their van disappeared into the bowels of the city.

He began to turn his head back to Bill. "Don't mov–"

Before the words left his mouth, Brody felt the sting of a full-handed slap. Bill caught him blind, the blow knocking him back a pace.

Bill took off at a slow jog. "C'mon fatboy! It's just like chasing the ice cream man down the street!"

Seething and stinging, Brody lumbered after the man, screaming into his radio. The van behind him rounded the alleyway corner and vanished, swallowed by the passing traffic.

The single explosion may have elicited a frantic shriek from the audience, but the aftermath rendered most catatonic. Shocked silence blanketed the atrium as the messy crowd checked for blood and wounds. Instead, they found themselves wiping cake and frosting from their faces, dresses, and tuxedos. Mayor Crowley and his cabinet had stood frozen, completely soiled with icing, staring at a sizable inflated airbag that now rested in place of the once celebratory cake.

As Marian regained her composure, she looked upon the stage to find the odd thing gently deflating. Like some comic book action bubble, the fabric of the bag read only, *"BANG!"* Suddenly a realization emerged. She shot a look back toward where the bakers were bunched yet found nothing but tech equipment. They had disappeared.

Chapter 18: Pruning

Captain Hogan paced the length of his office like a bat trapped in a hallway. He huffed and puffed and ran a hand over his face seemingly at each pass. Merv sat quietly on the other side of Hogan's desk, as instructed, and watched the show. He was good and high from a few bumps of coke and a nip back in his office. His face was tingling towards numbness. Hogan had been going on about something for forty-five seconds, pausing his fury here and there to blurt out words. Not until his voice escalated did Merv really start to listen.

"I don't want to hear about this! I don't ever want to about hear this! I don't need this! I got enough of a headache from the Mayor over this museum fiasco, okay? Some fucking whacks blew up a cupcake or somethin' and City Hall's losing their shit. Same ones that hung that damn banner that clogged up traffic. Now they want an investigation. Last thing I need to worry about is my senior officers losing their heads."

"What do you mean? There's nothing for you to worry about," Merv calmly assured him. "No one lost their head. I didn't lose my head."

"No? Brian Taylor had something different to say about that."

Merv twisted his neck. "*My Taylor*? . . .What'd he say?"

"Said you assaulted a kid."

Merv's eyed thinned. *Are you fucking kidding me?* "Bullshit."

"Said you roughed him up real bad."

"I didn't assault no kid."

"No?" Hogan was standing with his hands on his hips, like a struggling parent.

"No. Not now, not ever."

"So what, then? *Your* fucking deputy made it up?"

"Fuck if I know. But you bet your ass I'm gonna find out," Merv snapped.

"*Relax*, Hammer." A hand slicked Hogan's hair back. "Taylor came to me. He was very upset. He wants to request a transfer. Something must have happened. Just tell me what happened."

That's why he's been checked out. That fucking coward. Merv played dumb. "I have no idea."

"No idea?"

"No."

"So he just made it up?"

Merv threw up his hands. "I don't even know what the fuck we're talking about. I'm starting to get irritated."

"I said *relax*! I called you in to sort the issue out not set you off, alright?" The Captain was flailing his limbs about. His arm pits were soaked with sweat.

"There is no issue."

"God Almighty," Hogan mumbled angrily as he kicked at the floor. "This *fucking* museum!" His head looked like he'd fallen asleep in the midsummer sun.

Merv raised an eyebrow. "Well what'd Mancuso have to say about all this? You know if one's with me so's the other."

Since Taylor and Mancuso had been assigned to Merv, it was clear who'd last and who wouldn't. This Taylor kid was baggage from the start, with nothing but pathetic presence, poor ability, and deplorable "morals." As the weeks went on it took most of Merv's being not to send the kid packing. *And now this. . . It seems you want to choose you own destiny, kid. Come get it.*

Mancuso on the other hand was a warrior, through and through. He and Merv even went on some "extracurricular" tasks last week. He was a good drinker, good company, and had a moldable attitude. He had been in the shit and emerged the victor. He could hang around here.

"Mancuso had no idea what I was talking about."

Merv relaxed. *That's my boy. My fucking talent.* "Well, there you go."

"No, not 'There you go.'"

"Then what? What are we even talking about here?"

"Listen, I don't have time for this shit. If I don't have corroboration and an accompanying complaint, I can't do shit. You know that. But I'll tell you right now, God damn it." Hogan said, pointing in Merv's face. "If whoever-the-fuck comes in for whatever-the-fuck happened, you're suspended. That's it."

Merv tossed his head aside. "Mark."

He threw his hands up. "That's it!"

"Mark, nobody's gonna come in for nothin' because nothin' happened to nobody. C'mon–"

"Ah-ah-ah-ah." A palm went up. "I don't wanna hear it, Hammer. Say 'Okay' and get the fuck out so my blood pressure can level out for once this week."

Oh, Taylor, you motherfucker. You have no idea what you've done. . . Merv twisted a frown and replied, "Okay."

He stood and exited the Captain's office.

You've provoked the wolf this time.

Soon Merv was sitting across from Taylor at a window booth at the old *32nd Street Diner Car.* The morning was bright and the diner was amidst its brunch rush, with a packed "bar," crowded tables, and a few couples awaiting placement by the hostess. As far as establishments go, Merv would have never stepped foot in the place on any ordinary day. It was cramped, full of pathetic people, the food sucked, the coffee sucked, and the place didn't even have a liquor license. He chose it for situational irony.

Taylor scanned a menu as Merv stared holes in his head. He hadn't told Taylor to order but the man supposed to do so anyway. The nearly empty cup of coffee, single red apple, and lit cigarette sitting in an ashtray before him constituted Merv's breakfast. The smoke seemed to curl around Merv's head. Presently, a tickle formed on his nose, which he rubbed.

"Do you know why we're here?" Merv asked.

Taylor kept thumbing through the menu. "No, I don't."

In a fucked up way, Merv had respected the lofty risk but what could Taylor have possibly expected? Some sort of reprimand? Suspension? Demotion? A meeting, a powwow, legal action? Merv had been given his second Medal of Valor when Taylor was probably having wet dreams in his dinosaur pajamas. Merv pulled out his hunting knife and placed it on the table with a clink.

"Put the fucking menu down," he commanded.

Taylor eyed the knife and obeyed. After a moment's hesitation Merv calmly sliced a section of his apple. He'd rather have reached across the table to stab him, but that was bad sport.

"We're here because you have a problem," Merv explained blithely. "And today we're going to solve it."

"I have a problem?"

Merv placed the fruit in his mouth and began to chew. “Oh, yes. A big problem,” he said between bites. “You don’t know what it is, do you?”

“Not really, sir.”

“I’ll tell you. It’s the way you think.” He swallowed and began to slice a second section. “You think you know the type of man I am. You *think* you’ve got me figured out. Which is why you’ve acted the way you have. You think you have an idea of what it means to be a cop in my unit. You thought that by telling Hogan about our project a couple weeks back you’d get ahead. You think you somehow have power over me. You think you can’t be touched. You think your hands are clean.” Merv looked at the chunk of apple in his hand and paused. It had its origin sticker still on the skin. He looked back to Taylor, and ate the piece anyway. Taylor squinted in disbelief. “And I think you’re *wrong. Dead* fucking *wrong*.”

Merv swallowed and placed his cigarette in his mouth and pulled hard. Smoke left his mouth like a breath of mist on a subzero morning. Taylor looked like he was figuring out a calculus equation in his head, blinking and looking across the Formica table. He made a few attempts to reply, but Merv quickly reengaged.

“Allow me to tell you what else I think. I think that I don’t fucking *like you*. I think you’re a cunt. I think that if I kept you on board here and gave you the benefit of the doubt, you’d do what cunts do - you’d worm me out to Hogan again. You’d *scheme*.

“I think you have no idea how many people I’ve hurt. Or how many families I’ve destroyed. How many children I’ve kidnapped, or mothers I’ve violated, or fathers I’ve murdered. I think you’ve never seen evil.” Merv placed his knife in his mouth and sucked some juice from its blade. “Those are things that I think,” Merv continued. “They’re things I’ve been thinking since I had the displeasure of meeting you and since I suffered the insult of having someone of such a low caliber assigned to me. *You’re a disgrace*.” Merv’s voice burned like acid. “And as of this morning, these are things I’ve decided to sort out.

“You see, you’ve pissed me off.” He drew from his cigarette and grimaced. *“I’m mad,”* Merv snarled and blew smoke out of his nostrils like a charging bull. “Now I have plans for you. And your family. You wanna know what they are?”

Taylor heaved. *“Sir,”* he said, slowly raising his hands, “I don’t know what was said to you.”

Merv spoke over him nonchalantly. "For you, I'd probably just start by cutting your cock off." He shrugged. "I like that kind of shit. I dunno what to say. It's fun to me. From there, I dunno. I haven't decided yet. Maybe rape your wife. See what she tastes like. Maybe your daughter. Maybe both. I got a video camera, y'know? I could film it and make you watch. Or maybe just have you there watching." Merv scratched his beard. "If I cut your eyelids off, you–well. . .you get the picture."

Taylor rose out of his seat to leave, giving off the slightest tremble. Suddenly, he froze, stuck in a squat with his thighs touching the table. Standing across the diner car was Mancuso, arms folded in a furious presence. He mouthed the word 'sit' to Taylor. People passed through the space between them and out the glass door freely, some with full stomachs and smiles, others with hungry eyes. They were jovial and ignorant. Taylor glanced back to Merv, who sliced another section of his apple with a quick stroke of his knife.

"Sit the fuck down," he ordered. *"Now."*

Taylor lowered himself onto the cushion. The crunching sound spilt from Merv's lips again as he crushed ripe flesh with his teeth.

"Anyway, get this. This one time I, uh, barred the doors and windows of a guy's brownstone and lit a fire in his basement. He was a witness in a particular. . .*incident*." Merv laughed. "Kind of like you. He wasn't home, but unfortunately for him, his family was. They suffocated before they found a way out. Firefighters found claw marks on the walls and shit. It wasn't good. But, you know, hey, at least he didn't need to pay for cremation, right?"

His voice trailed off and he raised his coffee cup for the passing waitress to refill. Taylor was an image of creeping dread. He was trapped, cornered by wolves, unable to flee, unable to scream, left only to await his uncertain fate.

The waitress slid to the table and poured a hasty eight ounces while Merv reached in his jacket. He removed his tin flask and unscrewed it.

"Um. I'm sorry, sir, but you can't do that here," the waitress petitioned.

Merv paused and curled his index finger, beckoning her close to him. "C'mere."

"Um."

Merv raised his brow. *"C'mere,"* he repeated playfully.

The girl leaned in as he craned his neck towards her ear and whispered. She giggled and rolled her tongue over her smiling lips, pulling back slowly. Merv held her gaze for a moment until she walked away shaking her head. He stared at her ass. A twist of the wrist dosed his coffee with liquor. He took a sip, returning to the matter at hand.

"I got two of my guys - you don't know 'em. They ain't cops. They're. . .worse. Hah." He sliced the last section of apple, leaving a rectangular core. The piece stuck to his knife blade, which he guided towards his mouth and bit. Merv continued as he chewed. "Eastern European, actually. Balkans. Real fuckin' whackjobs. I'm talkin' if I told them to they'd torture you for two weeks. Or until you gave out. Whichever came first. They like that kind of shit. I do too. I'd come check on things, help out, y'know? See what your screams sound like."

Taylor breathed deeply. "Sir, just hold on. I think that–"

Merv couldn't contain his sarcastic laughter. "There you go. There you go, Brian. Thinking again. I thought we talked about this. That's a *problem* of yours. My men don't think, they just fucking *do*. But you're not one of my men." He waved his knife as he spoke. "You see. . .you *think* you know who you've fucked with." Merv leaned in with the apple core in one hand and his knife in the other. His expression turned severe. "But you don't. I'm *crazy*. I'm a *savage*. . . You're a fucking worm. And you don't belong here."

Taylor was pressed rigid against the pleather booth. Merv sat back and looked at his hands.

"Oh!" he cried in astonishment. "Check it out!"

Merv turned the apple towards Taylor, showing a tiny brown worm squirming towards an opening in the core. The flesh around the worm was rotted.

"That's you!" He pointed with the tip of the knife and spewed a burst of laughter. "There you are! Oh, Fate," he mumbled, "you never disappoint."

Taylor swallowed hard and shot a glance towards the window. Outside, Marcus and Rodney were leaning on the hood of their cruiser with folded arms and stares to match Mancuso's. Taylor was truly trapped. Merv maintained a looney look until his attention was returned. And then he placed the core in his mouth and chewed, worm, seeds, stem, and all. The bolus shifted with a grinding sound, protruding mostly from a favored left cheek. He swallowed casually while Taylor stifled a gag.

The restaurant was oblivious to the hostility. Kids laughed at the next booth and a man turned a newspaper page. Busboys and waitresses went about their duties. It was all just a common morning in the diner car.

But in the booth, Merv's knuckles had blanched white around the hunting knife, and he was slowly pointing the tip across the table towards Taylor's taut, ghostly face.

"Let this be a kindness I'm extending to you. If you ever step foot in my precinct again, I'll use Melinda and Abagail as my new fuck toys."

Taylor's eyes widened at the naming of his family.

"I'll rent them out. And then I'll fucking kill you."

Ernest and Robin sat down to their first meal together since Robin's release from the hospital. The time since his beating had been a span of stress and utter loneliness for Ernest. Robin was distant and unavailable, leaving St. Augustine's in the mornings only to return in the late hours of the night or not at all. It was evident that something was changing in him and Ernest feared Robin would soon reach the point of no return if he didn't intervene and help the boy. He prayed over it daily, finding an alarmingly miniscule amount of guidance through his faith.

Each man sat in their usual chairs enjoying a light meal of vegetable curry over rice which Ernest had made to be easily chewable for Robin's damaged jaw. It was a quiet evening, yet the kitchen felt uncomfortable, even tense at times. Robin was displaying his typically casual demeanor, but Ernest was treading lightly, as if the floor was a shell of thin ice which could consume him if he took a wrong step. It was the very first time Robin seemed like a stranger.

The banner that was hung two weeks ago had created a stir among the regular churchgoers and varying rumors and interpretations followed. The lunch crowd at the Soup Kitchen buzzed about it as well. The public seemed not to know the culprit, but Ernest's knowledge was far more intimate than the common man's. Its timing was all too convenient. Its message was all too familiar and suggestive of one and only one source: Robin. *And now the news reports of trouble at the museum*, Ernest worried. *It's all too easily connected. Coincidence is among the Lord's many languages. Today I fear that language is one of testing and confrontation. The time has come for answers.*

Ernest cleared his throat. "How are your injuries faring?"

Although Robin was walking and talking normally again, his outward appearance still showed bruising, redness and some swelling. His bloodshot eye had lessened to a mild pink hue, thankfully. Ernest knew the boy was in pain even though he masked it remarkably well.

"They're fine," Robin answered neutrally. He held a folded newspaper in his left hand and a spoon in his right.

Ernest knew which article he was reading so intently. Again, Ernest attempted to initiate him. "Have you gone for your follow-up at the hospital?"

"Nah, there's no need. I'm fine."

"Alright. . ."

Ernest scooped a spoonful of food in dejection. Any opportunity for real conversation recently, especially over how Robin had sustained his injuries, was impeded by shortness and his new unpredictable schedule. The church felt vacant again and although Ernest had found volunteers to handle the Soup Kitchen operations, the dynamic simply hadn't been the same. Perhaps he was only being selfish in wanting influence over Robin, but his heart told him the benefit was mutual. He missed the man he knew, not this distant person before him.

"I'm glad you're recovering well. Haven't seen much of you these past weeks."

"Yeah, I'm sorry about that. I've been real busy with Jon and Wil."

"Doing what?" Ernest asked with a raised brow.

Robin replied without making eye contact. "We're working on a project."

"Oh? What kind?"

"We're thinking of reviving the May Day Festival. That's why I was asking you all those questions about it last week."

Ernest paused. 'All those questions' constituted a mere seven minutes of back and forth about the festival's history, meanings, and traditions. It had been more of a report than a discussion. *Sounded like a forged alibi to me.* A twinge of aggravation rose in him.

"Is that true?"

Robin looked up. "Uh, yeah, of course. It's gonna take a lot of effort, so we're trying to figure out what needs to be done."

"The May Day festival isn't some Soup Kitchen that can be thrown together in one weekend. It means *many* things to *many* people. What type of preparation have you begun?"

"Um. Logistical. . ." He trailed off.

He is dodging my inquiries. "Go on," Ernest insisted.

"What?"

"What *else* have you been doing?" An accusatory tone had come out of him, too quickly to be censored.

"We've been preparing, Ernest."

"You once told me, 'We are not at mass, you can speak freely.' I might offer you similar advice in this moment."

"I'm not following."

Ernest dropped his spoon and raised his voice. "I'm not stupid, Robin. First that banner goes up and now a real crime has been committed. What's going on?"

Robin's eyes showed an eerie look of amusement. "If you have something to ask me, then ask."

Ernest mustered some mental fortitude. He knew the answer that lay at the end of his question and the terrible fallout that could erupt. "Are you responsible for what happened at the museum last night?"

"Yes."

Ernest blinked and ran a hand over his face. *Oh, Lord.* "I don't understand how you intend to justify–"

"I don't expect you to understand," Robin interrupted. "Which is why I won't argue with you over it. It's begun and we won't stop."

"What has begun?"

"Change," Robin said simply and nodded. "It's happening now." He returned to his food and newspaper as if he was finished discussing the matter.

Thoughts cycled in Ernest's mind as he struggled with a way to approach a continuation of the discussion. *The boy is hurting, even if he isn't showing it. Try to be his comfort, not another person to shove him. Try.* Ernest chose his words carefully, perhaps more carefully than he had in many weeks.

"I am sorry for the pain you have endured, Robin, and I've noticed for many weeks your growing anger towards the powers that be. I've always admired your passion, but I tell you here and now, son, I've felt as you've felt and I know all too well the consequences of succumbing to anger. It leads to destruction and most often hurts those you never intended to damage. There are other ways to achieve whatever goals you have. *Please* exercise peace."

Robin looked into space for a moment before responding. "Peace is a result. Not an agent for change. I wish it were different but this is the only way."

"Since I've known you, you have viewed these problems as a war. But I fear you've fallen well short in your understanding of what that means. It means pain and suffering. It means violence. No matter your cause, that's never the answer. These problems *can* and *should* be addressed with reconciliation at the helm."

"No. Reconciliation occurs when both sides have addressed the problem. You and I know that's not the case. There's only so many times I can tell you that acceptance permits victimization and that blame also lies heavily on the shoulders of those who choose inaction." Robin tapped his finger on the table. "Your generation hasn't done anything about it. So ours will. It's going to change now. . . That's it."

"Are you telling me that there is nothing I can say to change your mind?"

"Yes."

"Then you're leaving me with no choice, Robin. This is a house of God and a house of peace. I will not tolerate your behavior, nor be associated with it. As long as it continues, you are no longer welcome here." Ernest couldn't bear to look into the younger man's eyes any longer. "Remove you things, please."

Robin rose from the table. "There's always a choice," he said. "You taught me that." Without more, he was gone.

Chapter 19: Sanctuary

Beautiful stone and woodwork, massive ceilings, and wrought iron window frames, all mood-lit and warm, hugged Marian with a familiar embrace. This was her sanctuary, a refuge void of interruptions and time sucks. Her grandfather had brought her here, to the City Library, along with the museums and parks, too. Her favorite exhibit had been the one about medieval arms and armor, but other girls used to make fun of her for it. A closet nerd, you could say, the artifacts alike to those of high fantasy novels she'd read as a child never ceased to amaze her. She would travel the shelves of the library deciding on her next series of heroes to follow, consumed in the unknown adventure waiting to be experienced.

Now she came here to work. The office was full of distractions and negativity: the horny intern always 'checking in' on her, the wandering eyes of the other litigators, her diplomas on the wall evoking memories of excitement or heartache, her office phone perpetually ringing in her ear like the aftermath of an exploded grenade. Here she could focus and relieve the tensions of the week. The calming environment reinforced that warm feeling she'd had here since childhood and promoted a general single-mindedness, perfect for productivity. To her, this place was an anomaly of tranquility in the center of a chaotic symphony that was her city.

She sat quietly at her regular table, leaning back on the meager leather cushion the chair offered. As the days between the museum incident and the present grew, her feelings toward the event mutated from those of terror to ones bordering on comedic enjoyment. Marian's mental snapshot of the Mayor, and especially her boss, Herb Hanser, covered from head to toe in cake and frosting would never fade from her mind. The next day at work she hadn't been able to help herself from asking Herb if he wanted her to pick up any pastries for him while she was out for lunch. He hadn't enjoyed the slight, but she sure did.

Despite the "terror"-laden news reports she reasoned in her head that the intention behind the act hadn't been harm but "artistic impact," if you will. She couldn't place a motive but she knew if harm had been intended the result would have been *far* different. Her dress could have been splattered with blood and brain matter instead of cake frosting, and her psyche could have been bent for life instead of realigned. For that, she was actually grateful.

She hadn't been able to read the message on the airbag from where she sat, but the news had eaten it up. They said it was the second 'Few Against Many' message, whatever that meant. She could still remember the lines:

You'll act as though this was forced on you
But you can't have your cake and eat it too
Not of rich, nor of poor, nor of middle standing rule
Ignore any longer, and go the way of the fool

Fallout from that night consisted of more than just a prospective reevaluation. Ending things with Dalton was a natural outcome, but secondary to the event itself, which seemed to be affirming all her subsequent decisions. They met the following day, she with hopes of making a lasting emotional impact. To say the meeting was anticlimactic would be a bit of an understatement. His unaffected, detached, laidback reaction did eat at her. She felt robbed of her redemption, of some sort of victory over him, of the feeling of seeing him lose what he'd never have again in his life: a genuinely great girl. As much as she had tried to end things as the victor, that night had been his last - and perhaps his most hurtful - jab at her.

Single. The word meant freedom for some and prison for others. Marian was not necessarily in either category, though. She handled herself well both in and out of relationships, but the simple combination of her current attitude towards romantic possibilities in her daily life and foreseeable future seemed bleak enough to make her hesitate. Add to that that her friends joked that she was unapproachable, that she suffered from "bitchy resting face," and tended to attract assholes, and one had the formula for a unique self-esteem issue. Regardless, she was strong enough to handle that on her own.

The papers spread on the tabletop in front of her were calling out to her, but feeling the urge to pee, Marian ruled that her work could wait for the moment. She decided to stretch her legs, hit the restroom, and take a quick stroll through the library's labyrinth of shelves in hopes of clearing her head.

On her way back from the restroom, she passed the door to the rare book room. Always locked, a small desk off to the right adorned with a dimly lit lamp could be seen in the dark room through two slender glass windows on either side of the door. Bookshelves lined the remaining visible edges and a few armchairs could be seen in the shadows. Above the door, in fancy maroon lettering, a quote read, "Draw near! Draw near! Ten thousand yesterdays are gathered here." She had always enjoyed that quote, though to this day never bothered to learn of its source.

Marian sat down in her chair and adjusted her thin dark-rimmed glasses to comfort. From her second-floor vantage she could see the main desk and lobby of the library, full of communal tables, along with the lower section of periodicals. Study rooms lined the back wall, continuing out of sight, but she rarely used those. From a study room, you couldn't observe the subtleties of library life on slower nights like this Friday night, when her favorite thing to do in between thoughts was to people-watch. One ascertained a decent amount of information about a person from their body language, especially in a setting like this. She had found that, in general, elderly ladies browsed the New Arrivals shelf or stuck to Mysteries, while most men typically chose Fiction, both contemporary and historical, and Biographies. These were the type of people who flew through books, tackling several per month. Her grandmother had been exactly the same way. She'd come home with four new books each week and every so often would take out the same book twice simply because she'd forgotten she'd read it already. Anomalies existed, as with any population, but probably the easiest to spot of these were college students. There was no telling where they'd be browsing, and they didn't seem to know half of the time either.

When Marian looked up again from her work to check her watch, it was 10:27 p.m. *Just about closing time.* She stood and stretched. *I hope it isn't raining again.* As she bent down and gathered her things to prepare to leave, she heard the grand entrance doors close sharply, followed by the light tap of footsteps on the marble floor. *A little late to be returning books.*

Without thinking, she looked up from her bag and momentarily locked eyes with a man strolling towards the front desk. *That's a first. No one ever looks up here.* He wore jeans, a light jacket, boots, and a baseball cap resting lightly on his head. *No one that good looking anyway.* She continued to watch him as he turned, approached the desk, and leaned in to speak with the clerk—an elderly lady that had closed the library every Friday night for the better part of a decade. His question must have been brief, for within seconds their exchange ended and the man began walking towards the section of the library beneath Marian's balcony. *And where are you headed, handsome?*

Marian unconsciously glanced back at the clerk and did a double take. Much to her surprise, something the man said had made the elderly clerk chuckle. *That woman's ice cold. I don't think I've ever seen her smile in my entire life!* She followed the intriguing man as he approached, hoping to catch a better glimpse of what was hidden underneath that hat of his. As if acknowledging her internal request, the man removed his cap, ran his hands through his hair and placed it backwards on his head.

The motion made Marian freeze in utter disbelief. *Oh my God. . . That's him!* Her eyes squinted and her mouth opened in awe. *That's the baker from the Museum. It's him!* That motion, the hands through his hair, the backwards hat, was exactly as it had been that night. As soon as she had made the connection, the man disappeared under the balcony.

His path underneath her would lead to the computer lab, library offices, or, more directly, the staircase between the main level, her current floor, and the basement. Startled, she remained frozen, waiting to see if the man emerged from the mouth of the staircase behind her. Ten seconds went by without any change. . . Fifteen. . .

Fuck it. I have to.

In a split-second spell of courage she sprang up from her table, leaving her bags half packed, and tip-toed to the stairs. She descended quietly to the landing of the main floor and scanned the desolate computer lab. Only two people occupied the rows, neither of which were the man - the baker - she sought. She hesitated for a moment, like a child having to go into the basement alone for the first time, nervous of what lurked below.

Another flight down and her boots met the carpeted basement floor. It was one of the most outdated sections of the library. The orange carpet must have been as old as she. The shelves and tables were odd leftovers, remnants of various renovations done over the generations.

Feigning aloofness, she skimmed the terrain for a moment in an attempt to pinpoint where the man had gone, well aware that this was easily the most ridiculous thing she'd done in a while. Some commotion off to her right drew her attention. She crept towards it, her movement soft and graceful as she guided herself past a number of bookcases, touching each one gently as she went. Ahead, the end of the row opened onto an area labeled "Maps, Surveys, Drafts, & Blueprints." She could hear growing sounds of a repetitive movement, like books being shelfed, and placed herself just inside the last aisle in the hall to covertly observe the scene.

Through a slim, chest-level gap in between shelves she could see the man's upper half. He had dropped his jacket on the floor and was gingerly searching through the many racks in front of him, sliding each tube out halfway to read a sticker describing its contents. Some moments later, the man nodded and extracted a single tube from the shelf.

At first, it appeared that he was checking to see if anyone was watching him, his head swiveling this way and that. Then Marian realized that he was, instead, searching for a table or flat surface on which to lay the tube's contents. He walked over to an oversized podium on the far right of the room and removed a massive open book from its angled surface, replacing it with the unrolled contents of the tube. She watched him scan through the first sheet of paper, mark a section with his finger, and thumb through several sheets to another. For her to tell what he was looking at would require x-ray vision or clairvoyance. *Is it a diagram? A map?*

Without a jacket, now, she could better make out his physique and stature. He stood maybe six feet tall with an athletic build. A white t-shirt form-fitted his figure, hugging developed, but not overly defined, muscles. Despite the season, he was a bit tanner than she had originally imagined, with the same scruff of beard she recalled from the museum on his face. In the realm of looks, she approved. *I wonder if he thinks anyone saw him. I can't believe he'd show his face this soon after the event if he thought otherwise.*

After fifteen seconds of silence she collected herself, took a deep breath, and walked around the end of the bookcase in an effort to appear like she'd been in stride already and was oblivious to anyone else being around. *Seems harmless. I've got to mess with him. He needs to know he's not so slick.*

The courage she mustered up to confront him came from two places: her innate desire to right the wrongs of the world (see current profession), and her comfort in the current location. In her mind, she had a monumental home-field advantage that tilted the odds in her favor. If this situation had unfolded in some random coffee shop, or on the subway, her glass of courage might have looked half empty rather than half full.

She casually moved her hands from book to book, then tube to tube, inching her body closer to the podium where he stood. She snuck a look out of the corner of her eye. A portion of the heading on the paper was blocked by the man's forearms but she managed to make out the first letter "B" of the first word, and "Memoria" in the second. She frowned. The rendering looked to be a field of some sort, however.

The man finally looked her way. As he released his hands from the sides of the papers, they rolled in on themselves, causing her to miss the rest of the label.

"Hi," he addressed her with a squint. "Do you need help?" he politely added.

Marian's eyes shot to meet his gaze. She blinked. *Even more handsome than I thought.*

"Oh, do you work here?" she said, putting a hand to her chest. When called for, she could play stupid quite well.

"No. . ." The confused look on the man's face made Marian feel confident she had the upper hand.

"Oh, maybe not then," Marian said, showing sudden disappointment.

"Are you looking for something in particular?"

"That's so sweet of you to still want to help me. How chivalrous," she said.

The comment was meant to be sarcastic, but Marian worried he had missed the undertone as the man began to look around. She could tell his patience was running out and she did not want him leaving before she could put him on the spot. She had to act quickly.

"Actually, I'm looking for something. I think you can help me."

"Shoot," the man said amiably.

All at once, the reality of the situation closed on her and a rare case of nerves started settling into her. Here she was, face to face with the 'baker' himself!

"Um," she smiled, deeper than she meant to, and looked down for a second. "I was wondering if you knew of a great recipe for a birthday cake."

'A great recipe for a birthday cake'? Nice punchline, idiot.

"Oh, try looking in the cookbook section," the man said, pointing to the ceiling. "Upstairs."

Marian cursed herself, but found herself maintaining the charade. There was no indication that he was nervous, or that he had even caught on at all. In fact, he sounded a little disappointed at the request.

"That's not what I meant," she said.

"I don't follow. Cookbooks are upstairs. I promise," he insisted with a smile.

"I'm not looking for a cookbook," Marian replied. She noticed some bruising around one of his eyes.

He squinted. "Uh, still don't follow."

"Well you're a baker, right?"

The man squinted deeper. "No. . ."

"That's funny" she chirped, "because I saw you last week. At the museum. You delivered that cake on stage. I've gotta hand it to you, *explosive* flavor. . ." Marian said, staring right at him with a challenging stance.

If the man was nervous, he only showed it for an instant, in a subtle widening of the eyes. "I think you have me confused with someone else."

"Mm. Don't think so." A smile formed on her face. *Now I've got him.*

"Well, congratulations," the man said lightheartedly, "you've solved your first mystery, Nancy Drew. Don't bother turning me in, though. You'd be wasting your time."

"Oh yeah? And how's that?" *He'd look much better without that stupid hat on.*

The man chuckled gamely. "You're obviously not too familiar with the Justice System."

"I am a lawyer," Marian said bluntly, aggravated by the slight. Her smile turned dry.

"A *lawyer*? Let me guess, estate planning?"

"Guess again," Marian said in aggravation, now feeling as though it was *her* having to defend herself.

"Can't be in the criminal field," he continued. "Contract law?"

Marian shook her head.

"Med Mal?"

And again.

He snapped his fingers. "I got it – dog bites."

She stared at him and fired her ace in the hole. "I work for the District Attorney."

"Oh that doesn't count," the man said, as if dismissing a person claiming that they hit a hole-in-one on a mulligan.

"How does that not count?" Marian pressed, her voice creeping a little higher than permitted in a library.

"Because you're a public servant. You get to keep your job even if you suck. It's not like the private sector, where people choose you based on merit. You're assigned cases no matter what."

"Actually, my track record is one of the best in the city. And at my level I choose exactly what I pursue."

Marian absolutely hated when people challenged the validity of her profession. It was clear the man was trying to turn the tables. And it was working. Slightly. It was as if this man was a secret member of Dalton's family, just reveling in the fact that he could use her career to put her down.

"Well you must be pretty important, because I've never heard of DAs being invited to a party like that."

"Told you, best in the city."

"Is that right?"

"That's right. What would you know about who gets invited to those things anyway?"

". . .If I'm this. . .*baker* – as you seem to think – wouldn't I know who I'd be fucking with?"

She looked back and forth between his eyes, searching for a tell. She came up empty. "Maybe. Maybe you're just lucky. Or stupid."

"I'm lucky *and* I'm stupid, but not like that."

"Oh, I don't know about that. I spotted you. You can bet there were others."

"*D. . .A. . .*" he muttered in a thoughtful tone, ignoring this last comment. "Well, then you're educated on a little thing called evidence," the man said with a smile.

"I am. And I'm the best kind. A material witness."

"I suppose. . ." The man shrugged off the challenge nonchalantly, turning back to the papers as if the conversation was boring him. "Doesn't matter. I'd deny it. With an alibi."

"Security cameras," Marian stated plainly.

The man froze in place for a moment, a smile forming on his face. He turned his hat forward and pulled it low on his brow. He then turned and looked up to face Marian with only that bright, devious smile showing. It was a look that might intimidate most, but she saw it differently. That wasn't a look of intimidation; it was one of adventure, confidence, and masculinity. It gave her a rush.

"Can't get caught if you don't look up," the man said in a new, firm tone.

They were staring at each other when suddenly a voice came over the intercom:

Ladies and gentlemen, it is now 10:45 p.m. We will be closing in 15 minutes. Please bring your items to the front desk for check out or return them to a cart in a timely fashion. Thank you.

The orders were still echoing in the bowels of the library as the man rolled up the papers and returned them neatly to the stacks. Marian cursed herself again, as she never did catch the title of the file.

Noticing her watching him, he said, "Nurse Ratched's orders."

"Does that make you Randle?" Marian asked, catching the reference to one of her favorite novels.

The retort made the man pause for a second. He smiled subtly. "So, this place is therapy to you too, huh? Same time next week then?"

Marian blinked, and with a tip of the hat, he left.

Chapter 20: Draw Near, Draw Near

Marian awoke in a spasm, the jolting motion nearly flinging her laptop off her thighs as she came out of an unexpected slumber, flustered and disoriented. Stillness encircled her as was typical of the City Library at that time of night. Friday evenings were always the quietest.

She cursed herself in frustration. To doze off while working was a rarity for her, but when on occasion she did slip, it was always due to poor preparation. She had skipped her evening coffee, chose the coziest leather chair available, and positioned herself a bit too close to the repetitive droning of an air vent. It was an effective lullaby, a trifecta of drowsiness.

This night was the culmination of a week of hell for Marian. From the minute she stepped into the office Monday morning, she was swamped with case files and depositions. To make matters worse, one intern quit and another found a full-time job, leaving her team shorthanded.

Even though her workload was frying her mind, she kept up with a new workout plan each morning, bright and early. Marian had enjoyed exercise since she was a teenager, and carried her habits of those years with her into her twenties. Blessed with a petite figure, she never *had* to work out but enjoyed staying fit these days mostly to combat the endless junk food temptations that existed in office life. A probing mind may have associated the regimen reuptake to her recent change in relationship status, though Marian wasn't advertising that as her reason. Regardless, couple the unforeseen "hell-week" with her new fitness routine, and you were left with an exhausted woman. Since Wednesday she had dreamt of her off-day on Saturday, with its open-ended morning in the fluffy warmth of her bed.

Marian gathered herself, rubbed her eyes, and looked lazily around to see if anyone had noticed her less than graceful awakening a moment earlier. Her usual table overlooking the lobby had been occupied by two women, so she was seated at one of four desks lining the southern wall of the second floor. When nothing but orderly bookshelves and vacant desks met her glances, she stretched out the remaining stiffness with a grunt. A quick look at her watch divulged that her snooze had only lasted about thirty minutes or so. *At least I didn't nap the entire night away,* she thought. Fortunately, it was only 9:14 p.m.

After blinking free of her visual cloudiness, she absently moved a delicate finger toward the touchpad on her laptop, hoping to awaken the blank screen that had joined her in sleep. Instead, her finger landed on a folded piece of white paper. *What's this?*

She unfolded the paper to find a message in neat handwriting.

Draw Near, Draw Near
Ten Thousand Yesterdays Are Gathered Here.
Will You Be Guided By Courage
Or Frozen By Fear?

What the. . .? Marian squinted in confusion as the fog of her nap continued to dull her usual sharpness. *Draw*– The reference suddenly clicked in her mind. *Oh. . .* She sat up in her chair and swiveled around again, slower this time, in search of watchful eyes through bookshelves and around corners. Nothing. She looked back at the page and took a deep breath, her heart pumping ever so quicker. *Could it actually be him?*

Over the years, Marian had dealt with off-beat flattery during her nights at the library. Some men's advances were more audacious and shameful than they realized. Most recently, a wormy man mustered the courage to hit on her by asking her to sign her name next to a portrait of Aphrodite on a page in a Greek mythology book. He even brought a pen to get his point across, but she had been so surprised that the volume of her laugh froze the section of the library, scaring the poor man away. She looked at the first line of the letter again.

Draw Near, Draw Near

This was different. This wasn't an advance, no, this was an invitation. Even though he had told her he would be here the same time this week, Marian had talked herself out of the chance that he'd actually show. But his words were an obvious reference to the rare book room, just around the corner from Marian's desk. She stared at them again and bit her lip in thought. *Maybe just take a quick peek to check it out.* With newfound energy she closed her laptop, sprung out of her chair and headed in for a closer look. Rather than barging in, however, she decided to make a trip to the bathroom and investigate the room on the way. A quick glance in the mirror was mandatory before she committed to something this intimidating.

As she approached the room, she noticed the door was slightly ajar. With each step closer, new bits of information became observable. A lamp was lit on the desk positioned in the right corner of the room; a figure appeared at the desk, becoming more discernable as she passed. Her heart started pounding.

Holy shit, he's actually here.

Out of the corner of her eye she saw him - the "baker" - relaxing with his feet up on the desk and his hat low on his brow. The glance was quick and discreet, and in a flash she was past and on her way to the restroom.

Marian had been too nervous to pause at the door or make any slower of a pass, but she had definitely confirmed his presence. Her mind was racing. *How did he manage to find me* and *write that message? Who cares, he was thinking about me.* A smile formed on her face at the thought. *He* did *say he'd be here. A man of his word. Now that's a rare find. How did he get into that room, though?* Despite her best efforts, the clerk had rebutted Marian's inquiries about the rare book room on numerous occasions, always claiming the room was being cleaned or was 'temporarily unavailable.' Not only had he made Miss Ratched laugh the once, but now he had succeeded twice where Marian had failed often.

Inside the restroom Marian paced for a minute, debating how to proceed. *Why does he still wear that stupid hat? Was he sleeping? I didn't get a close enough look. . . I bet he would say "because of the security cameras." I've got to go in, but what do I say? Don't be awkward. Just go, he's definitely inviting you. What am I doing? The guy is a basically a fugitive. . . But he didn't do anything that bad - you know you think it was funny.* Marian argued the point with herself for longer than she cared to think.

Finally, after calming her nerves slightly, she looked in the mirror at her complexion and checked her hair. Surprisingly, it only needed a quick toss to appear orderly.

Marian decided to find a middle ground. She wouldn't let this opportunity pass, however risky, but would proceed with caution. This man was dangerous after all, no matter how intriguing. She reflexively looked up at the ceiling, and decided to see what the gods of chance had in store for her tonight.

Leaving the bathroom slowly, Marian came upon the entrance to the rare book room. She pushed the door open slowly and peeked through the crack, ready to announce herself. To her surprise, the room appeared empty. *Where did he–*

"Can I help you?" said a voice from just over her shoulder.

Marian squealed. Jumping in her boots, she spun around and found the man standing right behind her, looking into the room as if he wanted to see what interested her in this new territory.

"Hi," she breathed, showing a mixture of aggravation and surprise. Her hand found its way over her heart, as if that would slow its beating.

"Hello." The man smiled in amusement. "Fancy seeing you here again."

He stood before her confidently, with arms folded across his chest. He held his hat by its brim in one hand, the softer fabric of the cap hanging loosely on itself. It was the first time she was able to appreciate his looks without the interference of headwear. His face was young, handsome, and welcoming, but showed minor smile lines on the corners of his eyes and the beginnings of creases on his forehead. She could swear that he had experienced some sort of light injury to his face, though. She couldn't quite discern his age. Mid-twenties if she was to guess. His eyes were darker than she remembered, and sparkled in the bright fluorescent lighting.

"You scared the shit out of me," she said, slowing her breath.

"Are you. . .*allowed* to be in this room?" he asked, jokingly pointed a finger.

"I've never seen it *open*, let alone been allowed inside," she said.

"Yeah, it's off limits unless you're a scholar." His tone was condescending in a facetious sort of way.

"A scholar *and* a baker? You just get more and more interesting."

"Just a baker," he said, smiling again. "But Miss Ratched thinks otherwise."

"I could call you a creep with that message you left me," she said, crossing her arms as well.

"You were sleeping. It would've been rude to wake you."

"Mmhmm," she noised while staring him down. *Creep*, she mouthed.

"Seems like you're doing a little creeping of your own around here."

"Stop it. How the hell did you get in here?"

"It's a secret."

Marian raised her eyebrow to challenge the remark.

"Something tells me you've been denied before," he wagered.

"Only like ten times. Miss Ratched usually snaps at me and sends me packing."

"Eh, don't let that bother you. It's not you. It's her." He laughed. "As for a secret. . ." He shrugged. "You catch more flies with honey, right?"

Marian stared at him, her lips motioning to say something further, but she stopped herself.

"Would you like to join me?" he asked sweetly.

She hesitated again and glanced inside the mysterious, shadowed room. *Careful. . . Shut up. Just do it.* "Let me get me stuff."

When Marian returned, the man had already set up a chair for her beside the desk where he sat. He had resumed his reading, noticeably absorbed in a book, and she quickly set her things next to him and took her seat. To Marian, the initially stark contrast between them was palpable. While he was relaxed and comfortable, she was rigid in her seat, unsure of how to proceed. She decided to fill the uncomfortable silence with something, anything to calm her nerves.

"Whatcha reading?" she asked.

He looked over amiably. "I'm reading *The War of the Worlds.*"

"Nice. I've never actually read that one."

"I used to read it every summer when I was a teenager, but it's been a while." He smiled and turned his attention back to his reading.

"Revisiting an old favorite?" Marian blurted to keep his attention.

He looked back at her. "I couldn't resist. This is a first edition, with an original foreword from H. G. Wells." He held the book cover to expose the marking. "It's not in other versions, so I'm hoping that after reading the foreword I can reread the book and have a different interpretation."

"Interesting," she said, pulling her laptop out of her bag.

He pointed at it. "You shouldn't do that in here."

"What?"

"Work," he answered with a laugh. "You've never been in here, right? Take a look around! There's some real gems."

Marian pursed her lips and conceded. "Fair enough."

At his direction, she stood and began to let the setting's ambiance sink in. The lights were low, as if to keep shadows over all the precious treasure this room protected. There were three freestanding bookshelves in a section to the left, and floor-to-ceiling shelving on the perimeter. She was charmed to find a rolling ladder attached to the wall shelving, allowing one to explore the collection's upper reaches. As she flashed her eyes about, small markings indicated that older magazines, newspapers, and journal articles were housed in the right-hand shelves and the room's books consumed the middle and left-hand side of the room. It was a bona fide book worm's room, reeking of knowledge and history. Folks who treated the library like the magazine rack at the local newsstand would not flourish here, and in fact, would taint its reason for existence. She would *have* to figure out exactly how he managed to get in.

Marian started her serpentine stroll through the shelves, passing volumes of all shapes and sizes. Each time she came to the end of a row she looked back subtly to see what the man was doing. At the end of the third row, she caught him looking up at her only to quickly refocus on his reading. She couldn't prevent a smile from growing, having caught his wandering eye. It was overwhelming to think that she'd find a perfect book among such treasures, and she quickly assured herself that no decision could be a failure. One book caught her eye, though, and she impulsively grabbed it. *The Autobiography of Benjamin Franklin* slid from the shelf, welcomed by protective hands.

When she returned to her chair she opened the book carefully, finding the first pages in the format of a letter to Mr. Franklin's son. But try as she might to enjoy the old text, she found herself distracted, repeating lines, and looking up often to see what her counterpart was doing. He seemed isolated and uninterested, without the slightest acknowledgment of what text Marian had chosen. She found this disappointing at first, but after a minute's consideration realized that she admired him for this quality she so uncommonly saw in others: full and pure submission to narrative. Most miss out on the intricacies authors work so hard to deliver, but his eyes thinned and widened as they traced the text, telling of some sight or smell or feeling being experienced within his mind. It was a quality she thought she possessed herself, the current moment notwithstanding, and hated to break him of it. *What else goes on in that head of his?* Her awkwardness got the best of her and she prodded him with another icebreaker.

"Busy week delivering cakes?" she asked.

He closed the book, marking a page with his finger. "Still working on a client list. Any suggestions?"

"Yeah, my boss," she said.

A smile formed on his face. "Alright. I'll look into it."

"I was kidding," she blurted, troubled by the sincerity she had detected.

"You sure?"

"Yes."

"I'll hold off, then."

Again silence took hold of the room. He wasn't cold, but seemed to be deferring all conversation starters to her. She was used to men calling to her, asking her the questions, and seeming interested in what she did or how she lived. But as her mind circulated for a quality topic that would sustain conversation for longer than a few lines, she realized how comical it was searching to start a conversation in a library, and with the passing time Marian's uneasiness ebbed. She sank deeper and deeper into her book and reached the moment of detachment, that ultimate submission to the text that is the highpoint of reading. It came in stages, like falling asleep and dreaming a place where time had no bearing. Over the next hour, and beyond, Marian would surface only occasionally to change position and look up at her partner, finding comfort in the mirrored image. It was the first time all week she had felt relaxed.

Eventually, the 10:45 announcement broke them of their hypnosis. They shared a look that, to Marian, held meaning. He offered to put her book back, which he did quickly, while she gathered her belongings. Closing sentiments streamed through her mind without her being able to settle on a viable option. Before she could say something in haste, he approached and spoke.

"Thanks for joining me tonight."

Marian stood and met him. "Thanks for inviting me. But next time. . .just ask," she said with a smile. It was returned and acknowledged with a nod of his head.

"Alright. Same time tomorrow?" he asked boldly.

"Tomorrow is Saturday."

"Do you have other plans?"

Marian hesitated. He was calling her subtle bluff, his eyes expectant. And she had zero plans and zero plans to make plans.

"Same time tomorrow, then. . ." She trailed off, hoping he would finally add a name to that wonderful face of his.

"Robin," he said.

"I'm Marian."

"See you tomorrow, Marian."

The following evening Marian entered the library at about twenty minutes past eight. While she made most library trips in somewhat questionable clothing found in her hamper or balled up on the floor of her apartment, perhaps a little smellier than was appropriate, tonight she had taken longer to get ready than she had for the birthday gala at the museum. It was a matter of finding the perfect outfit, hairstyle, and amount of makeup to fit the scenario. Looking effortless can require a great deal of effort.

Up at the rare book room, Marian was surprised to find the lights off and the door locked. She quickly looked past her reflection in the window to see if Robin was behind her again, but saw only the outline of shelves. When she turned, a thought snuck into her mind. If she could manage to get in before Robin arrived, the move might impress him. He surely must know how difficult it was for the average person to gain admission.

A clever smile and a quick stride brought her back down to the main desk, where she found Miss Ratched organizing book returns. The woman was handling the books with the utmost care, but the way she looked at them - with a scowl, really - convinced Marian that she hated the things. Marian cleared her throat gently. The librarian looked up, offering a tilt of the head as Marian's only cue to speak.

"Hello," Marian said with as much compassion as she could muster. "I would like the use the rare book room this evening. Would you be able to help me?"

"Name?" asked the librarian, as if Marian had not asked this same question ten times in the past.

"Marian."

The librarian glanced at what looked like a sign-in sheet and then back to Marian. "Follow me."

Marian was stunned. She had prepared a whole story about needing the autobiography of Ben Franklin for a research paper she was writing. This type of success was unprecedented and completely unexpected. *I'll take it.*

Marian deferred the lead, God forbid the librarian change her mind halfway to the room. The pair had just made it up the stairs when out of nowhere she spoke to Marian with—was that a touch of lightness in her voice?

"So you're the new graduate assistant?"

"I'm sorry?" Marian said with confusion.

This caused the librarian to stop abruptly and turn to face her. The lightness receded. "Wilson said there would be another graduate joining him tonight."

Wilson? Puzzled though she was, Marian decided to play along. "Oh, yes. That's me, sorry. I just started on the project last week."

The librarian huffed, but seemed to buy the story. "What's the project?" she said, continuing to walk without turning back.

"Um, how nonverbal cues, like facial expressions and body language, can communicate more information than spoken language."

"Oh. Well. Here we are."

She opened the door with an overloaded, jingling keyring. Marian frowned. *What else does this woman have hidden behind closed doors?* They had stepped not five feet into the room when the librarian turned to face her.

"Wilson will explain, but make sure everything is returned to where it came from. I do nightly sweeps of the room and entrance is a privilege, not a right. Treat it with respect and the privilege will remain available."

"Thank you, Miss. . ."

"Just let me know if anyone else tries to gain access without permission. I will put a sign up in case." She was on her way out before Marian could respond.

Marian took a moment to look around before walking toward the desk. This time she noticed a beautiful area rug centered in the entryway. Its foundation was red with three dark concentric rectangular borders framing an elaborate hexagon in its center. It was as close to a fractal pattern as one could get with hand looming, Marian guessed. *How could I have missed this?*

She walked along the edge of the hexagon, as if some place in her mind really believed the center would swallow her whole.

She set up her station and started to brainstorm ways she could surprise Robin. *Or is it Wilson? What I really need to know is: what am I doing around a wanted man?* She realized how hypocritical it was for someone like her to allow a criminal to roam free. Even more so, she was interacting with this person. And even more, enjoying it. A lot. Before getting too far off track she ended up deciding to just enjoy the room until he showed up. Marian had just situated herself at the desk when Robin walked through the door with a look of surprise on his face.

"I'm impressed," he said, smiling as he strode over the hexagonal rug.

"I had help from someone named Wilson. Do you happen to know him?" Marian said, trying to hide her excitement that he had kept to his word and came.

He laughed. "Wilson. . .Wilson. . .yeah, sounds familiar."

Marian tilted her head questioningly.

"I promise my name is really Robin."

"Ok *Robin,* tell me. How did you manage to get the VIP pass into this room?"

"Alright, so," he begun, settling himself in a little more, "when I was in college I bonded with a literature professor I had. Aside from teaching a great class he was a carpenter, craftsman, poet, artist, musician, a true renaissance man - I mean he could do it all. One of his more quirky passions was Old English, which he spoke fluently."

"Like, Shakespeare Old English?"

"No, like *Beowulf* Old English.

"Oh, wow," she exclaimed.

"I know, right? He used to read us passages and have our class analyze the similarities and differences between Old and Modern English. He'd always say that the same lines in a poem read or spoken in another language can have a drastically different impact on a reader. He encouraged us to read other languages, even if it was phonetically, to see how we felt about it."

"Interesting," Marian said with genuine curiosity, though she was waiting for a punch line.

"So we began talking one day about where his love of Old English came from and he said it stemmed from a library at his graduate university, which had a similar room as this. It was a little less guarded, though." He nodded in the direction of the librarian's desk. "Anyway, he put me onto this room, and as it turns out he's kinda well known around here. So if I ever want access I just let him know and he makes it happen."

Marian bobbed her head, impressed at this man's supposed connections. "So who's Wilson? Your professor?"

"It's my stepfather's name."

"Why didn't you give your name?"

Robin shrugged. "Because. She'll never know me outside of this place, and I get a kick out of it."

Marian gave him a sidelong glance.

"Oh, yeah right. Like you don't do that," he teased. "I bet you always give a fake name when ordering a coffee."

He smiled at her facetiously to which she shook her head. *This one's going to be trouble*, she mused, if only facetiously herself.

Chapter 21: Oxytocin

Pete's Righteous Pie was crowded but not packed when Marian and Robin arrived the following Friday night. Marian thought it odd that while the place always had customers, it seemed to be less busy around typical dinner times. Thirty-minute lines were not uncommon in the early evening when people would rush in to pick up an after-work pie, and even longer ones were seen when parties used it as a late-night stop on the drunken trail home.

The space was on the smaller side, with a row of countertop seating at the bar and tables and booths in the remaining area. A fire flickered through the opening of a domed oven near the rear of the restaurant and neat, pale brick wrapped the walls like smooth paper.

Marian's favorite memories were coming here with her friends and ordering the "roulette" pizza, where the choice of toppings was left up to the pizzaiolo. It was suspenseful and exciting to see what surprise was in store, and despite that one time she met with a concoction that included anchovies, she had never been disappointed. Perhaps tonight would turn into another memorable "roulette" night. She'd make sure to specify her aversion to those salty little fish, though.

She had grown closer to Robin in the past week, having wiled away the hours last Saturday talking about everything from Walt Whitman to Robin's dubious theories about how "All criminals commit crimes but not all who commit crimes are criminals." She found herself wanting to pick his brain, find out why he had done what he did, and learn more about who he was. But it didn't yet feel like the right time to pry. They had made plans to meet away from the library this week.

During the workweek, on Wednesday, she had the urge to revisit her second, more secret career as a quasi-private investigator in the office, but the failure of her first attempt still had her hesitating. Part of her wanted to quit, wanted to start over. She was getting burnt out and feared that further exposure to such a cyclical pattern of nonfulfillment would begin to develop serious long-term effects.

But tonight, Marian had left it all behind. The air was crisp and refreshing and her steps had an anticipatory bounce. She wondered if the emotions he was stirring up inside her were of a genuine nature or merely her fancy. Doubts had occasionally whispered their convincing messages to her at work, but she had done her best to put them to rest by going into their date tonight without expectations. Then he had surprised her with a Christmas present, a contraption called a hand release meant to be used when shooting a bow, and swept her away to *Archery Adventures*, Fort Dearborn's Premier Indoor Archery Range (so the sign said). Marian had never heard of the place and hadn't known anything like it existed. The last time she had shot a bow was during a P.E. block in high school, when it had snapped on her forearm so hard she lost the courage to try again. For an hour Marian attempted valiantly to hit the bullseye at a distance of only fifteen yards but without much success. Out of twenty shots she was mostly able to hit the five ring, but her eyes kept twitching shut at release so she felt like her percentages didn't count. Robin had been impressed nonetheless, and was quick to commend her as she improved. As for his shots, each was clustered close to center. It was clear he had some experience, but he embraced his role as teacher, and his demeanor never ventured into the realm of cockiness or overconfidence. She appreciated that. Humility was an attractive quality if not overbearing or feigned.

Presently, a pitcher of frothy, yellow beer arrived almost immediately as they sat. She had caught Robin glancing about the pizzeria more than once, as if something new was drawing his attention at each pass.

"Man, this place is cool," Robin said as he poured their first drinks.

Marian smiled. "I thought you might like it."

The two raised their glasses and Robin paused, staring straight into Marian's eyes. "Prost."

"What language is that?" she asked. "Czech?"

"'Cheers' in German. To go with our lagers."

She smiled. "Prost."

Marian wasn't a huge drinker, but did love a beer as much as the next girl - too many martinis and Cabernets in the world of high society had gotten dull over time. Robin ordered some brand she had never heard of called *Bearport.* He said two of his buddies had turned him onto it. The taste was bright and crisp and it finished clean, with a great balance between bitter and sweet. She thought it'd pair perfectly with dinner. *Righteous beer for righteous pie.*

She watched Robin's face as he continued to take in the parlor. A lovely smokiness from the wood fired oven seeped into the brick pores while the rumble of conversations from the booths and the whooshing of waiters and waitresses to and fro added to the sensory symphony. The place had character, kind of like *Archery Adventures.* He turned to her and caught her staring.

"You know, I always had this dream to go on a Pizza Quest," Robin said.

"What, try every pizza spot in the city?" Marian asked inquisitively.

"Yeah, and rank them to make a list of my favorites. Leave no slice uneaten."

"I love that," Marian said with another sip. "How would you do it? Like, read reviews to try the best ones out there? There's gotta be a thousand places in the city, no?"

"I think that'd take some of the fun out of it. I feel like it'd be better to discover them on your own, y'know? Or through word of mouth."

"Okay. So what would you do, just rank them from best to worst?"

"Oh, Marian, it's much more scientific than that," he said with pretend disappointment. "You have to first consider style, then presentation, crust, cheese, *sauce*!"

"A whole category just to rank the sauce?" she said disbelievingly.

"Marian, if pizza was a symphony, the crust would be the players, the cheese the instruments. . .but the sauce would be the *music.* It brings the two together in harmony. At least in my opinion."

She rolled her eyes playfully. "You take your pizza very seriously."

"Pizza Quest *is* serious. Or it will be when it starts," Robin laughed.

Marian smiled. "Well consider this our first entry. Let's order."

"Let's!"

It didn't take much for Marian to convince Robin to go for the roulette pizza, but he also ordered a single slice of plain. "For Pizza Quest research," he said. She laughed it off and finished her first beer, happily playing along with the adventure. But she wouldn't let the fun distract her from learning more about this man.

"So I'm curious. How did you become so good at archery?" she asked as Robin topped off both of their glasses.

"I used to spend most summers and winter holidays upstate with my uncle. I had a lot of time to practice."

"Are you a hunter?"

"Yes."

She nodded at the development. "Have you ever. . .got. . . anything?" she asked.

"Yeah," he answered. Marian sensed a soft hesitation in his response. "Does that bother you?"

"Not really. I just don't think I've met someone who actually hunts and has. . .killed something." She had no other way to circumvent the word this time.

Robin gave her a shrug with his hands and said, "Now you have."

Another question crept into her head. Maybe her need to always press for information was the reason why she became a lawyer in the first place, but she had to know more. "Why do you do it, if I may ask?"

He took a sip. "It helps me stay grounded. To see the world as a larger entity than the very human-centric city we live in. I think that when living in an environment like this it can become easy to lose a sense of reality."

"Don't you think our society has developed so that we don't have to hunt for food to survive? Aren't there other ways to stay grounded?" She said this not to be combative, but rather as a statement to continue the conversation.

"While there are many pros to that development, to some degree I think that it makes us more wasteful," Robin answered. "We're removed from the process so food holds less value to those who can afford it relatively easily."

"In what way?"

"When you have access to food without expending the necessary effort to procure it, it's also a lighter blow to our conscience when it's wasted. How many packages of chicken have you thrown out? How many half-eaten burgers or sandwiches have gone bad in your refrigerator?

"Knowing what it takes and being a part of the process is important in order to fully appreciate what you have, y'know? Unless you're a vegetarian, the act of killing still has to happen in order for you to eat. We just have the ability to pay someone else to do it. It's another way to soften the blow to our conscience."

Marian nodded, waiting for him to continue.

"Some feel that hunting is cruel or brutal. But I wonder if those same people know where their food comes from. The conditions most animals live in, in order to provide the masses with food, will always be worse than the wild—where they live a truer life in nature. A free life. It's called 'hunting' and not 'slaughter' for a reason. In fact, I find it respectful to the animal if I. . .*do* the *job* myself."

"So, in a way, you do this to keep your conscience clear?"

"Maybe? Maybe the right phrase is that I do it to keep it normalized, so I don't get desensitized."

"Okay. I can buy that. So why do you think hunting gets such a bad rap?"

"Honestly? I think it's because people are weak-minded. Having the power to take something's life is an immense responsibility. It forces you to be sensitive to the matter; at least it *should* force you to be. Some people don't want to be that in-tune with the cycle of life. It's a heavy burden and it's not something I do with a light heart. So I, like practically ever hunter you'll meet, make sure to use 100% of the animal as to not diminish the importance of the event. All meat is eaten; skin can be made into a rug or a blanket, etc. Most people want a steak with no eyes to show up on their plate and without any thoughts to go with it. . . It's very convenient to remove your emotion from the facts."

"I can't find much of a way to disagree when you put it like that. Unless people don't eat meat entirely, it seems hypocritical to be against hunting. Yet I still can't help feeling squeamish when I think about it. I dunno. I just love animals," she confessed.

Robin warmed her with a smile. "I understand that completely. And I think it's a minority of people that speak out against it. I think the majority aren't against it because of what I outlined. But the loudest voices are those in dissent and those are the ones we hear the most. It's an inherent flaw in information gathering."

"I hear that. Like with restaurant reviews or something. Of course the people who were most dissatisfied are going to want to say something. You never hear from the people who are like, meh, pretty standard meal."

"That's right."

The arrival of their pizza and another pitcher broke the conversation. Robin's eyes lit up as the waitress placed the tray between them.

"Holy crap," he exclaimed. "That looks pretty righteous."

Marian beamed. "Told you."

He inspected the pie to determine what surprise had been laid before them. "Is that. . .?"

"Oh," Marian exclaimed. "I think I know what this is."

The waitress chimed in, "It's our Caprese pizza. Light marinara, fresh mozzarella, roasted heirloom grape tomatoes, an aged balsamic vinegar reduction, olive oil, fresh basil, and some grated pecorino romano as a finish."

It was a beautifully sized pie with a bubbly and lightly charred crust. Steam rose off the molten cheese like morning mist off a lake. Once she had placed Robin's plain slice off to the side, the waitress was on her way. Marian formed a smile. Robin mouthed, "Oh my God." And they dug in.

Halfway through their third pitcher Marian was feeling the flow. The pizza was fantastic, as was the dinner conversation (a laugh over what their final meals on death row would be, leading to a list of favorite restaurants in town), and Marian happily let Robin finish most of the pie, as it was obvious he had quite an appetite. She found that curiously attractive and a gap in discussion allowed her to admire her date as he went to work on the very last of their food. There was something about this man that had her feeling hooked. She couldn't tell if it was his unique charisma, his charm, his mysterious smile, or his presence. There was just something *else* about him. Whenever their feet occasionally nudged under the table, neither was quick to retreat. An urge was coming over her.

"Okay, so sauce," Marian said, wiping her mouth clean for the third time.

Robin furrowed his brow and let out a deep sigh. "Okay. I made sure to test the plain slice first. Based off my expert opinion, I'm going to rate it an eight-point-five out of ten."

"Hmph. Pretty low for what I consider the best pizza in town. You saying I have bad taste?" Marian jabbed, hoping to defend her honor.

"No, no, no. You have wonderful taste. But I can't rate the first place on Pizza Quest a ten out of ten."

"What?! That's the most flawed logic I've ever heard! You are purposely downgrading what could be the best pizza of your life because of a technicality?"

"We've yet to establish a standard, Marian! I can't be throwin' out tens on the first night. The Quest will be gospel."

"Oh my God. . ."

Robin raised a finger. "This is what we'll do. We'll allow for certain return trips once the standard has been set. That way a precedent will be in place and the ratings will hold more weight."

"*Fine.* I suppose you're onto something there."

Robin was preparing to pour the last of the third pitcher when the waitress came over to ask if they would like a fourth. Robin declined immediately, a move Marian didn't see coming. She found it to be quite the show of restraint on his part. As he poured, Marian noticed him starting to squint at the television above her right shoulder. She turned to try to decipher what had caught his attention. The shot was of a judge leaving a courthouse surrounded by reporters and camera crews. The caption read, "*District Court Judge Martin Fulson to return to work after acquittal.*" Marian's heart sunk. It was like the clock had just rung midnight at her ball.

"Oh, wow. I thought that guy was headed for jail," Robin said with surprise.

"*Yeah.* . .shoulda been," Marian said with a thick layer of bitterness. She chugged her beer.

Normally Marian would maintain confidentiality, but in this case, she just didn't care. She was dying to let loose about the injustice at work and the difficulties she dealt with on a daily basis, especially with no one in her life to vent to. Up until now. Couple the beer with how comfortable she was feeling around Robin, and out came the details. She was a boiling pot with a sealed lid. Eventually she had to rupture.

"What happened? You weren't included in that case, were you?"

"I was. But my involvement was quickly *ex*cluded."

"I don't understand."

"I was assigned to it early on. I read the entire case file and had the preliminary legwork rolling on it – it was a fucking slam dunk. One day, out of nowhere, my boss took the case over and it closed immediately. Magically, out of thin air," she motioned theatrically, "the exclusionary rule was cited by defense – as in our evidence was obtained illegally, therefore prohibited by law for use in court. I didn't find any problems when building the case; not with the dates, the methods. . .and I'm an *excellent* lawyer."

"So he was let off intentionally," he clarified.

"Yes."

Robin leaned in. *"How?"*

Marian continued without restraint, "All you need to do is forge an evidence document. If you change a date so that evidence was collected before a warrant was sent out, or press a cop to change their story about the legality of what they saw and when they saw it, or. . .anything like that – boom. All evidence from that point forward is deemed inadmissible."

"That's outrageous. Wouldn't people find out about the forgery? It can't be that easy, can it?"

"Just because it doesn't happen often doesn't mean it's difficult. You need several confidants at several levels so that all the work is clean. That's really what holds most people back. Well, that and a conscience. But yes, it is that easy."

"So someone must have wanted him free? Or someone did him a favor?"

"If you were going to make a deck of cards of the corrupt people in this city, the Mayor would be the Ace, my boss could be a King, and that jackass would be the Queen."

"*Wow.* Unreal."

Robin had both elbows on the table and was leaning toward Marian, as if she was telling her story at a whisper. It was as if he somehow shook off the effects of their beers and was taking mental note of every detail. Marian was oblivious to the change in demeanor. She had barely made eye contact with Robin during the outburst, and was so far into her rant that she had no thought as to what the information she was sharing could do.

"What did this guy do anyway?" Robin asked. "I never got the full story."

"The short of it is he received kickbacks for sending kids to jail. It's actually something that has happened in other cities too, but this guy was utterly ruthless with it. He's the one that caught a lot of flak a while ago for making comments about how the kids were similar to dogs. It was disgusting."

"*Oh yeah.* I remember reading about that. That's this guy?"

"Yeah. I've worked with him before. He's a horrible human being."

"Un-fucking-believable."

"You have no idea."

"Why hasn't anyone called bullshit?"

"To who? The DA? He's the one who requested the warrant. City PD are the ones who carried it out and found the evidence. Could take it to the FBI or something, but it's hard to prove with that many people working against you. Plus, the FBI won't get involved unless there's clear evidence or basically a widespread vote of no confidence in city leadership. Neither is happening anytime soon. . . Imagine the retaliation when you accuse that many officials."

Robin merely shook his head.

"It's easy to miss since these guys are very good at what they do, but I pick up on the signs. I connect the dots," she said matter-of-factly. "It's why my boss doesn't include me in these types of things. Most of my cases are lemons."

"That's absolutely ridiculous. I dunno how you do it. It's like you're stuck. The people you're supposed to be able to tell about this injustice are the people actually carrying it out!"

"Exactly! It drives me insane!" she said with exasperation.

As Robin let the richness of the conversation sink in, Marian started to come down from her high. The fuzziness of the past few minutes started crystalizing, and she began to regret the amount of venting she had done. But man had it felt good to finally say that.

"I–I'm sorry I went off like that," Marian said with a regretful tone.

"Don't be. *I'm* sorry you have to deal with bullshit like that every day."

"Kind of deep stuff for a first date," Marian said in an attempt to lighten to mood.

"Third date. It's okay to get deep on a third date," Robin said seriously.

"Third?"

"You don't count the library as dates?" He took a sip.

"I guess I will. But if we're on the third date I think that's the sex date so. . ."

Robin almost spit out his beer. Then he could not stop himself from laughing. Marian joined in and the laughter lifted the spirits of the table a little bit.

"How about we start with a walk home, and we'll see where the forth date takes us?" Robin said.

He grabbed the bill away from Marian's side of the table. All Marian could do was smile and nod.

Chapter 22: Damaged Justice

"The guy's a wreck," Mancuso said. "They had to give him some sort of sedative to calm him down." He laughed. "Had his wrists and feet strapped to the bed when I got here."

"Mm," Merv grunted and pulled on his cigarette.

The sun was shining out on the hospital veranda, bringing some unlikely warmth to the January day. Mancuso leaned against a brick wall with his body angled towards Merv. He had reached Fort Dearborn General a good fifteen minutes earlier to learn what he could of the situation. Merv was quickly realizing that Mancuso's information was rather thin, of no fault of his own. The story of the crime was already being muddled to save the victim any more embarrassment.

"Apparently he's some big judge," Mancuso added. "Can't say I've heard of him, though. Fulson is his name."

"Yeah, I know the guy. Not personally, but I've testified before with him presiding. He's a raging fag, I mean, queer as a three-dollar bill."

Mancuso chuckled, packing his lip with chewing tobacco.

"He's one of those dudes that got married and somehow managed to get his cock up once to pump out a kid - just to fortify 'the visage,' y'know? Needless to say," Merv grew a sly smile, "I'm not necessarily concerned about his wellbeing."

"Well whatever happened, it's got him spooked like I never seen. Not scared, really - well, scared I guess. Just. . .whacky. I dunno."

Merv puffed. "They're trying to hush what happened so it doesn't get around. But it's too late - the media was there before it was all wrapped up. Hogan said they found the guy on the steps of his courthouse in a dog crate with a collar on and shit smeared over his face."

Mancuso burst out in laughter. *"What?"*

"I'm serious. There was a food and water bowl in the crate. Guy was left with only his underwear and socks on. A note hung from his collar."

"What'd the note say?"

"Forget the whole thing, but the last lines were something like:

Bespoke arbiters of punishments unjust
Shan't receive the public's trust
They shan't don wig, nor gavel, nor gown
Instead laid bare, this shit-nosed clown."

Mancuso raised an eyebrow. "That's fucked up. . . Why the crate, then?"

"It's literal. There's some audio tape that was made public where Fulson compared the kids he sent to jail to stray dogs. Said something like, 'If you keep them in cages, they can't multiply, they can't attack anyone, and they're no longer a nuisance.' It's like sending dogs to the pound. Round 'em up, get 'em off the streets, and forget about 'em."

"Can't say he's wrong."

"Of course he ain't. Still makes me wonder, though."

"What's that?"

"I'm trying to figure out if he had the shit mustache *before* or *after* they put him in the cage. I mean, he could have been nose-deep in a butthole when they kidnapped him."

Mancuso shook his head and spit a stream of brown saliva onto the sidewalk. "Hogan's gonna want an investigation, no? Heard there'll be a press conference this afternoon. What's he want us to do with the guy if he's still hysterical?"

"Fuck Hogan. I'm not worried about it," Merv said dismissively. "If he talks, cool. If not, I'm gonna hit a bar. The guy's a faggot. I really don't give a fuck. Until Hogan specifically tells us we're on the case, it's business as usual."

"Works for me." Mancuso looked Merv up and down. "You're spritely this morning."

My talent. Merv looked over and winked. "You know me. Piss and vinegar, my man."

Mancuso chuckled away and Merv's thoughts strayed for a moment while he finished smoking. He had the itch to black out or score some pills. Just the itch. Part of him wanted to get into a fight. Another part wanted to find a new hooker. He was bored for some reason he couldn't place. *Guess I'll wait to handle that after the press conference, or else Hogan will have a hemorrhage.*

"Alright," Merv announced, tossing his cigarette butt. "Let's go see what we can get out of him."

They rode the elevator to the fourth floor, passing several uniformed policemen in the hallway. Merv had never minded hospitals, unlike most. They were places for the weak and the dying, sure, but that only helped Merv to relish in his own capabilities. He had cheated death time and again, had healed from injuries faster than any doctor had seen, and felt only power when walking through the halls of the dying. He long ago resolved that when the inevitability of his death finally came, decades from then, suicide would be his sure method of choice. Not because of pain or suffering, or in lieu of it, but in spite of it. It was his life, he'd end it himself. Like a man.

The men approached a nurse altering a chart on the door of a patient room marked thirteen. The door was flanked by two additional uniforms. Merv eyed the nurse up and down, pausing at her ass.

"Excuse us," he said.

The nurse scurried out of the way, and he and Mancuso entered the room. Inside were two additional nurses and the balding old man, Judge Fulson, propped up in his bed. He seemed rather calm, which Merv supposed was due to whatever meds they had juiced him up with. *I wonder if they left some pills...*

"We're going to need a few minutes with Mr. Fulson," Merv announced.

Mancuso decided to flash his badge. *He'll learn.*

"You can leave that chart with me."

The women obliged as Merv pulled a chair over and took a seat beside the man's bed. They locked eyes, he and Fulson, and then Merv thumbed through his chart.

After a moment, he said, "I understand you've had a rough day, Martin."

The judge shook his head erratically. He mouthed some words, but nothing audible came out. Merv flipped a page briefly and then dropped the chart on the bedside table. His eyes caught a miniature paper cup on a grey tray. He peeked over and saw the shape of two pills. *Well what do we have here?*

Merv turned quickly and inspected the man. There were no bandages, cuts, scrapes, slings, casts, or visible injuries of any kind. His neck was mildly chafed from the collar, and he still stunk slightly. Otherwise, he appeared wholly unharmed. Merv inwardly cursed Hogan for making him do a job that a rookie could do. He wondered what the Captain's angle was here, but knew that if he began thinking too hard about it, he'd get angry. Merv decided, instead, to do as basic of a questioning as possible. None of this was worth the aggravation.

"Would you like to tell us what happened today?" he asked plainly, not bothering to record the conversation.

Fulson stared straight ahead as if he was too ashamed to make eye contact. "I don't want to talk about it," he said in a whiny voice. He swallowed. "I think I've suffered enough."

"Indeed you have," Merv lied. "And in–"

"I–I'm not talking about it. Just leave me be. I don't want to talk right now."

"Hey, hey, hey. Look at me. Us?" Merv motioned between himself and Mancuso. "We're not here to embarrass you. We're here for information. Because we want to find who did this. And we can make the punishment much greater than what any court decides, you understand?" It was an empty promise. "But we can't do that unless you talk to me. Start from the beginning. What happened?" he asked again, grabbing what was nearly the last of his patience.

Fulson seemed to struggle with what to do a moment longer, but soon managed an answer. "It was before dawn. They kidnapped me outside my home and took me. . .somewhere. I don't know where."

Merv waited a dozen seconds for more that never came. "Can you describe them to me?"

"No. They put a bag over my head before I saw any of them. They were so strong. I tried to fight back, but. . .they forced me."

He rolled his eyes. *This guy is fucking useless.* "How many were they?"

"I heard three voices but only saw one, once they let me see again."

"So you saw one of them?"

"No. He had a hat on and something covering his face. I couldn't tell where we were. It was outside. Maybe a rooftop somewhere. Then he started saying things to me."

"What kind of things?" Merv tried to blink away his frustration.

"They asked me if I've ever heard of 'F.A.M.'"

Merv squinted and looked over his shoulder towards Mancuso, mouthing 'F.A.M.' Mancuso shrugged.

"What is 'F.A.M.'?"

"Few Against Many. It's them, those three."

Merv's head rose in understanding. *Hogan had a hard on for them the other day.*

"He said they were representatives. He went on about what it meant." Fulson shook his head. "I don't know. I was too scared. They were berating me. He was rambling."

"About what?"

"About. . .me. He knew things from my case. . .started condemning me, convicting me of things like it was a sentencing, like it was some big joke. They laughed. They disgraced me. Not just with what they did, but what they said. They kept calling me a dog." Fulson's breathing quickened. "They kept saying something about 'damaged justice.' It was insane! It was just insane!"

"Alright. Just take a second to relax. We're almost done. They kidnapped you, took you. . .*somewhere*, engaged in a dialogue with you, but you didn't see any of them, and then what? What happened next?"

"Then they took my clothes off and they put me in a *cage.* They treated me like an animal. They gave me commands and. . ." Fulson's face curled like he was ready to break down. "I just want this to be forgotten." His eyes were tearing and his mouth quivered. He turned his head away to look out the far window.

"Martin."

"No. Leave me *be. Now*!"

Fuck this. Merv exhaled and stood to leave. "We'll have some other officers in to question you when you settle down."

He slid his chair beside Fulson's bed and paused, noticing the miniature pill cup. Once Fulson had closed his eyes, Merv snatched the cup, put the pills in his mouth, and turned to Mancuso.

"Let's go."

"Wil, you're gonna miss it!" Jon hollered.

He and Robin were lounging on the wraparound couch at Wil's apartment as evening set in over Fort Dearborn. Wil had been in the bathroom for twenty minutes while the trio awaited a press conference in response to their early-morning shenanigans with the Judge.

"I'm strugglin' in here, guys," Wil called from beyond the door. "How long 'til it starts?"

Jon cracked open a *Bearport*, emitting a spray of foam. "Another minute or two."

Wil made a distant groan. "Oh, Jesus."

"What'd he eat?" Robin asked quietly.

"A whole pizza."

"When?"

"Earlier. While you were sleeping."

Another all-nighter had left Robin napping away the afternoon, the third day of such a schedule, required of the guys in order to finish their reconnaissance, preparation, and event. Its execution had gone exactly as planned, truth be told, and the news coverage had lasted most of the day. Despite Robin's fatigue, he was quite pleased with how smooth everything went.

Presently, Robin and Jon watched Channel 3's live coverage of a press conference assembling. An empty podium came into frame with a backdrop of a blue curtain and the seal of the City of Fort Dearborn centered above.

Wil was incorrigible. "I'm never going back to Pappy's again, guys. Pure evil is coming out of my ass right now."

Robin and Jon both had a laugh.

"Guess that's off the list for the Pizza Quest," Robin commented to himself.

"It's probably just stress," Jon muttered.

"This isn't stress, Jon," Wil yelled. "Stress doesn't make you practically bleed from your butthole, okay? I know stress. Believe me."

"You were freakin' out a little bit this morning. Even more than me," Jon hollered. "Just sayin'."

Wil groaned. "Yeah, well, whatever."

"You *were* freakin' out this morning, though," Robin said to Jon.

"I couldn't help it. You don't think smearing dog shit in his face was a little too much?"

Robin shrugged and made to speak but Wil interrupted.

"It wasn't too much. It was just right. Fuck that guy. A little humiliation is fuckin' peanuts compared to what he's done to people, okay?"

Robin looked back to Jon. "What he said."

"You were on another level, though," Jon added.

"Yeah, man," Wil called. "You went off on that guy. He must've felt the size of an ant. I was trying so hard not to laugh but I couldn't help it."

"I'm not wrong," Robin argued. "Like you said. Fuck that guy. He needed to hear it."

Robin followed Jon's lead by cracking his own beer. Since he left St. Augustine's he'd been crashing at Wil's apartment. It had been downright enjoyable for a while, but privacy was nonexistent. He had a few lines on apartment vacancies some blocks away but hadn't found anything particularly worthwhile. Jon supposedly knew a guy whose mother had recently passed away and was looking to rent her apartment, which lay near Baker's Memorial Park. He and Jon were going to take a look the following week in hopes of striking a deal. The thought of Baker's Memorial Park reminded him of something that had fallen by the wayside while the trio had furthered the F.A.M. movement. He thought it a good time to chat before the press conference began.

He turned to Jon, knowing Wil could hear him well enough from the bathroom. "I want your guys' opinion on something."

"What's up," Jon beckoned.

"I think we might have a good opportunity on our hands if we get after reviving the old May Day festival."

Jon's head rose slowly in memory of the old discussion.

"We've got plenty of time," Robin continued. "I think if we work on it in between F.A.M. projects it might turn into something nice."

"The more we talk about it, the more it's beginning to come to life in my head," Jon admitted. "You might actually be on to something."

"Might be a great kickoff for the summer."

"We've got plenty of time," Wil unknowingly repeated from the bathroom. "That park looks like shit anyway. This'll be the way to get it back in shape."

A suited man came into frame on the television from the left side of the screen, striding towards the podium. He wore glasses and was dressed in a navy outfit.

"This guy looks pissed," Jon commented.

Following him were three men, one in uniform and two dressed in business-casual attire. They formed a line on the back wall behind the podium, with one familiar, bearded man positioned on the right of the screen beside a limp set of municipal flags. He stood with a bored, distant expression and a commanding physical presence.

"Anyway, let's think about it some more." Robin said, eyeing the formation briefly, squinting at the new faces. "I've also got an idea for a *major* undertaking for us involving a lot of money. You'll wanna sit down for this one."

Only when he looked back at the television did the bearded man's identity suddenly click. Robin leaned towards the television in disbelief. His face flushed and he felt a tingle run up his spine.

"Oh my *fucking* God," he exclaimed. "You've got to be shitting me."

"What?" Jon asked, startled.

"What?" Wil yelled from the toilet.

Robin's eyes were glued to the screen. "Oh my fucking God."

"What, Robin?"

Wil's muffled voice rose again. "What's going on out there? Did it start?"

"That's him."

Jon leaned in. "Who?"

The bathroom door opened, revealing Wil seated on the toilet with his pants around his ankles. "Did it start?"

"That's him!"

"*Who*, God damn it?"

"That's the cop who put me in the hospital."

Shock overcame Jon's face. *"What?"*

"Right there!" Robin stood and pointed. "Leather jacket, black beard. That's the guy. *Holy shit.* Turn it up. Turn it up."

Jon hastily snatched the remote off the table and cranked the volume. The voice of the man at the podium, who had just begun speaking moments earlier, became audible mid-sentence.

> *". . .official investigation and are treating the group known as F.A.M. as an organized criminal group. The crime and humiliating display this morning was premeditated, and we have determined its link to the explosion at the Wombach Institute in December. I've assigned our veteran detectives, who stand behind me, to the case and we are asking for any and all information from the general public. The investigation is ongoing and we are working on several leads. I've been made aware that a phone number will be shown at the bottom of this telecast. . ."*

Wil's belt jingled as he hobbled out of the bathroom with his pants halfway up. "Did they show his name yet? Where is he?"

"Right there," Robin pointed.

Wil squinted as he followed Robin's finger. "That guy?" He was out of breath. "Did they show his name?"

"I already know it."

"You do?" Jon asked, puzzled.

"Yeah." Robin sank into the couch cushion and ran a hand through his hair. His face turned austere. "That's Merv Hamstead."

Chapter 23: Starry Night

The gravel of the Odexut train station grumbled and gargled under Marian and Robin's feet as they distanced themselves from the departing train. They were about an hour's ride northwest of Fort Dearborn, a distance a city girl like Marian had traveled only a handful of times. Everything she ever thought she wanted was located in the city proper, but tonight's activity required the absence of such hustle, bustle, and more importantly, omnipresent light.

The pair followed the patchy, dull orange glow of parking lot lights to the main road. Marian took in what she could of the small town, trying to match it with Robin's description from the train ride. It was a pass-through town. A main street with two stoplights, a general store, post office, gas station, and a small school. To Marian it looked like Odexut was frozen in time.

The main draw of the town was a park a mere half-mile from the train station, Marian and Robin's destination that evening. It was a fourteen-acre clearing pitched ever so slightly in the southerly direction, as if Mother Nature herself had created stadium seating for music and theater performances. In summer, local bands and acts would utilize the park weekly, but in winter, a different kind of performance was put on: the enchanting display of celestial bodies dotted about in the night sky. The most vocal promoter of these winter "concerts" was the Fort Dearborn Amateur Astronomy Club, which publicized their trips up to the clearing whenever there was a noteworthy astronomical event. Members would bring telescopes and binoculars or, in tonight's case, just some blankets and hot chocolate to enjoy the event with the naked eye.

Marian was prepared for the weather, with thermals under her jeans, several layers under a sweater, a warm winter jacket, and a matching scarf, gloves, and hat. When Robin told her what they would be doing, between heavy make out sessions in the library last weekend, she was ecstatic. The Quadrantids meteor shower was one of the strongest annual meteor showers, but lesser known because the time of the year often hid it behind cloud cover or snow storms, and because of its short duration, peaking for only a night or two at most. Winter this year, however, seemed determined to bless admirers with the gift of crystal clear skies and, though brisk, quite tolerable weather during peak viewing hours. Robin had begrudgingly admitted how he knew of things of this nature, once being a member of FDAAC at the end of high school, to which she had laughed, kissed him again fervently, and affirmed it was a perfect date.

Presently, though, her demeanor toward the night had become tarnished by the news story that broke earlier that week about Judge Fulson. She had been picking up a coffee on her way to work when she first saw it on the television behind the cashier. The shock nearly caused her to drop her drink. Knowing full well she had divulged sensitive information to Robin sent a tingle up her spine. It felt like someone was watching her every move. That feeling haunted her the entire day and at work, it was impossible to escape the story. Her boss was snappy and at times she could overhear his pleas and protests on the phone, even behind a closed door. Someone wanted him to find out how it had happened. She had no concrete evidence, but knew logically that the information she spilled had caused Robin to carry out the crime. Since, she had avoided her boss at all costs in fear of revealing something that could implicate her.

At first she had wanted to cancel the date. How could she rationalize seeing someone who was actively committing crimes? In a vacant field, an hour away from the city, at night, in an unknown town? The museum incident was one thing, but what happened to Judge Fulson was on another level. Before hitting the 'send' button to tell him to fuck off and never talk to her again, though, she had paused. She had to know *why*. *Why* was he doing what he was doing? It caused her much stress, but she decided to go on the date and try to figure out why this man, a man she liked so much, a man who was so personable and charming, so fun and vibrant, so caring and *normal*, could do such a thing. And if it was just an eerie coincidence, she had to know.

After a few quiet minutes, they reached the park and entered through an iron gate, leaving the security of artificial light behind. A red glow appeared as Robin illuminated a flashlight to guide them to their destination, making sure to keep it low to the ground. He had explained to Marian on the train that in the spectrum of visible light, red is the least disruptive to one's eyes, thereby being the most respectful color to navigate by while allowing your eyes and the eyes of others to adjust to darkness. Waving a bright white light around the park was poor form, apparently.

In the dark, the park looked like an endless expanse without borders. There were small dots of red light scattered about, like buoys keeping them clear of a collision course with other parties. They passed a handful of people with telescopes, and one particular man who was set up with what looked like more machinery than Marian ever thought necessary for stargazing.

"I thought you said we wouldn't need a telescope," Marian said, lingering on the elaborate setup.

"We won't," he answered softly. "That guy is probably here to take advantage of more than just the meteor shower. Hard to pass up this clear of a night."

"What's all that other equipment for?"

He kindly shushed her, which sort of pissed her off, and said, "The more serious astronomers have telescopes with positioning systems or cameras to take pictures of the objects they find. Many come equipped with motors and computers. You target a few well-known objects as reference points and then the telescope will find any other object you want and track it."

"It finds the stars for you? Seems like that takes all the skill out of it. Didn't you mention something like that about gun hunters?" On a normal night, this would have been a flirtatious jab, but the tone she used now matched the wintry weather.

"Uh, yea I might've," Robin responded, noticing her attitude.

They found themselves a fairly level expanse, about a hundred yards from the nearest observer. She looked up before sitting and was surprised at how clear and star-filled the night sky was. It might have been the clearest night she'd ever seen. She took a deep breath, and tried to calm her nerves and put away her claws. But the claws remained.

Facing his red flashlight downward, Robin began to prepare their camp. He brought out a large blanket to lie upon and another to cover them as an extra layer of warmth. They sat and he removed a thermos and a little flask from his duffel bag.

"How about a little spiked hot chocolate to keep us warm?"

Marian noticed the shadows of a smile on his face. Still, his fire was met with ice. "I'm good. The blanket is fine."

He put the thermos and flask away and turned square to Marian.

"Is something wrong?" he asked kindly, the recurring coolness seeming to have finally got to him. "I thought you were excited about coming."

She became a little upset at herself for not having the guts to start the conversation on her own. Her attitude wouldn't get either of them anywhere tonight. It was time to get some answers. "Work was hell this week because of the judge thing. You heard what happened, didn't you?"

"I did. . ."

She tried to read his answer, to no avail. Having this conversation in the darkness was becoming a regrettable decision. His body language was indecipherable. "And?"

"And what?"

"You cannot think I'm that naïve," she snapped.

"I don't think you're naïve at all."

"So you thought I would be okay with being used like that?" She did her best not to let her rising heart rate raise the volume of her voice.

He huffed. "I didn't *use* you, Marian."

"Did you do it?"

A long pause followed. Marian flushed and bit her tongue. She could finally break through and start getting some real answers.

"Yes."

The word strangely felt like a burden lifted from her chest. The truth was always better than the fixations of the mind's free reign. It hurt all the same, though.

"Was it because of what I said? Do not bullshit me."

She was met with another pause. "Yes."

She was dying to see his expression. Was it one of remorse? Indifference? Pride? She would have to do with words for now.

"And I'm not supposed to feel used?" Her tone transitioned from one of confrontation to one of regret. "I had a direct role in causing that man pain."

Robin was still refusing to give much away through his speech. "Do you think he deserved it?"

"That doesn't matter. You used something I said to hurt someone. I mean, I didn't explicitly say I was telling you that in confidence, but I didn't think I needed to. I didn't think you would use that as ammunition!"

"Why did you tell me?"

"Because I trusted you, Robin."

"And you can still trust me. Trust is just what made you feel comfortable enough to say those things. Why did you *really* tell me?"

"Because. . ." she started without thinking. Why *did* she really tell him? It was a question she had asked herself rhetorically dozens of times since the news broke but refused to address. It was like questioning a one-night stand or a drinking binge and then going about your life without an answer, without learning from the experience at all. Now that she had to explain it to someone else, especially him, she was drawing a blank.

"I think you told me out of deep, perennial frustration," he offered, his voice kind, as it always was. "I think you told me because you truthfully wished he would be punished for what he did. You said it yourself. That guy is a scumbag. I admire you for following the rules at work when it could be easier not to, I really do. But, by no fault of your own, following the rules helps the people who *don't* follow them act free of consequences. You *should* have the power to change things from your position." He shrugged. "But you don't. I've decided that I do."

Marian sighed. It made sense, but she was not ready to admit he was right. She was never really upset that the judge was harmed, but at herself for her own culpability. Maybe it was because her role in the incident had come about almost by accident, or had not been a choice she made consciously. Take away that guilt and was she sorry it happened? Hell no. And as much as she hated it, following the rules at work did make her feel like others had no way of being held accountable.

"What am I supposed to do now?"

"You don't need to do anything. It's over with."

Marian fell slowly and rested her head on the duffel bag. She needed time to process her feelings before continuing the conversation. She felt a strange mixture of attraction and retreat, like she was on the cusp of taking some serious steps backwards in their relationship yet never wanted to be closer to him. She couldn't make sense of it.

Robin followed her lead and rested next to her. The pair stared blankly into the starry expanse until suddenly, a streak of light bolted across the sky like a quick pen stroke.

"Woah!" she exclaimed, grabbing Robin's arm underneath the blanket.

Marian was so removed, she had nearly forgotten the reason they came upstate. Another streak lit up the sky, and another. The shower continued its performance every ten to twenty seconds for a good five minutes, leaving Marian entranced. She settled herself as best as she could and thought about her man and his parallel life of crime. When the peak of the shower subsided slightly she realized she was still grasping Robin's arm and let go.

"I'm still mad at you," she said, trying to reengage in the conversation.

"I know you are."

"*Why* did you do it, Robin?"

It was the question she wanted answered most. She no longer regretted so much being in the darkness, and wanted him to feel as liberated as her, lying there before the infinite vastness of space. She wanted to expose herself through her words, yet use the darkness as armor for her feelings.

"Two reasons. One: because fuck that guy. Two, and more importantly: to make a statement."

"How is putting a man in a dog crate 'making a statement'?"

Robin chuckled. "That part was meant to be ironic, but it ended up serving a very specific purpose as a very literal shaming. The act took a man who relentlessly abused his position of power and reduced him to a creature. For all to see. It's very important," he finished, as if pointing out a fun fact.

"You're out of your fucking mind."

Her tone was becoming more playful, but Robin seemed to miss it. "Look, I'm not going to sit here and try from every angle to convince you that this is the right thing–"

"And I like it," she interrupted. "I won't try to persuade you to stop. I mean, we're past that anyway. You're already doing it. But I'm really hung up on something. It seems like. . . I dunno, it seems like you're warming up. What's the limit? Will this ever end?"

"Yes."

"When?"

"I'm not entirely sure yet, but I think I have an idea," he replied casually. "Maybe May Day–"

"Woah, woah, woah," she interrupted. "An *idea*? You have an *idea*? You *think*?" She laughed emptily. "Robin, people who *think* are those who sit on the sidelines, who debate and discuss, who theorize - they don't get shit *done*. You have to be more than that. You have to *know*. Those who *know* are doers, changers. Their goals have paved paths. You know as well as I do that open-ended plans aren't plans at all. They're just a string of actions. You have to realize that what you're doing has the potential to get out of control."

"The point is to take it to that level."

"You see, *that's* what I'm not okay with. Whatever your reasons are, they're not good enough for *that*. You need to set limits, Robin. You need to be absolutely sure on everything you do. You need to be safe and disciplined. You need clear direction - and that includes a destination." Robin was silent beside her. "I accept what you do or else I wouldn't be here but I'm very hesitant to *support* you. You have to ask yourself questions. Constantly. 'What am I working towards?' 'What comes next?' 'How can I make a difference without putting lives in danger?'"

"I've thought about this to the point of exhaustion."

"Well, then, that's not enough. You have to be *sure*. You're important to me and I know you're important to other people too, even without family. I may never fully understand what you're so pissed off about, but if you don't think *every single thing through*, there's only one of two places you'll end up." She took his silence as frustration rather than thought. "I'm just asking you questions you should have asked yourself already. Sometimes saying it out loud makes you see your rationale in a different light."

An audible sigh came from Robin. It sounded like the release of tension.

"It's just scary, Robin. . . " Marian pleaded.

"I'm scared too, Marian. Trust me."

"And that doesn't make you want to stop?"

"No. Fear keeps me safe. It has to happen this way. But you're right. Everything you've said is right. I *haven't* been doing enough."

He sounded regretful, but Marian wasn't wholly satisfied. "I just don't know if I understand the goal here."

"Believe me, Marian. It might seem like it, but I'm not doing this for recognition. I'm not doing it for fame or personal gain or legacy. I'm doing this because it's the only way."

"What does that even mean?"

"You and I both know the city is broken. Traditional powers of change have become orchestrated. Fixed. When the one place where change should occur puts itself before the people, it must be uprooted. The only way to do that is to embrace radicalism. Proper radicalism," he pointed out. "That's what I mean by saying 'the only way.' My friends and I are fighting for the disenfranchised, sure, but in doing so a greater good will come about. Change isn't always best done on a voting floor. It's the people's turn. And I'm giving the nudge.

"Look. . . I have learned, with some difficulty, that there are monumental moments in life that shape who we are as individuals. Permanently. It happens to us all. Watching my mom die is one of mine. It took some time for me to realize how impactful that experience was, but I've since learned that my system of values was overhauled. I became. . .different - I don't know how else to say it. I changed, I. . .decided that most petty things in life aren't worth the effort. I decided that certain big ticket things *are* and that those are what are worth putting my heart into. That experience also opened my eyes to the world outside of my old, narrow vision. Honestly, this movement is my way of exploring the new opportunities of my life. It's my way of trying to make a difference."

The conversation reached its saturation point and both breathed in unison. It made sense to her. It wasn't sympathy she felt, more so that perhaps Robin could open her up to a larger change in herself. Perhaps there was a way to learn from his example - not emulate but adopt a mindset and see where it took her. Her current ambivalence in her path at work could use a fresh outlook.

Robin reached his hand under the blanket and grabbed Marian's, giving an affectionate squeeze. "I'm *very* sorry for disrespecting you and using your words as a means to spark action. I didn't do that to intentionally hurt you. Marian, you take precedence over practically everything in my life, and the last thing I ever want is for what I do to drive you away from me. In any other situation, I'd stop what I was doing to prove that to you. It's just that this is already in motion. You deserve to know everything and I won't hide things from you. . .that is, if you're still willing to be with me. You don't need to answer that right now. How about we just enjoy some of the shower before we head back? I promise we can finish the discussion entirely."

She squeezed his hand back, but remained deep in thought. Of course she wanted to stay with him. But he deserved to simmer in silence a little while longer, just for the stress he had caused her. Even though she thought about removing herself from him entirely, she knew it was an impulse that emerged from fear, not truth. She couldn't help it. She was falling for him, and those feelings made fear and hesitancy go by the wayside, even if he was an outlaw. She focused on the stars, and watched meteor after meteor flash through her vision.

Eventually, her head felt as clear as the sky. Somehow, an unlikely thought tumbled into her mind and she cracked a mischievous grin, just like her man always did. She finally knew of one way to make a difference in this fucked up, beautiful world.

In one movement, Marian rolled on top of Robin, straddled his hips, and pinned his arms down beside his head. He let out a grunt out of surprise as she pressed herself against him and she dove in for a hard, warming kiss. They lay there under the stars and shared a feeling through unspoken language. Their lips parted as strands of her hair fell lightly around his cheeks and ears, framing their faces in an intimate cage. From on top of him, she stared into his eyes, lit only by moonlight.

"What would you do if I told you about someone who perfectly fits your. . .agenda?" she breathed. "Would you do something about it?"

Robin's hands slid into hers, interlocked, and squeezed tightly. "Coming from you, I'd make it my priority."

Marian smiled and bit his lip. "Let me tell you about a man named Shane Lackley," she whispered.

Chapter 24: Golden Parachute

Shane Lackley marched into the colossal lobby of the Dwyer Building as if he owned the place. As the Chairman of Lackley-Andersen Investment Securities LLC, one of the region's premier investment firms, Mr. Lackley was accustomed to making such an entrance with such an attitude. Of late, however, his movements had become a touch more casual. Six weeks ago the National Securities Commission caught wind of a major reporting error from within the firm, prompting an investigation. Subsequent findings yielded indications of questionably favorable performance and fraud allegations constituted a majority of the growing case against the firm. According to public information, totals were unconfirmed, liability was without direct aim, but the developments had unquestionably caused dire circumstances for many major investors.

When the allegations broke, the Board of Directors voted to have Shane step down from his post. "An early retirement" they called it, but not before giving him a comfortable severance package for time served, a common practice of upper echelon national companies when chief officers "relocate." Outside of the office, an official investigation was mounting, but those things took *time* and, historically, similar investigations had a track record of fading away if the evidence trail was weak. And Shane was an excellent bookkeeper.

And so, Shane clomped his way through the lobby in what would be the closing weeks of his career. Despite his imminent departure, he wore the same costume as always. Power suit, power tie, power gait; it was his way of life. The morning's *Financial Times* was folded in his hand, hiding the *Legs* magazine that lurked below, his true morning read. His phone was pressed to his ear. On the other end of the line was his mistress, a stunning young girl who more than made up with physical favors what she lacked in intelligence.

The call was at its tail end, having lasted the entire car ride to the office. He walked into the lobby elevator as he said his parting words, assuring her that their plans for the weekend would leave them exhausted and sore. Shane slipped the phone into his inside jacket pocket and assumed the dominant male elevator pose: head pushed back slightly to thicken the neck, wide flatfooted stance with hands crossed over crotch, wristwatch exposed.

As the doors came to a close to lift him to the fifty-first floor, a gigantic hand slid through the diminishing sliver of lobby, stopped the doors in their tracks, and forced a slow retreat to their housing. A behemoth of a man walked into the elevator dressed from head to toe in a dull brown uniform. He wore a low hat, which pressed his shaggy ear-length hair against his head, making a small curl of the strands. Behind him came a dolly that held an oversized cardboard box matching the color of his uniform.

"Apologies, sir," the man said in a deep and booming voice as he positioned himself on the opposite side of the car.

Shane gave no audible reply and resumed his pose. As the large man settled his cart, the elevator doors once again emerged to seal the men inside. But like déjà vu, another hand slid through the nearly closed doors and forced them open. He thought he heard the doors sigh on the way back, as if wondering how many more times today they would be required to repeat their task.

The two men who entered next wore standard Dwyer Building custodial uniforms and carried what looked like an electrical supply bag and a carton of miscellaneous construction materials. Intrusive laughter came with them, breaking the peaceful, albeit boring, elevator music within. They appeared uncharacteristically short next to his original elevator mate, but Shane assumed he looked just as short in their eyes. Though aggravated, he held his stance in the presence of the silent giant and the raucous duo that had joined him. The main elevators were reserved for employees and guests, not workers nor delivery men. These three belonged in the rear freight elevator. He supposed he'd take a minute to scold the incompetence that warmed seats at the lobby desk once he finished his morning read.

". . .so I go, '*wrecker*? I barely *know* her!'" one janitor said to the other as they both laughed and positioned themselves inside the car. "Woah!" the same janitor exclaimed upon noticing the giant delivery man. He stammered dramatically. "Look at *this* guy. 'This elevator ride is presented to you by the color *brown*.'"

The other began a soundless laugh, awaiting another joke. Shane observed the scene apprehensively as the doors came to a close, sealing him into the budding fray.

"Check it out, though," the first janitor pointed. "Put some medals on him and it's G.I. Joe, True American Hero. Seriously, look at the *head* on this guy. Hey pal, what d'you have to *step* into your shirts every morning? Oh, wait - button-ups only, that's it."

He nudged the other smiling janitor and they both turned to face the doors. An awkward silence followed. Shane wished, for the sake of himself, that the barrage had subsided. Not five seconds went by, though, before the man's voice interrupted the hopeful calm. Shane's pose began to stiffen.

"Hey, so I was making a sandwich for my girlfriend yesterday and asked her, 'Do you know the difference between jelly and jam?' She shrugged, so I go, 'I can't jelly my cock down your throat!'"

The two men laughed again as the joker made a thrusting motion with his pelvis to hammer home the punchline.

"This guy knows what I'm talking about," he said, pointing a thumb at the large delivery man.

The giant made eye contact with the joker and folded his arms, a quiet warning to cut the act. It went unheeded.

"Hey, Big Brown, lemme ask you something," he continued, looking over his shoulder at the behemoth. "I always see your trucks double-parked outside with like three or four parking tickets on the window. You guys have to pay for those out of your own pocket?"

The behemoth, turning his head slowly and staring, replied with a simple, "No."

"Yeah, figured. I bet you just pass the cost on to the customer or somethin'. Fuckin' shysters." The joker shook his head and looked forward.

Shane eyed the giant, whose face presently contorted. His chest heaved, pushing his folded arms out to a once unimaginable distance. Shane glanced, then, at the digital readout and saw that they were only passing the twenty-first floor. A sense of dread filled the air.

"Probably why they make you dress like a walking piece of shit," the janitor snapped. "Can't afford nicer uniforms with all those tickets - I mean, seriously, I could wipe my ass on that thing and the only sign of it would be the *smell.*"

Suddenly, the behemoth reached swiftly around his dolly and slammed the 'Emergency Stop' button on the control panel. Shane was unsure if the jarring motion he felt was due to the strength of the blow against the elevator or the momentum from the screeching halt. He braced himself against the railing and backed into the corner, eyes wide with alarm.

In an instant the behemoth had grabbed the joker by his collar and thrown him against the elevator doors. "How are you going to wipe your ass when I break both of your *fucking* arms?" he growled.

The little man froze in shock and let out the smallest squeal, raising his arms in submission the instant he was lifted.

"Hey! Hey! Relax!" the third man broke in, hands on both the behemoth's arm and his co-worker's shoulder. "He just likes to bust balls. It's a misunderstanding, that's all."

The large man's grip began to loosen as he looked back and forth between the two janitors.

"C'mon, he isn't worth it. Look, where's that package going? We'll help you find who you're looking for."

Shane, still firmly planted into the corner, slowly began to reach for his cellular phone, readying to dial the security desk. The delivery man considered the offer in the tense silence, then slowly lowered the custodian. He snatched the box off the dolly.

"It's an express delivery for. . ." He checked the label. "Shane Lackley," the man said in a deep tone.

Shane froze and squeaked, his mind screaming 'oh shit' but his words coming out meek. "Uh. That's me," he yelped.

The trio turned to look at Shane together for the first time, void of the shock that should have come when he revealed his identity, for they knew precisely who he was.

The three figures staring back at him were menacing, like a row of executioners coming to take him to the gallows. Looking more closely the men he realized that each had a hat pulled low over his brow, casting deep shadows over his eyes. Smiles formed on each of their faces. Confusion paralyzed him as it suddenly dawned on him that not one of the men had chosen a floor upon entering.

With unexpected speed and strength, the two custodians seized Shane, knocked the phone out of his hand, and pulled him closer to the behemoth, who began opening the oversized box. He flipped over the cardboard tabs, revealing a glittering golden fabric inside.

"You've been expecting this," the behemoth said.

He reached for the elevator controls. A pull of the 'Emergency Stop' button put the elevator back in motion. Shane watched as the large man cancelled the glowing icon for the fifty-first floor with a double-click and reset their destination to the uppermost floor.

Wind whipped through the heights, across rooftops and spires like the cold breath of a sleeping giant. Jon's hair fluttered, though pinned by his brown hat, and he initiated a memorized folding sequence on the large glittering fabric before him. Wil worked alongside him. They had fluffed the golden canopy in a wide pebbled space on the Dwyer Building's rooftop, surrounded by the Financial District's many towers. Presently, it lay in a shape resembling a flat cone with its apex removed. At its base, cords stretched like miniature tributaries to a grey pack some yards away.

Behind the men, facing the roof's edge, were Robin and the trio's dapper hostage. Robin held a notepad and paced to and fro before a seated Shane. Not a minute earlier, they had removed Shane's blindfold and the duct tape covering his mouth, making him aware of his conundrum. Robin's sardonic speech was loud, but his volume could be distinguished little in such a location.

"Prior to recent developments, seventy-nine percent of Lackley-Andersen's holdings, that's twenty-three *billion* dollars, consisted of investments from twenty-one major charities, twelve hospitals, four small pharmaceutical companies and, *dear god*, the civil service of the City of Fort Dearborn." Robin eyed him scornfully. "Backed by analysts and expert testimony, new findings claim your company has deliberately misrepresented earnings, modified its balance sheets, reported complex and misleading transactions, and, worst of all, entered fake trades. My, how easy it must be to steal people's money when they entrust it to you. Since this evidence broke, many of said charities have halted operations, two have closed completely, one of the three hospitals is on the verge of bankruptcy, and the unions are initiating a bailout plea. Losses are estimated in the tens of billions. These are. . .*not* numbers to be proud of. It's amazing how deeply affinity fraud runs, is it not?" He glanced down at his paper again, then back to Shane. "The rest of the money you stole was from rich people. Forgive me while I wipe away a fake tear on their behalf. I will say, however, even *they* deserve not what you have committed. Please, oh please, do not misunderstand me. I do not have a vendetta against the rich - no, no, no. I am here to teach you a lesson on ethics in the workplace and show you that your actions are *offensively* careless, like. . .a faucet left on all night. Your wastefulness is heinous and an insult to those in need. It simply will not stand."

"What do you want with me?" Shane breathed submissively. He had been distracted as Robin spoke, frantically examining the situation that was unfolding.

"What do you *think* we want?" Robin mocked.

"*Money*? Tell me and it is yours. I swear to God it's yours."

Laughs cut through the air.

"Somebody wasn't paying attention. . . Why is everyone so quick to bargain with money?" Robin asked ruefully. "Does money make the world go 'round? Hey, Bill, what do you think makes the world go 'round?"

"Pussy" Wil yelled, focused on his work.

"What about you Mr. Lackley?" Robin requested. After a handful of "ums," Robin continued, "Based on your reading material today, I would say you vote the latter." After a pause, he proceeded with a hardened tone, "I'll be truthful. People like *you* are the reason people like *me* fucking *hate* money. You are a *monger* and a thief of the lowest caliber. The very last thing I want from you is *money.*

"Money is a tool that has only as much value as that for which it is used. Your actions have devalued that which inherently has little value itself. . .leaving it worthless. An individual's *will* has value," he explained, "and if enacted with such a tool as money, it can do marvelous things. A fool I may be in many aspects of life, I am no fool when facing the reality of a capitalistic society. Our environment requires money to continue to function. I may not like it, but I realize and accept this without reservation. What I do *not* accept is ruthless selfishness in which an individual—*that's you,*" he pointed and whispered briefly "—takes a massive shit on not only people, but companies and organizations that exist *mostly* to help others. Sure, charities are as much a business as hospitals are, and desperately present themselves as profitless as possible, but at their core they exist to aid humanity. *And sure* practically the only redeeming quality of a pharmaceutical company is what they produce. . .but do you see what I'm getting at here when I speak of *will*? . . .No?

"You have been targeted because you are the embodiment of immorality in the financial sector of society. Your profiteering and *greed* shapes thousands of lives - and don't get your hopes up, it's not for the better. You've rigged the almighty contest of Capitalism. You've cheated and wiped your ass with the very rubric of ethics - which doesn't make you smarter than the rest; it makes you a coward and a weakling."

Jon and Wil had prepared the Z-fold, and were now wrapping the bundle with cord. Any minute, now, they'd be finished. Robin decided to bide his time with one more point.

"To quote my favorite writer, 'You are what you do; thus, if you do nothing, you are nobody.' The point is this: our actions define us as individuals. I've already told you what you are, so it's only fair I return the gesture. Have you ever heard of a group called the Few Against Many?"

Shane's breathing picked up and he nodded. "In the news."

"Good! Allow this to be our formal acquaintance. We three are representatives of a population that has been dismissed, yet seems to suffer indefinitely at the hands of its disdainers. We are the will of that population. And the hand that acts out its will. Nothing more." He paused and looked side to side, as if deciding on what to say next. "You may not know it, but we're thieves ourselves," Robin said with a smug smile. "Though we do not keep that which we pilfer, we give. We are thieves of pride, attention, and fear. What we steal is used to inspire and incite. To stimulate. To–"

"Done," Wil announced, halting Robin's monologue. Robin gave him a nod and refocused his attention on the unfortunate banker, that smile still glued on his face.

"Do you like extreme sports, Mr. Lackley?" he asked.

"Please. . ."

Robin ignored him. Instead he stepped a pace and glanced over the edge of the building. He quickly pulled back, shivering at the sight of the ground from such a height.

"Which looks farther away: A building's roof from the ground or the ground from a building's roof?" He shivered again for effect. "I'll tell you what. Peek over that edge and you'll have your answer."

"This is outrageous. I–I'm innocent. Let's just sit, let's sit down and talk about it," Shane gasped. His panic was showing, and his eyes darted back and forth.

"You are sitting. And we are talking."

"I'm innocent. I swear, just–"

"You are as innocent as your actions, Mr. Lackley!" Robin snapped. "Are you truly claiming that there is such a thing as deliberate innocence? You're Ivy League educated and a Laureate. Act your *fucking* station, you prick. You insult our intelligence with such pathetic begging."

Jon and Wil had since come to flank Shane, Jon holding the big grey pack and Wil holding a wide three-foot-long tube which had been stuffed with the glittering fabric. Out of the bottom end, a cord ran to the pouch of the pack. Through the very top of the cylinder, opposite the cord, ran a thin cable, threaded through the holes and then crimped onto itself, creating a tight bond. The remainder of the cable ran along the roof and out of sight.

"Society has a question for you, Shane, and we took it upon ourselves to ask you on their behalf. The question is this: *Where*. . .do you *get*. . .the *balls*?" Robin exclaimed.

"What?" Shane asked quizzically. His attention was split between the kidnappers, who were approaching him from either side.

"Do you know what a Golden Parachute is, Mr. Lackley, sir?" Robin asked as his posture stiffened.

". . .Yes," Shane admitted reluctantly.

"And you were offered one were you not? On the scale of eighteen *million* dollars?"

". . .Nineteen," Shane quietly, and with his head lowered in visible shame, corrected.

Jon brought the pack to Shane's back and began forcing his arms through the shoulder straps. Jon fought off the man's flailing easily and corralled him in place, at one point saying, "Believe me. You wanna wear this."

All the while, Robin had been speaking. "Well, I for one think you deserve such a gentle fall. It is a long way down from where you are. It'd be suicide to fall that far without protection. I worry that the protection you were offered isn't significant enough, though," Robin leaned ever closer, rubbing his thumb and forefingers together. "And since that fall from grace is upon you, I wanted to make sure you not only made it *off* the pedestal, but back down to reality."

Jon quickly ushered Shane to his feet, walked him to the precipice, and forced him to peer over the edge. Shane's eyes almost fell out of his head at the sight of the avenue below.

"Stop! I'll do anything you want! Anything! Name it!" Shane begged.

Robin looked at Jon and Wil, then back to Shane. "Jump without the parachute," he said with a stare that would temper steel.

"Oh, *God.* You're crazy! *All* of you!"

"Okay. Don't, then."

"There's no chance you'll get away with this," Shane threatened.

"I don't intend to. Enjoy your fall."

Before Shane could say more Jon lifted him off the rooftop and threw him over the side of the building like a ragdoll. Wil immediately pitched the cylinder after Shane, watching it soar towards the center of the void. After nearly ten stories and a lung-full of screams, all at once the cable connected to the top of the cylinder became taut in Wil's hands, and below the golden chute slipped out of its housing, catching the air like a magnificently glimmering sheet. Shane's body jerked and came to slowly float as the canopy opened fully, accompanied by confused wails and prayers.

The trio watched from the rooftop as Mr. Lackley's golden parachute sent him safely toward the street below, with speed no faster than a feather.

Merv leaned against a traffic pole, chuckling to himself between puffs from a fresh cigarette. Across the intersection, a suited man hung from one of the Financial District's many tall, ornate traffic poles, which had been built in the early '20s and ran the length of the District along 2nd and 3rd Avenues, towering over the city's standard streetlamps and traffic lights. The parachute attached to the man had somehow tangled its shroud lines in the mess of cables, suspending him some twenty feet above the intersection.

Traffic had been at a dead stop on 2nd Ave. for more than thirty-five minutes. Apparently, a box truck had swerved out of the way of the banker as he fell from the sky towards the intersection, setting off a chain of fender-benders and four minor accidents. Emergency responders were milling about, waiting too patiently for a ladder truck to make its way through the gridlock.

All the while the unfortunate banker hung helplessly, an image consumed second by second by curious onlookers and a flood of media personnel. The man surely knew he would be plastered on every television in the city throughout the day.

Merv had arrived five minutes earlier, and learned that three teams had begun sweeping the Dwyer building. He knew how useless that maneuver was, especially on a skyscraper, but it made people feel safe. Firemen and EMTs had been speaking with the man for some time. He had reportedly suffered a broken arm and dislocated shoulder, having swung into the post before he became caught. Thankfully his yells had ceased, but occasionally moaning and groaning could be heard underneath the surrounding commotion. Though the intersection had been taped off, the crowd of onlookers persisted.

Steadying a shaky wrist, Merv read 10:17 a.m. on his watch. His headache was surprisingly soft considering the amount he had consumed the night before and he happened to be dressed rather well, in a new blazer and slacks. Yesterday's fresh haircut and trim of his beard suited his uncharacteristic lightness this morning. He figured it all mostly had something to do with him running out of drugs earlier that week, a void that, luckily, he'd arranged to fill today.

"Hammer," a stern voice called.

Merv looked to his left and found Captain Hogan staring him down. For what reason the Captain was there, Merv hadn't a clue. Hogan waved him over, and turned to keep walking. Squinting, Merv pulled hard on his cigarette, flicked it away, and followed him, wondering what retardation waited.

Several strides behind Hogan, and maneuvering between some police vehicles, he watched as the Captain approached a black limousine with tinted windows. Hogan tugged on the back door and opened it, motioning for Merv to take a seat. Reluctantly, Merv entered and slid along the dark leather. Hogan slammed the door after him and rounded to the other side.

Sitting across from Merv, facing him on bench-style seating, was a balding man in an expensive suit. His cologne was subtle and his cufflinks appeared to be solid gold. In his lap was a small folded newspaper clip. The man looked up a moment after Merv's entrance and made eye contact, extending a hand to commence a formality of sorts. Hogan slid from the opposite side of the car into the seat next to Merv and shut his door, closing the men inside.

"Nice to see you again, Detective," the man said in a friendly voice.

"Mr. Mayor, it's a pleasure as always," Merv lied, hiding his confusion behind an assumed professionalism. Half of him was glad he hadn't yet had a drink and the other half wished he had never passed out the night before, so as to take the meeting under a pleasant curtain of booze. The whole of him gave a laugh at the coincidence of being not only sober, but well-dressed.

Mayor Crowley was a keen and treacherous man, who Merv had encountered several times over his career. He had seen cops less than he ran, quite literally, out of town at the Mayor's behest. If it was Crowley's prerogative, you'd find yourself out of work and facing any range of passive abuse. In this regard, Merv respected him; however, he'd done many favors for him in the early days, when Crowley was but a City Councilman, and in doing so, learned that regardless of station, Crowley was rather predictable. Afraid, Merv was not – he simply approached the unexpected meeting with caution. Merv glanced from Crowley to Hogan, awaiting the impending conversational dross.

"Well, gentlemen, it has happened again," the Mayor huffed, his practiced tone sounding almost regal at this point in his career. He was ever calm. "It seems like every few weeks I have news whispered in my ear and something. . .outrageous has happened. I hear those three letters attached, always associated. F-A-M. And every week I hold out with confidence in your abilities. I tell myself that this will come to an end quickly, that our finest men are working tirelessly to suffocate the cries of those three letters and restore order and peace. Today, I grow worried that my faith is too generous."

"Mr. Mayor, sir," Captain Hogan began uncomfortably, "I want to assure–"

"My time is limited here, Captain," Crowley interrupted politely. "Please spare me your assurances. We are past that point are we not?"

Hogan smothered what panic was likely baking inside him with an eager nod.

Merv cleared his throat. "Give it to us straight, Mr. Mayor. If you would."

Crowley eyed Merv for a moment and tilted his head. "Very well, Detective."

He shifted and crossed his left leg over his right, tenting his hands over the newspaper clip. Merv wondered how a man could manage that pose. If he tried it himself, his nuts would surely be squashed in a femoral vice. The Mayor seemed comfortable, though, and spoke coolly.

"This has. . .created an element in our city that will not be tolerated. Frankly, I don't give a flying fuck who's in charge. All I care about is putting a stop to this. . ." he motioned to the crime scene, "madness. There has been growing uproar in the Inner District these past weeks. What were once whispers have grown to an outcry of support for these fugitives. Protests have formed, not only in light of Judge Fulson's release. . . I can see the uneasiness in City Hall. A particular population is stirring, gentlemen, and it is awfully worrisome to my colleagues. If you think your hands are full now, wait until this comes to a head. You both can recall the riots all those years ago, can you not?"

"All too well, Mr. Mayor," Hogan said quickly.

"I am here because I'd like to hear what you know so far and what is being done to solve this escalating issue. I, myself, am a witness and *victim*, yet this group remains at large. Hell, I've practically *met* the bastards. I must say that the lack of development is disconcerting. . . Detective?"

"At this point, Mr. Mayor," Merv said, "our leads have slowed. With such a public display this morning, I'm hopeful that there will be a breakthrough. We've yet to question the victim, and it's too early to gauge what eyewitness accounts might surface. Additionally, a building like that, as well as those around it, is littered with security cameras and personnel."

Crowley held a hand up. "That's all well and good Detective, but spare me – I'm aware that this situation may provide leads. My worry is that those leads will yield nothing. If my worries prove true, then what? I'd like to know where we stand on this investigation."

"Currently, we're at a bit of a standstill. It's quite clear that their targets are premeditated, yet there's no distinguishable pattern. Security footage has been limited. Witness descriptions, when given, have been concurrent yet vague and rather fruitless. Our one hopeful lead has turned sour."

"Which was?"

"I'm speaking of the rookie who was attacked in the rear of the museum. Ortmann is his name. He interacted with one of them, even got a decent look at his face but. . .your pardon, sir. . .he's a fucking moron," Merv remarked coldly. "An eight-year-old could do a better job."

"Am I to believe a *policeman* has failed to provide a proper description?"

"The force ain't like it used to be. Verbatim, he said: 'I dunno, sir. He was wearing a hat and was mostly in the shadows.' He's sure that if he saw him again he'd recognize the man."

Crowley blinked rapidly.

"Seems to me he was so embarrassed he'd rather have it over with than anything else. No identifying characteristics other than speech, build, skin and hair color, and a name: Bill. Most likely fake."

"Go on," the Mayor pressed.

"Crime scenes have been rather clean - our forensic teams haven't come up with much from the museum nor the Fulson incident. The prints we have found do not match any in our system, unfortunately. We're hopeful of citizen aid."

"It's rather obvious at this point that these men are from the Inner District, Detective. Even I can deduce that."

"Rather obvious indeed, sir."

"So what exactly are you saying with all of this?"

"I'm *saying*. . .beyond that information, we have nothing."

Crowley's face hardened. "I'd like to read something for you, gentlemen." He reached into his pocket and removed a small note. He began in a stern tone:

"The standard of punishment is all but lost,
Since when must employees follow the rules, but not the boss?
I suggest those curb such flippancy, lest they forfeit repute,
Obey society's will or jump without a parachute.

"Am I next?" He turned to the Captain, then. "Are you?" Next he turned to Merv. "Are you? Who's the next one to be. . .hung from. . .a fucking bridge? Humiliated? Or *murdered*? What is next? Hmm? Family? What's the limit here? I, *Mayor*, feel threatened in my own city. It will not stand. It will not last. You will do your job, and swiftly, or there will be personal consequences."

Merv couldn't help but feel enjoyment watching Crowley squirm. None of these "victims," these fucks, mattered to him. Not even remotely. So some asshole got thrown from a building. So some faggot judge got a little retribution. So some rich cunts got cake batter on their five-thousand-dollar tuxes. So some poor, minority-riddled scum are getting pissy. So what? So fucking what? *I solve real problems, you twat. I chase criminals - not cowards who hide their faces.*

"Captain. Detective. I am here to tell you that your window for wrapping this up is nearing its end. This F.A.M. garbage has already beckoned the attention of the FBI. If we keep showing such incompetence, they will swoop into our offices - into our *lives* - and put their noses where they don't belong. It goes without saying that a Federal investigation is the very last thing *any* of us want. That includes you two. You have in the realm of days to make some arrests, or we will have an entirely different set of problems on our hands. Do you understand what I am saying?"

Merv looked over to Hogan whose fury was blatant. He looked like he was either going to punch Crowley or throw up. Maybe both. If Merv knew one thing in life, it was that Hogan despised the FBI more than Internal Affairs, Democrats, lawyers, and vegetarians combined. His face reddened at the very word 'Federal,' and he shifted in his seat, clearing his throat as if he wanted to scream out a rebuttal.

Merv didn't disagree with Hogan, per se, yet he found himself detached. These circumstances troubled him greatly, but the F.A.M. crimes were about as motivating as a traffic stop. As much as he had tried, he couldn't bring himself to care. The group's actions were a pathetic attempt at resistance from some wannabe criminals who had seen too many movies, who had delusions of some sort of societal change. He simply didn't take them seriously.

"Understood, sir," was all Hogan could muster.

"Detective Hamstead, I've always had confidence in your expertise, regardless of past incidences. You are the best there is and I need you," Crowley said in a fatherly tone, brow raised.

Merv nodded in appreciation. The sentiment made him wonder if he was being lazy. There was glory attached to this case that, though subtle, he supposed was unparalleled in this city. It wasn't a typical threat, and so there wouldn't be typical payoff. Perhaps he would phone Mancuso and start to give a fuck.

"I will do whatever it takes to end this quickly, Mr. Mayor. I will be employing. . .my most useful tactics. You have my word." The comment was made to hold Crowley over. Merv had yet to decide how he'd handle things, regardless of orders.

"Very good. I am prepared to make this worth your while, gentlemen. I am here to motivate you. Not issue threats or warnings. To put it plainly, deliver the outlaws and I'll see to it that you'll be taken care of. Detective - the medals that were stripped from you will be returned and you'll be considered for a promotion. Captain - I believe a pay increase would be up for consideration. It's nearing high time, is it not?"

Crowley looked to both men individually and then dropped his head and took a pen out of his jacket pocket. He began to examine what Merv had deduced was a crossword puzzle.

"With your leave, sir," Hogan said, a hand on the door handle.

Mayor Crowley remained focused on his crossword and let out an "mmhmm." Merv glanced at Hogan. The both opened their doors to exit.

"Gentlemen," the Mayor added, his eyes on his puzzle. "If you fail, our next meeting will not be as pleasant."

Chapter 25: Heavy Work

Tall weeds and briars pulled at Robin as he strode through the brush. Had he not been wearing heavy denim pants, his legs would surely be crisscrossed in scrapes by now. Wil and Jon had already thanked him for the recommendation of attire, Wil especially. Many afternoons this March he had coupled a sweatshirt with shorts. And who could blame him. The weather permitted so.

A limited assessment of their surroundings would make one think the trio was well beyond the city limits, in some wooded place or forest. A variety of foliage, shrubbery, grasses, fallen leaves, downed trees, and the occasional item of trash filled Robin's view in every direction. Yet they stood no more than a few hundred yards from the ever-familiar Atlantic Ave. Baker's Memorial Park would need some tender love and care for anything resembling a restoration to come about. But the guys feared not. Today's rummaging was merely for getting their bearings.

"How'd the move go, Robin?"

"All settled. Had Marian over the other day actually."

The apartment Jon had informed Robin of had turned out to be a wonderful setup. Though the building and its amenities were staggeringly old, the space was rather lovely—a simple one-bedroom place on the fifth floor of a seven-story building, fully furnished and cozy, complete with a view of Baker's Park.

"Awesome," Wil said. "I'm glad we got to meet her."

"Definitely," Jon added.

"Same. She had a great time. Shit, now that I think of it that was only the second time I saw her this month because of our extracurriculars."

"That's it?"

"I mean, she and I talked about it, and it's not smart to have her around so often with all the heat we've taken on."

"Stop with that," Wil cried.

"I'm just talking worst case scenario."

"No one knows it's us. We've been ghosts the past few months."

Robin stepped over a skinny fallen tree. "That's precisely why people might think it *is* us."

"How do you figure?"

"Think about it - nights out, the Soup Kitchen and all. We go from being omnipresent to omni. . .vacant. You can't tell me people aren't at least speculating."

"Are you worried?" Jon asked.

". . .No. But I don't wanna have to worry." Robin squinted at himself. "Does that make sense?"

"Yeah," Wil answered.

"Alright. Hold here for a minute," Robin announced as the group entered an open expanse just south of the pond.

The day after Robin's stargazing date with Marian, the trio immediately began work on organizing the May Day festival. He had taken her words to heart that night, and lost plenty of sleep over her points and sentiments. But she had helped him see that this day, this festival, could be the perfect way to begin a healthy unification in the District. It made perfect sense. What followed was a legitimate action plan and full confidence and commitment from Jon and Wil.

"This is gonna be so sweet," Wil repeated as they scanned the area. He had said that exact same line probably ten times since they entered the park.

"So if my research is correct, this is where the main area was back in the day," Robin said, taking it all in. "It's obviously the largest of the few sections that still resemble clearings, so I think that we could have the landscapers clear it entirely and make a nice open field for the main attractions. The smaller sections will still hold vendors and things, but this is where the magic will be. Food, drinks, crafts, fun, you name it."

"We could even hold a concert in the fields down there," Wil said, pointing downfield.

"That's true."

"Don't forget about the flowers," Jon added.

Wil huffed. "You and you're fuckin' flowers, man."

"Its tradition, dude. We've gotta have 'em."

"We'll make it happen, Jon," Robin assured his friend. "We're blowin' this out."

"Well if he's getting his flowers, we've gotta do the art section. I'm tellin' ya, it'll be a hit."

Jon rolled his eyes.

"I told you five times already we can have the damn art section," Robin said. "You're in charge of it."

"It's gonna be so sweet," Wil repeated yet again.

"This is going to take a mass of workers, man," Jon decided as he once again surveyed the land. Imagining the finished product came easier to some than others.

"It'll be fine. What's important is that we've got the ball rolling here. All the quotes are in, so we know what it'll cost. Now it's up to us to plan the finer details and spread the word."

"You still haven't answered my question of how we're going to pay for this thing."

"There's two options. One: have someone else pay for it – and I have a plan for that. And two: pay for it ourselves."

Wil and Jon sounded a vocal alarm, but Robin cut them short.

"Before you guys lose your shit, I understand the blatant issue with that, seeing as we're collectively broke. But I have solutions. Which leads us to our next adventure, being the outlaws we are. . . Tonight, my friends, we'll have ourselves a proper discussion, full of plotting, scheming, and boozing."

"Oh, I'm gonna love hearing this one," Wil remarked skeptically.

Jon merely smirked.

"We've got our work cut out for us, boys," Robin declared. "On both accounts. Either way, the funds will be disbursed," he finished with a wink.

Steam billowed softly out of a wall grate like smoke from a dying fire. Shirtless, Wil slowed to a halt as he reached the empty alleyway a good mile northwest of Baker's Memorial Park, his damp skin glistening in the remaining sunlight of the day. He began settling his legs with a walk about the cramped area, interlocked his fingers over his head and laboring to control his breathing and heart rate. Before any thoughts could materialize, Robin's thudding footsteps came to a skidding stop from the opposite direction.

"You are. . .one fast. . .motherfucker," Robin said through heavy breaths. He attempted to walk around in imitation of Wil, but collapsed into a bent position instead, leaning his hands on his thighs.

"Imagine if I wasn't hungover," Wil replied with barely enough air to finish the statement.

They eyed each other lightheartedly. *Kid's gettin' faster*, Wil thought.

"I swear you have," Robin huffed, "the shorter route."

Wil shook his head. "If anything, mine's longer."

It had been two weeks since Robin revealed his plan for their next F.A.M. endeavor. To say it was the most brazen and utterly risky to date would be a laughable understatement. Wil literally spit out his beer when Robin dropped the idea. Jon nearly had a stroke. After some settling and deep discussion, though, the unanimous vote, paramount to their formalized decision process, was reached. Much of Robin's persuasions rang true with Wil. A symbol must fall, and they were to give it its first push.

Deep breaths echoed in the alleyway as steam continued to quietly escape from the wall. The air was dense, unsuitable for recovery but great training for their lungs. He, without a doubt, had never been in better shape in his life. They had run the route every day since their vote, training in accordance to Wil's knowledge of cross-country running from high school. Even though Wil always finished first, he refused to question Robin's work ethic. He wasn't just a thinker, this man, he was a doer. He turned his dreams and ideas into actions. And he was molding Jon and Wil into men of a similar caliber. Their movement gave him purpose. It gave him direction. For the first time in his life, he was proud of himself. Gone were the days of aimless struggle. Gone were the mornings of endless depression and the nights spent drowning sorrows and chasing happiness. It was all thanks to Robin. And the only way Wil knew how to return the favor was to give all of himself to their cause. Their training was grueling, even for someone of Wil's capabilities, but there is no greater motivator than fear. And it was fear of a very particular outcome that pushed them.

Run like they're chasing you.

A red 1976 National Motors Primo puttered along a busy street in south Fort Dearborn. It was a tiny box of a thing, with a missing rear hubcap on the left and a rusted, mismatched blue door on the right, requiring the occasional prayer and a heavy-handed smack on the dashboard to turn over. In short, it was a piece of shit. Wil and Robin had to barter with Wil's neighbor for the car, and despite their universal disregard for the law, this particular stage of their plan required upholding it. Grand theft auto came later.

Wil, who claimed he was a far better driver than Robin, held the wheel at ten and two, made sure to come to a complete three-second stop at every stop sign, and kept at least three car-lengths back from their mark. From the outside, theirs was just another vehicle among the traffic. Occasionally, Wil's acceleration became jerky, or he'd frustratingly brake in a way that caused Robin to brace himself, but both had shaky legs from the run that morning - and yesterday morning's and the day before, and so on. So the situation permitted some leniency.

Robin, with a composition notebook open on his lap, furiously tracked their mark's path. "What street were we on after the Deli?" he asked without looking up.

"Uh, I think it was Randolph," Wil answered, focused on the road.

"Okay. This is the same route as last Friday."

It was day twelve of "two-a-days" as they referred to them—running in the morning and reconnaissance in the evening. Anything in between was secondary.

"And this one is A876H," Wil said, getting a glimpse of their target before it turned down Hanover St.

Robin scribbled the letters and digits, repeating them under his breath. His notebook was meticulous, each of the five new headings recording a license plate number of a vehicle of interest. Below, the entry contained physical descriptions of associated parties, the time and location of specific events, routes, and other observations that may prove useful in the future. It was becoming rather apparent that from that night onward, opportunities for gathering information would be few. The following weeks would have to be spent on their "two-a-day" schedule until the time was right. It was like Robin said: "The fastest way to torpedo a mission was to corrupt their plan with flawed information."

"Alright," Wil said. "I'm gonna back off."

We'll be back for you soon, my dear Cavalier.

Jon flipped through some pages of a rather tedious manual. It was a task to focus so intently, especially in such an interesting locale: the rare book room of the City Library. It was the very first time Jon had been in the library, let alone such a "protected" room, as Robin had called it. He and Marian sat across the dizzying carpet from Jon, amidst their own reading material. It took a few minutes to grow accustomed to the silence and calm, not because Jon preferred socializing, but because such an activity was typically enjoyed by his lonesome. The significance of this place to them had been hinted to him at one time, and he hadn't wanted to tread upon their alone time. But Robin insisted.

The pair lounged sideways across two leather chairs, acutely angled towards one another, their feet hanging off the armrests. They swayed inches apart, as if yearning to intertwine. If either were to break their concentration on the literature on their laps and look up, they would most certainly be distracted by the other's presence. Jon, at the desk next to them, couldn't help but smile before returning to the book resting on his lap.

At first, he was awfully hesitant when Robin told him he had informed Marian of "everything." The action seemed worthy of a growling reprimand or some sort of flurry of yells, but in a flash Jon realized the ignorance in such an act. After all, Marian was involved in her own right. Willfully, now. That, in and of itself, became an instant source of comfort to Jon. Further, when the four were together, she never brought it up, never questioned them, and somehow because of this he knew that she would never jeopardize their safety willingly. Her questions of Robin were not part of a malicious attempt to incriminate them. Jon thought they came from a place of concern and genuine desire to be a part of his, and now their, lives. And that was all he could ask for from someone in her position.

Marian got up slowly from her chair and tugged on Robin's foot lovingly. "Gonna stretch my legs and go to the bathroom quick," she said, giving him a look that would melt a snowman in Siberia.

"I hate to see you go but. . .you know the rest," Robin replied flirtatiously.

Marian gave his head a soft push as she walked and with a quick chuckle she was off. Robin's feet hit the ground and a quick wince told Jon that he was still sore from the rigorous physical training him and Wil were doing. Without pulling his eyes from his book, Robin spoke.

"How'd you make out at the store?"

"Um, I priced some things out but I think I'm going to need some guidance here. There's like a dozen different grades to choose from. Not to mention lengths."

"Hmm," Robin sounded. "Just get fifty feet of something middle grade. Enough to hold around a ton. We don't have to go nuts with it. I mean, think about it. Doubling it doubles its strength, no?"

"Yeah, I guess so."

He looked up. "So if we get fifty feet that should be plenty."

It sounded fine to Jon. "Alright. I'll get it tomorrow. Where's Wil?"

"Welding." Robin already had his head back in his book, some high fantasy thing about a sword in a stone.

"Man, he doesn't stop, does he?" Jon said. "Who's handling the printing?"

"I'm taking care of that tomorrow." Robin looked up again. "You learning anything new over there?"

Jon glanced at his book. "Yeah, I'm gettin' it little by little. On my third read through."

Robin smiled. "If you put the book under your pillow you can probably learn through osmosis. Might be faster."

"Hey, I just wanna make sure I'm ready," Jon said without smiling back.

"It's not you I'm worried about."

To Jon it sounded as if there was a second part to that comment that never made its way out of Robin's mouth. Jon, on the other hand, had had his anxiety ratcheted notch by notch with each closing day. *Anxiety keeps one alert*, Robin had told him. He turned back to the book on the desk, entitled '*Operational History of the AS350 A-Star*'.

Chapter 26: Family Business

Madison Corp. occupied floors forty-five through fifty of the Enterprise Building in the heart of Fort Dearborn's Financial District. Though it was prime real estate for any business looking to make a name for itself using the prestige of its address, Madison Corp. no longer needed such a boost; they had long established their dominance in the corporate world and remained presently to stay physically close to large and potential clients. Not to mention they owned the building. . .

Wilson approached the base of the onyx tower as he had every day for twenty-five straight years - purposefully. He maintained his routine, making sure to say hello to the doorman, Fred, the morning security guard, Linus, and the elevator operator, Morrie, on his way through the lobby and up to his office. He knew them all on a first-name basis as well as the simple facts about each man's life, not because he genuinely cared but because those relationships might prove useful in the vastly unknown and unpredictable future. To Wilson, life itself was a business. And the fundamental rule in business was to build relationships, regardless of their immediacy or fruitfulness.

The elevator ascended undisturbed to the fiftieth, and uppermost, floor. The entire area was devoted to just five rooms: the board's massive conference room, the office of the President, Wyatt Madison, the office of the COO, Stanley Jandl, the office of the CFO, Edward Gibbons, and the office of the CEO, Wilson. The floor had its own private security guard at the elevator and an outer foyer with a personal secretary for each office. A marble fountain centerpiece dribbled in a relaxing rhythm, inviting those who entered to feel an often false sense of comfort.

With a peaceful tone, the elevator doors parted as if making way for Wilson's eminency. Turning right he could see Agnes, his secretary, and the concerned look that enveloped her face. His footsteps were deliberate and brisk, pattering the marble floor with pitched repetition. As he approached, he noticed the outline of a young man in sunglasses seated on the leather armchair near the door to his office. The individual rose and turned to face Wilson as Agnes rounded her desk.

"He said you were expecting him," she announced with a tone mixing concern and delight that only she seemed to have mastered.

Across the foyer was a man of similar size to Wilson, with a younger face and a fuller head of hair. The man's image was bolstered by an immaculately cut and custom-tailored suit, tortoiseshell sunglasses, and in his hand a copy of the day's *Financial Times*. The man raised his sunglasses and propped them on his head showing a familiar, though hardened, face.

If it were anyone other than Rob, Wilson would have inwardly remarked on their class and style. In this case, motives that were likely malicious, petty, or both made the outfit seem a mere pretense.

"He did, did he," Wilson stated, keeping his eyes focused on Rob.

"This'll be short. I know your time is valuable," Rob ensured with familiarity in his tone. His sly expression told Wilson otherwise.

"Was our last meeting somehow insufficient?"

"It's not about that. I'm just looking for five minutes," Rob insisted.

"You can't afford it."

"Then I'll owe you."

The two stared at each other, Wilson intensely and Rob expectantly. Wilson held for effect, the tension building in the entry, and finally exhaled in vexation. "Next time, have him arrested," he said to Agnes with a goaded look. He entered his office without holding the door.

"After you," Rob conceded with a smile.

If the masculinity and fortitude of Wilson's office correlated to his cock size, he would ring in just over a foot in pendulum length. Milton Berle himself would have nodded in approval. Fifteen foot vaulted ceilings, inset bookcases with immaculate hand-carpentered frames and molding, a stocked liquor cabinet and humidor, Persian area rug, and his prized Snooker table were but a few of the luxuries within. The lounge area itself was larger than most offices, and came with a furniture set fit for royalty.

Wilson's trapezoidal desk was more fixture than possession, constructed of rare sunken lumber salvaged from a Midwestern lake. Its shape and grain, making it appear deeper than it was in reality from a visitor's point of view, had a daunting effect on most. When Wilson was seated, the floor-to-ceiling windows behind him illuminated his silhouette in a manner reminiscent of Jesus at the last supper, the reflective glare from the day shining onto the potential client, deliberately.

Two paintings hung on the opposing eastern and western walls. To the west was a French impressionist study of a nude woman's torso, a virgin in form and figure, an unspoiled and unflawed embodiment of the spoils of success and the desires of all powerful men. To the east, by contrast, was a Japanese portrait, framed in bamboo, depicting two feudal warriors. The center figure was seated on the ground performing 'Seppuku,' ritualistic suicide by disembowelment for defeated or shamed Samurai.

With Rob in tow, Wilson approached his desk, the sun reflecting brilliantly off of the polished surface with the exception of a small fraction darkened by a shadow. The dividing line of light and shade ran sharply across the desk, created by the changing angle of the sun against a partly drawn window shade.

"Sit," Wilson commanded. He rounded his desk yet remained standing.

Rob slid a chair away from the glare, over to the side closest to the French woman, causing Wilson to sneer. This was a simple test he enjoyed putting potential clients or employees through. How big were their balls? If they were submissive to their surroundings, they were easier to intimidate and mold; but those willing to alter their environment had a much higher return on investment. Wilson hated admitting to himself that Rob might possess the skills of the latter. He continued standing, holding up his watch on his left arm and resting his right hand on the face.

"Shall I start a timer?" he said, wrinkling his forehead as he glanced up in Rob's direction.

"That's not necessary. Like I said, this'll be short," Rob replied, putting a foot on his opposite knee to suggest the contrary.

"Why are you here?" Wilson said bluntly.

"I have an investment opportunity for you."

"Not interested," he said without thought.

"Hear me out," Rob replied with a raised hand. Speaking slowly, he proceeded. "Now I, as much as you, realize that our history is mired in disagreements, some backhanded compliments, and. . .*rather* upfront insults. I am here because you're likely the only person capable of executing my idea to its full potential. And within that potential is benefit for not only you, but the entire city. What I'm proposing could change thousands of lives."

"Your mother was the philanthropist," Wilson stated curtly.

"I'm not pitching a charity. I mentioned this would benefit you, did I not?"

Wilson stood with his hands behind his back, peering out of the massive window with a look of indifference. He remained still for a moment, lingering in the vacuum of his office. In lieu of a response, he walked over to a bar cart by the east wall and poured himself a finger of scotch. Had Rob been a client, friend, or colleague, he'd have offered him a glass. He was none, so Wilson refrained from muddying the waters further.

"Right," Rob continued. "Firstly, let me ask you; are you familiar with the Inner District's history?"

"Yes."

"What are your thoughts on former Mayor Xavier and the scandal that transpired during his term?" Rob asked.

"I thought what happened was unfortunate and a poorly planned financial strategy. Blame faulty accounting," he answered disinterestedly as he walked over to his desk and placed the glass on the glossy wooden surface.

"That's it?" Rob said after a pointed silence. "Those thousands of lives ruined by a simple calculation error?"

"The benevolent intention was there. The realistic action plan, and subsequent execution thereof, was not," Wilson replied matter-of-factly.

"C'mon. I'm not a journalist. You're not going to be quoted in the *Times*. Tell it how it is. What happened?"

Wilson took a sip of his drink, utilizing the pause to analyze Rob. He prided himself on sensing the angles and intentions of others, but presently his predictions for this meeting held only questions.

"There's a point to this. Feeding me bullshit is only going to drag it out," Rob added coolly.

Touché. Wilson decided to answer honestly. The sooner Rob was on his way, the better.

"There's a maxim regarding my line of work," he began with a trace of joviality. "Maybe you've heard it, maybe not: Success in the world of business is deemed by the common man as obtainable, the wise man as relative, and the powerful man as irrelevant. To say Xavier thoroughly exploited that would be an understatement. Put simply, he gave the 'common people,' who at the time were a strain on the city, a sniff of the good life, and they *erupted*. Little did they know their hard work and investments were only benefitting him. He made out like a bandit, quite literally, and they lost everything. A powerful Mayor though he was, he then made a God-awful business decision that, as the years went on, turned criminal. . . Xavier was a pure politician and pure politicians are, among many other things, terrible businessmen - despite what some would have you believe." He finished his note with a sip of his scotch.

"So, besides the evident destruction of the District's collective well-being, tell me more about this business decision of his. Specifically what it was, why it failed, and what made it illegal," Rob prodded.

"The 'what' is as simple as the 'why.' 'What' it was, was a trap. Nothing more. Through propaganda and empty promises Xavier sold an elusive and unobtainable idea. 'The Future of City Living,' the program was dubbed. It was promoted to be a communal, city-run development project for the lower working class. The first of its kind, which targeted the Inner District for - at the time - its many suitable locations for demolition and rebuilding, it having been the site of some defunct industrial properties and vacant lots.

"I'll paint a picture for you: at the time, unemployment was at an all-time high. Fort Dearborn was experiencing what many referred to as 'an erosion of the classes,' which in plain English means a dwindling middle class and a widening gap between rich and poor. As any educated individual knows, such is the inevitability of capitalism. The point is there was a problem that required a solution. Enter Mayor Xavier and his plan, the gist of which went as follows: Using taxpayer money, he initiated a program where individuals and families that fit in a particular low-income bracket were given the opportunity to make a small investment. In return for your investment you received equity, an eventual brand new living space, and wages with interest - essentially a share of what you helped build, which in turn would gain great property value upon completion, ushering in businesses and a reestablished District. It was an 'everybody wins' sort of promise."

"So the people that entered the program helped rebuild the District?"

"Correct. If an individual had vocational skills, they were hired for construction and promised wages with interest. The goal was to reestablish the lower class as a valuable part of society while revamping an area of the city that needed a boost. But, as you may have noticed, they only made it so far. . . The real mastery of that fuck-fest was the sale. Thousands bought into it without batting an eye. It was *presented* as a business arrangement. You invest *X*, being time, an upfront monetary commitment, and labor; the city will provide *Y*, being employment, material, and resources; and you'll receive *Z*, being alleged compensation, return on investment, and a new life. And they rushed towards it, fought to be included in it." Wilson chuckled in recollection. "There was a waiting list, if I remember the articles correctly. It took but a mere taste for people to swallow the hook. All Xavier had to do then was pull. There never was an 'end.' There never was a 'future' - even though the signs said so. It was all a scheme to collect money and use time and propagating circumstances to unload a believable downfall, conveniently piling many already disenfranchised families from around the city into one dense District. There were claims of funding errors, zoning discrepancies, utility troubles. . . I recall a report about a sudden rise in copper prices. Any vague cause for delay was used. It was creeping normality, plain and simple. Instead of freezing everything all at once it was a series of snares that slowed the whole project down over the years until the final trap closed shut. If I was to guess, he needed to make it look like he spent all of the project money to quell any likely villainy placed upon him while somewhere along the line it was instead fed into a secure place.

"I'll guarantee people still think it was just bad luck. That they were victims to misfortune. There's no concrete proof but. . .it's clear as day. Luck had nothing to do with it."

Rob appeared to digest the information. "And the 'why'?"

"The 'why' to your question is because he established a flawed relationship where the only way to profit was to clean the entire group out. It was wholly one sided. Similar to a Ponzi scheme."

"If you were in his shoes, what would you have done differently?"

"Not have run for Mayor," Wilson barked with a laugh.

"Without the politics. And the illegality for that matter. From a business standpoint. . . Humor me," Rob said.

"From a business standpoint, I'll put it this way: When I engage in a business deal, I partner with people with whom I view the relationship as mutually beneficial. Acting unilaterally, or any way otherwise, is a flaw. . . The goal, *of all of this*," he motioned broadly around him, "is to repeat gains at minimal to no cost. The only way to do that is for both parties to benefit. Employing a 'single use and discard' venture is piss-poor business. If I operated under that pretense I would not be in business for long because of the enemies I'd have made. And so, back to our prime example: Xavier quite quickly entered the unemployment sector, albeit with heavy pockets. Should have been jail," Wilson concluded.

Rob's brow stiffened and he blinked in thoughtfulness. "Can't argue with that logic, although I'm not surprised. I'm sure your path to your current position was straight as an arrow."

Wilson put down his drink, unbuttoned his jacket and took a seat in his throne. *Let's cut the shit here.* He was about out of patience for the current conversation and its trite uselessness. His inability to predict its future and the fact that he had done almost all the talking had pushed him towards sourness. There was surely an objective here, and he knew Rob was likely leading him to a breaking point on purpose.

"Your five minutes are up. I hope you've enjoyed your history lesson more than I have. If you are holding out on the punchline, now's the time. Otherwise, you know your way out," Wilson said.

He watched as Rob got out of his chair, nodded his head, and turned. *Giving up so easily? I thought he had more in him.* Wilson followed him with his eyes as he walked a few paces away from the desk, stopped and spun his head about the office in a searching manner. He spotted the bar cart and, making a silent 'ah—ha' gesture, proceeded to walk directly over and serve himself a finger of whisky. Wilson smirked. *That's more like it.* Rob's knack for pushing the envelope, at least, was unwavering.

"That wasn't listed in your inheritance," Wilson added mockingly.

Rob turned around with a smile and took a sip. After the quaff, he displayed a surprised look, as if the whisky was better than anticipated and he hadn't been drinking it for several years already. He held the glass up momentarily to cheers Wilson over it. *Ever the showman.*

"I'll cut the shit. I think you, along with the rest of the city, are happy about what happened to the Inner District. I think the inequalities befit many, such as yourself. I think you enjoy the division."

"Enjoyment is far from what I feel, but don't get me wrong, that neighborhood and those people are a scar on the face of the city. Thankfully scars fade on their own. It's just a matter of time."

"Exactly. It's a waiting game for everyone else. It's that silent ignorance in hopes that one day it goes away."

"It will," Wilson hammered.

"So that's it. It's hopeless?"

"Like I said, it'll fade on its own. Time heals all wounds. Even that one."

Rob considered the words and finished his drink with a healthy gulp that seemed to invigorate and ignite passion in him Wilson hadn't seen since before Amelia's death. It was gripping to witness the animation as Rob walked back toward the front of the office. It was something Wilson thought Rob had lost forever.

"I completely disagree. Not only is it salvageable, but it's rife with opportunity."

"Try all you want, you can't shine shit, son."

"It's not shit. It's a gem that just needs some polishing again. I'll explain. I've been spending a lot of time in the Inner District and I've seen what everyone talks about. The sorrow, the apathy, the misery. But if you peel away those layers, at the core is a group of people ripe for the picking. Eager for the opportunity to regain a purpose. That purpose is the second half of a potentially long term, mutually beneficial relationship.

"Since we last met, I've been working hard to inspire them to reject their current social status. There are people in this city that have wronged them and continue to wrong them by standing upon an ignorant and corrupt pedestal. But there are also those in the District who are beginning to refuse that and want to change the course of the future.

"Our city's advancement has been stunted since the incidents that took place there. Sure, other sections have prospered, but the ignorance of the issues plaguing the District negates that progress. On a grand scale, yes, my idea is to basically do what Xavier promised, just without it being fraud. To legitimize it, privately. But that's not for years to come. Initially I want to do a small test."

"I don't like the direction of this conversation. I'm not a savior, and I will not become one."

"Relax. I'm not about to ask you to singlehandedly save the Inner District. I'm asking you to help me test my vision. That's all. Just a test. If it works, we'll reassess what's possible from there."

"Why this? Why there?"

"Because it's worth it. Because I care. And because it's my home now."

"I'm not buying it, Rob."

Rob's searched the floor, twisting his mouth. Then his head shot up. "Where does a society's future lie?"

Wilson eyed him levelly. "Peaceful coexistence and productivity."

"Wrong," Rob pointed. "That's a hopeful product. The answer is children and individuality. Children are the lifeblood – literally. Creating children is simple, though somehow you've managed to find yourself with only a stepson."

Wilson raised an eyebrow at the comment.

"Creating children *responsibly* is a-whole-nother discussion. . . Individuality, on the other hand, is what separates a community from a mass, a collective people from a mob. Individuality breeds creativity, creativity breeds expression, and expression breeds *identity*. This is a suppressed people we're discussing, a people without a voice, a people without acknowledgement. You can imagine how creating a true sense of individuality within a community is perhaps the most difficult task.

"First, you need a leader. Without leadership there is no society. It's simply the way we've evolved. I am by no means a leader there. But what I have become is a figure to some. There's a subtle difference. I do not presume to make rules or exact order. I act and as a result of my actions receive acknowledgement and endorsement. There are a number of individuals there that not only support what I do but crave more, consciously or unconsciously. My goal is to ween myself off my current path of action, and start a tangibly productive project. Boosting psyche and morale is one thing, but I'm interested in creating something physical to build upon. But I can't do it alone and I can't be the leader, at least not yet.

"The problem is these people reject common leadership because the last time they were met with it, they were fucking raped. It's a large-scale defense mechanism. Resistant though they may be, they're not without motivations and desires for betterment. They just refuse to trust that which has betrayed them.

"So rather than public funding, this will be private. They don't need to be trusting of a politician or some public scheme. Privately it's all business. Both benefit. There's no underlying pretense. No image to uphold. No one knows your name if you don't want them to. Hell, they don't even have to ask for it. Progress will just happen."

"I fit in where?"

"My plan needs a financial backer."

"I'm sure it does. Though I'm struggling to see how this is mutually beneficial."

"There's no guarantee that it will be mutually beneficial until we test the waters. And I have just the plan."

"Those who are competent enough to succeed do not need handouts. They make their own way."

"Fair point. But sometimes people just need to see a little third-party confidence."

Wilson raised his brow, nudging Rob towards a continuance.

"Everyone sees that District as filled with bums, degenerates, sorry excuses, and wasted life. I won't feed you bullshit, that element is there. But what I see much, much more of are carpenters, inventors, business owners, and teachers. . .*human beings*. . .all waiting for a small infusion they would then return tenfold. Imagine discovering the next big startup. Imagine that area in a condition similar to the Waterfront. The real estate alone is worth a serious consideration. The District just so happens to border some up-and-coming neighborhoods. People view it as worthless because they lack vision. Apply the right vision and it can turn into gold. And you'd have first pick."

"And second, and third, and so on," Wilson said sarcastically.

"Precisely. And others will follow suit wishing they had bought in earlier. Buy closest to a bordering neighborhood and move inward, renovating as we go," he said as an example. "Stop thinking I'm wrong and imagine I'm right. If these people gain your trust, the opportunities are endless."

"You're asking for a lot of faith. And you haven't given a dollar amount."

"The amount is insignificant."

"What happened to the money you were left with?"

"That money was used for other inspirational purposes," he said with that same slyness as his first words that morning.

Wilson pounced on it. "Like delivering cakes?"

The statement silenced Rob, his look suddenly that of a child awaiting a reprimand.

"You have always impressed me with your potential as a businessman," Wilson said, standing to look out the window. "You are professional, decisive, motivated, and instinctual. What trumps all those qualities is your presence. It's a tangible characteristic that separates a leader from a follower. A success from a failure. Your mother never wanted me to expose you to this life because it can be taxing and can compromise a man's morals. I'd hire you myself if our past was different and I hadn't made a promise."

"I appreciate that," Rob replied sincerely.

"Well, hold that thought. Aside from that puff of smoke up your ass, there's one particular thing about you that has the potential to nullify each and every one of those qualities. You're an idealist. That's what separates you from me. I am a realist. Realists thrive in business because they know when to say no. Idealists perpetually strive to see the good in situations. I've seen such men get caught up in deals I wouldn't touch if I was using someone else's money. Idealism clouds judgement, causes rash decisions that cost you money," Wilson then turned and warning with fatherly concern, "or puts you behind bars."

Rob stood and walked over to the window. His eyes met Wilson's, who glanced sideways at him, and then he turned to look out upon the expanding city. He spoke slowly and sincerely, in a tone entirely new to the conversation.

"I may be an idealist. But that does not mean I'm wrong this time. This will be the most important investment you ever make. It is my suggestion that you do not write it off immediately."

"And if I say no? Recently, people of my stature who say the wrong things end up taking a trip off the top of a building. . .and we're a little too high up for my comfort," Wilson said with a touch of sarcasm.

"This city is saturated with villains," Rob said, looking still upon the city. "And villains need to be reminded that they're not invincible. As much as we've disagreed in the past, those people who've been. . .*affected*. . .are nowhere near your stature. I'd say you have nothing to worry about. Regardless of your decision."

Wilson paused to once again admire the young man who was, among other things, his stepson. Their severed relationship did not mitigate the respect Wilson had for Rob's aptitude, vigor, and persistence. He had faced his recent challenges in life head on, despite some moments of immaturity and recklessness.

"No more discussion. No more persuasion. Tell me what my investment would be used for. Answer all of my questions honestly and directly. Give me the exact details. If I like what I hear, we'll talk money. If not. . .this meeting never happened."

Rob turned around and grabbed Wilson's whisky glass. He refilled both deftly and handed Wilson's back to him.

"It all started the last time we spoke," Rob said as he smiled and turned. "When I told you to go fuck yourself."

Chapter 27: First We Feast, Then We Felony

A weathered man moseyed along a sidewalk with his head hung low. Over his shoulder he had slung an old bag matching the color of his dingy and ruined clothing. It looked like it was a part of him, like he was a hunchback or something. Wil watched the homeless man walk by like one would a foreign vehicle - intrigued, but only momentarily so. A breath of wind blew the man's hair about and he shuffled to maintain his footing. Within moments he was out of sight. Something about him looked awfully familiar, but Wil only pondered it briefly.

He and Robin sat at a street-side picnic table beside the food-truck gathering that assembled every weekend in a vacant lot off of Atlantic Ave. Tonight's options were from trucks of Korean, Mexican, Polish, and Italian cuisine. There was a hotdog stand too, but Wil hated hotdogs. He and Robin split an Italian Combo from *Salvatore's*, loaded with delicious coppa, soppressata, mortadella, fresh mozzarella cheese, some pecorino for a salty bite, roasted sweet and hot peppers, and shredded lettuce. What truly made the sandwich, though, was their oil and vinegar-soaked bread. Wil took a bite and felt like he was about to levitate off his seat.

It was a chilly Friday night and wind gusts upwards of twenty miles per hour were in the forecast. Presently, the evening was calm save for a westerly breeze that cooled Wil's perspiration, but there was something else in the air too. The three men had evolved their movement from infancy into a true force of inspiration. As the weeks went on, many locals had grown confident. Some remained wary but what mattered most was that people were *talking*. Wil had always believed that a reputation built on mystique was far greater than one built on vanity, and so he worried that some knew it was them who had perpetrated the F.A.M. crimes. A legend grew from rumors and tall tales until it became larger than life. Thus, while the crimes were important and all, what truly mattered to Wil was the success of the May Day festival. Though they weren't unified yet, community was burgeoning on the streets like it hadn't in decades. Spring was rife with opportunity, and it was amazing to see Robin's vision grow in a manner of positivity and, surprisingly, peace. That is, for those in the District.

Wil folded the paper off his sandwich a few inches. Whereas he would have normally ordered a full one, they had each agreed on a half sandwich. Wil could only speak for himself, but it was obvious that he and Robin's appetites both were just about nonexistent. Dinner was more of a way to kill time before they set off on their final crime. His nerves smothered his hunger. Jon, however, appeared to be stress eating. He had already set a tray of noodles, pork ribs, and pierogis on the table, and was waiting for his order from the burrito truck. He was even threatening to get zeppoles for dessert.

Wil looked across the table at Robin, who was stern of expression and patient with his bites. He appeared to be in thought. The scar on his head was still pink.

"How'd your meeting go the other day?" Wil asked.

Robin looked up. "About as well as it could. Couple hiccups here and there but he and I got something worked out."

"Does that mean we can afford the flowers?"

"We can afford everything now."

Wil nodded softly. Robin had taken an important risk meeting with his stepfather. The festival would have happened regardless of the outcome, but securing funding brought it to another level - like nothing the District had ever seen. It was a matter of restoring the parklands. The city had no interest aside from allotting festival permits, so Robin took it upon himself to find funding to clear the land in time and hire local contractors to make the experience something special. Wil had never been a part of a project like that from concept to execution, he had never been allowed to have a say in anything important before. It was a brand new feeling of accomplishment. He couldn't wait for May 1st.

"Does Jon know?" he asked.

"Do I know what?" Jon inquired as he took a seat beside Robin, placing another tray on the wooden table, and immediately stuffed his mouth with a rib.

"We've got the money. I've arranged for workers to start clearing the park on Monday. The landscapers have about a week's worth of work ahead of them and then another few days of planting the following week. I'm hoping we can round up enough volunteers to get everything else in order."

"How many vendors have confirmed?"

"Sixty-five so far. Eighteen more are pending and I'm going to reach out to about twenty over the weekend."

"What's today?" Wil asked.

"April 17th."

"Is there enough time for everything to get done?"

Robin smiled. "Only if we're ready to work our asses off."

"What's that like?" Jon asked sarcastically as he dove into his meal.

Wil chuckled to himself. He and Robin's training schedule had concluded two days earlier. In all his years, Wil had never felt in better shape. The routes, dietary scrutiny, sobriety (for the most part), and attitude had come together to create two running machines. He'd wager that Robin could run a sub 5:30 mile now. The kid had dropped eleven pounds. They both looked lean. Wil curled his toes in his sneakers. He was ready to stretch his legs.

Jon took a monstrous bite out of his burrito and the table shook as he bounced his leg off the ground. He always did that when he was nervous. Wil couldn't blame him. The big man had a big job to do not three hours from then.

"We should reach out to Ernest," Jon said.

"That's what Marian said."

"Let's get him out to May Day," Wil suggested.

"I'd like to try to talk to him," Robin offered. "It took a little while to convince me but Marian had a few good points, so. . ."

"Marian got pretty toasty the other night, huh?" Jon asked.

"We all did."

Wil grunted. "I needed that. Our training has had me wound up tighter than a fuckin' fishing reel. I mean, I feel incredible, but I needed a night to unwind."

"We all did," Robin repeated before a bite.

Jon took a quick break from shoveling food in his mouth. "Marian's comin' for May Day, right?"

"Oh yeah. I've been mostly keeping it a surprise but she knows how important it is. We've talked about it."

"She can hang, man," Wil said.

The men finished their food in silence, letting the sounds of the environment wash over them. Wil could hear the tapping of a spatula and the sizzle and pop of meat on a hot griddle. The smell of the cuisines surrounding him was intoxicating. He tried to use the sounds to maintain some sense of calm as the seconds ticked closer to the inevitable. He glanced skyward and noticed a clear night. The stars seemed fainter than normal.

Wil bit his lip gently as his thoughts started to scatter. Robin had given him more responsibility this time around than on any of their other escapades. He felt a burden to perform like he hadn't felt since, quite honestly, the museum incident. Sure, each of their crimes had held inherent risk, but tonight had so many unknowns. There was no backup plan like with the judge. There was no secondary escape route like with the thief downtown. This was all or nothing. One hitch, one slipup from any one man, and it was all over.

Jon looked down at his watch and burped. "What do you think guys? 'Bout that time?"

Wil rolled his foil into a ball. *Fuck it all*, he thought. "Let's make like my parents and split."

"Just a sec. Before we go I wanna say something," Robin announced.

Wil noticed Robin's demeanor tighten as if he was readying a speech. It wasn't until then that Wil realized how quiet he had been since they sat down. He often wondered what went on in that man's head. Robin blinked a couple times and inhaled.

"I want you guys to know that I love you both. You're the closest thing to brothers that I'll ever have, and by far the best friends I'll ever make in my life. These past months have been fucked up in many ways, but I think I speak for us all when I say they've been the most important of our lives. Remember when this all started, how we promised ourselves that there would be a limit, that there would be an expiration date to all this? Well, it's here. It's two weeks away. It's May Day, baby. The festival is going to make all this worth it. Everything we fought for, everything we've worked for, all the risks, all the planning and sleep deprivation, all the effort, all the love, all the hate, all the willpower. But I won't lie to you. I'm nervous. I'm terrified. Tonight," Robin said, tapping the table with his index finger. "Tonight is the most dangerous night of our entire lives. This is it. This is our final one. If we fail, it may mean that all of our hard work was for nothing. Tonight we're going to give every inch, every pound, and every breath. Every second of every minute, every minute of every hour needs to be exact. Tonight we've got two options: jail or freedom. Let's make sure it's freedom."

Chapter 28: Disbursement of Funds

What would have been otherwise drumming footsteps was masked by vehicle traffic and cotton shoe-covers worn on each sneaker, leftovers from the restoration project at St. Augustine's. Gently, Wil and Robin treaded towards the parked Cavalier Securities truck. One at a time, they positioned themselves at the rear doors. Robin crouched left and Wil right, backs against the beast's steel shell.

The seconds passed like minutes and eventually, after numerous groans and squeals from the engine, the attempts from inside the truck to turn the ignition subsided. With a click, the driver's side door opened and out dropped a heavyset man, some loose pavement crunching under his weight. Scratching his head, he shut the door and hobbled around to the front of the truck. Robin peeked past the left rear quarter panel and watched as he undid two latches and lifted the hood in search of a diagnosis for the sudden stall.

A gust of wind cut through the air, turning up Robin's jacket collar. He turned to Wil and locked eyes with him through their black ski masks. Robin pulled a pistol out of his jacket, nodded, and rounded the corner.

Just then, Wil heard a commotion from within the rear compartment.

"Jerry?" a voiced called from inside the truck.

Silence. Then a second click sounded, this time the rear compartment's side door opening. The voice called again.

Wil smiled. *Ah my dear Cavalier, how you've lived up to your name.*

The kid inside the truck opened the side door fully and stepped out, taking a healthy breath of the crisp evening air. He shook his head in an attempt to orient himself and continued taking deep breaths as he walked around the door. The fumes inside had become unbearable.

"Hey, I'm serious, man, I'm getting exhaust in there or something," he said to Jerry.

Circling towards the hood, he found Jerry with outstretched arms positioned on the top of the truck's grill. A masked man in all black was visible over his right shoulder with a gun pressed to Jerry's head. Despite his lingering wooziness, the kid blinked once in surprise and acted on the situation in valiance.

"HEY!" he yelled as he drew his firearm on the assailant.

Immediately the assailant lifted his other arm and pointed a second weapon at him. "Don't move!" the kid said.

"Drop the gun," the assailant ordered in a heavy tone.

"*Don't* move!"

"Drop the fucking gun!"

"Let him go or I will shoot you!" the kid screamed. Just as he finished, the tip of yet another weapon touched his skull from behind.

"No you won't," a voice said softly. "Now drop the gun."

The kid froze, finding himself paralyzed by the sudden onset of grim circumstances. He was trapped and panic stricken. Silence hung for a moment.

"Not many options here, kid. One of them is to watch your friend die tonight," the first assailant said.

"You don't wanna watch him die, man," the second assailant muttered from behind.

"Drop you're gun and get on the ground before I drop *you*," the first ordered.

"Just lay down," the second muttered.

The back and forth commands exacerbated the kid's dizziness twofold and his heaving breaths became audible. He began to shake slightly, his nerves rooting him to the pavement. The two assailants locked eyes for a split second.

"You shoot, you die. Might as well be putting the gun to your own head," the assailant on Jerry announced.

"Shoot and you *both* die," breathed the other from behind.

The kid's gasps were vicious now and his eyes fluttered in terror. His pistol remained aimed at the first assailant, though its barrel shook considerably. Sweat began trickling down his brow.

"Listen to them, kid," Jerry pleaded. "J–Just listen to them."

"I'm not gonna say it again. Drop. *Your fucking.* Gun."

A whisper came. "Just listen to him, man."

"KID, YOU HAVE THREE SECONDS BEFORE WE ROCK YOU NOW DROP THE GUN AND GET ON THE FUCKING GROUND!" the man screamed. *"Three!"*

"Okay! Okay!" he piped between sharp breaths. Yet he held his trembling draw.

"Two!"

"Okay!" he said again. But the kid remained still, defying their threats and his own words. His body was like concrete. Just barely, he lifted the gun barrel in the beginnings of submission when–

He felt a pinch. Instantly, muscular control ceased. With a pained cry he dropped to the ground, releasing his weapon during the fall. Face first he hit the pavement while his body convulsed in a burning, vibrating agony that violently twitched his extremities. Vertigo ensued. . .

With a dozen passes, Robin duct-taped the restrained guards back to back against a metal pole. Meanwhile, Wil returned from a nearby alleyway with two huge duffel bags, wheeling one and struggling to carry the other. Gasping and cursing under his breath, he loaded the bags into the rear of the truck while Robin stepped away from their victims. In one stride, Robin squatted down and removed a plug from the vehicle's exhaust pipe. He tossed it to Wil, who tossed it in the side door.

"Let's roll," Robin announced.

Wil nodded, hopped in the rear compartment, and closed himself in.

In the driver's seat, Robin slid his seatbelt on and twisted the truck's key. The engine groaned and squealed, struggling to turn over. Robin encouraged it silently. Two further twists of the key sparked the ignition and the cab rattled.

"Yeah, baby."

"Let it idle for a second," Wil instructed from behind.

"I am."

"Now give it some gas to blow the funk out of her."

Robin obliged, and the beast rumbled and coughed. Finally, it was breathing normally after such a suffocating period of time. Robin put it in gear and began a slow roll onto the busy street.

"Alright," he said. "Now the night really starts."

Within moments, the dashboard radio buzzed. "Dispatch to Truck fifty-two. Jerry, can you confirm the status of the vehicle? I see you're moving again. Any damage to report?" called a womanly voice.

Wil looked up at Robin from behind the grated divider.

"Jerry, talk to me. I'm calling off the tow truck."

Robin hesitated a moment and picked up the receiver in response. "Jerry had a date with the pavement, sweetheart. Status of the vehicle is armed and dangerous, heading up Munson. Gonna see what this tank's made of so the damage report's. . .*gonna* change a bit," he announced into the radio receiver.

Wil's laughter could be heard from the rear.

"Who am I speaking with?" the dispatcher asked cautiously.

Robin smiled through his mask. "You, my dear, have the pleasure of speaking with the leader of the Few Against Many. Remember this day, for you are quite fortunate! Rest assured, we're simply borrowing your truck, though I fear it won't be returned to you the way we received it. . . You've got quite the payload back here. Be sure to know that I thank you for that."

"Are our men hurt?" the dispatcher asked.

"Unharmed, dear. Just in shock."

"The police are being notified."

"Aww you're too kind. Well, I hate to cut the conversation short but I must be going. Send my apologies to Jerry."

Robin cut the radio. "Alright. I'm gonna head towards the beltway. You get started on that money."

Merv threw the stall door open with purpose. His bodily need to empty his full bladder superseded his mind's desire to finish off the fresh beer he'd ordered back at the bar. Breaking the seal was always a victory for the body, and he took a wide stance as he directed a stream of piss into the bowl without much regard for aim. The forceful sound echoing off the porcelain drowned residual banter emanating from the bar crowd beyond the restroom door and tingling relief washed over him.

He'd been drinking casually for a while, maybe an hour and a half or so, and was growing bored as time carried on. Though the men's room was dim, his droopy gaze absorbed the scribbled text on the inner walls of the stall: a penis etched into the paint with a moniker reading "actual size," the standard "for a good time" phone number that dotted nearly every bar restroom he'd ever used, an obscene comment about a presumed girl named "Pat" above the empty toilet-paper roller. To his left he found a little quote etched into the metal wall. Though rusted, the text was neatly legible and looked to have been there for years on end.

money ain't everything
but having it is

He considered it briefly making a sound just shy of a chuckle. *Says the man that probably stole his money to get loaded here.* With buzzed delight, Merv decided to carve his own quote into the wall. His urine was at a dribble at this point, and so, with his manhood still exposed, he fished into his pocket for a permanent marker. In concise form, he wrote a limerick above the toilet, one hand outstretched to hold his leaning body while with the other penned the message.

There once was a man named Merv
Who had a thick cock to serve
He hit every G-spot
Even stretched a balloon knot
With his bulging phallic curve

Upon finishing the note, Merv looked down and realized he'd dribbled onto the toilet seat. He raised his eyebrows in disregard and zipped himself up, marker still in hand. As he was turning to push open the stall door, however, his eyes fell on three letters he'd seen far too often in the past few months. Letters that proved to piss him off regardless of his mood, for they symbolized the pathetic resistance; the pointless and exaggerated struggle. This outlaw fad, this revolting mania running on fumes perpetuated false dissention and protest. It wasn't a cry for help. It was a cry for hurt. Bold were the letters.

F.A.M.

One last time he used the marker, drawing a fat X through the letters. He pressed so hard the felt tip crushed under his weight and excess ink ran down the door in streaks. *Fucking cowards.*

The restroom door opened with a creak as Merv exited the stall. A tall man entered with long, greasy hair pulled in a ponytail, exposing a leathered face. He wore jeans and a black wife-beater. A sleeve of tattoos wrapped around his right arm and he was puffing on the tail end of a cigarette. With the urinal out of order, the stall was the only option for the newcomer. He passed Merv indifferently and entered the stall while Merv reached towards the door, skipping the sink. Just as his hand gripped the door handle, the man in the stall raised his voice in a tone of provocation.

"Ah what the fuck, man," he yelled.

Merv paused and waited. Had silence followed, Merv intended to leave the restroom peaceably and continue his onslaught of drinks. A single word further and there would have to be an exchange.

"Hey, asshole, you pissed all over the seat."

Quietly, Merv locked the doorknob and nonchalantly spun around to address the problem. Turning out of the stall, the man showed a riled expression and widened nostrils. He turned to Merv and spoke, meeting eyes and pointing in towards the toilet.

"Wipe the fucking seat. What's wrong with you?"

Merv stared a hole in the man, whose own pupils hinted at intoxication, with a heavy intensity. "No paper," Merv said curtly.

"No shit there's no paper. But you're wipin' this seat before I let you walk out."

Merv rolled up his sleeves exposing his thick, hairy forearms and cracked his neck on one side. "Sure about that?"

The armored truck hummed along. Behind it police sirens screamed, a dozen cruisers and counting howling in hot pursuit like a wolf pack mid hunt. Engines growled angrily and red and blue lights lit up passing storefronts and restaurant awnings like the fourth of July. The blaring noise overwhelmed the neighborhoods and echoed between adjacent high-rises, forcing the duo to yell in order to hear one another.

"Got a *lotta* heat already, *man*," Wil warned from the back with suspicion in his voice.

"No shit, Wil. I-I fucking *see that*," Robin yelled over his shoulder.

"Drive faster."

"This fuckin' thing's pegged."

"She's got some left," Wil insisted. "Any birds in the sky yet?"

"I don't see any. We're looking alright so far."

Wil shook his head as he peered back at the flashing lights. "I don't trust it."

"Relax."

"I swear to God, Robin."

"He'll be fine, Wil. You need to relax right now."

"If that fat fuck screws this up I swear to God I will butt-fuck him with a beer can."

"He's *fine*."

"One job!"

"He has more than one job!"

"*One job*! He has *one* fucking job!" Wil yelled holding up his index finger. "So help me *God* if that helicopter gets in the air!"

"He'll be fine, would you *shut up*?"

"He's never fine. It's always something with him."

"Don't get in my head with that shit. Jon will be fine, God damn it. Shut up and finish those fucking bills!"

"Finish the bills," Wil mocked. "I'm gonna cut my fingers off the way you're driving. You're scarin' me."

"You just told me to speed up!"

"Yeah, speed up. Not drive like you're warming the tires on a racetrack. Remember, I'm not strapped in. Fucking madman up here."

"Madman, yeah. Just wait. You haven't seen shit."

"Hey, you hear that, piggies?" Wil knocked on the rear doors. "We've got a madman in here, watch out. It's a miracle you even got this thing rolling. Where'd you learn how to drive? I told you I should be up there."

"Your mom taught me now shut up and undo those straps."

In front of Wil were three carriers holding the truck's payload. Twenties, fifties, and hundreds were separated into stacks by denomination and wrapped in Violet, Brown, and Mustard-colored straps respectively. To his right, piled unevenly in the small duffel bag, were a different set of bills. . .

Wil worked in haste to cut the strap off each of the many hundreds of stacks and place the loosened bills into a large black trash bag. Disregarding denomination, he worked randomly from top to bottom of each money carrier, abandoning scissors early on for the use of his fingers to rip the straps. With the first trash bag halfway full, he loaded several fistfuls of money from the duffel bag into it, shook it violently, and set it aside. The process was hurriedly repeated until all of the bills were loaded into three total trash bags.

"How we looking back there?"

"We're good. All set with the bags."

"We're approaching the south side of the park, maybe three minutes out. I'm gonna take 7th over to Memorial. That should give us enough room."

"Definitely. Tell me when and I'll give us a buffer for the turn."

"Thirty seconds," Robin yelled. "Get the spikes ready."

"On it."

Wil moved the three trash bags to the front of the captain's seat and crept to the rear of the vehicle, sliding the second duffel bag along with him. He unzipped the bag and fished out a star-shaped, jagged piece of iron. The bag contained exactly three hundred and ninety-nine more just like it. Four wicked, sharpened points to each, the homemade items were made from metal scraps and welded into a fearsome form of potential. Unannounced, Robin swerved around a double-parked car on the side of the road, sending Wil against the sidewall and spilling a few spikes on the floor.

"God damn it, Robin!"

"Now, Wil! Dump 'em out!"

"Jesus."

Wil hopped to both feet and threw open the back doors of the truck. A blur of blacktop whooshed by below while he pushed the bag to the edge. Kneeling, he held the bag on both ends and yelled towards the chasing fleet of police, immeasurably deep in number.

"Rain hell, boys!"

With some effort he dumped the bag on its end, spilling the objects onto the rushing street below. Bouncing and tumbling, the iron shrapnel dotted the road like salt from a plow truck, instantly shredding tires, cracking grills, and ricocheting off windshields in random calamity. Cruisers swerved and bumped one another. But deeper in the pack, as the shrapnel settled, was where the real damage occurred. A mass confusion of brake lights and deflations was disrupting the tight pack. Wil watched the ensuing destruction like it was on a giant movie screen before him.

"Hahaha! Not tonight, sweet princes," he yelled between laughs. "You'll have to tune in for the rest of this show. I'm sure your buddies will give you a play-by-play. Cocksuckers." He shut the doors and shuffled back to the captain's seat at the front of the bed. "Took out most of the squad. Never saw it comin'!"

Robin was watching the damage out of the side-view mirror. "That was all you, brother! Brilliant!" he shouted back. "Let's finish this thing."

The sink water ran warm and steady while Merv lathered his hands with soap. To his left, part of a man's body was visible through the opening below the bottom of the stall door. His upper torso was out of sight, but lifeless arms dangled to the floor on both sides of the toilet like a discarded doll. Inside, the tattooed man had been left unconscious over the bowl. His sopping wet hair covered a bloodied face and an even bloodier, now mostly toothless, mouth. The earlier flurry of hits had knocked him out cold but not before Merv made sure he tasted the piss he so vehemently wanted wiped off the toilet seat. As well as the toilet water.

Washing the filth of the man off of his hands, Merv breathed deeply in an effort to decelerate from the whirling fury he had risen to a few moments earlier. With clean hands he rinsed his face, grabbed the loose paper towel roll from the corner of the sink, and unrolled a wad. He dried his beard, eyes, and forehead before finishing with his hands. After discarding the towel he caught his reflection in the mirror and froze.

For the first time in weeks he took a close look at the man that stared back, the face that carried his twisted consciousness and callous intellect. An aging man was before him. Wrinkle lines on the corners of his eyes and across his forehead showed themselves regardless of how much he relaxed his face. His skin was leathering like hide left out in the sun. Grey hairs fought their way in between the thick mess of hair on his head and full beard. Balding he was not, though his hairline had receded more than he remembered. It fled from his forehead.

He found his gaze unbearable to meet. This man he saw was a stranger. An alien and a trickster. Age and stress, he realized, had turned him into something he didn't accept. The person inside was trapped in a body that wasn't his own. More like a mutilation of a man he used to be. *Fate, you wretched cunt. You twisted fucking cunt. You knew all along that this would happen, only to show yourself once it was too late. What is there for me now but the inevitable long road downward? I should end it early just to spite you.*

The sobering sight sickened him provoking a deeper, more dangerous rage than any fistfight could. Hatred, repressed and volatile, flooded him. His jaw tightened and water glistened over his eyes. He saw his father's features in the mirror. The features of a man he loathed, a man he cursed and rejected.

The fist he'd used so often as a cudgel of reckoning clenched once more and connected with the mirror that met his view. With a crash the mirror fragmented in a spiderweb of lines and cracks. Again he hit it. And again, harder as he went on. When he lowered his fist, a jagged hole the size of a grapefruit remained. Behind it the wall had caved in. He inspected the damage and found his reflection now divided into countless shards. The fissures split the edge of his head and hairs while the hole took the place of his face. *I shouldn't exist.*

Back at the bar he slammed the shot and beer that had been peacefully awaiting his return. Though small, it was a busy place, particularly at this hour. He slumped his head, and felt a gentle vibration crawling up the wooden stool. He reached in his jacket, which was hung over the stool, and fished for his phone. The vibration had stopped, revealing twelve missed calls. Squinting, he opened the phone to yet another incoming call.

"Yeah," he answered casually.

A panicked voice shouted on the other end of the line. It was Mancuso. "Sir? Where are you? We have a situation. Chase in progress. It's them!"

His eyes lit up with the newfound energy of anticipation.

"On my way," Merv announced into the receiver.

This is it. . . Oh Fate, how you tease me so.

Robin turned the truck northbound on Atlantic Ave. along the southwestern section of Baker's Memorial Park. The quiet avenue glowed from the pale streetlamps lining it on both sides like a runway. Ahead in the distance, at the end of the straightaway, the road curved sharply to the right and wrapped around a sizable corner lot.

"There it is! Get the bags ready," Robin yelled.

Through the truck's thick windshield Robin saw the lowly, vacant corner storefront come into sight and grow in size as he pressed the pedal closer to the floor. By then the pack of police cars had reassembled and regained the distance lost from other angles. Cruisers swerved and rushed at the truck, much more aggressive than before, as the ear-pounding sound of sirens returned to full blast as the road opened up ahead. One car pulled alongside the truck and Robin swerved, knocking it aside. Again it advanced in an attempted fishtail maneuver, but Robin slowed and bumped the car off the road.

"What's happening up there?" Wil hollered.

"I think they want that money back, Wil!"

"Fuck them! Let's see where the wind takes it instead."

"This is it! Let it fly!"

Wil slid to the back of the truck once more, dragging one of the black trash bags along with him. One at a time he opened the steel doors, exposing a scene not fully describable by words. Amber and blue flashes dominated his field of view at first. Then slowly the breadth of their debacle presented itself in its entirety, and yet so did the purpose of the act in which they had chosen to engage. Defiance burned deeply within him.

Snapping out of the momentary trance, he folded the trash bag's opening onto itself and by the fistful threw wads of bills out of the rear of the truck. Violently he flailed his arms, throwing the money into the air as they sped onward. Robin watched his progress out of the side-view mirror. He glanced ahead and then back to the mirror, ahead again and back to the mirror once more. The corner building was approaching too quickly for Wil to empty the truck of its contents in time.

"More! Dump it all, Wil!"

Acknowledging the order Wil took the garbage bag in both hands and stood. With one hand gripping the opening and the other on a bottom corner, he shook the bag out at the pursuing police cars. Then he released the hand that gripped the opening and pulled the bottom of the bag back with his other hand. Along with the rushing wind from the truck's open windows, the motion left the contents suspended momentarily in midair. Gusts of wind coming off the truck caught the bills like miniature sails, lifting them spinning and flickering away in the wind. With the same motion he dumped all three bags and watched as the bills scattered about in the wind in a cyclone of disarray.

By then the corner building and its accompanying turn were just some two-hundred meters away.

"Wil! Finish up and strap yourself in!"

"Roger that!" he screamed while shutting the back doors.

"We have impact in less than ten seconds."

"Blast through it!"

Despite the road's upcoming curvature Robin held the wheel straight while Wil buckled himself in the rear seat.

One-hundred meters.

As if anticipating the move, cruisers steadily backed off one by one, admitting a sizable space between the truck and the lead of their pursuit. Wil watched through the grated divider and clutched his backpack to his chest with white knuckles.

Fifty meters.

Peripheral sounds lessened in the intensity of the moment.

Forty meters.

In that instant, there were no sirens.

Thirty meters.

There were no thoughts.

Twenty meters.

There was only now.

Ten meters.

"HOLD ON!"

Impact.

The truck's front tires jumped the curb and mounted the sidewalk. Robin and Wil left their seats and levitated for a split second as the back tires lifted off the ground. In a thunderous, booming collision the armored truck crashed through the corner storefront, shattering glass and splintering wood with immense force. Old register stands and empty shelving were obliterated and tossed aside like toys as the five-ton beast rolled through the vacant space. Once completely inside the building, Robin gave the truck one more press of the gas pedal, striking a set of aisle dividers. The truck split the dividers in half and barreled towards the rear of the building. Inertia carried them crashing through a storeroom and finally settling to a halt with the front half of the vehicle exposed through the cylinder block wall at the very rear. A trail of dust plumes and piles of debris were all that remained in the truck's path.

Outside, droves of police cruisers screeched to a halt a ways shy of the building's exterior. In a wave, car doors flew open and officers moved into a standard defensive setup, anticipating a possible standoff. Guns were drawn, spotlights were lit, and the natural chain of command initiated between individuals scurrying about the maze of vehicles. All the while crisp currency still rained from above, floating gently in the soft gusts of wind like feathers in a breeze.

Behind the building, Robin and Wil hastily exited the truck. Though banged up a bit from the impact, they kept the pain inside, for their escape had only just begun.

With the rear of the vehicle still in the building, Wil jumped through the steel double doors and headed towards a service door several meters away. He met Robin in the alleyway behind the store, kneeling and working to remove his Kevlar vest. Wil followed in haste and slipped on his small backpack, pulling the straps as tight as they went. For extra support he clipped the shoulder straps together with a plastic quick-release clip and yanked it taut. The two looked at each other in the darkness through the eye holes in their masks and nodded.

"Let's go," Wil said casually.

They snuck through the perpendicular rear alley away from the crash site. A megaphone's faded echoes reverberated in space and Robin's ears picked up the words "surrounded" and "peacefully" between the wailing sirens and engine banter. Further they went, tiptoeing along. Additional sirens were approaching from both the front and rear, indicating a flank of sorts to surround the building from the north and south. They had but seconds to reach the end of the passageway before police would, in all likelihood, probe the scene forcibly.

At the end of the alley they reached a T-intersection. They made a right turn down another passage that lead to an open cross street, west by northwest of the grocery store and Baker's Park. Remaining in the shadows they stopped just before the passage terminated. Across the orange-hued road they could see the entrance to another set of alleyways astride a stretch of stores and row homes. A pair of cruisers sped by in the direction of the park as a rush of wind met the duo at the mouth of the alley.

"Once we make it across, it's full bore to the split point," Wil said hurriedly. "They're gonna chase us, but you follow my lead and I'll get us out of here. Just like we practiced. And remember. They'll never shoot. All we have to do is run." He turned to Robin quickly. "That's a promise." He gave Robin a wink and turned back to the glowing street.

"Let's do this," Robin answered. His 'pump-up' breaths were audible through his mask.

"Ready?" Wil called.

"Ready."

Wil stood and stepped out into the light of the street, holding his hand back at Robin to halt. He peeked right towards the commotion at the building's rear position, now roughly fifty meters away. Then he turned left and, with a start, immediately shouted, "GO!"

Illumination engulfed the two as Robin and Wil took off from the alley like they were shot out of the barrel of a gun. Halfway across the road a pair of cruisers skidded to a stop and four policemen jumped out and sprinted after them. Entering the next alley, commands filled the space.

"Freeze!" one officer screamed as they abandoned their idling cruiser on the street.

"In pursuit on foot. Two men. Dark pants, dark jackets. Masks," another yelled into his radio. "Alleyways off Garrison. Need immediate backup!"

Ensuing was a race for freedom shadowed by a race for glory. The officers ran in after them and lit their flashlights one at a time. The duo sprinted at a blistering speed rounding a corner with Wil slightly ahead. Robin trailed one stride behind and maintained while the officers followed apace, tethered in their pursuit. Their lit flashlights were held like Pony Express batons, lighting the alleyway floor and surroundings in wild, transitory bursts of light. Each momentary flicker saw the two fugitives gaining marginal distance on their pursuers, crushing loose gravel under their steps and splashing shallow puddles as they went.

The stretch of alleyway lasted several dozen meters before Wil and Robin rounded a left-turn corner. Clutter filled this passage. Dumpsters and old furniture littered the sides of the alley, some jutting about and making for near misses by both parties. Above, fire escapes and iron balconies caged the chase in a tunnel. The moon's glow lit the passages only enough for general awareness, but the duo ran the stretches like a practiced route. Flashes of light continued and the ever present and seemingly gaining footsteps pressed the pair onward. Six sets of shoes hitting the ground and steady breaths were the only local sounds. Sirens, though, provided a constant audible backdrop.

A fence loomed ahead.

In full stride Robin and Wil leapt for the top crossbar and scaled it with skillful finesse. They hit the ground running, but to their surprise found that the officers hadn't missed a step in dealing with the obstacle.

Their next turn led them down a pathway that opened onto an illuminated avenue perpendicular to their heading. Rapidly it approached, the uncertainty of its contents weighing on both men's consciousness. A wailing police cruiser raced by as they passed the halfway mark towards the opening, then a pair of unmarked vehicles followed.

The duo maintained their blazing speed, entering the street with reckless disregard for potential traffic. Entering the orange glow of streetlamps presented a momentary glimpse, a madness of rushing peripheral police cars speeding through the bordering cross streets. Halfway across, the sound of a nearby engine and siren grew louder.

The officers dashed into the street in pairs behind them. Suddenly, in the blink of an eye, the screech of a police cruiser's brakes sounded. The car narrowly missed the first pair, but sent the rear pair of officers hurling into the air like ragdolls. They rolled over the halting vehicle, their bodies landing on the pavement with a thud.

In the alley, the remaining pair picked up the pace of their pursuit. Despite begging radio queries, they were unable to specify their location. A heading, however, appeared certain to one of the policemen.

"Northbound!" he shouted breathlessly. "In the alleyways, God damn it!"

Any more of a response was a waste of precious of lung capacity. Maintaining a sprint of this distance was something rarely done outside of competition. But tonight, competition was taking its ultimate form.

Merv's brakes squealed as he pulled his vehicle up to pure chaos. The unfolding crime scene was worse than any description one could have relayed. Police euphemisms had long sickened him, and tonight they ran rampant across the radio waves. He hadn't seen this number of cop cars in one spot since. . .he wasn't quite sure. It was a disaster area. *Jesus fucking Christ. This is a nightmare.*

He jolted the car forward and pulled park-side onto the sidewalk of Atlantic Avenue, well back from the crash site. The road from there onward was blocked with vehicles and a bustle of foot traffic. When he exited his vehicle, the full experience of the event became vivid. Wailing vehicles were parked haphazardly along the road, still idling and glowing from their emergency lights. All along the road were bills. Thousands - no, hundreds of thousands - of dollars strewn across the street, giving the appearance of tile or some marbled brick surface. The gusting wind shifting bills made the ground seem in a constant state of mutation. Sensory overload though it was, Merv was quick to adjust. He walked into the fray in search of a reliable source of up-to-the-minute information. He found Mancuso and two uniformed officers in the distance and stormed over, forced to meander between parked cruisers.

"Give it to me straight," he announced.

"No perps yet, sir. We have uniforms inside clearing the building. They're combing through slowly," Mancuso responded. He had a walkie-talkie in his hand.

"Just fucking smoke 'em out and get it over with," Merv snapped.

The three gave him a silent, sidelong look.

"Get some units parked on the north end of this building, whatever the next cross street is. If they come out the back we need to be there," he ordered.

"Truck's empty," came through over the radio. "Team Two, check upstairs. Team One, with me. Watch corners."

Merv's focus had been on the storefront since the moment he arrived. While in the openness of such an environment he had to act according to his position. He wasn't a 'frontlines' man anymore, regardless of his superiority in these situations. His seniority forced him to helm the command.

"All of you, start getting the street cleared of these cruisers. We'll need a cleanup crew immediately. If too many of these dirt bags around here discover this money, all hell will break loose."

A uniformed officer came upon their group. "Sir! Patrolmen surprised the suspects behind the building while they were escaping. They're on a foot chase as we speak."

Merv's face lit up. "Where?"

The noise and commotion made shouting the only way to communicate. "They're in pursuit in the alleyways, north of here."

"Which alleyways? Where?"

"North, we believe."

"You *believe*?"

"We're not sure how many officers are pursuing, sir. The one's we've heard from have, uh, implied quite a desperate chase."

"What the fuck does that mean? Cut the shit."

"Uh, they're having trouble keeping up, sir. There wasn't time to provide us with details. This is developing."

"Jesus Christ. . .if they fucking lose them. . ." Merv growled. "Get me on the radio with them, and someone check on that fucking chopper."

"On it," Mancuso said, trotting away.

Merv turned to the other officer. "What are their names?"

"I'm not sure, sir."

"How many did they say they're chasing?"

"Two."

"That's not right," he mumbled, and then rose his voice. "There's got to be a third somewhere. Check the building again."

"They just cleared it, sir."

"Just check the fucking building." Merv turned his head, his glare landing on a dawdling officer. "You," Merv pointed. "What's your name?"

"Raymer, sir."

"Raymer, I want cars doing circuits through the streets north and west of here. We'll try to cut them off if they cross a street."

"We've got a dozen on that circuit already, sir."

"Double it. And get that fucking chopper over here."

"Yes, sir. All available units. . ."

Raymer's voice faded as Merv walked closer to the crash site, running his fingers through his beard. His eyes were darting back and forth, trying to envision how the events had unfolded, when suddenly Mancuso approached with a worried face.

"Uh, sir we've, uh, gotten word that our chopper broke down," he reported. "They're, uh, working on getting it in the air."

"What about the other one?"

"Five minutes out."

"Get the f–" He turned his head in disgust. "Get the fuck out of my sight."

He closed his eyes. *Oh you unholy motherfuckers. . .*

Snaking through the twisting innards of the District, the foot chase intensified. The fugitives leapt over an overflowing pile of trash bags blocking the narrow corridor. The cops did the same, keeping their composure and maintaining the difficult pace. They ran under an archway, a scattered remnant of the old city that still remained undisturbed.

They were losing their lead on the two officers as they crossed another street and entered an alleyway. What had started as an all-out sprint had turned into a jogging, long-distance chase extending over a mile from the crash site. Such effort had neutralized the initial adrenaline boost both policemen had harnessed and panting from all four men became audible. Ahead of them, a T-intersection approached.

"Here it comes," one of the fugitives shouted.

At the junction, they separated left and right respectively.

"Go left! I'm right," commanded the leading officer, dividing the pack into two individual pursuits.

To the cops' dismay, both men had picked up their previously slowing pace in a last ditch effort to flee. Two rights and a left. Or was it two lefts and a right? Was that the same cross street? The number of turns and streets crossed, the amount of focus demanded from a chase of this magnitude made keeping a sense of location dizzying for the officer following Wil. A straightaway and a left turn, followed by another straightaway, left him nearly depleted. Losing ground, he grunted loudly in frustration, using every ounce of energy he could muster to keep on the man.

"FREEZE GOD DAMN IT!"

But freeze, the fugitive did not. Instead he continued onward, unrelenting in his pace. Ahead, in the distance, the officer glimpsed him turn yet another corner, left now, disappearing in stride behind a dumpster and out of sight. Lagging, he took long, important seconds to reach the bend. As he finally took two or three steps past the corner, he was confronted with a baffling mirror image of another flashlight's glow rapidly emerging from around the opposing bend in the alleyway, a few dozen meters ahead. His fellow officer rounded the opposite corner, running straight at him. Dumbfounded, the two skidded to a halt. They met eyes under the light of their flashlights and shared a bewildered, wide-eyed look. They panted uncontrollably. Apart from the officers, the alleyway appeared empty.

They franticly spun their heads about. They scanned with growing futility the empty and undisturbed canvas of brick and mortar with their flashlights. Gasping with fatigue, they tried to communicate with each other but nothing more than a "Wha" was repeated from both. Steam billowed out of a grated wall vent between them in eerily peaceful contrast to their panic, and a blanket of stillness cloaked the stretch. The two perpetrators had seemingly disappeared. . .

Just then, in the hollow pocket of the alleyway, the heaving and coughing policemen were assaulted by the shock of a thousand lightning bolts. They dropped to the floor, convulsing.

Merv stood in the center of the avenue, surrounded by money. Blockades were being erected to prevent the residents from spilling onto the street, as the scene had become quite a theater for the many people that resided in the area. Merv was observing the crowd, his blood pressure rising, when a motion caught his eye. It was a little boy, waving at him with one hand and holding a fistful of money in the other, brandishing a smile like it was picture day at school. His amusement perked Merv up a bit. *This* is *all a huge joke, isn't it?* Merv then scowled. *But the joke's on you, kid.*

The majority of the police presence was focused on crowd control while a few dozen other officers had returned to the search for the fugitives in their cruisers. *Where is that fucking chopper?* A cleanup crew had recently arrived, and Merv watched as several available officers joined in the effort. Hastily they worked to combat the gusting wind that plagued the avenue and open parklands. He was sure that the effort would have to spill into the park to reclaim all of the bills floating around.

"Sir!" yelled a voice to Merv's rear. "Sir. . .we. . .we've lost contact with our officers. Their radios appear to have been disconnected. . . Detective?"

Merv didn't even turn to acknowledge the voice. Yells and whistles, engines humming and sirens blaring and wind gusting chilled air encircled him. A tempest had passed through and this, this was its result. Slowly and with a heavy head he looked at the sprawling stretch before him. At his feet, he noticed movement. Dancing gently, and floating inch by inch along the pavement, was a peculiar-looking bill among the assorted twenties, fifties, and hundreds. With a perplexed squint, he squatted down and plucked the bill from the surface of the road like a feather from some enormous bird. Blinking in disbelief, a terrible recognition overcame him, pulling with it a curtain of mortification and surging rage.

In his hand lay a phony three-dollar bill with a portrait of Merv's own face smiling directly out at him from its center.

PART 3: MAY DAY, MAYDAY

"There is no such thing as exaggerated art. There is salvation only in extremes." - Paul Gauguin

Chapter 29: Always the Acorn

A strung-out, weathered man lay as stiff as a corpse in the midst of a blank, cavernous slumber. A strange and spookily dark room had housed his body for nearly twelve hours while he treaded a delicate line between consciousness and coma. Within, the light of his life was flickering like a candle in the breeze. How he arrived there, he'd never know. Some form of a path had taken him there, surely, but which path depending entirely on the decisions he'd made in his life—the determining interchanges, boundless in in their number of exit and entrance ramps, on the highways of life.

The average person takes about five-hundred and fifty million breaths in a lifetime. But this man hadn't been an average person. That heaving, screaming, writhing mass that was him as a freshly born baby wasted a good hundred or so in the first minute of life. How many thousands more were wasted sucking on the end of a pipe? How many were smoke-induced coughs or overslept snores? How many were panic attacks that rushed his breath tenfold? Perhaps life was just a countdown chipping away to the quadruple digits, to those breaths that *really* mattered. If human beings experienced life with a ticking countdown of breaths visible in their minds, would they live their lives differently? Would they acknowledge the purposeful and abandon the petty, the inconsequential? Would they let that ten-millionth breath go in hate or in love? Would they submit to the nature of being and disregard the certainty, the ever-present irrevocability of death? The answer was simply: no.

At the age of nineteen, the man discovered intoxication and altered states of consciousness. He was a teenager without friends, without influence. Where some found alcohol or drugs through an older sibling or "cool" friend, he discovered both on his own and harnessed the use of each through his pain, filling an endless void. No one was there to tell him to slow down or check him when excess took reign.

In school, teachers preached that marijuana was a gateway drug. Reefer madness and the like were cautioned against, to preserve the mind of the nation's youth. He obeyed his teachers for a while, however, rebellion and autonomy developed inside him as it does in us all. The night he first tried amphetamine, it took that charge. It led him to real drug dealers and real drugs. Pot and so forth were child's play, a supplement or consolation from there onward. A natural progression, if you can call it that, was his route through consumables. From ecstasy, came coke and other uppers, then downers and hallucinogens, and on to specialty stuff like scoop and DMT and various prescription narcotics - synthetics and concentrates. He'd try anything once, because fuck it. It didn't matter what happened. At least he'd know if he liked it or not. Youth garners a feeling of invulnerability. He knew his behavior would someday lead to death, but no time soon, so he let the addiction take hold. He had welcomed it. Many years later, he welcomed it still.

Suddenly, he stirred. . .

Eyelids fluttered and a cough came. The man jolted awake on the floor of that strange home, that den, with alien bodies lifeless and unconscious around him. The blinds were half-closed. Moonlight peeked through the slats outlining the lumpy figures strewn about the floor. A putrid stench permeated the air and the room spun in his vision. It caused a nauseous, gagging rush through the dimness to find a bathroom, holding back the tightness in his throat. Instead he found a closet, where he proceeded to wretch his guts out. It brought him to his knees. The hurling was violent and unrelenting, shooting stinging surges of bile and mucus through his mouth and nose. He vocalized his condition through moans and distressful chokes as he lay rocking back and forth on the musty, stained carpet.

The night seemed endless. He would awake, vomit, pass out, awake, vomit, pass out, each time knowing less of that weird room in which he lay, each time watching a part of his soul spew from his mouth and swirl into the fibers of the carpet. Strange noises and visions vivified and encroached each time he woke. His hallucinations toyed with his sanity and the boiling in his stomach made it harder and harder to drift back into sleep. But once more he drifted.

In pure darkness he woke again, empty and muttering. He made his way from the closet, following the wall to open a set of blinds exposing the night sky. He needed air, fresh air. The light of the moon poked through the window, void of its companion stars. His weak hands searched for a handle, some grip to raise the window to free him of that stench and heaviness, but he found none. He pushed upward on the glass only to find its frame cemented shut. As he stared out of the window in defeat, the glass iced over in his vision, grey and opaque. It was cold to his touch. He pushed at it but it pushed back, so cold it burned. He yelled in pain and cowered away. Backwards he stepped and tumbled over a body on the floor. His back hit the ground with a thud and he lost his breath. The impact caused him, oddly, to taste the vileness in his mouth, the leftover vomit and refuse of his insides that caked his teeth and festered under his tongue. He coughed and spit at its foulness.

When he had caught his breath, he rolled on his side and moved to his knees to wake the person he had tripped over. He had to know where he was, how he got there. . .and how to get out. He shook and tapped the figure, calling at it and waiting for a response. The body remained stiff, though, as frozen as the window and as cold to the touch. He rolled the body over and met lifeless eye sockets and rigid features. With a scream, he recoiled from the corpse and squirmed over to another body on the ground several feet away. It left a small shadow from the setting moon's shine. This body had an arm crossed over its torso and the other arm was missing. It was hollow, with porcelain skin and plain, indistinct features. He shook the body violently, yelling for it to wake up, yelling for help. Then the head popped off and rolled a pace away. The man dropped the mannequin and slowly rose. He had a terrifying sense that he was being watched from the shadows, trapped in some funhouse nightmare. The hairs on the back of his neck stood on end and goosebumps formed along his thin arms.

Stumbling and mumbling, he fled in fear. Bumping along walls in the darkness, he tested doorknobs and hallways, searching feverishly for an exit. One door led to the next and so on. He felt like the rooms were repeating themselves, that the stench was getting worse and worse the farther he went. As he was about to give up and succumb to the belly of that place, his pocket caught a knob along the hallway's left wall. He tried the knob in desperation and opened a door onto a rush of crisp, brisk air. Gasping, he plunged into the night and staggered forward, down a set of stairs, and straight into a waist-high fence.

The fence caught him in the abdomen, holding his weight as he huffed full breaths of air. Nausea surfaced in him once again from the pressure to his stomach and he stood to hold himself, leaning on the railing with his hands. In a moment of clarity, recollection of his most recent bender came through in distinct, painful waves. Snapshots flooded his mind. He contemplated his actions and his condition, his fall from opportunity into this dreadful pit.

He became aware, then, of a sizable puddle in front of him as he remained leaning over the metal rail. The puddle shined with the residual light of the moon, creating a silhouette of the man's upper body against a shimmer of white light. Life's natural mirror. A man reflecting back was emptiness to himself.

The man turned away and slid down into a seated position. To his side were several metal trash cans. They shifted slightly from his movement, clattering. The man spent several minutes slowing his breath, slowing his thoughts. As his breaths settled, he felt constricting pressure on his left arm and looked down to find a woven band snugly fixed around his wrist. He remembered that, with some of the money he collected, he had purchased an inexpensive watch from old Harper's pharmacy near the western entrance to Baker's Park. Standing outside of the store that night, he had set the watch to match the electronic display on the Jung Tower, visible in the height of the Downtown skyline.

Presently, he turned the watch face into view, slowly pressed the little illumination button, and blinked furiously at the date, mortified at the disappearance of the last few weeks. His emotional response of that realization momentarily plucked him out of his mind's creations, and he began to weep, a desolate wreck.

Of all days to regain awareness, it had to be so close to that one. Of all days. Memories of and sadness over times past coursed through his mind, some truth, some skewed alterations of less important details. All, though, were depressingly positive. Depressing not because of their positivity but because of their unobtainability, their distance, and their unique value. His departure from the innocence of those days was like an acorn from a tree, beautifully budded to be shed down and cracked open, his heart chewed up, digested and shit out, leaving only a shell to remain, rotting for seasons to come; forgotten and insignificant like a natural process of life, never to return to that safe place on the tree of his past.

This was a sign.

That day of remembered happiness would be the day, for the spark of his life was fading and he wished it extinguished. For all his years he'd had control of his life taken from him by everyone and everything, never feeling unique, never feeling true individuality. Always the acorn. At last, he could control something, for taking his own life would be an act of control. And so he made his commitment. He would die that day. And he knew just the spot.

In the pre-dawn darkness, the man stumbled along a circuitous route past places ancient in his history. He passed the row-home, third one from the right, where he had lived with his mom, a drunk and a pill-head, after his dad left. He walked fifteen more blocks to the campus of his junior and senior high school, where one day a group of football players found him and a boy kissing in the locker room, stripped them, beat them, and urinated on them both. By dawn he slunk past the art studio he once owned, now rundown and vandalized.

There was a time in his life where he was considered successful, where he was given praise. In his twenties, after college, the man made a name for himself in the art community through his small studio in the Manufacturing District on the southern end of Atlantic Ave. His paintings and sculptures were featured in galleries across the city and beyond, with acclaim domestically and abroad. While the Inner District was crumbling around him, while people he knew were losing everything, he had flourished. At least on paper. Even as he spilled his psychological traumas onto the canvas, and harnessed the repression and evil he had experienced, addiction had kept its chokehold.

This was his mosaic, the mess of his life, only when viewed from afar it remained as jumbled as it did close up. The row of buildings before him was a mosaic too. Brick and sidewalk, windows and doors, and roofs and sky formed an indistinguishable assortment of pieces. Some grew larger than others, showing snapshots of his past. They were the bricks that were the foundation of his life.

Bricks, he realized. . .he needed bricks. So he walked across the roadway and into the rundown studio to find them.

Chapter 30: In God We Trust

The Devil is in this city. I can feel it. He taints us all with his touch, with his malevolence. From where, Lord, does He emanate? Show me. Show me and I will vanquish Him. Show me and I will do my part. As you see fit. Show me.

The 6 a.m. church bell rang repeatedly through the hall in an ominous rhythm. Ernest had been sitting on the left, second-row pew for four hours. Leaning. And Praying. Beyond him was his podium, a stand from which his sermons had echoed in this hall countless times. Hanging above and behind that stand was Jesus, bloody and omnipotent. He who died for our sins, He who forgave and loved unconditionally. He who was born immaculate and true. He who was merciful. . .

You gave me a clue. Ernest rubbed gently at a torn piece of paper in his hands, crinkled with writing faded from hours of consideration. Each pass of his left thumb showed a name and a number swiftly written on the worn loose leaf.

You gave me a chink, a weak spot in His stealth. He read the two lines of text, as he had a hundred times over, mulling the potential repercussions of his decision. *But to exploit that weakness is to sacrifice those I care for.*

Oh, he was like a son to me. The night he was beaten tore at me like my own Jack's beating. They were so alike, so poised. . . I can only praise you, Lord, for keeping Robin's life safe. Ernest's face crumpled into a look of sadness, then. *What happened to that bright young man who first walked into our home? The men that beat him, they beat his goodness out of him. They sullied him, Lord. They sapped his will, blackened it, and exacted it into him with enmity. They opened him to the Devil.*

He recalled the anger in Robin. How it never left him. *That night changed him. It changed everything. It brought this madness, this chaos. I didn't realize its coming until it was too late. It awoke a sleeping beast within our District and aggravated it into acrimony and thievery. Into discord. It all came from Robin. The Devil is in him, now. I can feel it. . .*

Numbness had reached Ernest's rear end and thighs over an hour earlier. Presently, it crept down his legs, causing the slightest tingle in his feet. The robe he wore was tattered in places and soiled. How long it had been on his body without a wash, he truly didn't know. A mirror was something his eyes had avoided these many weeks.

He looked at the cross above the altar, then back down at the paper in his hands once more. *I can reverse this discord. I can make peace if Robin is stopped. There is no justification for the madness he is perpetuating, no future in it. My duties as a godly man and as a citizen are being tested. If he is detained peacefully, justice can be served; by God and by State. He deserves this mercy. And I must help give it to him.*

I know, now, what must be done, Lord. . . This has gone too far. The boys are wrong. Have mercy on them, for they know not the consequences of their actions. They've been misled and shrouded in evil. Have mercy. Have mercy on them and have mercy on me for what I'm about to do.

He fingered the paper. His handwriting was sloppy, performed in haste as the information was being shown on the television. He couldn't miss that chance. *The righteous choice lies in my hands. I but have to pick up the phone.*

Ernest pursed his lips and reconsidered momentarily. He recalled the better days, when Robin was his guest. He recalled the bond, the joy, and companionship. He recalled his will to do well by and for others, to simply *help. He was a good kid. . .*

Is this your challenge to us all, Lord? Emotion? Have we all along been tested with our loves and our cares? Our humanly qualities are unbecoming of our duty to worship. But I choose to squander that which is human this day and praise only you.

I have been tempted so, have I not? Tempted and lost, I was, all those years. And I found you, O Lord. I found you, in all your glory and holiness. You had been waiting all along. I but needed to walk in your light. He too needs to walk in your light. But first he must be stopped and shown, as I was shown. He must atone as I have atoned.

The righteous choice, cursing that of temptation, is my path. I will not be a slave to my emotions, to my lesser, more human faculties. I will praise the Almighty. I will trust in you, Lord, as I have and as I always will.

It is time to do my part. No longer will I support criminals. My inaction makes me as guilty as they. My inaction is permission for this anarchy, this madness. My inaction becomes my old self - my bad self - not the man I grew to be. . . My inaction leaves us all weak.

Ernest clasped his hands together in prayer. *This day is my reckoning. Keep me steady in my righteous endeavors. Keep my community safe in these trying times. And keep the boys in your merciful embrace upon their demise. There is salvation for them. If only they trust in you. Lord, have mercy. Give me the strength to do what must be done in this dark hour.*

A dark hour though it was, streams of colored light pierced the dusty air above. The stained-glass windows depicting the Resurrection cast the outside white beams in an assortment of blues, reds and yellows. Slowly, as the minutes passed, they walked along the main buttress of the chapel until they came to shine their vivid colors upon thy holy cross. Christ gleamed radiant in the transmogrification. His body shone bright and magnificent with the rising sun. The sight was enough to bring Ernest's tired eyes to tears. He wiped at the streams but they fell and fell. *The time is nigh, old man.*

Ernest stood, blotted his cheeks, and spoke aloud. "Lord, I beseech you. Have mercy on their souls."

Softly, he exited the chapel and made for his study. He quickened his pace as he passed Robin's old room, and quietly stepped into his office. The phone lay dormant on his desk. He reached for the receiver and placed a hand around it firmly.

"And on mine, too," he muttered.

With a deep breath, Ernest snatched up his office phone and dialed directly from the worn paper in his hands. The line rang but once before a female voice answered on the other end.

"I would like to meet with Detective Hamstead," he uttered in a shaking tone. "I have information on the identities of the men who perpetrated the armored car heist. The men who call themselves 'The Few Against Many'."

Chapter 31: Baker's Dozen

Marian awoke in a warm bed to the sounds of songbirds outside. Even though the sun's rays were not yet bright enough to squint at, light had made its way into Robin's bedroom, illuminating the area in a pleasant mood. She yawned and rubbed at her eyes. Another night together was another night spent awake until the early reaches of morning talking, laughing, and being intimate. Marian still hadn't given herself fully to him, but she knew the moment was fast approaching. The recent weeks had been a test of will. In her heart, she wanted him more than air. In her mind, though, she was proud to have faced temptation and saved herself thus far. Their connection had benefitted tremendously, and the sexual tension they were experiencing was an intoxicating buildup to the eventual climax of their new relationship.

Marian stretched and listened for noise, wondering where her man had gone to. She sat up and checked her watch, which lay on the nightstand. It read 6:26 a.m. She set it back down and made her way into the living room in just her underwear and a t-shirt of Robin's from high school.

This was only the second time she had stayed the night at Robin's apartment on Pine Street since their relationship began, but she had found it comfortable from the start. She very much admired the high, tin paneled ceilings, creaky wood floors, and

Victorian accents. You simply couldn't find that kind of detail downtown.

Marian entered the living room and found Robin lounging at the far window with a pen and a yellow notepad. He turned to her and offered a smile that melted her heart.

"Hey you."

"Good morning," she replied softly, walking over.

He made room for her on the padded ledge and she curled up across from him, her expression full of admiration. They stared at each other contently.

"Ready for your big day?" she asked with a grin.

"I could barely sleep," he said, tossing the notepad aside. "Thanks to you."

"I didn't hear any complaints," she replied with a giggle. "I was half worried you'd left me to get started at the park."

"Never," he laughed. "The last of the vendors aren't arriving 'til eight to do a walkthrough. I was going to leave you around then," he said facetiously.

Marian inhaled dramatically. "Go, then," she cried. "I don't want you here. I can't stand the sight of you anymore," she said, looking out the window to cap off the joke.

"I knew this was hopeless from the start," he exclaimed. "I should have brought you to this place. . ."

Marian smiled his way before turning back to the window. His apartment sat quite a bit higher than the buildings next to his. Beyond them she could see Atlantic Avenue and the west side of Baker's Memorial Park. The clear morning showed the distant downtown skyline magnificently, the towering buildings half lit, half shaded in the light of the rising sun. Dawn offered a glimpse of the coming day's beauty. Tomorrow would hopefully be as beautiful.

Much to her chagrin, the bulk of the festival was covered by treetops and some peaked roofs. Only glimpses of the work being done in the park could be caught in the few times she came to see Robin here. From his window's vantage, she had a clearer view of the lake and tip of the south fields than anywhere else. Moreover, Robin had been incorrigibly defiant in letting her peek at the progress.

Her curiosity made its way away from the view to the window frame and surrounding architectural prominences within the apartment. When her eyes fell on Robin, he was staring at her. "Are you really not going to tell me where to meet you tomorrow afternoon?"

"I told you," he said. "You'll have to find me."

"Come on! I'm *al*ready going to be late and I haven't seen you much these past few weeks. You're going to make me walk around *alone?"* Marian would have to work late that night to have a half-day the next, despite pleading with her boss.

"Just trust me. Besides, you won't be alone. There'll be thousands of people there," he teased.

She gave him an irritated grunt that turned into a look of defeat.

"Come through the southwest entrance and just explore. I promise you'll find me."

"Alright, alright. I trust you. . . I'll be there around 2."

"Perfect," he replied with a nod. "We'll have the whole afternoon and evening together. I need to spend the first few hours on logistics anyway."

A thought came into Marian's head, then. "Have you heard back from your friend, Mr. Ernest?"

Robin smiled meagerly. "Nah. Unfortunately not."

She noticed the regret in his voice. "I'm sorry."

"It's alright. I can't blame him."

"Do you think he's still upset?"

"I'm not sure. The door was locked so I tried sliding a note through the mail slot. I asked a couple people nearby if they had seen him, but they hadn't. I thought he'd at least get in touch. I just wish I could have another chance to explain some things."

"Well, maybe he'll come. And if not today then maybe sometime soon. It seems you two were close enough for an attempt at reconciliation."

"Maybe when things get a little calmer he'll reach out."

Marian glanced at her wrist instinctively, only to find her wristwatch missing. She'd forgotten to put it on upon waking. "What time is it, Robin?"

"Quarter to 7."

"Okay. I'm going to get some clothes on. I have to go in a few."

Marian stepped lightly into Robin's bedroom and shut the door to a crack. She put her jeans on one leg at a time and pulled Robin's shirt off, folding it neatly and setting it on the corner of his bed. A look around his bedroom found it modestly decorated. In just a few places hung mementos of his past - pictures mostly. He had recently framed one of them and placed it beside his mirror, one Wil had taken the first night they had all gone out. She and Robin were sipping a can of that Bear beer, staring into each other's eyes with arms intertwined. She smiled at the snapshot and the memory it conjured. Beside it was a picture of him and his mom from when he was a child. They were faces from another life, a happy life. She could see her brightness in him.

When she finished dressing, she tossed her hair and returned to the ledge in the living room. "I want you to know that I'm really proud of you."

Robin smiled at her in awe. "The last person to tell me that was my mom. Thank you."

"Well she'd be proud too," she added, and kissed him.

Often were the mornings where Marian wished she had a chance to meet his mother. Who was it that could raise such a wonderful man?

"I don't know if I've ever been more excited for anything in my entire life."

"All I know is that if you're involved, it's going to be amazing."

"Thank you. Having you there only makes it sweeter. We're going to have the time of our lives." He cracked that sly smile of his that Marian loved so dearly. "I added something at the last minute–"

Unexpectedly, Robin's front door opened and Jon spun into the living room. He held a flat pink box and a tray of coffee cups in his hands. Immediately the pair by the window smelled the sweet aroma of breakfast treats. Round ones.

"Yo!" Jon called.

"Hey," Robin called back. "Whatcha got there?"

"Oh-ho you know what I got here," he replied, before adding quickly, "Hey, Marian."

"Hi, Jon."

"Got us our favorite donuts, my man – and lady. Y'know, for the occasion. Our guy even threw in an extra one in the dozen for me. I think its cinnamon filled with jelly. Marian you're gonna freak over these, you have no idea." Jon set the box and tray on the breakfast bar.

"I've heard. . ." She lifted her head slightly to get a look as Jon opened the box. "Oh God! Look at those. Oof. I have such a sweet tooth."

"Thanks, Jon," Robin said with a laugh.

"Yeah, no problem. I couldn't sleep much anyway."

Marian slid off the ledge and walked over to the table of goodies.

"Coffee?" Jon asked.

"Yes, please," Marian said, accepting a paper cup graciously. She browsed the donuts with a finger on her lips. Glazed, frosted, powdered, filled, and sprinkled options created a dazzlingly colorful assortment. "Which one should I take?" She wanted them all.

"The glazed is a staple, as Robin likely mentioned."

"Hey, no lobbying!" Robin called to Marian facetiously. "You must choose on your own."

She made a face at him and turned back to the box. "Mm. . . I'll try that one."

Jon handed her one coated in cinnamon and sugar. "Snickerdoodle. A wise choice."

"Where's Wil?" Robin asked.

Jon took a seat on a stool at the counter, grabbing a donut of his own. His had rainbow sprinkles. "I dunno. I thought he'd be over here. He's probably starting early over at the park." He took a bite.

"Probably. The guy hasn't shut up about the art section for three weeks."

"*Holy crap,*" Marian exclaimed in pure enjoyment as she took a bite. Her eyes closed, savoring the sweet fluffiness in her hands.

The other two laughed, taking enjoyment in her enjoyment.

"It's gonna look sweet. I took a sneak peek last night."

"You did? Ah you dog! He's been guarding it like it was the last slice of pizza in the city."

"I know," Jon laughed. "He got too excited and wanted to show me. It's. . .not bad, man. Not bad at all. The kids will go crazy for the finger painting. The parents," he shrugged, "oh well."

"Good," Robin said as he stood and walked over to the counter. "Weather'll hopefully hold out too."

"Fuck yeah it will! High of 78 tomorrow, baby. Low humidity."

Marian laughed. Jon's excitement couldn't be contained and he appeared to be buzzing from caffeine. The recent weeks had solidified her ease around Jon and Wil. They all had only hung out a handful of times, but each proved to be a blast. The guys were genuine sweethearts and, though a touch vulgar, always went the extra mile for her to feel welcomed and comfortable. Not to mention Wil was a riot. His "mental hospital" story was far and away the hardest she had laughed in a long time. Robin hadn't even heard it, and laughed just as hard.

"Alright. Time to go," Marian said after finishing her donut.

Robin turned. "When will I see you?"

"Two o'clock tomorrow."

"Three it is."

She shook her head and kissed him quickly. "See you at four," she said on her way to the door. "Bye, Jon."

Chapter 32: Lunatic Fringe

Dusk settled on the outskirts of town as three men stood in tense assembly at the city-side abutment under the Fort Dearborn Bridge. The towering structure shadowed them beneath brick and rusting, paint-chipped metal that spanned almost a mile across the New Orange River. Above, post-rush hour traffic coasted along the inbound/outbound lanes in a subdued hum. Two vehicles were parked, trunk to trunk, on the skinny dirt service road that ran along the shoreline to a pumping station a mile upriver.

The spark of a lighter put fire in the air. Merv leaned on the rear of his cruiser, puffing on the end of his freshly lit cigarette. He wore a sweat-stained wife-beater, dark cargo pants, and military-style boots. Despite the approaching evening chill, a layer of perspiration was evident on his brow and upper body. His same ragged black beard coated his face but there was something quite different about the man. He'd shaven his head, and looked menacingly brutish. He had a lupine presence. Something sable and inhuman lingered in his eyes.

Standing across from him were Ted and Marty Aksakov, two men he hadn't seen in some months. Ted and Marty stood calmly against the rear of their own car - positioned left and right respectively - as they listened to Merv's disjointed address. He had summoned them two hours earlier, demanding a meeting as soon as possible.

Ted spoke English fluently, with only a minor twang of an Eastern European accent. Marty, on the other hand, would convince you he was a mute, he spoke so infrequently. Merv had heard him argue once in the background of a phone call and realized a speech impediment was what spurred him to silence. But of the many men Merv had met in his lifetime, these two were among the most calculatingly cold blooded he'd come across. Because of that fact, over the past seven years, and dozens of deals, their business arrangements had worked seamlessly and forged a mutual trust and respect between them that typically aided the occasions in which they met.

Tonight's situation, however, had begun edgy, without formalities. The pair of henchmen were growing increasingly uncertain of the task they'd been called to hear. This figure before them was some sort of embodiment of the man they'd known, some vacant representation, not at all who they expected they'd meet. His voice had a mysterious tone of accusation and suspicion. He seemed unpredictable. He seemed dangerous. They had heard that he had been humiliated by some kind of heist, that he had subsequently been off the grid for weeks.

Merv stood solidly, with his feet spread just wider than shoulder width and his arms crossed. Behind him, on his trunk, was a small canvas handbag. Not the kind a woman totes but a smaller, fold-over messenger bag of sorts. He had brought it from his vehicle, not a minute earlier, and set it there without a word. He studied their behavior, wondering and unsure, as he spoke. His brief proposal was heard. Then he got right to business.

"One-hundred K per hit," he hissed at them.

The man on the right whistled upon hearing the amount. Merv squinted at him, unsure if he had made the sound or not. Maybe it was in his head again. The man on the left spoke, then, distracting Merv from his wariness.

"Where you get that kind of money, Hammer?"

"What the fuck does that matter?" he asked suspiciously.

"That's a lot more money than usual. If you say you have it, then you have it. If you say you had to hit someone, who will then go looking for it. . .not as promising."

Someone got to them. Who? MacDunnah? Mancuso?

No, not them. Never.

How could they have gotten to them? Kill these two and we'll do it ourselves.

No. No, no. No. Not them. He's just naive.

"You're aware of an armored truck that recently shed its skin, no?" Merv asked, shaking free of his thoughts. He searched for signs of mal intent in their answers.

"Might be. Don't make us feel any better," Ted answered cautiously. "Hear the Feds found their way into that."

"Who told you that?" he snapped. "Diaz? Hernandez?" Merv blinked feverishly, his thoughts racing.

"News, Hammer," Ted laughed. "*News.* I do not know these men you speak of."

Relief washed over him and he laughed under his breath. "News, oh. . . Those Feds you saw are like fake tits. They make a big impression in the open but don't have any practical use. Don't believe everything on TV, my friend. Trust me."

"We trust you, but it is a fact. No believing necessary."

Out of nowhere, fury erupted in him. "It's a *fact*? Oh, I'm sorry," Merv said sympathetically, laughing at himself and shaking his head. "*You're* right. *I'm* wrong. I seem to be wrong a lot recently - I just can't seem to help myself. Maybe I've been wrong about you two. I thought you two were thirsty for a payday, Ted. I thought I got a call from you not three months ago looking for work. And three months before that, huh?"

Ted shifted uncomfortably and scratched his chin as he looked over at his brother. "Hammer, I was just–"

Merv cut him off, raising his voice and speaking quickly. "I thought I heard someone once say 'money's money.' I thought I had contacts that honored business arrangements. You know business, right? *You* offer services and *I* fucking pay you for them? I thought you were professionals. I *thought* there were two more savages in this city with a thirst as bloody as mine. Did I think wrong?"

"Hammer, listen. It's a lot of money. I'd like to make sure it will be there when the job's done. It was a question. Nothing more. Listen–"

"No, you *fucking* listen! Do I question you? Do I check up on you?"

Ted swallowed hard. His eyes were thinning. Marty folded his arms.

"No."

"Then which is it? I'm wrong? Or you're thirsty for that payday? Or maybe you just like calling me, huh?"

"We're here, ain't we?" The man was losing patience, his jaw showing rage forming.

"Yeah, your bodies are here. I think you left your nuts at home. How about you, Marty?" Merv turned with eyes like daggers, rubbing his nose. It felt like it was bleeding. "You thirsty? You find a voice to fill that useless head of yours?"

Marty met him unflinchingly, just staring that stare of his. Merv continued.

"Give a dog a bone and he wants the whole steak. Is that what this is? What happened to the pursuit of glory and reputation? What happened to. . .justice. . .?"

Merv stopped himself and stared off into space, realizing the prating clumsiness of his words. He had lost control again. At the same time, Marty spit on the ground and flared his nostrils. A standstill elapsed, mounting tension accompanying the heavy silence.

Nothing happened to glory. It is but there for you to skim off the scummy film of this city. Remember, glory breeds reputation.

And mine is thoroughbred.

"No. No. . . No, I'm sorry. I'm sorry about that. I know you're thirsty." He took a deep breath. "I know where your motivations lie and from where your questions were born. I know you're thirsty. Forgive me for that. Here's something to wet your whistles."

Merv grabbed the handbag behind him and threw it to Ted, who caught the bag without breaking his stare.

"Consider it an advance. Get the job done and it'll be added to the total."

Ted unzipped it and folded the opening on itself. Inside was a pile of banded stacks of fifty-dollar bills. The seconds ticked by without change.

"You have my word," Merv added, hoping for a response.

Ted fished through the bag as he stood, working his jaw back and forth. Marty was silent.

"Hmm?" Merv pressed, staring them down.

"Thinking."

Merv huffed and grabbed another cigarette from his pack, placing it in his mouth. "While we wait," he said with muffled sarcasm.

Traffic maintained a consistent droning sound as the meeting paused. In the distance, Merv caught out of the corner of his eye a boat jumping along the surface of the river's choppy break. Upriver, into the wind and against the current and the waves it raced, engaged in a desperate battle versus the unstoppable flow. Its engine whined and its hull crashed each time it landed over a wave. *Gas. Yeah, we'll need gas.*

After what felt like a minute, Ted closed the bag and rested it on the trunk behind him. "How many targets?"

"Everyone's a target," Merv mumbled as he watched the boat. He blinked. "Five. There's five."

The two men looked at each other again. And again they conversed through that unspoken exchange. "That's a tough ratio to sell us on. . . I don't like it."

"You make five-hundred and fifty K in twenty minutes. You like that ratio?" He stared at them one at a time, mimicking their silent discussions. Their eyes admitted what their mouths wouldn't say.

"Who?"

"Since when do you want names? Since when do you fucking care who it is?"

"Relax, Hammer. I was–"

"No," he interrupted. "No relaxing. I don't like your words. Don't ask me a motherfucking thing other than what's standard."

"Okay, Hammer. As you wish it. We'll need firepower for that many."

"Open your trunk," Merv ordered.

He didn't give the men time to question the command before he spun around and opened the latch to his own. A faint light emerged from within, painting the space pale yellow. The men suddenly noticed a pistol stuffed into the back of Merv's pants as he turned. They kept alert at his movements, which were quick and deliberate, as he grabbed the handles of a large duffel bag and lifted it, turning towards them with a step. Marty reached a hand behind his back and unlocked the latch of their trunk.

"Move."

Merv muscled the bag from his trunk to theirs, nudging the two men aside. With a thud he let the bag fall and tore the zipper along its U-shaped path, spreading the opening carelessly. A bright compartment light inside their trunk glimmered as ash from his cigarette fell like snow, landing on matte black metal protruding from within. These were the barrels of two assault rifles.

"Bushmaster XM15 Dissipater and a Hecker & Koch G3. Both converted to fully automatic."

Merv grabbed both weapons, one in each hand, and handed them to the men flanking him. Ted checked the Bushmaster's action and shouldered it, eying the aftermarket reticle. Marty just stood and watched the presentation.

"There's a fifty-round drum for each, three thirty-round magazines for the Bushmaster, and three twenty-round box magazines for the G3."

Under the rifles were two black items, side by side, flat and bulky in appearance. "Two Type III Aramid vests - large," he said in a cloud of smoke. Merv removed them and stuffed the vests further into the reaches of their trunk. He reached in the bag again.

"Two MAC-10s threaded for a suppressor option with two thirty-round .45 caliber magazines," he said as he laid them out and reached in again, "two Desert Eagles, four Mk concussion grenades, four No. 76 incendiary grenades, two M18 smoke grenades, two pairs of tactical binoculars, two black balaclavas, and two pairs of all-weather shooting gloves."

"I didn't realize we are going to war."

Merv looked at him like he had two heads. "Then fucking realize it already. Think I'm paying you for a hit and run? . . .Now, I sewed watch faces into the back of each left-hand glove," he informed, showing them the custom job. "It'll take a minimum of–" He paused and blinked. *Seventeen minutes.* "Seventeen minutes from the time you open fire to the time the first responders arrive. Give yourselves no more than twenty-two minutes to get out and on the road."

Marty gave a simple head nod. In his language, that was equivalent to a vigorous "yes sir."

"Your targets will be armed, and there will be armed men among them - maybe a dozen. Expect resistance, understand? Make sure to put a few extra rounds in them. I want 'em to stay down. Nothin' they'll have can go through those vests and with your explosives you'll be able to pick 'em off like birds."

Marty hung the G3 on his shoulder and reached into the bag. He gently moved two grenades aside and removed the Desert Eagle. He pulled the slide and released it, loading a brass round into the chamber.

Ted spoke for him plainly. "I do not think this will be an issue."

"Good," Merv replied. He reached in and grabbed a vest, laying it flat over the duffel bag. "Tomorrow night there's a festival," he said slowly and with loathing as he reached in his back pocket and removed a folded stack of papers.

He spread the papers flat, unfolding them to show a satellite image on the top page. Streets and avenues were marked in bold lettering. Highlighted lines marked a large opening on the map's rectangular centerpiece with an X.

"You'll enter through the park's east gate here," he pointed to a smaller X, "and take this route to the square. I paced out the area. The square's seventy-two meters at its widest point. It has three main exits I've marked - here - and a wide path leading to the lake - here. The two positions you'll take are the least travelled exit points and offer the best vantage, marked here where the east path ends and splits. At eight p.m. sharp you'll find your targets across the square, to the west, in the area of the three marks. Keep your eyes open and bring hell. Understand?"

He slid the map aside and spread out five pages on the flattened vest. Each was an enlarged portrait—three smiling, candid headshots and two mugshots.

"Who are these three?" Ted asked.

"High priority. You don't know 'em."

"But I know these faces," Ted remarked as he pointed to the remaining two pictures. "Consider them extras, though equally important," he said. "There will be hundreds of people in the square so a clear shot may not present itself immediately, or at all. Your window to engage is only a few minutes, so take any shot available and don't mind the masses," Merv added.

"What is it you mean exactly?"

"Meaning a hundred could go down in the crossfire and I wouldn't fuckin' worry about it. The more people you kill, the better chance you have of hitting your targets. You have explosives and hundreds of rounds for a reason." Merv rubbed at his nose. It still felt like it was bleeding. "Also, meaning you'll have cover to escape with the crowds. There's no cameras, no security, no patrol. In and out in twenty minutes. Max. Dump the weapons and gear when you're done and ride with the darkness." Merv looked at the men looking at each other. "I expect you to be out of ammo by the time you leave. Consider leaving town for a few months. Understand?"

"It will be done," Marty announced in cold, broken English as he closed the trunk. They were the only words Merv had ever heard him speak in person. The two eyed each other like a mirror of madness.

"I have full confidence in you. Any questions?" Merv asked hurriedly as he walked over and sat down on the edge of his open trunk.

"Where do we collect?"

"Usual spot. Midnight, tomorrow night. Keys will be on the front left tire. Money will be in two file boxes in the trunk."

The men made to leave, still holding the rifles.

"Hey," Merv said.

It was dark by then. The only light in the area came from the trunk of his cruiser, his body a black form against it, seeming to overtake the source itself. His cigarette lit up cherry red and bounced as he spoke.

"Do this for me and you're rich men. . ." *Kill them all.* "Kill them all."

Chapter 33: The Dynamo of Life

It was just shy of midday when the strung-out man floated his way to Baker's Memorial Park. He had intended to stroll through the last important remnant of his past, replaying those few distant, joyous memories once more. This old park was the only place he ever loved. And so it was here he decided he would die, to remain a part of it forever. But once inside, what he came upon stopped him dead in his tracks, floored him. It made his knees weak and his breath catch. The hallucinations were back.

He knew what day this was, what it signified in his life. It was May Day. The day that held easily the fondest, most cherished memories he'd ever known. It was the ever-ephemeral evocation of love his soul was left with. It was the sole shred of sentimentality in his self. And it, like so many other things, was being taken from him. Somehow, his weak frame found a familiar bench to cradle him, and he sat there sobbing, his eyes a river of despair.

The vision wouldn't stop. The park around him was a shining testament to its former beauty, yet somehow more brilliant than ever before. The bumpy, fractioned trails were restored and conjoining. Where weeds and intrusive shrubbery once grew, now immaculate grasses and time-worn trees filled the landscape. The hallucination mocked his memory, for it was drug-induced, nothing more than an episode of delusional recall, enhanced and vivified by his addiction. One last teasing fantasy for one last day alive.

He watched from his old park bench, before a tranquil pond with two cinderblocks and a hand-wound length of wire at his feet, waiting for the visions to assuredly and inevitably vanish. Over an hour had gone by since he first sat down, yet they endured. He couldn't bring himself to believe the possibility that what he saw was real. It just couldn't be.

Rising laughter, music, and pleasant commotion from the festival carried across the lake to him. As the day went on, more and more people filled the pathways and areas with stands and vendor booths. The scene was out of a painting, with flowers in bloom and greenery stretching its limbs, basking in the fullness of the spring season. Across the pond, a group of children chased one another around a pink blossomed tree. It looked like two boys and a girl with a bow in her hair. The man had a vision, then. He saw himself among those children. It was decades ago, when he was but a child himself. He chased and was being chased, he and them an image of innocence. His and their hearts knew no evil.

He shuffled his feet and scraped his shoes on a solid, rough object. Tying the cinderblocks to his ankles would be enough to drag his frail body to the bottom of the pond. He just needed to swim out far enough to drown. That and make sure the length of wire tied to his feet wasn't too long, he guessed. . . A scowl drew itself on his creased face. He always *guessed*. Everything was a stupid fucking guess. No more guessing, he told himself. Just death–

"Mister?" a sweet voice called. "Are you okay?"

"Wha. . .uh. . .?" the man replied as he lifted his head out of his hands and quickly wiped away his tears with the sleeves of his shirt.

In front of him were three children, two boys and a girl, with timid expressions on their faces. His confusion was pure. Strangely, embarrassment and a sense of self-consciousness crept up on him.

"Uh–I–uh. . . No–well, yes. I–uh, I was–uh just. . .sitting. . ."

"Happy May Day," the boy said. "Do you want a flower?"

The man looked at the boy, then the flower, then back at the boy, squinting contemplatively. What type of delusion was this?

". . .Flower? Uh–well. . .*yes*. . .? Yes. Yes," he said, watching the children carefully in an attempt to determine their materiality.

"Here you go," the boy chirped. He handed the man a little bundle of goldenrod with three daisies imbedded in it. They were beautiful.

"Oh, thanks - thank you."

The man gently took the flowers and smelled them with a touch of caution. The aroma was mild but distinctly pure, yet another sign that the experience could be real. A pause ensued while the man inspected the flowers further. They were tied together with a strip of burlap. The children looked at each other and the same boy spoke again.

"Mister, why are there bricks by your feet?"

"What?" he said as he glanced towards the ground. "Oh, these-uh. I-uh, I-uh. . .found them here. They're, uh, not mine." He swallowed hard, covering up the lie as best as he could.

The children exchanged another look and, after a moment, the little boy asked, "Do you want to come to the festival with us?"

"*The festival*? Is it, uh, really. . .real? Uh. . .is it happening?"

"Of course. It's so much fun," the boy exclaimed. The others smiled in agreement.

"It *is* fun. . ." the man remembered. "Uh, okay. Yes. I'll go. . ."

"C'mon! There's all kinds of games!" the little boy yelled as he led the pack in a prance towards the festival.

The man stood slowly, and dried his eyes. He looked down at the bricks that framed his stance as the kids resumed their jovial banter. It was real, they said. Really real. *I can always come back*, he told himself, and made his way towards the little stone bridge that traversed the skinniest section of the pond. The trip to the bridge had its difficulties, as he glanced back at his bench a few times, hesitant about where the children were leading him. The three little ones waited for him on the other side of the pond and waved him along.

"C'mon!" they yelled. "There's cotton candy!" They giggled and ran farther along.

As the man reached the peak of the curved bridge, he stopped in his tracks, scanned the fairgrounds, and turned to lean over the railing, letting the kids go on a little ways ahead. His heart was racing and he needed a moment to settle. The water below him was shallow and still. In the distance, a duck swam by with its ducklings in tow, sending divergent curtains of rippling water behind them. *It's all about the children*, he thought. Out of the corner of his eye he saw the little kids over to his right, seeming to be patiently playing until the man arrived. What mattered more than their future, than protecting their innocence?

He looked down at his reflection. Life's natural mirror. Where blackness had met him hours ago, this time there was substance. The man that looked back was disheveled and worn out. His clothes still had structure, but his skin and hair were oily. His face was thin and sickly. His eyes, though, still held their lovely iridescent blue hue.

The man he saw in that reflection was the man he was inside, spent and worn, but not the man he could be. There was the slightest draw of potential in that reflection. He was sick, he was unkempt, he was ragged. . .but none of that had to be permanent. The festival sounds were growing louder now. It was real. It was all really real.

A single tear ran down his nose and hung there for a split second. When it succumbed to gravity, the tear dropped to the pond and struck the middle of his reflected face. A ripple in the water emanated from him. He pondered that moment and realized that he too could make waves, if he but took action. Purpose started to sneak its way into his shattered mind. It filled the cracks inside him and cemented them together, repurposed and repaired. The afternoon, he decided, was to be spent not only in glee, but in search. But first, he needed to cross the bridge.

He found himself rooted. The act of crossing was symbolic. The walk he would take was emblematic of a betterment of his self. He had yearned for this moment, pleaded for it year after miserable year in the bowels of his consciousness. And it never came. For him to stumble upon it, for it to be all but in the palm of his hand while he was on the brink of death was an experience in the realm of the surreal. A dream. Was this but another disguise, tempting him as he'd been tempted his whole life, only to reach a foul stink of truth in its core? There was only one way to find out. And this feeling was too bright to dampen with doubt, too awesome to shield himself from. No more would he watch the goodness of life, though scant, pass before him with only a consideration. Today, he decided to choose, for choice is the mother of purpose, and purpose is the force that powers the dynamo of life.

With a gasp and a deep outward breath, he formed a smile, and those subtle, unused creases on his face came back to life.

"Start living," he said, and took one step forward.

Chapter 34: May Day, Mayday

The afternoon sun flared like a beacon in the vast, pale spring sky as a beautiful young woman entered Baker's Memorial Park. Fresh excitement and stimulation enveloped her as she walked through the grassy southwest entrance, her hair dancing in the breeze like the wisps of a wind-caught willow tree.

Marian's steps were casual and light. She wore a loose-fitting tank top that bared her sun-kissed shoulders and fair chest. Petite shorts exposed the length of her legs and the leather sandals wrapped around her little feet allowed sneaky blades of grass to kiss her toes with each step, tickling her from time to time. A few meters through the gate she stopped and absorbed the inspiring transformation before her.

The decrepit park she'd only seen at a glance was completely renewed. It captivated her, drawing wonder and delight from within as she surveyed the new, vibrant landscape. The wide entryway was edged with simple, yet dense flower arrangements backed by patches of tall wheat grass. The wrought iron gate behind her was overgrown with vine aside from delicate trimming that exposed the park's namesake at the top of the archway. Colors across the spectrum came alive in the motion of the festival, from both the people and nature itself. Greens and oranges, reds and yellows, blues and purples, browns, pales, and tans, each of a light and dark shade, animated the scene. It felt to her like nature multiplied.

The ingress was bustling but not overcrowded. Scores of people were making their way into the festival proper, some pausing to greet friends or familiar faces, some laughing and holding hands as they walked. There were several attractions to experience in the entrance area, but Marian knew she had to wander the inner paths to find the heart of the day's charms. Her initial search for a map of the grounds was fruitless, but as she walked through the open area, around and between people, she spotted a painted sign giving simple directions to several main points within. The park's amorphous lake was highlighted, as expected, as well as a large section just south of it labelled "Main Square & Maypole," and a small area beside the lake labelled "Flower Gardens." There were several winding routes to the Main Square from her position, along which there were openings that, though unmarked, she deduced were additional sections of the festival containing attractions and booths. Just as she was moving to leave, she noticed a quote etched into a board just beneath the map.

"Give fools their gold and knaves their power,
Let fortune's bubbles rise and fall,
Who sows a field or trains a flower
Or plants a tree, is more than all."

With a "hmm" she smiled and turned away from the map, thinking of the different paths to take. Whichever she chose, her search for Robin would take her throughout the festival, it seemed. *I'll find him. He can't hide all day. . .*

She made for a random path, a good fifty feet away, where she soon noticed a commotion ahead. Festival-goers were being received by staff handing out handmade macramé bracelets. A welcoming gift of sorts, she presumed. Some were brightly colored, some were earthy and plain, but all were woven by hand and knotted gently around accepting wrists or ankles. Marian walked over and was greeted warmly by a handsome boy.

"Welcome to the May Day Festival," he hailed. "Would you like a bracelet?"

"Sure, I'd love one. How much?" Marian asked as she reached for her pocket.

"They're free. Which color would you like?"

She looked through the options and with slight hesitation chose a bracelet woven in white and green thread.

"I like that one," she chose with a pointed finger.

"Here ya go. I made it myself," he said as he tied it around her left wrist. "Have fun!"

As he walked along to the next person, she looked down at the favor once more, and straightened it on her wrist so the knot faced inward. Marian continued along, observing the arrangements of flora, both native and introduced, all of which were presented so naturally they seemed entirely organic. Flowers grew in abstract formation, grasses outside of walking lanes and trails stretched for the sky uncut, and old oaks, pines and furs, maples and birches, elms and ashes sprinkled the upper landscape, fighting for real estate in the sun's light. Marian soaked it in, in pure happiness.

Though the festival was well underway, Robin had assured her that by the time she arrived, the best would be yet to come. His encouragement allowed her to remain causal about the event itself and focus on her true excitement for merely being able to share the afternoon and evening with him. The festival and all its wonders was an added bonus. And so she continued without expectation and with an open heart.

The shaded pathway opened before her lined with beautiful wildflowers and tall grasses. It was skinny, maybe allowing for four people to walk through abreast, and paved with flat, angular stones. Marian wandered along the right side of the path admiring the flowers and reaching her hand out once to brush the petals and stems with her fingertips. The motion reminded her of childhood.

Just as she reached the end of the pathway, her attention was grabbed by the sweetest of voices.

"Miss!" it called.

Marian turned her head from the flowers and found a girl with long, light-brown hair trotting over to her.

"Miss, come here, come here," the girl said, grabbing Marian's hand with a pull.

"What's wrong, sweetie?"

"Nothing," the girl laughed. "Follow me!"

She bounced with each step, giggling, and led Marian across an open meadow, weaving between groups of festival-goers.

"Where are we going?" Marian called in amusement.

"You'll see, c'mon!"

Passing busy booths and attractions the girl moved hastily with Marian in tow. They nudged people as they passed, evoking a "sorry" or two from Marian but moving so fast she hadn't a chance to meet their eyes. She laughed aloud at the silliness and spontaneity of the situation and her little leader joined her in delight. The girl led her towards a thicket that sat behind and between two vendor tents. Until they were upon the trees, Marian hadn't noticed the pathway at all, which caused a bout of consternation within her.

Under two crossing, shoulder-high tree limbs and through an abruptly curved path, a pocket opened among the pines, evergreens, and flowering geraniums. The girl led her into the clearing and introduced her to a gorgeous middle-aged woman in a white dress sitting gracefully on a stool. Beside her was a wicker basket that held an assortment of white flowers, a bundle of thin, leafed twigs, a spool of twine, and scissors. A patch of sunlight brightened the tree-lined area, illuminating the woman and her belongings. In her lap was a circular formation of twigs that she was tying together with a length of twine.

"Nana! I think I found her!" the girl announced upon their arrival.

She released her grip from Marian's and stood beside her, both catching their breath from the hurried pace. The woman looked up, then, and met eyes with Marian. She studied Marian briefly before a smile appeared on her face.

"Welcome! It looks like you've been nominated!" she said in an angelic voice.

"What have I been nominated for?" Marian asked, bemused and taking in her new surroundings.

"You, my dear, have the honor of being selected for the May Queen Pageant. My little darling, here, and her sisters are in charge of nominations. She must think you're *very* pretty."

"Of course she is," the little girl exclaimed as she walked toward the woman. "Do you have her gift ready, Nana?"

"My gift?" Marian inquired while remaining at the entryway.

"*Well*, we have a tradition to help all nominees stand out," the woman explained cheerfully. "*And* in just a bit you'll see what it is. It's almost ready but I wasn't expecting you so soon! Sit with us and chat for a moment."

"I'm flattered. What are you making?" Marian asked, beaming.

"You'll see, dear. Sit! Tell me about yourself. What's your name?"

"Marian."

"Marian, I'm Amy and this is my granddaughter, Quinn," she said, gesturing towards the girl.

"It's a pleasure to meet you both," Marian said, seated now with her legs crossed in the grass.

"Likewise," Amy replied.

She finished tying the knot on the ring in her lap and pulled two lengths of leafed twigs and a single flower out of the basket. Quinn sat in the grass beside her working on her own craft. She took a flower out of the same basket.

"So, Marian, this is your first May Day festival, isn't it?"

"It is. I hadn't even been familiar with the celebration until recently, but from what I hear this used to be quite an event."

"It was indeed," she said as she began to tie the twigs around the circular formation. "From the time I was a child until I was about your age it was everyone's favorite part of the year. The whole community looked forward to the festival and prepared for weeks. . . It's a deeply rooted tradition around here. And I once thought I'd never see it again."

"What was it like when you were younger?" Marian asked.

"Different. A lot bigger." She laughed. "More people, more vendors, more flowers if you can believe it. On a few years the streets were closed down for a couple blocks in every direction, it was so large. The spirit was the same, though."

"I'm glad to hear that. It's been described to me so vividly. It's one of those things where I would be sad if today didn't live up to the tradition."

"Have no fear, there won't be any sad people today," she said as she took a second white blossom out of her basket and began tying it in place.

A moment of pause elapsed. Then Marian's curiosity of this setting, this woman and her granddaughter, this *pageant* got the best of her.

"Can I ask what this May Pageant is?"

"Oh!" Amy burst out in laughter. "Forgive me. I don't know why I thought you knew already. I must really be getting old. Yes," she said deliberately, "yes, you may certainly ask. The pageant this year is just for fun. My granddaughters are out choosing a couple girls and later tonight we'll all meet by the May Pole and the four of us will act as the pageant board and choose a Queen. It will be at 7 p.m., but don't feel obligated to come. Like I said, it's informal - just for fun this year."

"Ok, whew. I wasn't sure what was required of me! I was worried that I had some obligations to uphold."

"I'm sorry. I'll remember to tell any other girls right away. Not to worry, Marian. The only obligation you have to us is to keep looking beautiful," Amy said with a big smile. "Now, it used to be quite an event. The May Queen would lead a parade, receive a sash, flowers, and was usually the envy of every girl at the fair. It was all in good sport, but girls would take it pretty seriously. Since this is the first year that the festival is back, we're just having an honorary 'pageant' to keep the tradition alive. . . Oh, this brings back such great memories," she finished while looking down at the flower arrangement in her lap.

"It really is wonderful be able to witness its return. I was never given a clear reason as to why it ended, though."

"Well," she glanced over at her granddaughter, "that's a little less of an upbeat topic for a day such as this. I'm sure you're at least a little familiar with the history of this area, no?"

"A little bit, yeah."

"Let's just say when things went south a lot of great things disappeared around here. And the festival was one of them."

"I understand," Marian said with a nod.

"No matter, it's back now. And I have a feeling it's for good."

"I get that feeling too. The right people are behind it."

"You know them?" Amy questioned with a mixture of wariness and curiosity.

"I do, yeah."

"Interesting. You're a lucky girl," she said knowingly.

"We're all lucky."

"Indeed."

The two shared a smile and held eyes, understanding each other in an unspoken way. Amy took her fourth blossom and began to fasten its base into the interwoven twigs.

"You know, to see this festival, this park. . .these *people* come back to life is truly surreal. It feels like I'm somewhere else. Somewhere far away."

"I know what you mean. I've taken just a handful of steps through the entrance and I'm already amazed at the transformation. It's like nothing I've ever seen."

"Haven't you been through?"

"Not yet. I only just arrived when your granddaughter grabbed me."

"Oh, *Marian*, I'm sorry to keep you here. I didn't know that. . .*but,"* she said as she worked, "you've been selected! And like I said, it's tradition, so you'll have to forgive us."

Quinn looked up from her creation with an expression of mild worry.

"It's okay! I'm enjoying myself. *And* the company," Marian assured her, sending a smile to little Quinn.

Quinn returned the look and refocused on her flower corsage in the making.

"Are you here by yourself?" Amy asked freely as she selected another crisp, pale flower from the basket beside her. Marian watched her hands as she worked, admiring how skillfully she managed the delicate arrangement.

"I'm meeting someone."

"Is it a special someone?" she said with encouragement that struck Marian. The woman must have taken notice of her mild reservations during their conversation, and seemed to be coaxing her answers out of her. The personal nature of the question made Marian think deeply of Robin and a longing assumed her mind. She glanced at the ground in shy thought as she pictured his smile in her mind's eye.

". . .Very special. Yes," she answered. The shift in subject matter caused her tone to change. Amy noticed.

"He must be quite a man to have you so enamored," she offered.

Marian smirked and drifted away again. "He's one of a kind."

"So. Where *is* the special man?"

Marian laughed at her answer before she gave it. "He. . .didn't tell me where he'll be today, so it seems I have to explore. He made it a point for me to search for him."

"Ah, he's playing hard-to-get, huh?" Amy joked.

"In a sense," she laughed. "I think he has something up his sleeve, but I'll find him."

"Are you in love?"

"Um," Marian blinked hard several times in surprise. The question caught her off guard and in the instantaneous silence she debated whether to answer truthfully or not. Her comfort level around her new friends was high and her certainty was true so with honesty, and a deep breath, she answered. ". . .Yes."

"Then it is no search. You've already found each other."

Marian smiled acceptingly, visibly letting some tension out of her body.

"You look like you were holding that in so hard you could burst with it," Amy commented.

"You could say that," Marian replied, realizing that this moment was the first time she'd ever voiced her feeling aloud.

"Does he know how you feel?"

"I'm not sure. I haven't told him yet."

"You know," she started in a motherly tone, "a part of me envies your position. New love is the most powerful and unique of all emotions. You may never be more vulnerable in your entire life. Scary, huh?"

Marian took a deep breath. "It's terrifying," she said not without distress.

"And *that* is beautiful."

"I suppose. . ."

"Maybe think about it like this: These emotions make you *feel*, Marian. To the extreme. It's raw and unconditional. There is no greater anticipation in all of life than pledging your love to another and hoping for it to be returned. Cherish it."

In lieu of an answer, Marian exhaled deeply.

"Are you afraid of being hurt?" Amy asked.

"I don't know. It's just that he's not. . .typical. I can see myself getting lost in him, and I'm afraid that if he leaves for some reason, I'll be left with nothing. Emotionally, that is."

"You'll always have something, Marian. It's better to hurt than to feel nothing at all. The moment you feel nothing, then you're truly lost."

"I guess so, but that doesn't really make it less intimidating."

"Love should be intimidating. It asks qualities of you that you may not know you possess. If you're scared, well. . .love should be scary. When we commit to something or someone, there is always a possibility of heartbreak, of failure. In that fear we learn to push ourselves to a higher level. . . Try all you want, love can't be controlled. Sometimes, it's like a wave, y'know? You're just along for the ride. That can also be a hard truth about love. Sometimes it's fluid. Sometimes that wave loses its strength and carries you no more. And so you wait around, maybe swim along, hopeful that another wave will pick you up and carry you away. Other times, from nowhere at all it sweeps you up, spins you around, and brings you straight to paradise. So all of your fears, all of your terrifying unknowns, I think they come from experiencing a lack of control. Stop trying to control that which is uncontrollable. I think there are certain things that we all need to surrender to. And you're experiencing one right now. Surrender to it. Love greatly or lose greatly – it doesn't matter as long as it is done *greatly*."

Marian considered the unusual sentiments. They were truths, surely, but were they realistic? It was aggravating to know how easy it was for her to speak those tough truths to someone else, to be the one uninvolved. . . But, wait. No. Amy wasn't *uninvolved*. Knowing those truths wasn't *easy*. Those words she spoke were from experience. *She has loved as I've loved and more*, Marian realized. *She has lost as I've lost and more.*

A deep feeling of need emerged in her, then – the need to trust those around her, the need to surrender, and the need to feel. It was like an injection of pure invigoration. Life was but a series of 'nows,' not 'thens.' Now, she decided, was the time. This day was to be her leap, her effort, her wave to ride.

"Today is the day, isn't it?" Marian asked aloud.

"Only you know that. But I have that feeling," Amy replied with a grin.

"Today's the day. . . *Tonight*. . ." Marian trailed off.

Amy smiled in admiration. She steadily wrapped a final blossom around the ring and wound it in place with thread. With a push and a twist, she tested the ring's rigidity with a smirk that Marian interpreted as approval.

"You're going to stand out even more than you already do. What do you think, Quinnie?"

"Definitely!" she replied with a thumbs up.

Amy rose out of the stool and motioned for Marian to follow. They stood before one another, near equal in height.

"Oh, you remind me of someone so much. It's uncanny," Amy said.

"Really? Who?"

She laughed, then, and showed her teeth in a wide smile. "Me. Do us proud, dear. I was named May Queen for three straight years when I was your age!"

Amy lifted the circlet of flowers with both hands and placed it ceremoniously upon Marian's head. The thin headdress sat like a crown, framing her face with her long flowing brown hair. The white blossoms, eight in total, were evenly spaced around the crown and alike to a clementine in diameter. It was elegantly made, nothing short of tasteful, adorned with subtle leaves between the flower buds that added a kind of native substance.

"There. You belong in a fairytale," Amy said with a beaming smile and recollection written in her eyes.

The sentiment exalted Marian to jubilation, and she hugged Amy in thanks. She smiled at Quinn and blew her a kiss, then made to leave the little pocket of nature with a warm feeling of joy.

"Remember, Marian," Amy said, causing her to stop and turn. "May Day is about love and new beginnings. Go to him. And maybe we'll see two you soon."

Marian smiled back and passed a deliberate nod their way. "You will."

She emerged from the hidden grove and stepped into the busy expanse ready to begin her journey through the parkland. Her reentrance into the crowd after the unexpected detour made her feel in a dreamlike state. Sound was amplified, movement more dramatic, but all the while she felt calmness as she walked. Marian had an aura about her. She was absolutely radiant, as if the light of the day followed her and bathed in her existence. It wasn't the angle of the sun and it wasn't the imagination of those around her. Her eyes sparkled and her smile had others beaming without thought. She was a true beauty.

The crown lay delicately on her head and the breeze of the afternoon carried her with it. Her initial reentry into the festival had been still clouded with thoughts, but in short time her mind settled into clarity. She walked without a clear destination, but now more than ever she had a yearning to find Robin.

She navigated around a circle of people in conversation who'd stopped in front of an intersection. Beyond them, she was presented with three routes to take deeper into the festival. Signs marked each path but she paid them no mind, simply deciding instead upon the far right path.

The skinny lane she entered began as ferns and high grasses, empty of people. She rounded a bend, and what she came upon made her lose her breath in awe. The section was lined in its entirety with hundreds upon hundreds of blooming white flowers. Rockcress, Sweet Alyssum, Lily-of-the-Valley, and Queen Anne's Lace reached for the heavens, complementing her crown in their magnificent purity. From afar the mass of tiny, droplet-sized petals looked like a dusting of fallen snow or some knitted fabric woven in a pattern of impossible complexity. The configuration was so lovely and so densely intricate she couldn't help but stop in her tracks and absorb the beauty surrounding her. Little bees hummed from flower to flower as she gradually made her way along, glancing about. Patches of shade veiled her as she walked, her face frozen in a look of wonder.

Marian next entered a section of the festival with booths and stands aplenty. Upbeat commotion and laughter drew her curiosity the moment they became audible, inviting her further with each step. Half a dozen picnic tables sat in the middle of the square, each packed with people sharing an afternoon snack or enjoying the treat of live music. She followed the sounds to her left, where an old man strummed an acoustic guitar on a small terrace between a refreshment stand and a patch of high fescue. The limbs of an old oak tree shaded the man in places while he played his soft tunes for passersby. Marian pondered what venues that troubadour had performed, what cities he'd called home.

The faint squeaks of chirping birds could be heard between the notes of the music. It was a song beneath a song. Some flew overhead, from tree to tree, while others hid themselves in a faraway game of hide-and-seek. She looked above and watched as an orange-breasted bird flew over the center of the square, swooping into a blossoming Dogwood tree. A child startled her as she brushed by Marian holding a container and a bubble wand. The girl ran with the wand in hand, a trail of glistening, floating orbs tracing behind her. Two friends chased the little girl, the group laughing between breaths as they ran off toward a skinny pathway. Marian giggled as a straggler, a little boy much younger than the others, emerged running after the three with determination.

She stepped forward and glided along the perimeter of the open area, discovering new vendors and artisans as she went. An elderly woman sat under a canvas canopy while she worked on a sculpture of some sort. In her hands was a bundle of thin copper wire that she was twisting into a tight braid. Intrigued, Marian lingered to browse the merchandise while the woman worked on her piece. She toiled quickly, with deft fingers, to form what began looking like veins or perhaps branches of a tree on a frayed end of the braid. Before long, the woman fanned and flattened the bottom of the sculpture, presenting a miniature, foot-tall, copper oak tree. The trunk was about the thickness and length of a roll of quarters. The flattened bottom "roots" stretched in every direction, some six to eight inches in diameter, and the sprawling branches spread out every which way, even exposing individual strands of wire at the tips for detail. She set the artwork on a stool beside her and looked over at Marian, picking her out of the several observers as if knowing she'd been there all along.

"For hanging earrings," the woman said invitingly as she removed her own dangling bauble and hung it from a tiny branch.

"It's beautiful," Marian replied with a smile.

After a brief conversation with the artist, Marian departed and continued to the next booth, where two children were having their faces painted by a man and a woman. The little girl in the stool closest to Marian had a near-complete white flower arrangement painted on her cheek. The man painting her dipped his brush in paint and moved to finish his work. She snickered as the brush touched her cheek, then causing the man to chuckle and encourage her to hold still just another minute longer.

Amused, Marian laughed to herself and strolled along, imagining the tickling of the paintbrush on her own face. She surfed through the remaining attractions over the course of ten minutes, aloof and content as a spectator. As she walked along she found herself glancing about in search of Robin but only noted other, foreign eyes catching her form.

At a far end of the square she reached a fork, this time choosing to go left. Partway along, the path narrowed considerably, with room for no more than two people to fit side by side. As the path tapered, moss-covered roots and rocks made up the boundaries like an uneven green carpet. Before long, she was walking through another section and came upon a cozy counter to her right where a line of people were queued up for frozen treats. The young woman behind the stand leaned down and handed two children popsicles while their mother, baby in arm, watched in smiling approval. Marian thought it near time to indulge in one or more of the delicious offerings she'd encountered since her adventure began. She browsed the stand, named *Dana's*, and found a chalkboard hanging with several items listed on it in freehand. The menu offered ice cream, popsicles, three flavors of homemade Italian Ice, chipwiches, and chocolate-covered bananas. The lemon Italian Ice was calling her name.

As Marian was perusing the menu she felt a tug at her shorts and looked down to find a little boy staring up at her with big brown eyes. He was shirtless and barefoot, with just a pair of denim overalls on.

"Hi handsome," she said with a smile.

He smiled back with chipmunk-sized cheeks and held up a single, red carnation toward her. Marian studied the offer and giggled.

"Is this for me?" she said as she knelt down to his level and teasingly raised an eyebrow.

He exaggerated a nod and handed the flower to her. She placed her nose near the tip of the blossom and inhaled.

"Thank you," she said sweetly as she accepted the gift. "It's beautiful. Where did you get it?"

The boy turned and pointed towards a tall flowering tree some distance across a walkway adjacent to *Dana's* little stand.

"Him," he said coyly.

She followed his finger and found the shaded silhouettes of a man and a little girl facing each other beneath the tree's sprawling, vibrant limbs. Several people crossed her line of sight before her view cleared. Through an opening, she recognized Robin.

He was leaning over and offered flowers to the little girl, who wore a white sundress and a pink bow in her hair. She looked awfully familiar. . . As the girl reached up to accept, her heels came off the ground and he whispered to her through a cupped hand. She trotted off with a beaming smile, dress flowing in the quiet breeze. Robin stood, then, and met eyes with Marian, likely checking on his little messenger's progress. The moment they saw each other their faces opened up into glowing smiles and a look of allure passed between them. Marian stood, rubbed the boy on his head, and left him as he ran off.

She had spent her afternoon casually searching for her secret love only to be the one found by him. She could feel it in that moment, the magnetism between them. It was pure. And it was enough to make her want to run to him. But the moment was too special. Marian was entranced, lulled by the sight of his resplendence from afar.

Marian understood, then, that her unlikely acquaintance, Amy, was right. She hadn't been searching. She was being guided. Her inklings that afternoon weren't born of her own thoughts, but rather brought upon by his pull. The chords of love wound tightly around them, even though their feelings had not yet been spoken. She knew it in her heart. Amy knew it by her body language. And the time would soon come when Robin would know it by her words. But not yet. . .

Heart fluttering, she walked across the grassy stretch and over the stone walkway towards the tree. She approached Robin and stood before him in momentary silence. Even though the pair had seen each other just yesterday, Marian couldn't help but think he was somehow greater, more alive and vivid, more present in this moment. He stood out. He attracted her every sense and pulled each thread of her attention.

In that silence, his look towards her became enamored. In that moment, she was his, and he was hers. On that day, they were one. That sparkle in his eyes gleamed more brilliantly than ever. That mysterious, ever-present smirk on his face, at last, made sense to her. It affirmed her deepest wishes. *He loves me.*

She looked at him in awe and savored that moment, tucked it away. It was hers forever. Theirs, eternally. She wanted to explode with feeling but her composure held. Patience, she had learned, would make this moment, this precipice of expression of love in each other, linger. This tipping point would last this day until she was ready to plunge into the beautiful unknown. And so, she held onto those words, and instead broke the silence with an expression of her admiration.

"You did all of this?" she asked brightly, searching his eyes.

He smiled again and nodded gently, a smitten look remaining on his face. She shook her head just slightly in wonder. She moved to caress his cheek, feeling the skin on his face and his soft growth of stubble. Robin grabbed her hips gently and inched her forward. The motion was graceful and smooth as she acquiesced, and they pressed their lips together in a kiss with heavy, closing eyelids.

Around them pink petals floated feather-like to the ground. The flowering tree shed its bounty upon and about them, cloaking the couple in a tender nimbus like a winter's flurry. Time stood still. The connection was realer, the kiss more meaningful than any Marian had yet known. It conveyed love and it evoked lust. Warmth flooded her. When it was over, Marian slowly withdrew to look upon him once more.

"You're amazing," she whispered.

Robin rubbed his thumb lightly over her cheek as she looked at him expectantly. He peered into her eyes, unblinking, and for the first time that afternoon, she heard his voice.

"Walk with me."

Wil lounged against an oak tree, back a ways from the crowd of people before him. The oak's canopy shaded him but for a bar of sunlight poking through the tree limbs and onto his chest. He was in an open area of the festival near the big pond. He had designed the northwesterly section himself and managed to have a small truckload of equipment donated by a local supplier to really tie it all together.

It was meant to be a place for anyone and everyone to create art. There were thirteen easels, boxes of different sized canvases and papers, free oil paints and acrylics, pencils, brushes, charcoal, sculpting clay, and even cans of spray paint. It was an all-around success, with people of all ages taking their turn at creation. Wil even did a piece earlier in the day that he had later leaned against a nearby tree. It was a graffiti riff of a *Bearport* label showing Blotto, the infamous inebriated cartoon bear, sitting in a flower garden playing a harmonica - dandelions about his feet and a foamy stein of beer between his outstretched legs, of course. Wil chuckled at its ridiculousness the entire way through the painting. Where was the old bear's plane this time?

Presently, Wil watched, along with dozens of others, as a man finished a remarkable painting. It was an oddity. The man was clearly homeless or poor beyond even Wil's comprehension.

His clothes were ragged, his arms were like twigs, and his hair was oily. But his skill was that of an absolute master. Wil couldn't get over the sight. Every stroke was perfect, every color was intended, and he never once backed away to consider the work. To Wil it was a performance unlike any other he'd seen. It was downright beautiful.

It took some effort to figure out what the man was painting at first, as it was awfully abstract. Then, an hour in, a lightbulb went off in Wil's head. The homeless guy was painting the festival, obviously, but it had some other sort of formation, like a metamorphosis. Judging from the crowd's demeanor, no one else had figured it out. They were inquisitive, always searching for different angles to view the thing. The man finished up by signing his name at the bottom of the painting and turned to a gallery of clapping people.

Wil lit a cigarette and adjusted his backwards hat. It was Robin's old green camouflage one that he had lent to Wil. He figured it felt a little like having a hand-me-down from an older brother, even though he never had one. Plus, Wil knew it looked better on him anyway.

Some casual strides had him on his way to meet the painter. Surely he could learn a thing or two from such a master. And if not, maybe he could at least get the guy something to eat.

Jon took a deep breath and let his body settle into heaviness. He occupied a bench in the rear of the flower gardens, simply watching the afternoon unfold. Joy and surprise were emotions he'd never tire of seeing on people's faces. They came in a steady stream, mostly from the main square, to walk the gardens and take in the gamut of colors. The landscaping was truly breathtaking. There were more flowers in this one place, on this one day, than Jon had seen in total in his entire life. There were tulips, daffodils, rose bushes, daisies, marigolds, black-eyed susans, and carnations, to name a few. There were perennials too, like yarrow, sage, peonies, iris, and bee balm, which was great for attracting hummingbirds and butterflies. The grass walking lanes were immaculate, the bushes were trimmed to exact symmetry and the flowers were planted in rows with a precise number per patch. It was the only place in the festival that was manipulated in such a way. Jon appreciated the deliberate decision for that to be so.

His interest in farming and agriculture had always been something he was somewhat open about, but his love of flowers was something he had never once shared. It was a private passion, which he took his time in learning for fear of ridicule or being the brunt of jokes. It was an annoyance he dealt with often in life - the expectation to be the manliest man alive simply because of his size and strength. He liked trees and flowers and animals, and resigned himself to keeping it all inside. At least he could enjoy them on his own. Like today, for instance. He had spent the morning labeling each species of plant in the gardens with little signs that stuck into the dirt. It was a last-minute touch inspired by the Fort Dearborn Botanical Gardens. They always had the best displays. *Maybe next year we can bring in orchids*, he thought.

A light draft came from across the pond and grazed his face. He breathed deeply again. It was a hell of a day, with a temperature that made you forget temperature existed. It was like–

"Hi Jon," said a soft voice, interrupting his thoughts.

Jon looked over and froze. A gorgeous young woman stood shyly before him. His stomach felt like it had levitated upon recognizing her, and his words became stiff.

"Hey," he managed, and stood to meet her.

Her face was one he hadn't seen in what felt like years. How it managed to grow more beautiful with age, he couldn't say.

She curled some strands of blond hair behind her left ear. "Um. I just wanted to say congratulations on all of this. You've really done something great here. . .with everything."

"Thank you. Um. How'd you know. . .I was involved?"

She smiled and shook her head playfully. "Everyone's kinda figured. I mean, word gets around 'round here. You know that."

"I guess you're right." Jon cycled some initiators in his head but nothing stuck.

"Y'know," she said, "my mom used to tell me about these festivals and how they were about love and bringing people together and new beginnings and everything. So I just thought that maybe we could take a walk and talk to each other." Her eyes found the ground, and then shot back up to Jon. "I think I owe you an apology."

Jon smiled and walked over to her. "Sure, Jade. I'd like that."

Robin and Marian walked hand-in-hand along a quiet stone pathway leading to the main square. Dogwoods and cherry blossom trees bordered the path, sprinkled with patches of wildflowers growing in yellow, purple, red and white. A breeze followed the couple, causing a whisper in the petals above as if the trees had taken notice of the lovers and venerated their closeness.

The day had barely scratched the surface of the late afternoon and already, Marian felt like she had walked the grounds for hours. Rather than exhaustion, it was a carefree sense of presence she felt, as if time, schedule, and worry had vanished from memory. There was only happiness, all else was nonexistent.

Halfway along the trail, Robin looked over and asked, "So this is it. Is it anything like you expected?"

"I don't have the words," she admitted, rubbing her thumb over his. "It's like we're in another world. How did you do it? Who did all of this work?"

"I went to see an old friend a few weeks ago and convinced him to make a small investment. We obtained a festival permit that week and got to work." Marian made to speak but Robin continued, "The trees were already here. We just needed to clear the pathways, make room for the different sections, plant flowers, offer booth spaces, and promote it. It's amazing what word of mouth can accomplish."

Marian's eye caught a pair of orange-and-black butterflies sailing to and from some flowering bushes.

"I ran into a local landscaper and mason a while back," Robin continued. "We talked for a few hours one afternoon and I hired him as a consultant and subcontractor. I had him supply laborers and put him in touch with one of the planners I hired to go over the vision of what we had in mind. He's old enough to have been to a few of the original festivals and was, I mean, invaluable help with the really important details and rounding out the vision. I'm going to make him a member of our committee next year."

Next year. She smiled again. *He really has been thinking ahead.*

Laughter and commotion grew louder. Marian could see movement through the sparsity of trees. "You said you went to see an old friend. Who is he?"

"He's my stepfather."

Marian squinted. "I thought you were on bad terms."

"*I* was. But I've come to understand him a lot better these past few weeks. He's not a bad guy. He does care – about me and about more than I ever gave him credit for."

"I'd like to meet him sometime."

"I'd like that too. He won't be here today, but we should arrange something soon."

Marian squeezed his hand. "Good."

They arrived at the south end of the main square to find crowds of people enjoying the day. It was easily the most populated area Marian had seen since she entered. The square had plenty of booths, like the other sections, but it was much larger. A tall wooden pole stood in the center braided in fabrics of all different colors. It was the very center of the festival. Marian supposed this was where the pageant was to be held later that evening, and hoped Amy would forgive her if she was occupied with Robin during that time.

Many other tree-lined paths opened onto the square from the west and southeast. Past the Maypole, due north, a wide lane exposed the park's pond and on both sides, between the passing traffic, she could see the beginnings of two bright sections beside the shoreline. *That must be the flower gardens*, she figured.

Robin led her through the crowds and past vendors of all kinds, booths with children's games, and a man and his daughter (presumably) playing a duet on a piano. She had noticed other free-to-play instruments set up through the grounds that made her wish she had kept up with her lessons. It would have been wonderful to impress Robin with a song. Partway through the square she began to notice smiles, nods, and fond looks directed their way. It took a moment to realize that the people were acknowledging Robin. She was sure that as the organizer he'd garner some recognition, but as people shook his hand and offered thanks her fascination grew. Community like this was something she had never been exposed to. Strangers didn't feel entirely like strangers, more so friendly, albeit unfamiliar, faces. It was a safe place, this square.

They wandered hand-in-hand for a while until Marian suggested a snack break. After sharing a delicious set of kebabs from Robin's Turkish friend, she was craving a cool, sweet treat. She ordered the lemon Italian Ice while Robin excused himself to say hi to Jon and Wil. As time passed, she grew restless as to when she would have some alone time with her man. She watched him, Jon, and Wil standing nearby in a triangle chatting. Robin had his arms casually folded, nodding to people and shaking hands as they walked by. She watched the three companions relish in their accomplishment, enjoying her spot, for the time being, as a distant observer. This moment was important for them, as best friends, and although she wondered what words were said in that conversation, she knew they weren't hers to hear.

Wil threw out a quick line, causing Robin and Jon to sway in laughter. *Always the joker, that one*, she thought, and smiled. Wil cleaned up nicely for the occasion, even in a plain white t-shirt and jeans. Why he wore that hat of Robin's, she couldn't say, though. She smirked. It did fit him a lot better than Robin.

Eventually, Wil left, waving goodbye to Marian before he went. She waved back, and soon after, Jon had departed too in the opposite direction. Robin turned, then, and made eye contact with her. They shared a smile and met each other halfway. *Now is my best chance*, she thought. *Get him alone.*

"I was thinking," she said. "We should go somewhere for a few minutes and talk."

"Well. . ." Robin said, checking his watch and glancing up at the approaching dusk. "I have a surprise for you."

She smiled. "Another?"

"Just one more," he returned. "And we actually have to leave the park for a little while but I promise - it'll be worth it."

"We have to leave?"

"Trust me. Okay?"

"Okay. I trust you," she said.

That mischievous smile grew on Robin's face. "Let's go."

The pair walked hand in hand west out of the main square and towards the exits. They passed children as they went, chasing fireflies with their last spurt of energy in, what had become for all, a magical day.

Darkness fell as Merv's boots thumped against pavement, scraping gravel with his heels repeatedly in a foreboding rhythm. His pants were crinkled above his boots' exposed tongues, and he wore his leather jacket open, revealing a dark Kevlar vest over his white tank top. Flanked by Mancuso and MacDunnah, he tore his way across Atlantic Ave. towards Baker's Memorial Park.

In each of Merv's hands was a metal jug. They sloshed and swayed with each step he took, seeping fumes from the loosely threaded caps like incense spread by a pastor. Sloshing and thumping were the only noises from the group, as Merv's briefing identifying Robin and his men, with the help of intel from the strange old man, had held enough dialogue for the day and then some. Words belonged in the air or on a page. Tonight was about action.

As the triad stole into the fairgrounds, Merv did a sweep of the entranceway. It was mostly empty except for a young couple that caught his eye in the faint distance, walking towards another exit. Merv stared at the girl's ass as they shrank from view. Before she disappeared entirely, he noticed a crown of white flowers sitting atop her head in delicate fashion.

No roses tonight, you cunt. Only thorns.

Merv's movement was leaden and his conscience was numb. His eyes were glazed over and bloodshot. He let his cigarette fall from his mouth and took an exaggerated, severe breath of air.

"Clean," he mumbled with a scowl that turned into a sneer. "Not for long." He turned to Mancuso, a sound of sloshing arising and settling as if quieting itself for his words. "Get into positon," he commanded lightly. "When you see flames, just start shooting."

And he walked off into the darkness.

Robin led Marian across Atlantic Ave. under a colorful dusk. He gripped her hand tenderly as she followed him up the road a block and onto Pine Street. The laughter, music, and joy emanating from the festival became hushed as they entered his building and paused as the elevator doors closed.

"Your surprise is in your apartment?" Marian asked skeptically.

"No, no, no," he replied and pushed the button for the top floor. "You'll see."

He spoke no more, holding only his devious smile. She pressed him with curiosity, but he merely shook his head.

"This better be good," she warned.

The doors opened with a ding and Robin pulled her into the hallway. They sped along the carpet and reached a heavy exit door labeled 'Do Not Enter.' Through the door was an iron stairwell to the roof.

"Are we allowed up here?" she couldn't help herself from asking. Unsurprisingly, she was ignored.

Marian followed him up the last steps and onto the rooftop, feeling like a teenager trespassing on some old property. The terrace was unexpectedly clean and orderly, from what she could initially tell as they walked towards the edge closest to the parklands. All she could think about was the moment she'd confess her love for him. It made her heart race.

The rooftop gave a much grander view of the park than Robin's apartment window. From their current height, the entirety of the grounds was visible, and offered an angle that revealed the main square and several other prominent sections among the trees. It looked like lanterns were being lit in those sections and along paths between them. To the east, skyscrapers towered over downtown, their windows shining like a starry night of their own.

The pair passed a large skylight protruding from the roof, and Marian became aware of comfortable setting laid out near the foot-high barrier along the front edge of the roof. A sprawling blanket was spread out there, with two large, flat square pillows resting in the center.

"What is all this?" she asked enthusiastically.

"You will see, my dear," he promised. "Come sit with me."

She obliged, and held his hand on the way to the cushions.

"So. . .I brought you up here for a surprise. . .but I also wanted to have some time for us to talk."

"I was hoping for that too," she smiled.

"I wanted to tell you that I've made an important decision. I've decided that I'm done using crime as a means to make changes here. This festival was meant to build community, to give the people something tangible, something real to latch onto. And it worked. Now it's time for us all to move forward. Together. No more escapades. It's time for a more legitimate force to take action."

"You're finished now?"

"I'm finished. This is what everything has been for. All the energy, all the risk, all the plotting."

"All the crime," Marian added, chuckling.

Robin nodded. "Yes. All the crime. All the love and the hate."

All the hate, she thought.

"Look, I. . ." his words trailed off as a look overcame him that she'd never seen before. It was like a grimace. "I've never told you this before, but about six months ago. . .I. . .was beaten. Very badly. I, uh, was walking home, not far from here, when I went to break up what I thought was cops kicking the shit out of somebody - a man. But what happened was, from what I can piece together at this point, some sort of. . .trap. You see, a few days earlier I saw two girls being harassed by undercover cops and I stepped in. It got violent and what happened to me was payback for how badly I hurt those officers. Turns out that the man who I thought I was helping on the night I was jumped - he was a cop too. And he made it a point for me to learn my place in their world. I, uh, was in the hospital for nine days, I have nerve damage around my eye and my jaw still hurts even now, as I speak. The scar on my head isn't from an accident. They smashed my head into a dumpster and left me for dead."

Marian couldn't speak. She remembered the appearance of injuries when she first met him but the story was worse than anything she could have imagined. She felt like weeping for him.

"I'm so sorry," she said, and reached to run a hand through his hair and feel the face that she loved so dearly. "Who did it to you?"

"Some guy named Hamstead. It doesn't matter," Robin said dismissively.

Marian pondered the name, finding something familiar in it.

"I don't know why I haven't told you that," he continued. "I think I was worried that you would think this was all some sort of personal vendetta. I know that you know that's not the case, but I was just waiting for the right time, I guess. Ultimately it was a good thing, because it was the spark that got us where we are now, and I wouldn't change it for the world. I wouldn't change anything. Because if anything was to change, then I may never have met you."

She couldn't help but smile at him.

"Wanna know a secret?"

"Yeah," she breathed.

"The very first night we met in the library - the one where you snuck up on me - I was looking for something."

"It was a map of the park, right?"

"Yes but there was one other thing too. Until now I've kept it to myself. I don't really know why. I think that deep down I was worried I'd actually have to use it."

"What was it?"

Robin smirked and shook his head. "Blueprints of the subway system. There happens to be a line that runs underneath some important buildings."

"Which ones?"

"Mm. . ." he smirked. "Stock Market. City Hall. Few others."

"You're crazy," she laughed. "What would you have done?"

"That doesn't matter. My point is you taught me that going that far is unnecessary. I wanted to thank you. You've helped more than you can ever know."

"You don't need to thank me. The feeling is mutual, Robin. You've helped me every day I've known you."

They held each other's eyes for a moment. "I. . .I want you to know how important you are to me," he said. "I've had things taken from me in life – things that now only exist as memories. I can't tell you how worried I've been that if I fucked things up, you'd just become a memory too. . .and I want more than that. I can rob, steal, kidnap. . .do this," he motioned to the festival, "but I–I can't lose you."

"I don't want to lose you either."

"You're a once in a lifetime girl, Marian."

Marian flushed, tingly warmth flooding her body. The moment arrested her senses. She felt like she was floating. *It's time. Tell him.*

"I have a secret for you too," she admitted.

"Yeah?"

She met his eyes. "A big secret."

"Tell me."

Marian took a deep breath. "Seeing you today. . .being with you at the festival convinced my mind of everything I already knew in my heart. I've just been too terrified to go for it."

"Terrified?"

"Yes. The things you do are so powerful. And I was afraid. Until now. Until today. I'm not scared anymore. You don't understand. You're not like other people, Robin. You're *un*believable. Your spirit, your drive, your outlook on life. I've never met anyone more genuine. Not ever."

Robin showed a quirky smile then.

"Do you see how people look at you? Did you notice all those people today? Everyone you meet falls for you."

". . .And you?" he asked lightly.

"Me most of all." She blinked. "I'm in love with you, Robin."

Her breath caught in her throat as he stared at her. Those words, there was a lightness to them now. The buildup was so immense, yet the profession was as light as a feather. It brought a glaze of wetness over her eyes.

Robin slid his fingers into hers, an intensity overcoming him. "I'm in love with you too. I fell in love with you the moment I heard your voice."

They embraced each other. "I love you," she cried. "I love you so much."

Their kiss was honey, mellifluous and velvety sweet. Marian's emotions knew no greater confidence or affirmation. What is more precious than the undeniable connection with someone you've known for a matter of days or weeks? From the outside, it seems doubtful. From the inside, it becomes tangible. For her, it was the truest manifestation of feelings she had ever experienced. It simply *was*.

A thump echoed in the distance. . .

Boom!

In the sky above the park, a white and red firework exploded and bloomed in animated luster. Startled, Marian turned her head away from the kiss and inhaled deeply with a rush of elated surprise. She made to speak, but her words became caught in her throat, frozen by the dazzling display.

"Surprise," Robin whispered into her ear.

"Oh my God. . . *Amazing!*" she exclaimed at last, with laughter and a smile as bright as the flashing sky. She felt his hand grip hers tightly, and their faces lit up in color under that dark theater of the night.

The fireworks were magnificently vivid in the clear, star-speckled evening. Some traced thick tails of sparks like lounging palm branches and others had dozens of points that hung like wind-caught parachutes. One massive report stood out among the others, flashing an ethereal blue like some bioluminescent supernova. They rang on, multiples at a time. She saw shapes of Chrysanthemum flowers and falling leaves. It was a tribute to the festival and to this fairytale, this enchanted day in time.

Robin and Marian admired the show for a time in blissful contentment. She sat against him with her legs crossed, her hands in her lap, and her head resting on his shoulder, watching the grey streaks of aerials reach their height and explode. Wafts of sweet perfume still lingered in Marian's flower crown. Even Robin, who had orchestrated the show, seemed amazed at the spectacular variety of colors and profiles. He leaned back on outstretched arms with a look of pure happiness.

In the immediate stillness, and encased by the intensity of the show, Marian slid her hand across her lap and on to Robin's inner thigh. She paused for a moment and began rubbing him with sensuous invitation. She was decided. Tonight was the night.

Noticing her touch, Robin slowly took his eyes off of the show. He glanced down to her hand while he raised his own and placed it on her back, moving upward to caress her bare shoulders. She continued to rub him suggestively, inching her hand closer and closer to his pelvis, but stopped herself just shy of it. His fingers moved along her neck, to her cheek, then, and she leaned into him gently. She turned away from the sky and a dance ensued as they admired each other's figures, resisting the temptation to meet eyes. He followed her legs up to her breasts while she followed his chest and torso to his crotch, stripping one another with their gaze. At last their eyes met, glowing a deep red. Robin put a hand to Marian's head, softly removed her crown, and placed it next to her. A carnal intensity overcame them as they peered into the fires of each other's souls, longing for sweet embrace.

They kissed one another harder than ever before, sliding their tongues together through open mouths. Marian felt the weight of his hand rest on her thigh, matching hers on his. She nibbled on his lip and he grasped her hair and pulled. They kissed lustfully until he made his move, grabbing her far leg and guiding her on top of him. She straddled him. Marian grabbed his head in her left hand, feeling his hair between her knuckles as she rubbed a finger from her other hand over his lips, pausing in the tension of the moment. Her hands left his head, then, and gripped the fabric of his shirt, lifting it upwards. Robin raised his arms and his shirt came off in an instant. Before he had a chance to move, she had removed her tank top. A booming firework complimented the act, framing her body in pink luminescence. Robin's hands moved from her waist to the rounded curve of her ass, Marian grinding against him suggestively, feeling his manhood beneath his pants, her heart beginning to race. Her hair swayed in their movement, soft and gentle against his cheeks as they kissed. He slid one hand upward and caressed the small of her back, moving up to her bra. His fingertips felt like feathers against her skin. With a pinch, Marian's bra unclasped, exposing her bare back. The straps fell lightly over her slim biceps, and she took her hands off his body and let her bra fall off her arms. She expected him to move to grab her breasts but his hands returned to her waist and slid suddenly to her ass again, gripping her forcefully.

In no time his pants and her shorts were loose on their waists and their zippers were undone. She pushed herself off him and together, on the floor, they kicked their shoes off and pulled their pants down to their ankles, shaking their feet free of the fabric shackles. They sat up simultaneously and rose to their knees to embrace each other in another kiss, their naked bodies half lit by ever-changing color. Robin grabbed the small of her back with his left hand, pulling her closer. Marian put a hand around his penis and began to stroke him, feeling his thickness in her delicate fingers and palm. His breath became sharp, and he grabbed her breast with his free hand, squeezing her and rubbing his thumb lightly over her nipple. She stroked him and inhaled sharply as he pinched her nipple and pulled, moving with him in the heady boundary between pleasure and pain. She tightened her grip on his penis and pulled him in, feeling it press against her. Robin ran his hand from her breast downward, then, caressing the skin of her belly with his fingertips. Her heart pounded as she felt him slide between her legs. In that moment she pulled her head away from him, and they stared at one another, and his lips parted just barely as she felt him over her wetness. His touch was soft at first, then after a playful second he applied pressure. She exhaled sharply, her face an image of deep, heavenly desire. Her chest heaved as he rubbed two wet fingers over her. She licked her lips and closed her eyes, audible breath sneaking between the booms of the fireworks above. He rubbed further and slid a finger inside her. Marian moaned sharply and rested her head on his shoulder. She bit down on his neck, grabbing his hair by the roots and pulling his head aside. She scratched at his back as he slipped deeper inside her. Her hips were bending in pleasured response to his movements. It was too much for her to bear any longer. Marian bit his neck again, then his ear.

"Fuck me. Fuck me, Robin," she moaned, and put her forehead on his, the two gasping together. "Fuck me," she commanded.

Robin grabbed her beneath her thighs with both hands and lifted her up onto him with ease as he sat back on his heels. She straddled him and opened her legs, feeling the underside of his penis slide between her lips. She grinded against him tightly, holding the back of his head. They stared into each other's eyes, lost in their euphoric fantasy. They felt only each other. Not the roof, not the air, not the breeze, not time, nor space. Flushed, she relished that pause, the second precipice of their adventure in love, the mounting crest of a wave, the true burning flame of their passion. It was overpowering. Marian licked her lips as she watched Robin lick his fingertips, still wet with her, and reach down to cover the tip of his penis in saliva. He pulled her hips up, and she lowered herself onto him as she felt the pressure of his thickness enter her. She moved down just a little, pausing to tease him, lifting her eyelids just enough to see his expression. Their passion flared, too extreme to control, and he grabbed her hips tightly, pushing himself inside her further. The move spurred her excitement to unbearable levels and she submitted, taking him in entirely. The lovers collapsed to the floor, then, and began their sublime ballet.

Their journey to love that day would be remembered by each as the most intimate moment in their life, a consummate union transcendent of mere words or feelings. It was the raw physicality of love, the ultimate expression they were capable of. They had said the words, but now they had acted them. Above, a silver-lined cloud floated by the moon, and the pair entered rapture as one, baptized in pure ecstasy and a spectrum of radiant phosphorescence.

"I love you," they sighed in unison.

A little boy worked on his cotton candy while the night sky erupted in color and sound. He never heard anything so loud, or saw anything so bright in his entire life. Except the sun, he guessed. The cotton candy was getting his right hand sticky, so he switched to his left and wiped the other on his overalls. Above, a quintuplet barrage of reports exploded and brought James's attention skyward. Mommy told him earlier to be patient and wait for the grand finale. She said it would be worth the wait. He wondered if it was starting. Another barrage exploded in a range of hues, their bangs and booms orchestrated so that the sky was never long without color. They looked like flowers blooming in the sky, or a thousand fireflies blinking in random beauty.

Everybody was so surprised when the booms started happening. People stopped in their tracks and looked up as if angels were coming down from heaven. The "oohs" and "ahs" lasted for a little while, and eventually everyone fell into silence, watching and admiring. No one expected the fireworks at all, but they had been going for twenty minutes already.

It was more amazing than when the money fell from the sky. His mommy said that was a very important moment for them. She and Dad collected five thousand dollars, but she said that wasn't the reason, that he wouldn't understand until he was older. Dad only cared about the money, though. He wondered if this was an important moment for them too. No one was speaking. . .

Little James Jr. finished his sugary treat and considered the sticky paper tube in his hand. He guessed he should find the garbage pail so he wouldn't have to hold it any longer. He looked down and twisted his face in deliberation. If he left it on the grass his dad would yell at him again, so instead he looked around the dimly lit square for a place to throw it away, turning his head this way and that. Maybe he could wash his hands after he threw it out. He searched around the area for a bin but too many people were blocking his view. The dangling bulbs strewn throughout the open area made it bright enough to see and be aware of people and places, yet dim enough to make it an effort to spot details like a garbage pail. Maybe his mom would help. He turned around and tugged on her shirt, but was dismissed with the wave of a hand. Her eyes never left the fireworks.

James Jr. looked at the paper tube again and sighed. A glow of orange caught the corner of his eye, and he turned his head left, then, and saw a man in a white shirt, jeans, and a backwards hat leaning against a post on the outside of one of the booths, across the way. He had his legs and arms crossed, casually enjoying the fireworks show as he puffed on a cigarette. The same orange glow appeared again as he took a drag. James Jr. watched his motions as he lifted his right arm up to his lips and removed the cigarette, exhaling smoke through his mouth and nose.

The man took his eyes off the show and blinked a few times, as if sensing James's watchful eyes. He turned his head and glanced over at James Jr. and the two met eyes for a moment. The man beamed broadly at the boy and winked. Then the man returned his attention to the fireworks with a look of satisfaction on his face.

BOOM!

James Jr. jumped and his shoulders met his ears. As much as he loved the bright colors and sparkle of the show, there was one type of firework he hated. The small white fireworks were frighteningly loud. They hurt his ears and his chest and happened so fast that no matter what it always surprised him. Dad called them mortars. He hated the mortars. Dad said that if he watched closely he could see them coming and he could anticipate one because the flash came just before the sound. It scared him anyway.

BOOM!

James Jr. looked back near the lounging man for a garbage pail, noticing one just behind him, half out of sight. Just before he moved towards it, his eyes were once again caught by the same type of orange glow, only this time the glow came from a few paces to the left, buried in the shadows. At first he thought his eyes were tricking him, that maybe it was like when he looked at a lightbulb for too long and the dots remained in your vision. So he kept watch for a few moments to make sure that he wasn't going to walk over into somewhere scary.

B-BOOM!

Again, the same glow appeared from the darkness. This time, a figure stepped out of the shadows, exposing half of his body to the light. He was standing just a little behind the lounging man, staring into the back of his head. The half-shadowed man was disheveled, with a buzzed head, full black beard, jeans and some sort of thick tank top. His arms were bare. James Jr. watched as he stood there for a few moments, his eyes never leaving the lounging man's head. After five seconds or so, the shadowed man pulled his cigarette out of his mouth, turned his head back towards the shadows, and flicked the butt into the darkness. Almost immediately after, flames appeared.

B-B-BOOM-BOOM! BO-BOOM-B-BOOM!

The sky grew furious with glittering pyrotechnics, the grand finale beginning, while at the same time the ground and booth beyond the shadowed man quietly became engulfed in flames. They crawled up support beams and began torching the fabric walls of the booth, spreading outward across the ground at an alarming rate. James Jr. watched as the shadowed man slowly brought a short shotgun out of the darkness with his left hand. He assumed the trigger and grip with his right and held it at his hip, pointed directly at the back of the lounging man. After a moment, the lounging man, who had been fixated on the show, noticed the sudden fumes, heat, and flickering light of fire. He spun around with a horrified expression, and made the slightest movement towards the blaze before stopping in his tracks as he noticed the imposing, shadowed man.

James Jr. watched as a look of recognition came over the young, startled man as they locked eyes. They stared at each other, neither moving in the literal and figurative heat of that moment. The startled man blinked and moved to raise his arms, visibly torn between the growing danger of the conflagration and the imminent danger of that terrifying man. The startled man had his arms halfway above his waist when, without warning or cause, there was an explosion.

BOOM!

This time, the explosion came out of the end of the shotgun. The man flew backwards like a ragdoll and fell onto his back, squirming around slightly. James Jr. stood stunned, his eyes glued on the shadowed man with the shotgun. The look on his face was terrifying. He was smiling and the fire around him lit up his eyes like how the devil must look.

At first, James Jr. didn't hear the screams. It took a second or two before they reached his ears between the din of the fireworks. Still, though, his eyes never left that man. A pumping motion dropped an empty shell from his shotgun onto the grass. The man gently loaded another round into the chamber and turned to look at the crowd of people scattering about the square like ants. Almost instantly, his eyes met James Jr.'s. His smile remained as he raised his gun again and pointed it at James, the fire covering the entirety of the booths behind him now and spreading violently.

James Jr. felt a forceful tug on his overalls from behind. He could hear his mother screaming franticly as she dragged him closer and moved to turn and cover him. Until her body was in front of him, he kept staring at the man. Those eyes gleamed like sinister jewels from the fiery depths of hell. That shadow over him - it was death's shadow, a grim aura.

James's mother's screams were piercing, echoed by the fleeing mass, intermittently audible between the periodic dissonance of the fireworks. The very last instant, the very last millisecond before the shadowed man disappeared from behind his mom's hip, he saw the explosion come again from the end of his shotgun. And then her screams stopped.

Robin and Marian cuddled atop the building like old lovers. Both welcomed the breeze the evening brought to them as it cooled the damp skin on their naked bodies, glistening with sheens of sweat. Robin kissed Marian gently on the neck and shoulders as they lounged, she in the cradle of his body. She nuzzled against him and rubbed the arm that lay across her bare chest. She couldn't have imagined a more perfect first time.

When the fireworks finally subsided, the pair was left staring at each other in the light of the moon. A sparkle lit up Marian's eyes, her face decorated in loving satisfaction, but slowly, second by ticking second, peripheral sounds began to dig their way into the pair's trance. Screams and pops, remote cries and cracks, tones of *terror* wrenched them out of their moment. The two searched each other's faces, checking to see if the other had heard what they had. Perhaps the fireworks were still ringing in their ears? Robin squinted at Marian as her sparkling irises were overcome with a deep, flickering orange glow, her cheeks gradually turning a tone of faded auburn. His look turned to one of panic as his attention shot over to the fairgrounds. Marian followed his eyes and witnessed it too. A great fire raged. And in the background were screams and gunshots.

They stood. Robin froze, speechless by the sight while Marian unconsciously cupped her mouth with her right hand. Her eyes started to water.

"Oh my God," Marian cried. "Oh my God, no. Oh, *fuck*, *Robin*!"

"Holy shit. No. . . Oh my fucking God! No, no, no!" Robin shouted, his mind racing a mile a minute.

On instinct alone he sprang into action. He scrambled to put his underwear and pants on, skipping the zipper entirely. His breaths were audible between the pops and shrieks coming from beyond. He threw his shirt over his head and stomped into his shoes while Marian called at him, asking, pleading for him to respond. His rage drowned her out until she shook him.

"Robin!" she cried.

He snapped his neck towards her and saw the fright in her eyes, in her posture. He blinked furiously.

"Stay here. Stay here," he breathed. "If I'm not back in a few minutes, go somewhere safe - go down to my place, go home, anywhere."

"No! Robin, don't go," she shrieked as he began to turn away. She held onto him and pulled. "Robin, *no*. Don't leave me here alone. Please don't go."

"This is bad. This is so bad. I need to help, I need to get help. They're *screaming*. I have to go in," he cried in a rush. Tears were welling in his eyes, now, and his head was shaking visibly. She was terrified for his life. She knew those bangs to be gunshots and she heard the terror in the screams, the shrill register of children. It wasn't fear of a fire. It was the witnessing of murder. People were being killed down there.

"Listen to me! Do *not* move from here. I'll be back, okay? I promise. *Okay?*" They kissed each other forcefully, him tearing and her sobbing, now. "Okay?"

"No, no," she cried again as he pulled away from her. "No," she wailed.

She watched him abandon her on the rooftop through a screen of tears, naked and powerless.

Merv squatted in the bushes with his shotgun held flat against his chest. Women and children, and even men, screamed far and near. The shadows of fleeing masses ran against patches of bright orange fire. Nearby, the square was crackling with gunshots and half of the booths were burning. His earpiece had been filled with frantic banter since the first explosions and shots rang out. Hernandez, Mitch and Kingsley were incinerated in an explosion minutes ago, it was reported. Seconds later, smoke bombs were filling the middle of the square and rounds were hailing towards his men through a screen of thick grey haze. And people.

"I've been pushed back to the mouth of Position Two. Taking heavy fire! I have Marcus down and Jim was hit in the head! Sergeant, we need backup!"

Another explosion rattled from the square, the first isolated one since the fireworks ended. What sweet irony that surprise had been for Merv. His smile lasted for the entirety of the show, feeling like God himself had intervened to prolong this deed of death.

More yelling buzzed in his earpiece. Someone was hit, someone was confused or in pain, and someone was low on ammo. They whined. He heard their words, but not really. He was busy listening to the pure voice within. It commanded murder. It only yelled '*die*.'

Merv retraced his steps along the path he had travelled not thirty minutes earlier, and rested behind a tent. More crackling shots came from the square. He struck a match and tossed it at the burlap wall beside him, soaked in gasoline earlier in the evening. It lit up immediately. It was the thirteenth tent he had set on fire in the past three minutes and forty-four seconds, by his watch. Three minutes and forty-six seconds by now.

He stood and hustled around the now blazing fabric into an open area, bringing his shotgun to his shoulder. He pumped out six shells of buckshot into a fleeing group. Six bodies went down. Those were the last shells he had of the box of twenty he'd brought. He discarded the weapon and moved on to the .45s in his shoulder holster.

"Suppressing fire! I need Marcus's body drug back God damn it!"

Rodney had been doing most of the screaming over the radio. Merv was tired of listening to it. He sprinted through the trees, hopping ferns and fallen branches into a small pathway south of the square. Flowers were all around him. He snuck up the pathway towards the fiery mayhem. He thought someone said they'd hit one of the gunmen, and he wondered absently if it was Ted or Marty. Probably Ted.

The path curled once and abruptly opened onto the square. It was a warzone. People still crawled and limped for safety. Bodies were everywhere. Dozens. Hundreds. Shots continued in volleys from both sides. The remains of one of the smoke bombs were dissipating but the fires raged, adding their own blackness to the land. It smelled like burnt paper and cooking meat. There was a tall pole in the center of the square burning like a beacon. It was beautifully scorched, lighting the area a deep orange and red.

Merv hunched down and noticed Rodney huddled over a body while yelling into his earpiece. When Merv approached, he started screaming some nonsense at him as he tried to reload his pistol. Merv grabbed him by the collar, put a gun to his head, and squeezed the trigger. Pieces of skull sprayed about. He dropped lifelessly.

Bullets whizzed by overhead. He could hear the whistle-like noise, so close that he plunged to the ground. He was surprised to find the ground wet, until he saw the blood spraying out of Rodney's head and realized he was being soaked by it. The hissing bullets ceased, directed elsewhere. Merv took a huge breath, sprung up from the ground and in an all-out sprint dashed across the southern part of the square. Smoke from the flaming booths, tables, and bodies screened him from sight. Having reached the far side, he dove into the tall grass and rolled, catching himself in a kneeling stance. He checked his watch quickly. Eight minutes of hell had elapsed. Time to finish was running dry.

His eyes darted back and forth, searching for the remaining gunman. Muzzle flash lit once and drew his attention dead ahead. Then it repeated ten times over, blasting away at his men across the square. Merv snuck closer through the grass into a set of trees, took aim, and lit up the gunman with a few rounds. He realized too late that he'd equipped them with heavy duty body armor, and dropped to the ground as the automatic fire turned his way. He rolled, extended his gun and aimed higher. The shot sent the man's head back like a bowling pin, and he fell. Merv ran over, grabbed the man's gun, one remaining magazine, and called into the radio for the first time that night. He was right. It was Ted that had been killed first.

"Cease fire! I've got the last gunman down. Cease fire! Cease fire!"

Merv crawled out of the woods. The square was a firestorm. The air stirred with smoke and glossy heat. He held the rifle at his hip and came upon his remaining officers at Position One. Mendoza and Valentin had held their ground. MacDunnah emerged from the smoke to Merv's left, nursing his arm. Mancuso was nowhere to be found.

Mouths moved. Sounds likely came out. Merv ignored it all. He was caked in dirt, sweat, and Rodney's blood. His eyes were as wide as bottle caps, and he stared off into nothingness. And then he spoke.

"Where's Mancuso?" he boomed.

The bodies shook their heads and shrugged blandly. Then Merv erupted. His rifle howled ballistic fire at them all. And they all went down. He walked over to one that was squirming and put a shot in its head.

Die.

And another.

Die!

And another.

DIE!

And then he walked back into the fires.

PART 4: WAITING FOR A FUNERAL

"Beyond this place of wrath and tears
Looms but the Horror of the shade,
And yet the menace of the years
Finds, and shall find me, unafraid."
- William Ernest Henley

Chapter 35: Hello Darkness, My Old Friend

"As the hours come and go, new developments at this ghastly scene have followed. The death toll has risen to staggering numbers; however, the cause of the fires and gunshots has yet to be pinpointed. We now bring you the mayor's press conference, live, for what has been dubbed the 'May Day Massacre'."

"Thank you all for being here at this hour of the morning. I would like to begin by saying this situation is still considered an active scene and a very active investigation. I would like you to please understand that the information we have for you at this time is quite limited, and our ability to field questions will be limited as well. In addition, as the investigation continues and new evidence is uncovered, reports may vary or change to reflect the latest findings.

"I will debrief you on the major points and then allow Captain Mark Hogan of the Fort Dearborn Police Department to field specific questions about the crime scene. We will conclude with Fire Chief Ralph Buchanan who can fill you in on the details of that aspect of the event. First, I will begin with how we got here.

"Sometime around 8:30 p.m. last night, during the grand finale of a fireworks show, a fire started near the central attractions of the May Day Festival in Baker's Memorial Park. To be clear, initial reports do not suggest that the fireworks were the cause of the blaze; however, with such a large area to cover, it may be some time before an exact source is determined. An arson investigation is underway as I speak.

"Now, in regards to the reports of gunshot victims. . . We are very much dependent on witness testimony and forensic reports

before any concrete leads can be pursued. It is an extremely grisly aspect of this horrible crime that I find rather difficult to speak of.

"I do find it significantly necessary, however, to raise further awareness of a rather particular set of criminals in our midst. We are all aware of the escalating situation our city is facing with respect to the terrorist organization known as F.A.M. This organization, which has brought such outlaw filth and chaos to our fair city, has eluded authorities for far too long. Their capabilities have proven to reach farther than once presumed, their poisonous message has been underestimated, and their resources have seemed to grow exponentially. At this time, they are our prime suspects in this case.

"Make no mistake about it. This tragedy, this massacre *will be branded as the most devastating incident in our city's history. Our initial reports indicate that upwards of one hundred civilians lost their lives last night. But I can guarantee that number would have been higher if not for the training, bravery, and* heroism *of our officers and our first responders.*

"Before I let Captain Hogan field your many questions, I find it necessary to say we are counting on the public's support in this investigation to bring justice where justice is due. As always, Captain Hogan will give a hotline for any and all information regarding last night's atrocities. Captain?"

A distant chattering of voices coming from the TV whispered through the air of what was ordinarily a noisy space. It was just past noon, though, and Merv was the sole customer of the lonely bar on the outskirts of town. Or perhaps the heart of town. Or was he across the river in New Orange? He honestly had no idea. The voices coming from the wall-mounted television talked of death and destruction and of a fire that had claimed the lives of over one hundred people just hours ago. Questions were asked, speculations were conferred, and developments were communicated, but still nothing concrete was known of the situation other than the visible devastation and rising death toll. At least to the outside world. . .

Although Merv was staring in the television's general direction, he hadn't once looked up at it. He simply looked ahead into nothingness. His body was slumped over the left-hand side of the U-shaped bar. He propped himself up with his elbows, a position he had maintained for over an hour at the corner stool.

He wore a hat low, hoping to cover his face from any and all eyes. Underneath his hat was an expression that matched that of a snowman left out during the spring thaw. Droopy eye sockets and cheeks seemed ready to melt off his face. His vision was blurry, as if there was a haze to the air. It had been following him ever since the fires the night before, and he wondered if all that smoke had somehow damaged his sight.

A phone rang behind the bar but he gave no notice. On the second ring the bartender shouldered it.

"Yah," she said, listening, then shooting a sidelong glance at Merv. She hung up, and walked behind the wall of liquor that lined the back of the bar and out of sight.

Had there been anyone else in the establishment, they may have assumed Merv was there because of the loss of a job, a loved one, or even because of the tragedy from the night past. Each assumption would have been correct in its own way, but really Merv was there because drinking was the only thing he knew how to do. It was second nature. The day would begin, and so too would a buzz. Today, though, each time he tried to bring the bottle to his lips, nothing happened. His arms wouldn't move. He had touched the bottle once, but it felt cold and harsh. A once shameless narcissist, now all Merv felt was mortification, a nameless dread that stalked him and with which he hadn't the fortitude to cope. An hour had gone by as he watched his beer sweat and sweat, soaking the napkin on which it sat to a wetness matching that of his underarms.

Over Merv's right shoulder, the bar's front door opened. He turned to the sound and beheld a white light glowing through the frame like some heavenly furnace. It caused him to squint, and though his eyes were watering, he held them open, for a blink might serve to wink away that divine apparition.

A body walked into the bar outlined in shimmering pallor from the world outside. It started as a speck at the center of the light and came to blot it out as it approached, a tapping noise on the wood floor accompanying each step, drawing closer and closer to Merv in his stool.

God? Is that you? Merv wondered.

Finally, the tapping stopped and the figure sat a few stools to his right. A voice accompanied it.

"You look like shit, Hammer," it said.

The identity of the figure revealed itself to Merv a moment later, hitting him with recognition in an awful way.

"Oh. It's you," he lamented, returning his blank stare forward.

"It's me," the figure said with a voice like iron.

The door shut and the light disappeared. Captain Hogan was dressed in a suit and tie, freshly shaven, and wore a new pair of eyeglasses. He looked content and resolute, positioning himself upright on the spineless stool.

"What are we drinkin'?" he asked.

Merv looked down at his untouched beer, noticing the dewdrops streaming down its brown surface. He didn't have an answer so he assumed his former stare across the room.

"Heard you left the hospital against doctor's orders," Hogan pressed instead. "Didn't have time to come by. How're your burns holding up?"

Captain Hogan eyed Merv a bit longer during the ensuing silence. A bandage was wrapped around his right wrist, disappearing under his shirt sleeve and ending near his elbow. His neck was pink, and some scorched patches were noticeable in his beard. After a moment Hogan traced Merv's line of sight to the television on the far wall. Thinking he was watching the program, Hogan studied the display. The station's ticker running along the bottom of the screen passed some information that caught his eye.

"Looks like the FBI pulled some more F.A.M. reward money out of their asses," he chuckled, looking about the empty bar. "There a bartender in this place or what? What'd you do with her, Hammer?" he pressed. "Huh?" Hogan leaned forward and peeked under Merv's low brim. "Maybe she–"

"You ever think of how," Merv started suddenly, "*evil* it is to accept a reward for turning in a criminal?" He kept his gaze forward, the ends of his lips curling up. His voice was like sandpaper scraping stone. "We bribe people to 'do the right thing,' to be moral, to be decent. The concept of offering a reward isn't only a copout for us, it's a copout for them. We get to pay someone to do our job for us and they get to disguise their immorality with the illusion of being a good citizen by accepting money." His tone lightened. "It's like it's a job. Makes them feel important. That's the psychology behind it. That's all. A reward signifies submission, how we've long given up hope in the population. It's fucking pathetic. But it also embraces evil. And that I love." He laughed weakly. "We should offer a reward, and when the person comes forward they should be arrested for withholding information. Then put the rat and the crook in the same cell together. . ." He shook his head. "But here we are. That's why I like beating it out of people. So they know, for days and months afterward, what they've done. So they can reflect on their immorality. That's how I get people go out of their way to call me. Not through money. Through my fist. Through hustling. Leaving no stone unturned. Let's see the FBI do that. Lazy fucks."

"That's an interesting take but, you know, to be honest, I'm not here to discuss the morality of reward money."

"Then why, Hogan? Why are you here exactly?" Merv asked irritably. "Why the *fuck* are you here?"

"Well, I came for a couple reasons but I suppose I'll get right to it. I have a quick story for ya - if ya don't mind: One of the few survivors of," he motioned to the television, "those who were found. . .was a child named James Espinoza Jr. He was found alive underneath his mother's body across from what has been determined as the origin of the first fire - Arson investigators are amazing, aren't they? Anyway, he must have hid there for hours. Firefighters brought him to EMT personnel and he spent the night in the hospital getting cleaned up and having a few tests run. There were an initial set of questions asked by hospital employees - name, age, etcetera. It took 10 hours but he finally began speaking. I questioned him myself. He gave a report of everything he witnessed. Now, remember, this is an eight-year-old child, but he described things better than ninety percent of adult witnesses I've come across in my career. He stated things so simply, like telling a story from school or the bus stop. You know what stuck out, Hammer? He kept repeating what the man who started the fires looked like. He said he looked into his eyes and saw the devil. He said the man killed everyone around him. He said it was you. Not by name, of course, but he described you perfectly. Even though I knew, I still lined up five photos for him. We had an artist show what you'd look like without your hair. I showed two photos of other men and received no response. Then I showed him your face. And the boy began to scream."

The Captain paused, expecting Merv to respond. Instead he just stared ahead.

"I've seen some shit in my day. Thirty years' worth. But I've never. . ." Hogan trailed off and shifted in his seat. "I walked through the grounds just this morning. As the sun came up. Looks like a bomb went off - looks like images of war. People are still wandering the streets. Stunned. I've never seen such loss, such emotive misery. I even saw first responders crying."

An empty space took over the struggling dialogue for a moment.

"To be honest, you're a bit clearer than I thought you'd be. In the head. I thought I'd find you incoherent. Or incapacitated. Even dead, maybe."

"I'm dead sober. That's about it. Hell, I haven't even had a cigarette."

"Why'd you do it?"

Merv tried to clear his throat. "You know why. Control. Everything, always, is about control."

"It's clear you started the fires, but I can't quite figure out how nine of our men were murdered. I don't think anyone can."

"I, uh, don't remember it all that well. But. . .I was visited by someone. I don't know who, but he gave me identities and a location. A when," Merv said, a searching tone arising in his voice as if remembering details as they came. "When I got hold of a photo, something snapped – I, uh, lost it. I recognized them and right then and there I knew they were the ones who humiliated me during the, uh, heist. So I decided to destroy them. Not kill. Destroy. It was the only way to get control again. I had the intel, and I just. . .acted." Merv put his hand on the beer as if to drink it, but quickly removed it.

"How?"

"Hired a few killers. Guys I knew. Told them where to be and when. Geared 'em up. Promised big money. They were never leaving the park alive, so that didn't matter much. Then I got a few of our guys on board, got 'em rowdy. On edge. I just. . .tricked 'em. Pitted the two groups against each other. I marked a few of our guys for the hitmen and told our guys they'd meet resistance – to be ready for a shootout. I set up a firefight while I burned the place to the ground. . . Those kids that did the heist, the leaders of F.A.M., they targeted me. They hit me personally. So I returned it. I made it personal. If you want to destroy someone, you take what's dearest to them and you. . .just. . .ravage it. Make them watch, make them helpless. Take away control in a situation they most desperately need control over. That's, that's what I did."

Merv looked at the Captain, really looked, for the first time that morning. Those black eyes stared at Hogan under the dark shadow of his hat's brim.

"I killed one of them, you know," he said.

"You killed a lot of people."

"No. I killed one of *them*. One of *them*. I shot him in the chest."

"Why did you kill our men?"

It took many seconds for Merv to answer. "Because they laughed at me. Because they wanted to see me ruined. Because they knew too much. *I* didn't kill them though. Well, I killed a few," he laughed. "I set them up to die. *Mainly*. It was part of the plan I think. I'm not really sure. . . It's coming back a little. The killers I hired shot most of them. I finished them off when the hitmen were killed. It was, maybe, like a crossfire that happened. Oh, that's right. The purpose was to slaughter the innocent as revenge."

". . .You've said."

Merv looked over, unaware that he'd been repeating himself. "They really are useless, those people from there. From the District."

"I think," Hogan started, "you've managed to commit the most heinous crime I've come across in all my life."

"Call it what you want, but there was strategy here, Hogan. I brooded over this. I scouted it. I fucking knew that place in and out. Where the most people would be and when, where the funnels were, entrances, exits, fuckin'. . . I lit it up. It was so *easy.*"

Hogan grew a mocking face. "How's it feel?"

Merv stared at the bar. "There's nothing to report." Then he looked to Hogan. "At the end of the day, though," he said, "I was just following orders."

"What is this? A guilt trip?"

"Just know, in some ways you're responsible too," Merv replied quietly.

Hogan's face dropped. He leaned in, got close. "Are you fucking stupid, Hammer? Of course I'm responsible. All that pressure from me, from the Mayor, set a plan in motion that would not only destroy *you* but this entire F-A-M horseshit that's been going on. I *knew* you'd explode. It was written on your face. And when you did, I knew you'd take them all with you." He sat back and folded his arms. "I'll admit that losing our men was a bit of a curveball, but I'm sure you managed enough damage that this group has seen its last day."

Merv let out a drawn-out breath in response.

"As much as you live for outsmarting the system, you're incredibly predictable. For fuck's sake, you could have just put the guys in jail and been done with it. You said it yourself, you knew they'd be there," Hogan huffed. "I–whatever. Give the man that needs rules a rule-less world and he sucks everyone in. Everyone but me."

Merv's face flushed as Hogan smiled at him with pride. His judgement had surrendered to rage. Mortification sawed through his mind. He couldn't stop his head from shaking.

"You seem confused," Hogan said plainly. "I used your own tactic against you. I had you do all the work for me. I just underestimated the collateral damage."

"Doesn't make sense," Merv said.

"Sure it does. You cannot exist without rules," Hogan said slowly, leaning in again and using his hands to illustrate his point. "You must be the exception, the–the irregularity. Only within the confines of a structured code of ethics do you thrive. Hell, you break every rule you meet, but with*out* those rules your motivations self-destruct. It's like a forest fire. The more trees there are, the stronger it becomes. Remove the forest and in time it burns itself out. It becomes ashes. *You're* the fire. I just removed the forest and waited."

Merv zoned out like some student being lectured by a principal. That is, until the Captain reached into his pocket and placed something on the bar.

"I have the building surrounded by forty officers," he said as he slid handcuffs across the wooden surface. "I told them you'd come out peaceably."

Merv glanced at the cuffs and took a slow sip of his beer. It was the first drink he'd had all day. He returned the bottle to the soaked napkin, blinked, and nodded to no one. His jaw worked back and forth in a sawing motion and his cheek twitched. Merv resigned himself to his fate. His time was just about over.

"Just do me a favor," Merv asked in a tone that bordered on pleading. "Don't put me on the news like those degenerates." He rubbed his eyes. "I can't handle that, man. I can't handle that shit."

"Let's go," Hogan said.

Hogan stood, sliding the stool backwards as he did. Merv followed suit, removing his hat and placing it on the bar next to the barely-touched beer. He stared at the shackles for a few seconds, and click by click closed them over each of his wrists. He took a deep breath and turned to the Captain, extending an open hand. His right hand reached forward invitingly, his left hung up limply by the chain.

"It's been real, Mark."

The Captain paused, pursing his lips. To see Merv eaten away to but a shell of his former self brought an ounce of pity out of Hogan. He felt an odd sense of sincerity in the air. Their eyes met.

"Yeah. It has," Hogan said, grasping the inviting hand.

The movement was a twitch. Merv tightened his grip on Hogan's hand like a vice and yanked him forward, as quick and as violent as a lightning strike. As he yanked, he stepped into a head-butt and connected with Hogan's face. His nose crunched against Merv's forehead and a woeful grunt accompanied the crack of impact. Hogan dropped to his knees, stunned, knocking a stool over during the fall. Merv grabbed him by the collar and dragged him away from the bar. He spun behind the kneeling, struggling body and wrapped the chain link of his handcuffs around Hogan's throat. A knee to the back of Hogan's neck sent him to the floor, fumbling for reprieve, for air, for a way out of the metal trap. The knee pressed and the hands pulled. Merv's arms and eyes bulged with force and madness over Hogan's body. Merv was heaving and mumbling incoherent curses in tongues unknown, drunk with savagery. The flailing body looked like a tired fish out of water, flapping because there was nothing else to do but flap.

Time disappeared.

When Merv came to, his hands were numbing at his wrists and Hogan's face was purple. At some point, he was standing rigidly over the lifeless body, absent of the memory of having stood. He didn't bother settling his breathing.

At the bar he put his hat back on, pulling it low. He had a blank look on his face. Any semblance of a soul, any remainder of humanity had been extinguished. He was gone.

Merv walked to the door, opened it to blinding light, and strolled into awaiting captivity.

Evening came quickly while Marian paced across her living room. She passed a framed picture hung on the wall weeks ago of her and Robin on the fourth stop of their Pizza Quest. The couple each had a slice stuffed in their mouths with a goofy face to match. It had been her turn to choose the spot that day, a place called *Furnace*, and they ate so much that they had to put the Quest on a minimum one-week hiatus just to recover.

Marian wandered into the kitchen and felt the cold tile press against her bare feet. The sensation momentarily brought her out of her mind's cycling worries. She checked the fridge, as she had done about twenty times that day, hoping to find some hidden treasure-trove of junk food she may have missed the other nineteen times.

Left to her own devices, she became plagued by her imagination's limitless potential. After the allegations, Robin and Jon had thought it safer if she didn't know where they were. Fears over them had her feeling like a caged animal, and the television was her window to the outside world. Channel 3 had been playing all day, showing a number of reports, some witness interviews, and the progressive withdrawal of emergency response teams from the scene. Some remained to continue investigations and cleanup, but she found it odd how quickly much of the police and FBI presence had dwindled.

Earlier in the day, around noon, Marian made herself some macaroni and cheese. On television, coverage showed that peaceful vigils and mourning had commenced near a few of the entrances to Baker's Park. At first the people came one by one, some placing personal items against the walls like teddy bears. Others placed flowers, letters, signs, or pictures commemorating a loved one. A candlelight ceremony was to be held that evening, it was said, and the crowds gained and gained as the hours passed, until there was a sea of people in the streets. There must have been over a thousand people there. The camera angles on the ground were rather poor and the aerial shots made pinpointing an individual impossible. She just wanted to see Robin's face.

I hope he's okay, she thought over and over. *Please be okay.*

She hated the name the reporters were giving the tragedy. "The May Day Massacre." It made her feel horrible inside, hammering home a reality she wished she could reject. Every time she heard the phrase, she felt like cringing.

At ten minutes to six, Channel 3 cut from the studio anchors to the familiar press room in city hall. An empty podium was all the camera showed for thirty seconds. Then suddenly Mayor Crowley approached. His face was milky, like he had just seen a ghost. Marian increased the volume.

"I will make this address rather brief. I will not be fielding questions at this time. I have called this press conference to announce that an arrest has been made in connection to the massacre and fires that took place at the May Day Festival yesterday evening."

Oh God, Marian thought. *Robin. . .*

The Mayor drew a ragged breath. *"A sole individual was apprehended by police several hours ago after the murder of Police Captain Mark Hogan, a distinguished thirty-year veteran of the force. Captain Hogan was killed in a valiant attempt to detain the suspect around twelve o'clock this afternoon, and was pronounced dead on the scene."* He huffed again. *"The man in custody is our own Sergeant Merv Hamstead, also of the Fort Dearborn Police Department."*

An audible commotion stirred in the press room. Marian's breath caught in her throat as she connected the name. *Hamstead? Wait. . . Oh God, no.* It only took only a moment for the tears to overwhelm her.

"Sergeant Hamstead was the lead investigator in the search for the F.A.M. terrorists, of whom I must make it a point to clear of any initial connection to these heinous crimes. While the search for the terrorists is still an active and high-priority investigation, former Detective Hamstead has confessed to the premeditated murders of all nine police officers, dozens of civilians, as well as starting the fires that claimed the lives of countless other innocent men, women, and children of our city.

"The atrocious actions of this man are contemptible and do not represent the values of Fort Dearborn's fine Police officers, nor the standard of ethics of those in positions of authority across the city.

"Our thoughts and prayers are with the families of the victims of this tragedy. We at city hall mourn your losses as if they were our own. Thank you."

Marian sobbed on her couch, unsure of how she got there. She knew what was coming. She knew this would catapult Robin and Jon into madness, into unbridled anarchy. *Of all people responsible, why the police? Why him?*

Word of Hamstead's arrest and confession sent Robin and Jon into pure lunacy, trying as they were to grieve their slain friend in the midst of avoiding arrest. Discovering a connection, however minor, between the massacre and their F.A.M. exploits dragged them both through a grinder of gut-wrenching disgust and guilt, as if they alone had brought death to so many innocent people. The three-dollar bill incident during their heist was something they had laughed over in passing and mostly dismissed the moment it was over. For them, it had been a last-minute addition to a much larger project. It had been Wil's idea. "Because fuck that guy," they had agreed. They both knew in their hearts that their actions never justified a response so inhuman. Embarrassment did not permit murder. Not even murder permitted murder. But it did permit anger.

Everyone knew more people than just Hamstead were responsible. One man? Please. It had been a killing field that night. There must have been a dozen shooters; everyone who had been there knew it, and those who hadn't took little convincing. The peaceful crowds gathered near Baker's Park that afternoon were emotionally destroyed and ripe for provocation. Whether they knew it or not, they were a spark away from action.

Robin and Jon instigated a riot, plain and simple. It didn't take much. Nothing but a small spur, a buzz, just a few charged words. Then the community got rowdy. . . Word of the uprising spread like wildfire through the crowds. Robin noticed runners taking off and returning in numbers. Within fifteen minutes the meeting point and time was known by all. Within forty-five, the mob was assembled and marching. People handed out bandanas, kitchen towels, earplugs, and some eyewear. Those who could, armed themselves with rocks, sticks, bricks, and bottles. Others brought gasoline. It was guerilla-like.

First, Crowley installed a dusk-to-dawn curfew. Then, once the mobs were recognized as such by police, he announced a State of Emergency. Predictable and welcomed. The people were itching for such a fight. The police had burned their world, their children, their wives, husbands, and best friends. They had burned their peaceful, deserved celebration and their hopes and dreams. Now it was time to burn them back. It was time to fight fire with fire.

The march had gained twenty-three blocks before it was met by riot police on Phoenix St.'s broad strip just past the border of Old City and the fashion district. The initial clash on Phoenix took some time to erupt as both sides sized each other up. Robin would never forget that line of officers, navy-clad with shields, helmets, goggles, and batons. Soldiers against civilians. It began in waves, quick bursts of aggression. Eventually the mob got bold, overeager to flex their muscles. Someone threw a rock, and then someone threw a brick. Before long, the riot police were responding with force.

It felt like a game. When the resistance became too great, the mob would retreat and relocate. Attack from a different angle. The game lasted a few hours, aided by nightfall, seeing not one arrest until just before midnight. The initial spirit and stamina impressed even Robin. He knew it would taper off eventually, but it didn't matter.

By one a.m. helicopters hovered overhead, some news, some police. Sirens were omnipresent, though somehow always distant. They sounded like a baby's whine in the vacant street, echoing off windows and the sheet metal shell of parked cars. Other than the clashes, the city was like a ghost town. Not a soul was in sight.

Robin and Jon were slinking down a sidewalk towards Forester St. when suddenly an explosion rang out. Robin looked up the street towards the clash and started jogging nearer. Yanking two bricks free from a layer of sidewalk broken apart by persistent tree roots, he hopped on the hood of a parked car and climbed to its roof, hurling both pieces one after the other into the front lines of the riot police. His throws were returned with the thumping discharge of smoking gas canisters from the rear of the pack, spiraling overhead. He screamed at them and pointed and waved a vicious middle finger. Moments later a black ball-like device came over the frontline and exploded into a nearby group, knocking a few people to the pavement. They were shooting tear gas over the crowd, and pushing them into it with stun grenades. Another one exploded. Robin felt the concussive wave in his chest. *Slick sons of bitches*, he thought.

Behind the mob, the lamp lit street glowed orange as the tear gas rose and rose into a heightening wall. Forester St. was compromised. They needed to escape before it was too late.

"This place is fucked!" Robin yelled to Jon from atop the car. "We need to go or our night's over!"

He dismounted and they retreated towards the only exit - through the gas - while covering their faces with bandanas. They say teargas is odorless, but it's not. Though faint, it has an indescribable smell, kind of like old gunpowder or a spent firework. Mildly sulfuric but also acrid. It's strange and lingers on clothing and hair for days. Robin managed to protect himself from it rather well but even the slightest whiff felt like breathing needles. Eye contact stung like pepper spray, causing his eyes to water uncontrollably. At one point he had to hang back for almost thirty minutes until the symptoms became bearable. He was lucky to have only had mild exposure.

They eventually reached Phoenix St. to find absolute mayhem. Cars were burning, trees were burning, helicopters swooped and crossed, and blasts erupted. It was *loud* - even with earplugs. The frontlines had become sinuous on both ends. Where the police had maintained a solid front for hours, the constant pressure had taken its toll on the mob. Their line appeared weak, even exposed in spots. By some stroke of luck, the wind was in the rioter's favor that night too. Any tear gas shot their way drifted mostly northwest, away from the mob in what looked like a diagonal direction, just kissing the outer ranks of police near the left side of Phoenix St.

Robin, Jon, and the others immediately joined the rear of the mob. Just behind the lines was a chest-high pile of shrapnel and bricks, a cache of street ammunition. There was a bubbling feel in the air. Robin anticipated a final standoff, a tide-turning effort, in this very spot, in favor of whichever side could outwit and outlast the other. The thought left his mind carelessly, though. Nothing really mattered anymore. Only damage. One can only have so much taken from them before they snap and retaliate at all costs. Robin armed himself and entered the fray, looking to unload.

Suddenly, the wind swirled and a volley of tear gas tumbled through the sky, landing and rolling into the center of the mob. It swelled away from the canisters, and Robin cursed as he was pushed backward. Then out of nowhere, a skinny kid in black appeared wearing a gasmask. He swiped a smoking canister off the ground and lobbed it back into the formation of riot police. It soared, streaming a trail of vapor, and disappeared into the mass. The mob cheered and hollered, and another brazen, unmasked kid mimicked the action.

Throughout the night, the riot police had stalled and regrouped at times, but this was the first chink in their armor. Gas billowed from within their lines, and they separated, dispersed even, retreating some fifty meters. The mob roared hysterically, sprinting the distance and lobbing more rocks, bricks, and bottles at them. Any leftover canisters were kicked aside to let the wind take the gas far away.

A victory though it was, the riot police were well trained. They reformed their lines and marched again, banging their batons on their shields in a battle song of sorts, drumming in perfect unison. Unbeknownst to the rioters, a small number of armed reinforcements had trickled through the lines carrying shotguns. Rocks and debris rained down with fury, battering shields and helmets, but the police held fast. When they regained their lost ground, the police halted. Audacious off the successful push, the rioters advanced and provoked the lines with shouts, targeted throws, and cursing motions.

Steadily, over the shoulders and between shields of those in the frontlines, black barrels extended outward. There was a pause, the quickest of lulls, and then they barked. Muzzle flash lit the line like a row of cameras. Ten rioters buckled to the pavement and dropped. Everyone flinched at the sounds of gunfire, blindsided by the escalation of force.

People immediately dragged the fallen bodies away from the frontlines, but the police reloaded and picked off as many as possible. The once cohesive battle cry dissolved into panicked yells, and within seconds, the rioters were pulling back to take shelter behind anything, even flaming cars if need be. Robin and Jon distanced themselves by backpedaling, yet kept an eye on the police. Another round of fire took more rioters down. The shooters stepped out past the line of shields and pumped their shotguns, advancing with quick strides. The fight was lost. It was a flee-or-capture situation. Robin had turned to run when suddenly Jon let out a scream.

A knock startled Marian awake. She sat up from her couch and rubbed her eyes, checking her wristwatch for the time. The little white dial read half past eight in the morning. Again, the knock sounded as she rose and approached her door, apprehensive of whom or what lay beyond.

Crossing the living room, she passed the muted television recapping aerial footage of the riots. Dots of fire glowed on the edges of a wide street and small figures scampered here and there. The riots had calmed significantly once police gained position, pushing the mob away from the downtown area. At least that's what the news had said. The number of arrests being reported climbed by the hour and by five a.m. the fires had finally been extinguished. It looked like some semblance of calm was returning to Fort Dearborn.

What had been a snug ponytail now hung loose on Marian's right shoulder, and a pink, creased imprint covered one side of her face as she gripped the brass doorknob and turned. She peeked through the gap permitted by the engaged chain lock. Immediately, Robin's form came into view.

"Oh my God." She unlocked the door and swung it open. "Come here," she gasped and jumped into his arms, nearly knocking him into the hallway.

He had a strange smell to him and his neck was damp, but she squeezed him harder than she ever had. Robin only returned the embrace lightly at first, but when she wouldn't let go, he tightened his arms around her and buried his head against hers. She felt the gentlest kiss on the side of her head. It was almost enough to make her cry.

"You almost gave me a heart attack," she whispered.

"I know," he answered.

Marian noticed Jon, then, and went to give him a strong hug. He grunted when her body met his and she recoiled. She had missed a makeshift sling on his right arm.

"*Jon*, what happened to you?"

"Uh, took a rubber bullet to the shoulder. I'll be alright," he assured her.

Marian looked each of them up and down. She had been so overcome with relief that she hadn't realized how disheveled and worn they looked. These were shells of the men she knew and loved. Whatever had happened last night, they needed sanctuary.

"Come on. Let's go inside."

She shut the door and glided to the kitchen to put a pot of coffee on. The men collapsed, Robin on the couch and Jon against the wall, sliding down to the carpet. With safety finally secured for them all, it felt like the entire room was letting out a breath it had been holding for the better part of a day.

Once the coffee was done, Marian handed each of them a cup and took a seat next to Robin. He had since removed his soiled shirt, showing a bruise or two and some irritated skin on his shoulder. Jon was like a sculpture, clearly in physical pain. There was a defeated, shell-shocked look hanging over them. She thought that if she could just get them to talk, maybe they'd begin to heal - in one way or another.

"There were helicopters passing overhead all night," she said after a sip. "I kept wishing I'd somehow recognize you guys on the TV, as stupid as that sounds."

Robin formed a one-sided smiled, but it was Jon who spoke. "Funny part is you probably saw us and didn't even realize."

The television was still running, though none paid it any mind. There was nothing those clowns could tell them that they didn't already know. Marian bit her lip and tried again.

"What happened yesterday after I went home?"

Robin and Jon locked eyes briefly and each bowed their heads. It was as if they were ashamed.

"Too much to tell," Robin said.

"Okay." She let it be for now. Perhaps when life's surface recovered from this thrown stone, the reflection of events would become smooth once more. "Do you want to rest? Do you–I don't have much food here, I'm so sorry. What can I do for you guys? I just want to help."

"I don't know," he sighed. "What's there to do anymore? I just don't know what it's going to be like back in the District. I'm so worried about this overshadowing what happened on May Day."

"Oh, nothing could overshadow that."

He ran a hand through his hair, and Marian's breath caught. Flashbacks of the museum and the library, their first encounters, played like a video in her mind. She couldn't help but smile.

"Last night cheapens everyone's death. Even Wil's. Doesn't it?" Robin said.

"Wil would have done the same thing, Robin. You know that."

"I feel like I should be ashamed for being so reckless. I'm not even talking about the riots. Just with everything."

"Don't doubt yourself. You have nothing to be sorry for." She looked to Jon. "Neither of you."

"I feel like it's all destroyed now. It's all ass-backwards. This was all just supposed to. . .it's just gotta end. I don't have any energy left. It can't be this 'us vs. them' anymore. It's gotta stop."

"Then maybe it's time to stop," she offered in a tone as light as a feather.

"I don't know. I don't know what to do. I don't know what to do right now."

She rubbed his back with a concerned, sympathetic look. How she loved him so. "They need you, Robin."

"But I gave them me and what they got was. . .a pissed off kid. What they got was riots. I didn't help. I was just another person in the crowd. I–I'm not enough. They need a leader now."

"But they still need *you*. You are more than those things. You can still help."

He began to breathe heavily, she noticed. "You can stay with me as long as you want. Both of you. You know that. But this might be the most important time of this entire mess."

Robin sniffed and brought his thumb and forefinger to the insides of his eyes.

"Maybe you can call for peace. Maybe. . .maybe it's time to have a funeral."

"I don't know how to do that," Robin replied through his hands.

"I think you know someone that does," she said quietly. "You both do."

Robin lifted his head and held her in his eyes for a moment. Then he exhaled sharply and looked to the floor.

"I should've gone to see him a long time ago," he reflected, looking over at Jon. "We both should have. Let's clean ourselves up and take a walk."

"Are you talking about who I think you're talking about?"

Robin nodded. "Yeah. It's time. It's time to go see him."

Ernest stood at the desk in his study drawing deep breaths. The blinds were askew, letting fragmented bands of light leak in from the outside world. The light carried messages of grief and suffering, and though bright, he dwelt on the shadows that grouped together on his desk and about the room. Only in the darkness could he find answers.

The study had a thin layer of dust covering the surfaces of all the furniture, as if the room had been abandoned for some time. Ernest's presence was a disruption of sorts. After a frantic search for a most special gift, a thick leather-bound Bible, his bookshelves were in disarray. Volumes were strewn about the room and a table was upended. Glass lay broken in a far corner. The Bible, though, now lay plainly on his desk. Noticeable on the lower half of its front cover was a slim gouge that dug deep through its pages.

The Bible had been given to him by the local pastor on the day of his son Jack's death. In slanted, cursive writing the pastor had written the following words to Ernest on the inside front cover:

The path is dark, but God is the light

The path is cold, but God is the flame

The path is rugged, but God is your footing
The path is tiring, but God is your energy
The path is confusing, but God is your map
The path is dangerous, but God is your armor

Ernest thumbed the indentation in the Bible's front cover.

"Are you listening to me, God?" he cried aloud. "Armor! Armor was what you were supposed to provide me with!"

Thirty years ago Ernest lived not ten blocks from the church. His son, and only child, Jack, had been a strong, powerful man with endless potential. He was his father's son, full of the same characteristics, personality traits, and habits. Unfortunately, among those qualities numbered addiction. He was a genuinely good kid with genuinely human problems, and while his path had been promising, his drug dependence led him to an untimely demise. Jack had been beaten to death during a deal gone terribly wrong.

The town called it a tragedy, but deep down Ernest was convinced it had been fate. The funeral proceedings were a blur, however, the one thing he remembered was being consoled by Pastor Lucas Obervich, his predecessor at St. Augustine's. Obervich was a man of few words, not because he had little to say but because the words he chose carried such great impact, he rarely needed to use many.

It was Pastor Obervich who gifted the Bible and wrote those words to Ernest. At the time, Ernest had been a secularist with no need for a Bible and little understanding or want of how it was supposed to heal him. The most use he gave it was to even out the imbalance in his coffee table so it did not wobble and create a hazard during late night drunkenness. After stubbing his toe one too many times, he opted to throw it into the bottom of the nearby lake for its lack of functionality or purpose to his seemingly lost life. It did nothing but remind him of the funeral.

On his way to do so, as fate would have it, he was jumped by a robber with a knife. The struggle ended with the knife impaled in the Bible's front cover, the attack thwarted, and Ernest suffering no major physical damage. It was the most profound experience of his life. He had felt God for the first time—divinity intervene, the *energy* and *presence*. The devil's work had named him that night, but it had been the Lord who had saved him. It was only fitting that his path back from the lake led directly past the church. And on that path his life as a reformed man and future pastor in the vision of the Lord began. . .

Ernest paced. "My armor was to protect me from the devil. From his *treachery*. Where is my armor now? Have I not served you with righteousness and love? What is this judgement you've wrought? What is this death I've taken part in?" The words echoed through the room and out into the halls of the vacant church.

He was unable to escape the outcome of his actions that dreadful day in the precinct. It plastered every news outlet, cried on every sidewalk, and haunted his ghastly dreams. What he thought had been an act of courage had instead caused the worst incident he'd ever come to know. The mercy he sought those weeks ago had been just, it had been righteous. He had asked it for himself, for Robin, and for the boys. But the Lord had not granted it. The devil had his day.

The news report of Detective Hamstead's confession shook Ernest to the core of his being. He was convinced he had met with the devil, felt it in that man's presence, but could not stop himself from engaging. His memory was fragmented, but he knew his informing led to a massacre. He was tricked; tricked into believing that bringing Robin to justice was God's work. He now knew that the devil had dressed in God's clothing and led him there for exploitation. The only way to cleanse his wretched soul was swift and honest judgement.

His desk was clear except for an empty flask of vodka, overturned picture frames, his deactivated office phone, and that very Bible. In his grasp was leftover rope from the renovation project last year. The rope was rough against Ernest's skin, made of some burlap material that itched. Its ends were frayed like the ends of his sanity. It gave him a coarse welcoming.

Although he was alone, he spoke aloud, for the audience of his final sermon need not be in the room to hear the words.

"Judge not, is our instruction. But we must all be judged when the time comes," his voice boomed. "And my time is *now*."

He pulled at the rope with force, undoing his failed knot completely. He had never tied this particular knot before and was on his twelfth effort, learning as he went. It was an exercise that no one taught aloud, and if tied correctly, no one ever tied twice.

He realized he had opened the Bible, perhaps during his tirade, to the Book of Revelations, Verse 21, Line 8. He did not read from the page, as he had the passage memorized.

"Ah, yes. Look. The *cowardly*. The *sinners*. The cowardly have been consigned to that fiery lake! Your words were *true*! I *saw* it! They burned for their sins! But what of *me*? Have I been left a survivor? Or is my fiery lake forthcoming for my work with the devil? Perhaps my punishment is far greater? Or am I absolved? Am I to be *praised* for my performance? You give me no answers, Lord. You make me beg. . ."

He began the knot again, shaking his head. His look was one of disgust.

"I couldn't have been among the cowardly, I couldn't! Else *I* would have burned too. But my '*courage*' led me to the devil. So what, then? What of *my* actions? What of *me*?"

He put harsh emphasis on the words that coincided with pulling the rope taught, and expelled breath as he released tension from it. His eyes were focused on the job, but his mind was racing with punitive words for the Being that would soon pass almighty judgement upon his life's work.

"Our lives are a painting, Lord. Every day we add strokes of color and the image changes as we build those layers." Ernest paused and looked skyward. "When you look at my painting, will you see an image of hope? Or an image of destruction? Will you look upon my work with pride? Or with embarrassment? Have these last strokes of mine been black?

"No. . ." he whispered, refocusing on the rope. "You needn't answer now, for your answer is clear! Out there!" he shouted, pointing at the window. "That is what you think of my painting! The result of MY actions! The result of MY courage! Your answer is clear! Oh, but I have a rebuttal to the gauntlet which you have thrown. All is not lost, I assure you."

His hands worked of their own angry accord, and the knot began to take shape in a way no other before it had. He was closing in on success.

"I asked for *mercy*, not oblivion. I asked for your righteous *aid*, not to be an agent of death. I prayed for your *guidance*, only to find absence. You left me ripe for the picking. . . You be*trayed* me. At first I thought it was your anger that brought such fire to the land. Brimstone, I thought it was. I thought it was your punishment to those sinners. I thought I had your *favor*. I thought I was *spared*. But no. It is as I feared. . . I was abandoned!"

Ernest reared vigorously with a completed and reliable knot in his hands and a sense of victory oozing from his entire being. His robe, soaked in sweat, grime, and filth, swayed heavily with his thrashing. He gripped the rope tightly in his right hand, Bible in his left, and walked to the other side of his desk.

"Sinners have burned, yes. But what of the *children* among them? Children haven't the faculties to sin. They are innocent, so fragile and innocent. But they too burned. Such death disqualifies your presence that night. It wasn't brimstone. It was hellfire! And I granted it. I was his pawn, given up by you, Lord, for compulsion. I am no angel of death. I am wretched. I am a *puppet*. The devil is in this city. . .and he *used* me for his deeds. Now blood is on my hands that cannot be washed clean by humanly means."

The outburst swelled as he paced around the room like a leashed dog awaiting the return of its master. Ernest cackled crazily and held up his fashioned noose, a wild stare taking hold of him. A phantom breeze caused him to swirl around several times with his robe trailing behind. He sought the tangible form of God and assaulted the room with his voice, yearning to be heard. At long last his attention fell on a small crucifix hanging on the wall beyond his desk. Noose in hand, he pointed to the effigy.

"*You*! *You* taught me! Offer my body as a living sacrifice - THAT IS TRUE WORSHIP! Glory is given not to those who attempt to bring lives prematurely to the gates of Heaven! They are imposters! Sinners! Blasphemers! Their work is unjust! Their cause is faithless! They are the devil's sycophants! And I know the devil's work too well now."

He was screaming, and the once clear image of the crucifix blurred as tears welled in his eyes. Fading though it was, the almighty outline remained. Ernest focused on that vision, ignoring the tears running down his face and steadied his shaking voice for another chapter of his sermon.

"I deny him!" he cried. "I will be tricked no more! I praise only You!"

His tirade was reaching its pinnacle, the strength in his voice becoming irresolute. His thrashing and pointing, his accusatory lecturing drained his stamina. His shoulders sunk slightly and he began to speak introspectively, as if he was challenging himself to confront the validity of his argument.

"It is one who makes the ultimate sacrifice of one's self, and *only* one's self, that is ready for redemption, ready for judgement," he said with exasperation. The inevitable was upon him.

He directed his glance above where he stood to a portion of the ceiling where the tiles had been stripped away. He wiped the tears from his eyes and focused on the exposed pipes that ran above those tiles. Ernest bent down and began to stack books unevenly beneath the opening in the ceiling, speaking all the while.

"But will it be enough, Lord, to wash away my bloody sins? For the blood on my hands is that of the People."

The jumbled stack was knee-high. He steadied himself and stood on the wobbly pile, reaching the height of the ceiling and anchoring the rope around the thick pipe with two half-hitches. A tug proved its strength. Ernest continued.

"The time has come to have my demands answered. I must now enter the darkness for you, Lord," he cried while slipping his head through the loop. "Enter the darkness and begin the final journey to our formal confrontation, where glorious light awaits. Light is brightest when darkness surrounds it. You are that light. I have lived that darkness. My résumé is set in stone, but will this last line confirm your favor? Or has the devil marked me?"

The noose was snug around his neck, strengthening the throbbing pulse through his skull. He hugged his Bible close to his heart, and with his right hand double-checked the integrity of the knot. Satisfied, he returned his hand slowly to cover the wound in his Bible. Crying, staring into the blinds, the lightness and darkness there now blurred like an audience fighting to view his sacrifice. He spoke sentimentally.

"Will my impact on this world fade or will the ripples of my convictions endure?" A further rush of tears welled in his eyes, and he stared blankly into the nothingness. "Will the darkness be swift, Lord. . .or everlasting?"

A kick tumbled the stack of books, and in utter silence, Ernest dropped. His body flailed and his pulse spiked. The Bible fell as he grabbed the taught rope reflexively with useless strength. Kicks and jerks added a slight rotation to his movement and he began to pivot away from where the light and dark layered the room. A vision appeared through his fluttering eyelids, a scene of angels and demons fighting to claim him. In those last instants, those last fleeting flashes of life and light, the darkness set upon him unrelentingly.

Chapter 36: Waiting for a Funeral

The air felt as thick as vapor. Strange heaviness now lay over the place that so recently had lightened every soul who walked its paths and fields. The laughter was all gone. Things once green were blackened. Grasses, trees, flower patches, and shrubs bared their wounds, and the faint smell of ash drifted through the wind in waves. Robin thought he would have choked were it not for the community of people present bearing the burden with him. Dead things lingered, but on this day the living had come to share in their pain.

Robin stood atop a short stage in Baker's Memorial Park. He wore his best suit and his face was freshly shaved. For nearly a half hour, he had been watching as thousands of people filled the south fields to pay their respects to the victims of the May Day massacre. It was the first time the public had been on the fairgrounds since.

The stage was simple, holding a single podium and microphone only. He wore a solemn look on his face, for the recent days had held little sleep, minimal rest, and even less peace. His feet ached and his left eye twitched every now and again from heavy fatigue. Despite the squeezing lethargy, his nerves kept his pulse high and his mind alert.

Some distance away were maybe two hundred or so chairs, in two shallow rows, intended to seat the elderly. If they had been any closer, the seated mourners would have been invisible, swallowed up by the surrounding, standing mass. They fanned out on all sides, indistinguishable but undeniably whole. There was a news presence beyond the final rows of gatherers, surely eager for a story to report from this bold gathering. Robin could feel the cameras on him, even from afar.

His sight was true and free of tears that morning, and it appeared that the vast majority of people had arrived by then. It was 9:37 a.m. on a Wednesday.

Robin approached the podium. He reached into the pocket of his suit jacket and rubbed at a special letter. Having a little piece of her there with him was like being clothed in support. This week had been the first time he had thought of his mom in. . .a long while. Since her death, every so often he'd find himself wondering what she'd have said if she had seen him in a particular moment. He usually dismissed the thought, resigned that her would-be words were meaningless, nothing but a feeble attempt to cope. But today he knew that reasoning to be immature. Thinking, imagining what she'd say, was what kept her alive in his mind. It was what made her carry on inside him after death. It was all he had of her. Today, he imagined she'd have smiled and told him to finish what he had started. She'd have said there was nothing to fear when guided by love, that failure only hurt when an action was made without heart. Robin smirked at the thought, likely the only face resembling a smile for quite some distance. She'd have been right, of course. He loved this place. He loved these people. For all its problems, for all its rough edges, for all its scars, blemishes, and history, there was love. In spite of the hate, or perhaps because of it, there was love.

He wrapped his fingers around the edges of the podium, locked his elbows, and scanned the crowd of what looked like an infinite number of eyes set on him. Observing their colorless dress inspired a moment of reflection while he waited for the mass to settle. When he and Jon learned of Ernest's suicide three days earlier, their emotions reached the limit of human experience. Each of them, individually, snapped. The result, besides broken furniture, doors, glass, hearts, and voices, was a realization. His death would be the very last to come from this tragedy. The uprising would end. The violence would end. Instead, a voice would lead the victims, the people of the District, to a resolution with the opposing powers. And Robin would be that voice.

Hindsight was a motherfucker. Most knew it all too well, and Robin was no exception. Marian had been right: what they had needed the morning after the massacre was a funeral. But he had let emotion dictate his actions. They all had. Unbridled anger is one of those things that doesn't allow for argument, it doesn't allow for reasoning. It only allows damage. In hindsight, this funeral should have happened days ago.

Now he and Jon had their opportunity to do right by the people and the departed. Directly in front of the stage lay one hundred and twenty-three white caskets lined neatly and orderly in rows. Each had a single white rose laid upon its center, Jon's subtle touch commemorating the fallen. One section of the flower gardens miraculously survived the fires and Jon had made sure to utilize such a fortuitous finding. However difficult it had been to bear the facts of the ordeal, Robin and Jon had taken charge of organizing the ceremony, and one of their tasks was to represent the fallen. Perhaps the saddest detail of the presentation was the staggering number of child-sized caskets. There must have been fifty of them.

The May Day tragedy had touched people from all walks of life and all parts of the city. There were faces among the mass that had rarely stepped foot in the Inner District before today. Their presence was evidence of how deeply the deaths had reached, how individuals throughout the city were connected to that day forever. Whether relatives, friends, or sympathizers, they too mourned the senseless loss. The ceremony's time and date had reached all of them by word of mouth. Robin had barely needed to post a single flyer. They were here because this day was personal. They had been waiting twenty-five years for it.

A rush of memories flooded him then. He remembered Germany. He remembered his first, sleepless night at St. Augustine's. He remembered the moment he met Marian and the moment he fell in love. He remembered the stress, the theft, the actions both ridiculous and proud, and he remembered May Day. The life *and* the death. Years from now, what would he remember about this day?

A humid breeze brushed by Robin's neck and eased him back to reality. He felt that his underarms had begun to perspire and he stifled a creeping sense of doubt, steadying his breathing as best as he could. The podium held no papers. This was a speech that had to come from the pure emotions of the moment. He leaned forward, bringing his mouth inches from the microphone. His voice boomed over the parklands, calling all to attention.

"Ladies and Gentlemen, Children and Elders," Robin began. "I want to thank you from the bottom of my heart for your presence today in the face of ultimate grief and adversity. I stand before you a beaten man, among an endangered People, in the heart of a fractured city. The tumultuous events of the past week have left me contemplating exactly how we got to where we are today. It's an incredible. . .*mountain* of a task to attempt to comprehend all of that which is involved, but I tried nonetheless.

"The way I look at it, the situation we've found ourselves in is the culmination of the disconnected relationship that exists between the city proper and our forgotten District. Decades ago, when this District was exploited, a new way of order set in that quickly came to dominate life itself.

"The people were brave. They fought against it, but after enough time reality can weigh heavily on a person and they can become listless in a world that was once full of possibility. It's one of the gifts of the human race: adaptability. It's a strength, surely. People have the uncanny ability to survive by being able to change practically everything about ourselves to best suit what's around us. But that gift of adaptability is a flaw if the environment we are in is one that should never have been created in the first place. In our case, adapting to the environment created complacency and capitulation, two characteristics no *united* mass would ever have toward this oppression.

"With a little help, the general acceptance among us has been replaced by defiance and a questioning attitude. A paradigm shift has occurred, one which has truly been a sight to behold. Through the actions of a particular group, we've been shown that survival is not dependent on adaptation - that we don't have to surrender our autonomy. Instead, we've seen that another option exists, one where we can rise up and force our *environment* to adapt to *us*.

"And there we have our conflict. That overbearing part of our society that was once seen as invincible and untouchable - seen as *dominant* - was proven to be merely human. They're now exposed, their faults are recognized, and what we have fell victim to is their backlash. Plain and simple.

"Let's be clear. The barbaric actions of one man do not represent the intent of each and every heart in positions of power and control. But the anger behind it, the drive, and the hatred - even if passive - has been there for so long. *Too* long. Should we be surprised that when we tried to shape our environment, the keepers of our environment rejected us? Should we be surprised that our keepers replied with violence on perhaps the most meaningful day we've had in decades? I don't think so. . .

"Yet it happened. In the most horrific way imaginable. Awful doesn't begin to describe it. Unfortunately, we reacted in a rather awful way ourselves. Don't get me wrong, I was a part of the riots. I lost control, too. I burned things, too. I went ballistic. Hell, I helped incite them, truth be told.

"Our little temper tantrum, while thought-provoking, was one of disjointed actions and individual shows of force, barely scratching the surface of the armor we have spent so much effort weakening these past months. That we did not break through the armor is not a testament to its strength, but rather that, in haste, we chose the wrong weapon to fight with. We chose violence. And while I won't argue that violence has no purpose, I will argue that from this day forward, we must learn that violence does not work in a situation of this magnitude. It has no place in this fight anymore.

"The reason we must not continue to use violence is because violence is like a drug. It stimulates, and only when it's too late do we realize we're addicted to it and we use it until there is nothing around us to be violent towards. Then we become violent towards ourselves. It almost happened during the riots decades ago, and I worry that it might happen now - that further violence will lead to our self-destruction. Know our strength not by damage dealt but by power wrought through word and unity.

"Now, this all may seem quite hypocritical coming from me. For quite some time I have acted in the name of a rather violent group. Part of why I'm here today is to own up to my actions in front of all of you. I am the leader of the Few Against Many. I created it, masterminded it, and acted out each and every crime. Like some of you, I latched onto that name without questioning what it meant. I do not now, and will not ever, question the acts I committed or the motivations I had to commit them, because I believe in them with all my heart, but I realized something particular today. The Few Against Many. . .that name is *wrong* - so wrong. In reality, it is the exact opposite. *We* are the Many. *They* are the Few. Look at what we have here today. Look at how many thousands of us are here. If this isn't unity, then the word doesn't exist.

"I promise you, here and now, if we show courage instead of violence, if we show resolve instead of aggression, we will have our rightful justice by overwhelming, peaceful unity."

Robin backed away from the podium and took a moment to collect his thoughts. The pause felt monumental, toweringly so, like the hinge of his speech was about to break free and open the door to freedom. He rubbed at his chin and skimmed the faces staring his way, glancing over at Jon quickly. He leaned back in to continue.

"I've, uh, I've taken a good amount of time to think on what I'm about to say next. It's taken the help of those closest to me, the thought of you all being here, as well as the memories I have of those I've lost to bring myself to say it.

"I've realized in my life that individuals faced with death experience something profound. We become intimately aware of how fragile we are, how quickly things can change, and how our futures are more theoretical than anything else. Nothing is promised. And there's a lightness to that. . . I suppose the point is to understand this truth: the future is powerless to the present if we deem it to be. So all of our worry, our fear, our despair - it's nothing if we just act against it today.

"I've also realized that when we are exposed to an incomprehensibly inhuman act, our faith in humanity itself falters. We lose our belief in goodness. It's a defense mechanism, protection so that we never again find ourselves as victims. And I get that. We all saw things, heard things, felt things that no human beings should ever have to experience. We cannot un-see, un-hear, or un-feel. The only thing we *can* do is grieve for our losses together and ensure that we heal, leaving no one behind. We must not lose our belief in humanity. No matter what. Because when we stop believing in humanity, we stop believing in each other. Then, we've truly had everything taken from us.

"Yes, our celebration has burned, but we will have joy next year. Our children have burned, but we will never forget their faces, we'll never forget their names. We'll carry on humanity, bringing new children into the world not as replacements but in honor of those we've lost.

"We have a long journey ahead of us. So take time to remember. Remember the laughter and the smiles, because they will return. Remember the festival, because we will celebrate again. Remember that Spring is upon us - the time of renewal, the time where fragile things grow strong, where life wakes from dormancy. A life spent chasing Spring—embracing transformation, always striving to be better and to come out of the darkness and cold of winter—is a life lived to its full potential. That's the life we must live.

"Let's not trick ourselves or lie to ourselves. Change for our home and our city won't come easy. It won't come quickly. Our actions today are one step towards a brighter future. It may come decades from now, but that's okay. They are done in the name of our children, and our children's children. The youth among us and the youth to come, whose futures deserve to be fought for. If it's at the expense of mine, so be it. What will you say for yourselves?" Robin paused. "Chase Spring with me. Strive for betterment. Let us march, together, as a united whole. Let us deliver our cherished lost to the doorstep of their killer. March with those we must carry," he said, pointing to the caskets. "For justice, yes. But more importantly, for the future. It starts now."

As his final words rang through the park, Robin took a breath for what felt like the first time since he walked on stage. He then looked to his right, locked eyes with Jon, and nodded. The two stepped onto the grass and approached the casket chosen to represent Wil. They both waved to a few people in those bordering rows to join them, and then waved to others to attend the caskets to the left and right. The people obliged without a word or hesitation. Robin, Jon, and two others lifted, setting Wil's casket on their shoulders.

Robin, Jon, and the other frontrunners carried the caskets three-wide down the aisle. Behind them, one by one, the one hundred and twenty remaining caskets slowly rose off the ground at the hands of silent volunteers. Like gates opening, the crowd of mourners made way for the procession. As the last of the caskets entered the aisle, the front rows spilled in behind them, emptying one by one. The initial movement was slow, like a train coming out of the station, but Robin knew once they met the open road, once they gained a little momentum, their inertia would be impossible to stop. And so, the trickling white line of coffins stepped onto Orange Ave. with a widening trail of people marching in tow. Suddenly, it began to drizzle.

Robin led the procession out of the Inner District the same way he entered all those months ago, passing even the lawyer's office, which prompted his exodus, and which he had vandalized that first night out with the guys. He gave it no third consideration, focused only on the crucial objective. They stopped traffic, rerouted pedestrians, and kept the path moving forward toward their final destination at all costs. When Orange Ave. ended, a turn onto Phoenix St. soon saw remnants of the riots. Burned out storefronts were wrapped in caution tape, debris still speckled the roadway and sidewalks, and the trees - what was left of them, anyway - were mangled black shapes. The torched cars must have all been towed, but the gravel still showed stained outlines of ash and soot where they had been parked. Horns blared, drivers yelled, but the people held their formation.

The caskets were ten-wide as the procession turned the final corner onto Fort Dearborn Ave. The trip had taken almost an hour, but at last the ornate dome of city hall was in sight. It sparkled, even in the fog, like a beacon lighting the way. Grey clouds hung low like suspended puffs of smoke. They swirled and rolled ever so slowly, changing colors across the drab spectrum. From the way they moved, it almost looked like city hall was burning.

Moving his eyes downward from the dome Robin saw a blur of navy blue positioned in front of city hall's front steps. *Riot police.* He had expected as much. After all, units were probably on the ready in light of recent events. They seemed to be four or five rows deep, all brandishing shields, helmets, goggles, and vests, thoroughly prepared for the inevitable standoff.

From above, the scene was like a black and white river approaching a dam. The river crept and crept. The gap dwindled and dwindled. A repetitive thump followed them, like the beating hoofs of a battalion of warhorses. Helicopters thundered above, tethered to the unfolding drama. All this movement, all this sound, yet the wall of police stayed steady and statuesque.

At a hundred meters, gun barrels rose behind the shields and poked out from the line. It felt to Robin like each weapon was pointed directly at him. His pulse drummed in rhythm with the people's thumping footsteps. Above the rows of soldiers, standing in the middle of the mountain of steps, was a man flanked by some additional police. His shirt and tie made him stand out among such a uniform of navy-colored men. Robin refocused, praying to anything and everything that the lines would hold their fire. In moments, they'd be within target range.

As the black parade came within twenty meters, the riot police steadied and prepared for violence. He couldn't hear it, none of them could, but safeties unclicked and trigger fingers engaged. A few more meters and the police would end this march, these people, and the only hope for peace.

Instead, when the gap was no more than ten meters from the frontlines, Robin stopped. He motioned to Jon, and one by one all one hundred and twenty-three caskets were lowered to the pavement. Silence permeated, broken only by the quick cuts of helicopter blades, which stirred the wind and rain.

Robin's pulse was sky high, his breath was shaking, and his adrenaline was overexerted, but he steeled himself and coolly walked alone up to the menacing human wall. His vision swept across the soldiers and settled up the stairs on the oddity, an older man flanked by two officers with machine guns. *No rubber bullets in those.* The man's brow and sideburns were wet with sweat, and his shirt showed dots of rain droplets. Surely he hadn't been among those outside for very long. He had a Kevlar vest on over his shirt with three yellow letters branded across the chest: FBI.

They held eyes for an unknown length of time. Then suddenly the man shouted.

"Let him through," he ordered.

The soldiers in front of Robin split, forming a narrow lane through which two more approached, shouldering their shotguns, and patted him down. Finding him emptyhanded, they nodded and returned to their positions. Robin ran a hand through his wet hair, straightened his wet tie, and took a splashing step forward.

As he went through the ranks, they swallowed him row by row, trapping him beyond their wall. In eight strides, Robin had cleared their lines. A boiling cauldron of emotion overflowed within him. Step by step, he ascended the mountain to the man in the vest, all the while staring down the machine gun barrels ready to put more holes in him than a wheel of Swiss cheese. The two men locked eyes again. Robin lost awareness of his body. Somehow it lifted his field of view upward and onward. Four steps left. Three steps. Two steps. One step. Robin halted. He had to look up to face the man's icy gaze. The stranger's eyes blinked not once as he quickly scanned the sea of people filed down Fort Dearborn Ave., tracing from the far reaches to the middle, then to the caskets, and finally settling again on Robin. Deadlock ensued, as if both men were having a silent battle of attrition. Rain fell, hitting their faces without effect. Pressure built to the brink of jolting physicality. Finally, Robin summoned equanimity and inhaled. With a firm tone, he spoke.

"The Mayor will see us now."

Epilogue: Chasing Spring

"Alright, hon," Betty said warmly. "Let's see how well you can eat today."

She sat in a high stool and leaned towards a blank face, frozen and pale. It was a man's face, with dark hair and dark eyes that stared a thousand miles ahead. Betty held a plastic spoon in front of his face, maintaining her smile and warmth. The man opened his jaw and she slid a spoonful of mashed sweet potato into his mouth. She fed him like one would feed a baby, as the man had no control of his major bodily functions. He sat in a tongue-driven wheelchair but the staff resigned to push him around from his room to the common area each day, for he never once opted to use it autonomously.

Betty removed the spoon and scraped some excess food from his lips. The man swallowed and slowly opened his mouth again. His breaths had an eerie, granular sound like rocks falling on themselves.

A nurse intern, named Joy, sat with Betty in the bright white room, shadowing the day's workload. She was a lovely young woman that came highly recommended from the University program. Betty knew the man would soil himself a few hours from now and hoped that Joy would be able to stomach the process. She'd lost many aides because of that reality. Betty continued the feeding while Joy observed.

"Um–" Joy began, and then stopped herself.

"What's up, hon?" Betty replied, removing the spoon again from the man's mouth.

"I'm sorry. I was going to ask about his condition but I don't want to be unprofessional in front of the patient."

"Oh, don't worry. He doesn't listen to us," she said. "And he hasn't spoken in nearly two years – since the accident. Us nurses are the only ones who could answer your questions."

Joy gave a sympathetic form of a smile. "What happened?"

"Failed suicide. He hung himself in his prison cell but the rope snapped. Doctors initially supposed he had brain damage along with the quadriplegia but his scans show normal neurological activity. He's been an interesting case-study," she said and scooped another spoonful. "Most of our patients have the ability to speak but his vocal cords were damaged in the accident. The extent is undetermined."

"How long have you been caring for him?" Joy asked.

"I started here ten months ago." She turned to Joy. "Better pay than Hospice." She looked back to her patient. "And he's our *best* eater," she said with another spoonful heading to his mouth. "Isn't that right, Mervin?"

The man gave no shred of acknowledgement and simply stared aside, automated in his limited actions. He opened his mouth to accept the spoon.

Betty continued the feeding for a few moments while off to the side of the room, a noise came. Those black, empty eyes perked up ever so slightly and began tracing, foot by foot, across the clean, white room to the wall-mounted television. The volume had been turned low but his hearing was keen. A green landscape was being shown on the screen that caused the man to flush.

"That should be enough," Betty remarked. "He generally doesn't eat more than that."

"It's so little," Joy commented and subtly considered the man's frail figure.

"Yeah. . . He may be the easiest to feed but he never did have much of an appetite."

She started to collect the spoon and bowl when a grunt interrupted her movement.

"nnnnnnnn-nnnnn-"

Both nurses turned to the man in the chair. His eyes were swelling and his head shook gently. The noise he made sounded like a buzzing or a drawn-out groan and his mouth began foaming.

"Oh. . . Did you want more? You looked like you were finished," Betty said kindly and scooped more puree out of the bowl. She brought the spoon towards him and pushed it into his mouth but the man spit it out. Pulp ran down his chin and soaked his beard. He was a sputtering mess. Betty clicked her tongue in disappointment and grabbed a towel to wipe him clean.

"Perhaps not," she said.

"I think he wants to watch the television, Betty."

Betty glanced over in the direction of his attention, her eyes landing on the screen. "You want to watch TV, Mervin?"

"nnnnnn-nnnn," he groaned.

"Alright, let's wheel you over, then."

"nnnnnn."

Betty released the brake and spun him towards the television. She wheeled him closer, all the while hearing his faint groan. She parked the chair and took a look at the display. A newscast ran, telling of thousands of people who flocked to a celebration.

"Aw, look at that. Such a beautiful day for the festival," she said to Joy. "I'm gonna park you here for a bit, okay, Mervin? You can enjoy May Day from here."

"nnnnn-nnn"

"O*kay*. We'll be back for you later," Betty dismissed with a fading smile. She turned to Joy, who had the remote in her had. Joy turned the volume on the television up to an audible level for his enjoyment and set the remote on a table beside the wheelchair. They turned to leave.

"nnnn. . .nn. . .no. . ." Merv croaked.

The nurses stopped in their tracks and passed an astonished look to one another. "Oh my," Betty said.

". . .no. . .no. . ."

They rounded the chair to make sure of the words they had heard. Merv sat there shaking, spitting, and staring wide-eyed into the television. The news report panned across the bright landscape of Baker's Memorial Park and onto a sea of smiles.

". . .n-no. . .no. . .no. . ."

"Huh. I've never heard him speak before," Betty said absentmindedly and paused. "Good job, Mervin." She patted him on the shoulder, looked back to Joy and shrugged. "Would you look at that. You're good luck, Joy."

". . .no. . .no. . ."

Merv squealed on, but the nurses ignored and left him to his frothing stupor and the torture of his condition.

". . .*no*."

A gentle breeze crested a ridge and ducked into a shallow valley. Over tilled fields it rolled and scattered, spread and joined again, climbing gradually upward and upward to a bulbous hilltop. Leaves whispered from nearby trees and the breeze came to cool Jon's damp forehead as he pulled his hands from a patch of lush soil. His row of seeds was almost complete, terminating by the side of a dirt road just an arm's length away.

The morning sun shone brightly, giving promise of afternoon warmth worthy of summer clothes. Jon's overalls and boots would surely be too stifling come noontime, but luckily, most of his planting was taken care of, for his shirt was damp with sweat and his back was feeling the ache of being bent for hours on end.

He dropped three seeds into his dirt hole, covered it with soil, and patted it firm. On the road, a chicken trotted by. He noticed the old rooster considering him and he let out a chuckle. He then stood and reached in his pocket for a handful of feed.

"Here you go, buddy," Jon mumbled, sprinkling a palm's worth on the dirt road. Jon smiled to himself while the rooster pecked. Had it the ability, he thought the little thing probably would have thanked him.

With a stretch, he allowed his gaze to wander from the rooster to the surrounding farmlands. It was an undulating bit of land that Jon found purely serene. Sure, flatlands were easier to farm, but the rolling hills and thickets gave the land some character, a feel of individuality, as if one could attribute a name to a place. You got to know the land better that way, got to be friends with it.

The farm grew all sorts of things like carrots, onions, potatoes, string beans, assorted lettuces, radishes, tomatoes, cucumbers, kale, and eggplant. Plots of rye, wheat, and barley were on rotation in the far fields, apple and pear orchards were a quick tractor ride away, a proprietary beehive was tucked along a patch of woods, and they even had separate caves to age cheeses and grow different mushroom varieties under Randy's farmhouse. There was also a lovely horse pasture, spacious pigpens, and plenty of goats, but that was a much smaller operation, most of which was purely for leisure.

Jon and five other workers helped Randy year round with a dozen others on seasonal rotation, peaking at harvest time. This was his second spring on Randy's farm and to say it was the most peaceful, educational, and happy time in his life would be without exaggeration. Although Jon woke at four a.m. seven days a week, he didn't mind it in the slightest. Such was routine, which brought perks uniquely its own. There was something awfully special about being able to watch the sun rise every morning. He loved the air, loved the work, loved the smells, and loved to learn. To grow and to care for living things was his dream. Apparently, some dreams can come true.

Jon had learned to listen for the sound of birds waking in their nests, to take time to watch horses or pigs or goats shake off the stiffness of a night's sleep. They learn to expect your presence and, after a time, welcome it. It was far, far better than the car horns, smog, sirens, and concrete of back home. He did miss the people sometimes, though. Especially his friends. Maybe if he finished the day's work early he could borrow Randy's pickup and make the three-hour drive northeast to Fort Dearborn. He heard they were unveiling a memorial this year. Exactly what it was, he couldn't say but he knew the committee was in great hands. Last year's festival was somewhat subdued, what with the poor weather and the freshness of the tragedy, but thousands did gather, many vendors came out, and on the whole it still felt true to itself - like a celebration.

Today, however, was special for more than just the memorial. Randy's nursery, one town over, had been specially commissioned to grow flowers for the festival, contributing nearly half of the annuals planted that year. When he learned of it, Jon had thought of how exciting it would be to see the flower gardens again. A sentimental piece of him longed for that bench, that view from the gardens toward the pond, that peaceful seat in the lap of heaven. Maybe one day he could learn the flower business and handle the allocations for May Day. Maybe.

Jon finished up his row of seeds and walked over to his tractor, an old red German thing, and took a drink of water from his canteen. He reflected momentarily, leaning on the tractor like he had hundreds of times over, on how it had been two long years since that rainy morning at city hall. It saddened him to think that that had been the last time he and Robin were together. He wondered what he would have to say about the farm. *I bet he'd love it here. Hell,* Jon laughed at a thought, *I bet he already knows half of how to run a place like this, the bastard. 'My uncle taught me,' he'd say.* The laugh brought a follower and he shook his head.

To Jon, Robin was not only the smartest person he'd ever been friends with, but was the one friend in his life whose teachings kept on giving. With Wil, it was a matter of situational judgements. He was like an instinctual compass. You always knew where his poles were. Robin, on the other hand, taught Jon confidence. He gave him something more than a credo to abide by. He gave him the means to better trust his instincts and utilize his autonomy, applicable in all facets of life from relationships to work to personal growth. Whenever Jon found himself at a decisional crossroads, he thought of Robin.

He came out of his reflection, checked his watch, and frowned. *Ten o'clock. If I finish by one, that's thirty minutes to set up for tomorrow, thirty minutes to get ready, three hours to get into the city. . . Then what? Three hours back to the farm tonight and at it again at four a.m.? Ugh. . .* He huffed, the frown quickly turning into a smile and a following low laugh. It's not that he was hesitant to return, he was simply embedded in his new lifestyle. It held precedence over all else. It was his outlet and his love. With so much time to himself these days, though, he had grown acutely aware of how ridiculous he could be sometimes. *Don't be an idiot. It's May Day. Get your ass on the road. For Wil.*

Soft footsteps came to rest on a clean stretch of sidewalk. Toes exposed at the tips of leather sandals rolled and bounced spiritedly, like the hammers of a softly played piano. Marian stood on Atlantic Avenue shaded by an overhanging tree limb. The street was empty in the vicinity but pleasant and inviting clamor approached in waves. It sent distant promises of festival fun to be had.

A pair of birds chirped overhead, to which she smiled. They journeyed from tree to tree, chasing one another in some unknown aerial game and finally came to rest on a branch. She watched for a time while in the background, footsteps approached, lightly at first and growing to taps upon the concrete.

The taps settled beside her and fingertips met her palm and slid down her skin, interlocking snugly in her hand. She squeezed and the hand that met her squeezed back. A turn to her left brought view of Robin, who smiled at her and leaned in for a kiss.

"Ready?" he asked.

"Ready," she answered with a smile to match.

"Let's go," he said excitedly and the pair continued along.

As they walked, Marian nearly felt the need to pinch herself. It was only the third day since Robin had been released from prison and having him beside her, on May Day of all days, was simply surreal. They had spent almost every minute together yet her amazement hadn't worn. In a way, the two years without her love felt like they'd never end.

Following the march on city hall, Robin had pled guilty to an 'Inciting a Riot' charge and served 23 months in jail. Nobody knew exactly what had transpired in city hall that morning. Nobody knew of the meeting that took place, the painstaking arbitration, or the eventual settlement. Nobody knew how close Robin had been to failing. Nobody but her. . .

Robin had told her every detail in his very first letter to her from prison - all 20 pages of it. Where he had learned to negotiate like that, she truly didn't know and, frankly, had never thought to ask. She supposed it was from his stepfather, who she had the pleasure of meeting many times over, oddly, though, never with Robin. It always made her laugh when she thought of that fact.

For Marian, her two years saw tremendous change. The microscope focused over the slide that had become Fort Dearborn was of maximum magnification. The march on city hall resulted in swift scrutiny that had placed the city under a Federal eye. Investigations had reached every branch of government, yielding an unprecedented overhaul chockfull of prosecutions.

When Marian's old boss had been brought up on corruption charges and resigned, she stepped in as interim District Attorney. It was a burdensome process but her team worked tirelessly with the FBI to let justice's hammer fall. Presently, 11 of the 26 indicted city officials had been convicted. Trials of that sort were a lengthy, arduous process smothered with paperwork, mistrials, reschedules, delays, and, ultimately, bullshit. But she worried not. Their day would come. All would be held accountable.

All wasn't pie in fair Fort Dearborn, though. Class tensions flared at times and the Inner District had yet to become fully assimilated. The new leadership struggled to mend what was a dismantled gubernatorial body and trust levels fluctuated. But today, all was put aside.

As they headed for the park's southwest entrance, Robin abruptly halted. "Oh, *wow*," he exclaimed and pointed. "Look at Harper's."

Marian followed his finger to a place called *Harper's Corner Store*, wrapped in a modern façade and wide windows. A view inside saw only alternate lighting, as they were closed for the festival, but it was enough to see the makings of quite a nice market. Aisles were stocked and long, glass refrigerator doors lined a far wall. It seemed to her that a café was installed, too. It looked lovely.

She watched as he took it all in and noticed his eyes wander to the sidewalk. He got fit in prison, and though his hair was quite short, he looked every bit as handsome as she remembered. There was a mature, veteran look to him. She could see it in his eyes and in the way he walked. Presently, by the way he squinted at the sidewalk, it looked like he was envisioning something from his past. In a flash, his eyes shot back to the store.

"That's fantastic," he added and finally turned away.

Along their walk, Robin had commented countless times on particular changes he had recognized. An old bar was now a restaurant, a once vacant lot became a new apartment complex, and on and on. They had also taken a detour to pass St. Augustine's Church, which to Marian's knowledge had a new pastor. Robin hadn't bothered entering but certainly was happy to find the building in good shape. She loved watching him reminisce. Being a part of his joy, even as an observer, filled her heart.

The pair entered Baker's Memorial Park among a flow of pedestrians and took their time in walking to the Main Square. It was a special journey they had written about for two years straight, a dream of holding hands again in their favorite place. As expected, it was a much different walk than the one they had had two years earlier. Things once black were green and colorful, but there were scars if you looked for them. In time, nature would regain its shape and the spindly trees would grow anew.

"So," Robin said amidst a path of wildflowers. "We have all this free time. What would you like to do?"

"Hmm," she sounded. "I've been thinking about that actually."

"Oh yeah?"

"Yep."

"And what'd you come up with?"

"Someone once told me Germany is nice this time of year," she replied with a smile.

He laughed. "I more so meant 'what would you like to do *today*' but. . .now that you mention it, I can't think of anything I want more." He nodded to himself and looked over. "That would be amazing."

"You really wanna?" she asked.

"I really wanna. Let's do it. Let's go."

She bit her lip in excitement. "Oh my God I can't wait."

"We'll plan tonight," he said and wrapped an arm around her.

The Main Square was bustling. In short time, Marian found herself alongside conversation between Robin and festival-goers, so while Robin chatted, Marian decided to wander a short distance towards the center of the Square to observe the May Day Monument. A new, towering Maypole was erected and about its base was a circular formation of pavers hand-inscribed to commemorate each victim's name. Walking along she noticed that the bricks were placed in the formation of a large flower. She found it to be simply noble.

Suddenly, she flushed and her heart began to race as a realization took hold. She never had the courage to review the list of victims. Being here, having it in front of her held the potential for particularly devastating news. There were two special people that, if listed, would bring her to tears. Marian didn't rush, as to make sure not to be disrespectfully brief, but couldn't help but hesitate at each name. When she made it halfway, a voice came.

"It's Marian, isn't it?" the voice asked.

Marian spun to find none other than Amy, the very name she was so fearful of finding. It had been such length since the two had seen one another, and their minutes together so brief, yet Marian recognized her immediately.

She exhaled in pure relief. "*Amy.*"

Amy smiled. "Hi, dear."

They hugged each other tightly. When they separated, Marian had resumed her fearful look. "Quinn?"

"She's with her sister, Lily. We're all safe," Amy assured.

"Thank God," she breathed.

"I'm relieved in my own way, dear. I'm happy to see that you're safe, too." They held each other's eyes, silently acknowledging their special, serendipitous bond. Amy blinked and her eyes moved past Marian's shoulder. "Is that your man?" she asked and pointed.

Marian followed and then turned her head back to Amy. "That's my Robin."

A deep smile grew. "I should have known. It looks like our conversation was put to good use."

Marian smiled back at her. "It most definitely was."

They chatted for a time about life, sun soaked and happy. They exchanged hugs and ways to contact one another and before she left, Marian asked for Amy to send her regards to her granddaughters.

When Marian turned away, she found two other people hugging. It was Robin and Jon. Even from a distance she could make out the elation in their body language. Jon was as jovial as she'd ever seen him. The sight brought warmth to her heart.

Before she walked over, Marian took one last moment to observe the reunion. Regardless of the size difference between Robin and Jon, this was a meeting of giants. These men were known, they were legends around here. Their actions of the past canonized them in the present as if they themselves were walking monuments. People shared in the observance, knowing as she knew and smiling to match.

It's funny how the past comes through in the present. Though they were missing their friend, in death, Wil lived on in this place and in the two of them. He was as much of the F.A.M., as much of this festival as they were. Maybe more.

She knew that if she thought too hard on it, a peculiar form of frustration would rise. Perhaps she was merely oversimplifying, as one is wont to do, but thinking on the antics the three had shared made it seem unreal for it all to have needed to be taken that far. Even two years later, it bothered her. That three men had to risk life and limb, present and future, freedom and potential, simply to expose something as obvious as corruption was a testament to the nature of hierarchical power and to the flaws of modern governance. What they did wasn't an epiphany, it wasn't a godsend, and it wasn't charity. It was radical - not for the sake of the title, but for the sake of change. That's what proper radicalism does; it addresses a problem at its root, yanks it from its soil, and plants a new, fresher idea. They had been outlaws, Robin and his friends. And that's what it took. For Robin to recognize that fact and summon the courage to act upon it was perhaps a greater achievement than the crimes themselves. And until the end of their days, such outlaws as he and his friends, this town might never see again.

Made in the USA
Middletown, DE
05 May 2019